Modern Italian Short Stories

Edited by

MARC SLONIM

SIMON AND SCHUSTER

NEW YORK · 1954

Second Printing

La Lupa translated by D. H. Lawrence from Cavalleria Rusticana by Giovanni Verga, reprinted by permission of and Copyright, 1928, by Dial Press, New York.

The Petition from Don Camillo and His Flock, Copyright, 1952, by Giovanni Guareschi, reprinted by permission of Farrar, Straus & Young, New York.

LIBRARY OF CONGRESS CATALOG CARD NUMBER: 54-6670
DEWEY DECIMAL CLASSIFICATION NUMBER: 458

MANUFACTURED IN THE UNITED STATES OF AMERICA
BY AMERICAN BOOK—STRATFORD PRESS, INC., NEW YORK

CONTENTS

IV. THE NEW ERA   227

FOREWORD

The thirty-four stories in Modern Italian Short Stories are diverse in content and form; the characters they depict are extremely varied: they belong to different social strata and move in sundry situations. Geographically, the action of these stories takes place all along the peninsula, from northern cities to Tuscan vineyards and Sicilian hamlets, while chronologically they spread over several decades of our century. But they do possess in common that affinity of experience and attitude we usually call "national character."

To convey an image of Italy through the works of its modern writers was my primary purpose in editing this collection. I strove for typicality rather than completeness, in literary value as well as in illustrative significance. I aimed at offering a selection of stories which would make interesting and often exciting reading, while at the same time presenting the flavor of the Italian mentality.

The Italians have always preferred the short story to novels and long narratives. It has flourished in the land of Boccaccio and Bandello since the Renaissance, and its recent bloom in our times demonstrates the vigor of a national tradition. Most of Italy's great writers have excelled in this genre, and many of them have written nothing but short stories and novellas.

Of course, it would be quite wrong to claim that short stories of this selection, even though they are as many as thirty-four and are written by prominent living authors, can mirror all the facets of the reality of Italy. In general, this hardly ever happens in literature, and Italian writers, in particular, are not working toward the direct representation of facts and events. In many instances they even surprise us by remaining obstinately silent just when we expect them to be most eloquent. But they have their own reasons for assuming such an attitude. If, for example, they seldom depict the Fascist regime, it is not because they are avoiding a slippery subject, but because Fascism, in their opinion, evinced itself only as a very transitory episode. In the same way, short stories deal only incidentally with the urgent postwar situations—but then such features of the Italian scene as poverty and political instability, which strike the foreigner, are accepted by the natives almost as natural phenomena. It is quite possible that on account of these national idiosyncrasies, the vision of modern Italy throughout this anthology will not correspond to readers' preconceptions formed by our press or by the traveler's occasional glimpse.

Yet there should be no doubt of the authenticity of the literary testimony offered in this book. Italians themselves, and most authoritative ones, introduce us in these pages to a warm, gentle, and passionate people, for whom humor and irony are a shield against fate, a people moving easily from joy to despair and from anger to indulgence, without ever losing an emotional equilibrium of compassion, kindness, and equity. In these stories Italians appear as they really are—sober, hard working, as deeply attached to the family as they are to dramatic extravagance, and preserving intact throughout all the vicissitudes and privations their extraordinary zest for life—even in morbid introspection and fantasy.

In E. M. Forster's A Room with a View, an English lady tourist is extolling the smells of Florence. To her young companion who inquires whether these smells are nice, she replies: "One does not come to Italy for niceness; one comes for life."

This is what we come for, to a collection like Modern Italian Short Stories. And it is the same feeling of a living Italy that we find there.

M. S.

Modern Italian
Short Stories

1

THE PRECURSORS

Italy has played such a magnificent role in the history of Western civilization, she has supplied, for almost twenty centuries, such an uninterrupted flow of stupendous works of art, literature, and learning, that we cannot help looking at her as the land of glorious vestige and hallowed memory. Yet one of the most striking paradoxes in modern Italy is the discrepancy between the old age of her culture and the relative youth of her political existence. This long and narrow peninsula, the size of Arizona, smaller than New Mexico, has been the setting for the most eventful periods of European history, and the fountainhead of man's most spectacular spiritual achievements.

It was in Italy two thousand years ago that the Etruscans built their cities and the Greeks established their colonies of art, poetry, and wisdom. Here was founded the law of Rome, and the greatest world empire of antiquity. From here the early Christians, unshaken by sufferance and martyrdom, started their conquest of the European continent, and, from here, after the barbarian invasions, the Popes ruled the universal church. Mystical faith burned high in Italian convents and cathedrals of the Middle Ages, and during the Renaissance, arts and poetry, science and philosophy flourished in city-states, in Florence, Venice, Genoa, Milan, ultimately to be spread all over the world and to mark the dawn of new times. But despite all this extraordinary cultural activity, with all her legacy of paganism, Christendom, mysticism, and Renaissance spirit, Italy lacked political unity.

For almost fourteen centuries she had been split into dozens of separate regions, often ruled by transient conquerors and greedy foreigners, and torn by strife, war, and dynastic rivalry. Italy as a national state is of recent origin. In fact, it is one of the youngest in Western Europe; it was established less than a century ago, and Rome did not become its capital until 1870. The emergence of Italy as an independent and unified nation was one of the most dramatic events of the nineteenth century, and it seemed little short of a miracle. Although historians spoke of an Italian "rebirth" (the Italians called it Risorgimento-Renascence), it was actually the beginning of a new life, a difficult and laborious start.

The first years of the Italian kingdom in the late eighties were filled with obstacles and contradictions. Italy was a patchwork of different regions, such as Piedmont and Naples, Venice and Calabria, Lombardy and Sicily: each of them had led for centuries its own political life and developed its own characteristics and customs, enhanced by economic and social differences, and diversities of climate, soil, dialect, and tradition. The unity of the kingdom under the House of Savoy was achieved through bureaucratic centralization following the French pattern; and it was not an easy task to reconcile the older separatist tendencies with the requirements of the new state. Moreover, Italy had to make a place among more fortunate nations, and she was handicapped, since she stepped into the industrial revolution later than England, France, or Belgium. Her civilization was based on stone, marble, and handicrafts. She had poor equipment, an outdated economy, and a feudal class structure. She lacked most important natural resources—coal, iron, oil, and rubber. The poverty of her rapidly growing population and the scarcity of labor opportunities, leading to a large emigration, intensified the conflicts within the new state.

Italian patriots like Mazzini and Garibaldi, who, together with other Romantic intellectuals and idealistic noblemen, promoted the independence and unification of their country, were inspired by the glories of the past and the liberal ideas of their own times. But the statesmen and leaders of the kingdom of Italy in the eighties and nineties had to face hard political and economic realities. There was a bitter over-all struggle for power. While political parties within and outside the Italian parliament translated the conflict between the old and the new and the painful process of adaptation to changed conditions into social and political terms of struggle and agitation, Italian writers and artists expressed the spirit of the day in their own specific way.

In arts and letters, realistic tendencies clashed with pretentious Romanticism; the energetic stirrings of modernity were bogged down in provincialism and passivity. The legacy of the past stiffened into the rigidity of Academies, with their artistic canons and intellectual patterns, and the young generations had a very hard time in opposing tradition with innovation. The newly emerged middle class did fight against the sleepy backwardness of rural districts, but it lacked the dynamism of its European or American counterparts and was easily swayed by nationalistic dreams and the typically Italian individualism which often led to isolation and social aloofness. These contradictory and diversified tendencies in national life conditioned the rise and evolution of the main trends in Italian letters at the turn of the century. The young writers of the late eighties and nineties who wanted to break away from local provincialism were eager to rejoin the main stream of European culture. They rallied to the realistic movement, then prevalent throughout Europe, and, in the person of Verga, adhered to the naturalistic school of France—the country which since the eighteenth century had held a monopoly of literary influence over Italy. Yet Italian naturalism had its own national peculiarities and soon liberated itself from foreign tutelage.

Giovanni Verga—one of the key figures of modern Italian literature —was the founder of verismo ("vero" in Italian means "true"). This was a school which had deep roots in such works as Boccaccio's Decameron. Its impact is strongly felt today, particularly in the writings of postwar "neorealists."

A short-story writer par excellence, Verga evoked in his tales the very spirit of his native Sicily—a land that had been a Greek colony more than two millenniums ago, was later influenced by the Moslems and ruled by the Spanish, and in our times blended vestiges of paganism with Christian piety, and primitive passion with medieval custom. Verga described its shepherds who lead the flocks on rocky mountains, its peasants who toil in the fields under a merciless sun, its black-eyed women hungry for love—all these poor folk who live in a biblical world of poverty, pride, and superstition. In a way, he became the spokesman for these voiceless multitudes, and his "pessimistic humanism" reflected at the same time the moods of those upper classes to which he belonged by birth and education. The inebriation of the Risorgimento was wearing off. It was high time to look at life with open eyes and to cope with reality without bias and illusion. Naturalism seemed to provide an adequate artistic expression for such a bent. Verga's intention was to produce impartial documentation, objective descriptions of settings free from personal evaluations. Yet his dramatic narrative, despite the dryness, compactness, and sobriety which D. H. Lawrence admired in it so highly, had strong overtones of compassion and warmth.

Verga's verismo was not merely a literary manner; it became identified with regionalism as well as with populism. In fact, the head of the movement and his followers concentrated not only on depicting southern farmers, artisans, and laborers, the poorest and most neglected population of the kingdom, but paid a great deal of attention to all the differences in speech, dialect, mentality, and way of life which make every Italian region so curiously distinct from its neighbor.

At the turn of the century, verists and regionalists occupied an important place in Italian letters. Each province got its chroniclers: Naples—the tempestuous Matilda Serao and Federigo di Roberto, a writer of substance; the south—Luigi Capuana. The Abruzzi were favorites with Luigi Ciampoli, while Tuscany was Renato Fucini's territory. A strong impress of verismo can be also found in Italian music, especially in the operatic work of Mascagni, Puccini, and Leoncavallo; the book and the title, for instance, of the popular Cavalleria Rusticana are taken from Verga's story.

The populist motifs of verismo announced the democratic era, with its concern for the conditions of the masses, while its regionalism represented in a way the reaction of the Italian communal spirit against state centralization. But democratic institutions and liberal ideas were not too strong in a country which was unsettled politically and ridden with illiteracy and poverty, besides being strongly individualistic. The Romantic revival which took place in Europe in 1890 found its echo in various groups of Italian society—in the nobility and in the more active elements of the middle class—whose moods differed from those of liberals, democrats, and verists. English and French aestheticism was welcomed by traditionalists in literature who remained faithful to the ideal of pure form, while Nietzschean exaltation of the ego and aristocratic contempt for the common man were hailed both by young intellectuals and scions of old and new upper classes. The beginning of the twentieth century had brought about industrial growth in the north, an agricultural boom in the center, and a general improvement of living standards, and this relative economic prosperity sharpened the zest for life of the well-to-do and enhanced their love of sensation and pleasure. Their sensuous individualism was often accompanied by aggressive nationalism, and Gabriele d'Annunzio, whose poems, dramas, novels, and tales won international acclaim, became the main exponent of these new tendencies.

In his beginning as a prose writer, d'Annunzio followed in Verga's steps and depicted the poor folk of his native region of Pescara, on the shores of the Adriatic. But his lavish and highly contrived descriptions lacked Verga's moral concern and compassion. The regionalism and mythology of his tales were morbid and immoral. Voluptuousness and decay, sex and murder were d'Annunzio's favorite themes, and he elaborated them with an extraordinary verbal mastery. He initiated in Italy a whole aesthetic movement not unlike that promoted by Oscar Wilde in England and on the Continent, but with a greater emphasis on "demonism" and egoism and a deliberate appeal to nationalistic emotions. D'Annunzio glorified the rulers and condottieri of the Renaissance as models of the Italian national spirit and called on his contemporaries for a continuation of the great traditions of the past. He yearned for the role of poetic praeceptor Italiae, and talked of a Third Rome as the goal before new generations. Thus, in literary terms, he expressed those moods and aspirations which led first to colonial conquests in Africa and later to Fascist boasting.

The mixture of rhetoric, Nietzschean posturing, nationalism, and what Americans call "hamming" was not only typical of d'Annunzio as man and writer but also characteristic of the Italian educated classes. Eloquence, pretense, the affected voice, the inflated ego were symptoms of what has been often called "the Italian disease," caused by a blend of inferiority and provincialism. In any case, many Italian critics and thinkers, including important ones like Benedetto Croce, opposed

and eventually debunked the d'Annunzio myth. There is no use deny-
ing, however, that it had reigned supreme between 1900–1920, and
that it left a visible imprint on Italian prose and poetry. Moreover,
even the fiercest detractors of d'Annunzio had to acknowledge his
wonderful techniques, the sonorous musicality and the sensual paganism of his poems, and the contribution he made to the art of the Italian
short story—a genre the Italians had cherished since time immemorial.
Today the glamour and cold glimmer of d'Annunzio's style seem passé,
yet his hedonistic cult of art still holds certain attractions which one
can easily discover in the works of some young writers of the 1950's.
In their reaction against social concern in literature, in their negative
attitude toward neorealism, which they consider a mere rehashing of
verismo, there is a harking back to the author of Laudi, to his preciosity
and aestheticism.

As the precursors of modern literary trends, two other writers who
had reflected different aspects of Italian life should be considered along
with Verga and d'Annunzio. New sensitivity appeared in the works of
Italo Svevo, a Triestine businessman who had been more exposed to
Nordic artistic influences than most of his conationals. Friend of
James Joyce's and greatly esteemed by the European literary avant-
garde, Svevo started writing in the late nineties, but his influence is of
more recent date. All his novels and tales revolve around the same hero,
Zeno, the author's protagonist and alter ego, who is always defeated in
life by trivia and is given to monologues about his own inner experiences. His courageous and impudent confessions, filled with accurate
details and dry humor under a deceptively smooth stylistic surface,
made quite a hit in the twenties when a wave of interest in psychology
reached Italy. Svevo's subtle sophistication, his use of interior mono-
logue, and his stream-of-consciousness invention, his interest in the
subconscious and in psychological complexities made a deep impression on many young writers between the two wars (Moravia, Petroni,
Soldati, and others). Equally removed from verismo and aestheticism,
Svevo and his followers made up the Italian brand of the continental
psychological school in literature.

While Svevo's influence on writers was considerably greater than his
popularity with the general public (he appealed mostly to a limited
circle of connoisseurs), one of his contemporaries won universal recog-

nition. Europe and America hailed Luigi Pirandello as one of the world's greatest playwrights—although he was primarily a short-story writer (which explains certain conventionalities in his stage techniques). The twenty-four volumes of his tales, which encompass realistic portraitures of provincial pettiness, psychological explorations, satires, and paradoxes of wit and fantasy, form a chronicle of Italian life in the twentieth century—but they are also the expression of a sharp and tormented mind. A native of Sicily, Pirandello belonged to the southern tradition of abstract thinkers. The most important Italian philosophers from Vico, Bruno, and Campanella down to Croce and Gentile came from the Italian south. Pirandello was mainly interested in the whimsical and strange interplay of illusion and reality, in the syllogisms of wisdom and folly. In some of his stories, "The Bat," for instance, life becomes a stage, yet the stage reveals much more than life. Some critics suggested that Pirandello's paradoxes, his distrust of reason and rationality, as well as his reduction of thought and sensation to mere illusion, mirrored the attitude of Italian intellectuals. These felt so alienated from reality, so separated from the true life of their own country, so suspended in mid-air, that they easily identified themselves with the heroes of this sardonic and pessimistic writer. There is no wonder that his influence continued through the Fascist era when the intelligentsia suffered more than ever from awareness of this rift. In any case, Moravia, Alvaro, Bontempelli, and a great many other young authors fell under the spell of Pirandello's analytical, keen, and symbolic writing. Next to Verga, d'Annunzio, and Svevo, he is undoubtedly one of those great storytellers whose works prepared for the flourishing of Italian letters in our own times.

GIOVANNI VERGA

La Lupa*

TRANSLATED BY D. H. LAWRENCE

She was tall, and thin; but she had the firm, vigorous bosom of a grown woman, though she was no longer young. Her face was pale, as though she had the malaria always on her, and in her pallor, two great dark eyes and fresh, red lips that seemed to eat you.

In the village they called her La Lupa, because she had never had enough—of anything. The women crossed themselves when they saw her go by, alone like a roving she-dog, with that ranging, suspicious motion of a hungry wolf. She bled their sons and their husbands dry in a twinkling, with those red lips of hers, and she had merely to look at them with her great evil eyes to have them running after her skirts, even if they'd been kneeling at the altar of Saint Agrippina. Fortunately, La Lupa never entered the church, neither at Easter nor at Christmas, nor to hear Mass, nor to confess. Fra Angiolino, of Santa Maria di Jesu, who had been a true servant of God, had lost his soul because of her.

Maricchia, poor thing, was a good girl and a nice girl, and she wept in secret because she was La Lupa's daughter, and nobody would take her in marriage, although she had her marriage chest full of linen, and her piece of fertile land in the sun, as good as any other girl in the village.

Then one day La Lupa fell in love with a handsome lad who'd just come back from serving as a soldier and was cutting the hay alongside

* La Lupa means the she-wolf, and also the prostitute, the enticer.

9

her in the closes belonging to the lawyer: but really what you'd call falling in love, feeling your body burn under your stuff bodice, and suffering, when you stared into his eyes, the thirst that you suffer in the hot hours of June, away in the burning plains. But he went on mowing quietly, with his nose bent over his swath, and he said to her: "Why, what's wrong with you, Mrs. Pina?" —In the immense fields, where only the grasshoppers crackled into flight, when the sun beat down like lead, La Lupa gathered armful after armful together, tied sheaf after sheaf, without ever wearying, without straightening her back for a moment, without putting her lips to the flask, so that she could keep at Nanni's heels, as he mowed and mowed, and asked her from time to time: "Why, what do you want, Mrs. Pina?"

One evening she told him, while the men were dozing in the stack-yard, tired from the long day, and the dogs were howling away in the vast, dark, open country: "You! I want you! Thou'rt handsome as the day, and sweet as honey to me. I want thee, lad!"

"Ah! I'd rather have your daughter, who's a filly," replied Nanni, laughing.

La Lupa clutched her hands in her hair and tore her temples, without saying a word, and went away and was seen no more in the yard. But in October she saw Nanni again, when they were getting the oil out of the olives, because he worked next her house, and the screeching of the oil press didn't let her sleep at night.

"Take the sack of olives," she said to her daughter, "and come with me."

Nanni was throwing the olives under the millstone with the shovel, in the dark chamber like a cave, where the olives were ground and pressed, and he kept shouting Ohee! to the mule, so it shouldn't stop.

"Do you want my daughter Maricchia?" Mrs. Pina asked him.

"What are you giving your daughter Maricchia?" replied Nanni.

"She has what her father left, and I'll give her my house into the bargain; it's enough for me if you'll leave me a corner in the kitchen, where I can spread myself a bit of a straw mattress to sleep on."

"All right! If it's like that, we can talk about it at Christmas," said Nanni.

Nanni was all greasy and grimy with the oil and the olives set to ferment, and Maricchia didn't want him at any price; but her mother seized her by the hair, at home in front of the fireplace, and said to her between her teeth: "If thou doesn't take him, I'll lay thee out!"

La Lupa was almost ill, and the folks were saying that the devil turns hermit when he gets old. She no longer went roving round; she no longer sat in the doorway, with those eyes of one possessed. Her son-in-law, when she fixed on him those eyes of hers, would start laughing and draw out from his breast the bit of Madonna's dress,* to cross himself. Maricchia stayed at home nursing the children, and her mother went to the fields, to work with the men, just like a man, weeding, hoeing, tending the cattle, pruning the vines, whether in the northeast wind or the east winds of January, or in the hot, stifling African wind of August, when the mules let their heads hang in dead weight, and the men slept face downward under the wall, on the north side. Between vesper bell and the night bell's sound, when no good woman goes roving around, Mrs. Pina was the only soul to be seen wandering through the countryside, on the ever-burning stones of the little roads, through the parched stubble of the immense fields, which lost themselves in the sultry haze of the distance, far off, far off, toward misty Etna, where the sky weighed down upon the horizon, in the afternoon heat.

"Wake up!" said La Lupa to Nanni, who was asleep in the ditch, under the dusty hedge, with his arms around his head. "Wake up! I've brought thee some wine to cool thy throat."

Nanni opened his eyes wide like a disturbed child, half-awake, seeing her erect above him, pale, with her arrogant bosom, and her eyes black as coals, and he stretched out his hand gropingly, to keep her off.

"No! No good woman goes roving around between vespers and night," sobbed Nanni, pressing his face down again in the dry grass of the ditch bottom, away from her, clutching his hair with his hands. "Go away! Go away! Don't you come into the stackyard again!"

---

* When the dress of the Madonna in the church is renewed, the old dress is divided in tiny fragments among the parishioners; the fragment is sewn in a tiny heart-shaped or locket-shaped sack and worn around the neck on a cord, hidden in the breast, to ward off evil.

She did indeed go away, La Lupa, but fastening up again the coils of her superb black hair, staring straight in front of her, as she stepped over the hot stubble, with eyes black as coals.

And she came back into the stackyard time and again, and Nanni no longer said anything; and when she was late coming, in the hour between evensong and night, he went to the top of the white, deserted little road to look for her, with sweat on his forehead; and afterward, he clutched his hair in his hand and repeated the same thing every time: "Go away! Go away! Don't you come into the stackyard again!"

Maricchia wept night and day; and she glared at her mother with eyes that burned with tears and jealousy; like a young she-wolf herself now, when she saw her coming in from the fields, every time silent and pallid.

"Vile woman!" she said to her. "Vile, vile mother!"

"Be quiet!"

"Thief! Thief that you are!"

"Be quiet!"

"I'll go to the Sergeant, I will."

"Then go!"

And she did go, finally, with her child in her arms, went fearless and without shedding a tear, like a madwoman, because now she also was in love with that husband of hers, whom they'd forced her to accept, greasy and grimy from the olives set to ferment.

The Sergeant went for Nanni and threatened him with jail and the gallows. Nanni began to sob and to tear his hair; he denied nothing, he didn't try to excuse himself. —"It's the temptation," he said. "It's the temptation of hell!" and he threw himself at the feet of the Sergeant, begging to be sent to jail.

"For pity's sake, Sergeant, get me out of this hell! Have me hung, or send me to prison; but don't let me see her again, never, never!"

"No!" replied La Lupa to the Sergeant. "I kept myself a corner in the kitchen, to sleep in, when I gave her my house for her dowry. The house is mine. I won't be turned out."

A little later, Nanni got a kick in the chest from a mule and was likely to die; but the parish priest wouldn't bring the Host to him, unless La Lupa left the house. La Lupa departed, and then her son-in-law could prepare himself to depart also, like a good Christian; he confessed and took the communion with such evident signs of repentance and contrition that all the neighbors and the busybodies wept round the bed of the dying man.

And better for him if he had died that time, before the devil came back to tempt him and to get a grip on his body and his soul, when he was well.

"Leave me alone!" he said to La Lupa. "For God's sake, leave me in peace! I've been face to face with death. Poor Maricchia is only driven wild. Now all the place knows about it. If I never see you again, it's better for you and for me."

And he would have liked to tear his eyes out so as not to see again those eyes of La Lupa, which, when they fixed themselves upon his, made him lose both body and soul. He didn't know what to do, to get free from the spell she put on him. He paid for Masses for the souls in Purgatory, and he went for help to the priest and to the Sergeant. At Easter he went to confession, and he publicly performed the penance of crawling on his belly and licking the stones of the sacred threshold before the church for a length of six feet.

After that, when La Lupa came back to tempt him: "Hark here!" he said. "Don't you come again into the stackyard; because if you keep on coming after me, as sure as God's above I'll kill you."

"Kill me, then," replied La Lupa. "It doesn't matter to me; I'm not going to live without thee."

He, when he perceived her in the distance, amid the fields of green young wheat, he left off hoeing the vines and went to take the ax from the elm tree. La Lupa saw him advancing toward her, pale and wild-eyed, with the ax glittering in the sun, but she did not hesitate in her step, nor lower her eyes, but kept on her way to meet him, with her hands full of red poppies, and consuming him with her black eyes.

"Ah! Curse your soul!" stammered Nanni.

The Wake

TRANSLATED BY ADRIENNE FOULKE

Mayor Biagio Mila's corpse lay, fully dressed, on his bed, which had been moved into the middle of the room and surrounded by four candles; a cloth moistened in water and vinegar covered his face. Seated on either side of the bed, the wife and brother of the dead man were keeping watch.

Rose Mila was about twenty-five years old, a lovely, blooming woman of clear complexion, with a low forehead and long arching brows; the iris of her wide, gray eyes was flecked, like agate. Her luxuriant hair fell in heavy, rebellious curls and most often quite hid her throat and temples and eyes. Her whole person glowed with the splendor of health and her fresh skin had the perfume of choice fruit.

Emidio Mila, the priest, was probably of the same age. He was thin, and his was the bronzed face of a man who lives in the country under the full sun. A soft, red beard covered his cheeks; strong white teeth gave virile charm to his smile, and his light yellow eyes shone at times like two new golden coins.

Both sat silent, the woman telling the glass beads of her rosary, the man watching the prayers slip through her fingers. Both revealed that apparent indifference with which the Italian country people habitually meet the mystery of death.

Emidio said, with a long sigh: "It's hot tonight."

Rosa glanced up in assent.

In the low room the light shifted in response to the flickering candles. Now the shadows crowded together in a corner, now spilled across a wall, their form and intensity constantly varying. Although the blinds were closed, the window had been left open. The white muslin curtains stirred now and then, lifted by a breath of air. On the white expanse of the bed, Biagio's body seemed asleep.

Emidio's words sank into the silence. The woman bent her head again and resumed the slow telling of her rosary. A few drops of sweat beaded her forehead and her breathing was labored.

Presently Emidio asked: "What time tomorrow will they come for him?"

She answered in her normal tone of voice: "At ten o'clock, with the congregation of the Sacrament."

Whereupon they were again silent. From the surrounding fields the assiduous croaking of frogs and, now and then, the fragrance of sweet grasses entered the room. In that perfect stillness, Rosa heard a hoarse rattle issue from the corpse. With a gesture of horror, she started up from her chair.

"Don't be frightened, Rosa. Those are humors," said her brother-in-law, taking her by the hand to reassure her.

She grasped his hand instinctively and held it as she stood by his side. She strained her ears to hear, but averted her eyes. Inside the dead man's stomach the rattles continued and appeared to be bubbling up toward his lips.

"It's nothing at all, Rosa. Calm yourself," added her brother-in-law, nodding to her to sit down on the wedding chest covered with a long, flowered cushion.

She sat down by his side, still holding his hand in her distress. Since the chest was not wide, their elbows touched.

Silence returned to the room. The distant song of threshers rose in the night air.

"They're threshing by moonlight," the woman said, wishing with words to exorcise her fear and fatigue.

Emidio said nothing. The woman withdrew her hand, for the contact was beginning to cause her a vague sense of unease.

The same thought seized both, suddenly; both were gripped by the same memory, by the memory of bittersweet love from the time of their adolescence.

At that time, they were living in the Caldore houses on the sunny slope of the hill by the crossroads. A high wall of stones and clay bordered their cornfields. On the southern side, where the heat of the sun was more gentle and constant, a grove of fruit trees owned by Rosa's parents prospered and bore heavily. The trees flowered joyously in the springtime; crowning the wall, their silver and rose and violet cupolas curved against the sky and swayed in the breeze as if preparing to take flight; together, they made a drowsy, murmuring sound like honey-bearing bees.

In those days Rosa used to sing beyond that wall, screened by the trees. Her fresh, limpid voice gushed forth like a fountain under the blossoming crown of the grove.

During a long convalescence, Emidio had listened to that singing. Weak and fever-lean, he used to leave the house furtively to escape his liquid diet, hiding a big chunk of bread under his shirt, and he would walk along the wall, following the last row of corn, until he reached his favorite spot.

There he used to sit down, leaning against the sun-warmed stones, and begin to eat. He devoured the bread and then selected for himself an ear of tender corn; each kernel contained a minute drop of milk, as fresh-smelling as flour. The sensuous pleasures of taste and sound blended into a single sensation, infinitely delectable to the convalescent. And so, through those idle hours, surrounded by a warmth and fragrance that gave to the air the heady taste of wine, he found the girl's voice a natural food, too, through which, as with the physical nourishment absorbed by his body, he was reborn.

Rosa's singing was one cause of his recovery. And when recovery was complete, Rosa's voice still held its sensual power over the boy.

Still later, when the two families became more intimate, there arose in Emidio one of those wordless, timid, and solitary loves which consume the forces of adolescence.

In September, before Emidio left for the seminary, the two families went one afternoon for a picnic in the wood, by the river.

The day was mild and the three carts, drawn by oxen, passed by the flowering canebrake.

In the wood the picnic was laid on the ground in a circular clearing bounded by the trunks of gigantic poplars. The short grass was thickly splashed with small purple flowers which exhaled a delicate perfume; here and there in the interior of the wood broad patches of sunlight filtered through the foliage and, below, the river lay seemingly still in a motionless peace, a pure transparency in which the water plants slumbered.

After the picnic, some of the party scattered along the riverbank, others stretched out on the ground.

Rosa and Emidio found themselves together; they linked arms and struck off along a path traced through the undergrowth.

She leaned all her weight on him; she laughed, she snatched leaves from the twigs along the path and chewed their bitter stems; she threw back her head to watch the fleeing magpies. The movement loosened her tortoise-shell comb and her hair suddenly flowed richly over her shoulders.

Emidio bent over with her to pick up the comb. As they straightened up, their heads bumped lightly. Holding her forehead in both hands, Rosa cried out through her laughter: "Oh, dear! Oh, dear!"

The boy looked at her, and he felt how he trembled to the marrow of his bones, felt he had turned pale, and he was afraid that he must give himself away.

She tore a long spiral of ivy from the trunk of a tree and, with one rapid twist, bound it around her hair. Loosely secured, the green leaves, some stained with red, escaped here and there from under her heavy curls. She asked: "Do you like me this way?"

Emidio said nothing; he did not know how to answer her.

"Ah, what a pity! You've lost your tongue."

He wanted to fall to his knees. And as Rosa laughed with displeasure, he felt the tears almost brim to his eyes in his anguish over being unable to utter a single word.

They walked on. At a certain point, a fallen aspen blocked the path. With both hands Emidio raised the trunk, and Rosa passed under the green branches which hung for one moment over her, like a crown.

Farther on, they came to a well on either side of which were two rectangular stone basins. The trees formed a dense cloister of green around and above the well. Here the shade was deep, almost moist. The leafy canopy was perfectly mirrored in the water which rose halfway up the brick sides of the well.

Flinging up her arms, Rosa said: "How nice it is here!"

Then with a graceful gesture she caught up the water in her cupped hands and drank. Drops trickled through her fingers and scattered like beads over her dress.

When her thirst was quenched, she caught up more water with both hands and offered it invitingly to her companion: "Drink!"

"I'm not thirsty," stammered Emidio.

The girl threw the water in his face, biting her lower lip in a grimace of scorn. She lay down in one of the empty basins, as if it were a cradle, restlessly dangling her feet over the sides. Then, abruptly, she got up and looked at Emidio with a singular expression.

"Well, we might as well go."

They resumed their walk, returning in unbroken silence to the scene of the picnic. Blackbirds whistled above their heads, horizontal bands of sunlight crossed their path, and the fragrance of the wood rose to envelop them.

A few days later Emidio went away.

A few months later Emidio's brother took Rosa as his wife.

During his first years at the seminary, the young cleric often thought of his new sister-in-law. In class, while the priests were explaining the *Epitome historiae sacrae*, he daydreamed of her. In the study hall, while his neighbors, concealed behind the raised tops of their desks, indulged in obscene play with each other, he buried his face in his hands and abandoned himself to impure fancies. In church, while the litanies to the Virgin were chanted, he, following the invitation of the *Rosa mystica*, escaped far away.

And as he had learned corruption from his fellow students, the scene in the wood appeared to him in a new light. His suspicion that he had not understood, his regret that he had not known how to pluck the fruit surely offered him then, tormented him strangely.

Had it really been so? Had Rosa once really loved him? Had he really passed, all unknowing, by so great a joy?

And every day this thought grew more acute, more insistent, more beguiling, more tormenting. And every day he fed upon it with mounting anguish until, in the long monotony of priestly life, this thought became for him a kind of incurable infection and, before the hopelessness of the thing, he was seized by an immense despair, a melancholy without end.

He had not known!

In the room the candles were now dropping waxen tears. Stronger gusts of wind pushed through the shuttered blinds and swelled the billowing curtains.

Slowly overcome by sleep, Rosa's eyelids drooped; then, as her head nodded, she opened them suddenly.

"Are you tired?" asked the priest with great gentleness.

"I'm not, no," the woman replied and, rousing herself, sat up straight.

But in the long silence, sleep again took possession of her senses. She leaned her head against the wall; her hair veiled her throat; from between her parted lips her breath came slow and even. She was beautiful like this, and nothing about her was more voluptuous than the rise and fall of her breast and the shape of her knees, visible under her light skirt. A sudden puff of wind made the blinds creak and quenched the two candles nearest the window.

"What if I kissed her?" thought Emidio with an upsurge of passion, as he watched the sleeping woman.

Once more the chant of human voices spread through the June night with cadenced, liturgical solemnity, and from far away the responses, unaccompanied by any instrument, flowed back in diverse keys. The full moon must have been high, for the feeble inside light was unable to conquer the brightness that rained against the blinds and poured through the slats of the wood.

Emidio turned toward the deathbed. His eyes, traveling over the dark, rigid outline of the corpse, paused involuntarily on the hand, on that yellow, swollen hand, slightly hooked, furrowed with livid threads, and quickly he looked away. In the oblivion of sleep, Rosa's head slowly, slowly traced a half circle on the wall and sank toward the agitated priest. The woman's head drooped very gently and, because the motion slightly affected her sleep, the iris gleamed briefly between her lifted lids, then disappeared in the whites, like a violet leaf lapped by milk.

Emidio sat motionless, supporting her weight against his shoulder. He held his breath for fear of waking the sleeper and from the throbbing of his heart and wrists and temples, which seemed to fill the room, an immense, anguished oppression bore down on him. But as Rosa's sleep continued, a feeling of lightness spread through his body and he felt himself grow faint with an overwhelming tenderness as he looked at her throat voluptuously marked by a delicate necklace of flesh, and as he breathed in her warm breath and the female scent of her hair.

A fresh current of air, heavy with nocturnal perfume, bent the third flame, and quenched it.

Then, without further thought, without further fear, abandoning himself entirely to temptation, the watcher kissed the woman on the mouth.

At his touch she awoke with a start; she opened stupefied eyes close to her brother-in-law's face and grew very pale.

Slowly she gathered up the hair at her throat and sat, bosom erect, vigilant, staring before her into the shifting shadows.

"Who put out the candles?"

"The wind."

They said no more. Both remained seated side by side on the wedding chest, as before, their elbows touching, in painful uncertainty; with a kind of mental guile they diverted their conscience from judging and condemning what had happened. Spontaneously both turned their attention to externals; they invested a false intensity in this mental maneuver which did, however, match the tenseness of their bodies. And little by little a kind of inebriation possessed them.

The songs of the threshers continued and lingered long in the night air, response dissolving into faint response as the voices, male and female, joined in amorous composition. At times a lone voice rose high above the others, sounding a single note around which the harmonies flowed like waves around the central ripple of a flowing river. Again, at intervals, the metallic vibration of a guitar strung in fifths sounded at the beginning of a song, and between each repetition the measured thud of the threshing machines against the earth was audible.

The two people listened.

Perhaps because of a shift in the wind, the aromas were now no longer the same. Perhaps from the hill of Orlando there came now the powerful scents of the orange grove; perhaps from the gardens of Scalia the dense perfume of roses that gave to the air the savor of wedding sweets; perhaps from the swamp of the Farnia the humid fragrance of the sword lilies, a scent as delicious as is the taste of spring water.

Still the two people remained silent, motionless on the chest, possessed by the voluptuousness of the lunar night. Before them the last candle wavered suddenly and, bending low, dropped tears of melted wax. At any moment, it seemed poised to flicker out. The two did not move. They sat, fearful, watching with dilated, staring eyes the tremulous, dying flame. Suddenly the intoxicating wind quenched it. Then, without fear of the shadow, the man and woman as one turned toward each other in a gesture of avid desire, their arms entwined, and blindly, madly, their mouths sought each other in a wordless, breathless embrace.

LUIGI PIRANDELLO

The Bat

TRANSLATED BY FRANCES FRENAYE

Everything was all right. There was nothing so new and startling about the play that the audience was likely to take offense, and it was put together with a sure eye for effects. Among the characters there was a great prelate, a red-robed cardinal, to be exact, who gave shelter in his house to a poor widowed sister-in-law, with whom he had been in love as a boy, before embracing an ecclesiastical career. Then there was the widow's daughter, a marriageable girl whom His Eminence wanted to match with a young protégé who had lived with him ever since infancy, supposedly the son of a former male secretary, but in reality . . . well, a by-product of his youth, which no one could throw up against him now that he had risen so high in the church. To attempt further explanation in so limited a space would do the cardinal injustice, and besides, the young man in question was the invisible motivator of the second act of the play, where there is a highly dramatic scene between the cardinal and his sister-in-law, which takes place on a veranda, in the dark, or rather by moonlight, since before launching on his confession the cardinal says to his faithful servant, Giuseppe: *"Giuseppe, turn off the lights!"*

Yes, everything was all right. The actors were in good form and every one of them was in love with his own part. Even little Gastina was delighted with the role of the fatherless niece, who naturally won't hear of marrying the cardinal's young man and says so in a series of proudly rebellious scenes, which gave her a chance to reap an avalanche of applause.

22

In short, Faustino Perres was as happy as any author can reasonably expect to be on the night before the opening of his new play. If only a bat hadn't come into the story! Every evening of the Arena's summer season, the cursed creature either flew through an opening in the sloping roof or else woke up from a nest it must have built up among the bolts and points that held it together. At any rate, it swooped madly down, not over the heads of the spectators in the dark body of the Arena, but right onto the stage, where the footlights and spotlights irresistibly attracted it, and in front of the actors' faces.

Little Gastina was scared out of her wits. Three times in the course of the previous evening she had nearly fainted when the bat skimmed her hair, flying directly in front of her eyes, and the last time—Oh, my God, how awful!—the sticky, webbed thing whistled right by her mouth. It was a miracle that she didn't shout out loud. The tension of going on with the show while combatting the urge to follow the disgusting creature's flight with her eyes, to ward it off, or if necessary to run off the stage and take refuge in her dressing room left her nerves thoroughly on edge, and she swore that unless a way was found to stop this interruption of the play she couldn't answer for what she might do.

It was proved that the bat did not come from the outside but had its nest in the Arena, when on the evening of the dress rehearsal all the openings were closed and yet it made one of its desperate swoops across the stage just as usual. Faustino Perres was so worried that he begged the director and stage manager to send two or three workmen whom he offered to pay out of his own pocketbook to discover the nest and chase the insolent bird away. The director only flew into a rage and said he was fed up with Signorina Gastina's fear for her gorgeous hair.

"Her hair?"

"Of course, her hair! Hadn't you caught on? She's been told that if a bat flies into your hair a sticky substance on the wings makes it impossible to get it out except by cutting. Now, do you understand? That's all she's got on her mind. When she ought to throw herself into her role and forget all such foolishness!"

Foolishness? A woman's hair? The gorgeous hair of Signorina Gastina? The director's harangue only increased Faustino Perres's terror.

Oh, my God! If that was why little Gastina was so scared, then his play was as good as done for!

Just before the dress rehearsal Gastina was sitting with her elbow propped up on her crossed knees and her fist under her chin, resolved to give the director trouble. Very seriously she asked Faustino Perres whether the line in the second act: "Giuseppe, turn off the lights!" couldn't be repeated several times in the course of the play. After all, turning off the lights is the recognized way to get rid of a bat. Faustino Perres felt a chill run up and down his spine.

"No, I mean it!" she insisted. "After all, don't you want your play to give a perfect illusion of reality?"

"An illusion? No, that's not it at all. Art creates reality itself, not an illusion!"

"Very well. But if art creates reality, the bat destroys it."

"What do you mean? Why?"

"Just because. Just imagine that in real life you have a family quarrel, a scene between husband and wife, mother and daughter, a question of money or anything you like. And in the middle of it, a bat flies into the room. Well, what happens? I can tell you. The quarrel is held up; either the light is turned off, or the opponents go into another room, or else somebody fetches a broom, gets up on a stool and tries to knock the bat unconscious. And then they forget what they were quarreling about and gather around, half smiling, half disgusted, to look at the creature and see how it is made."

"All right, that's everyday life, if you like," objected Faustino Perres, with a frozen smile on his lips. "But I didn't put any bat into my play."

"Maybe you didn't, but the bat got into it, willy-nilly."

"There's no need to pay any attention."

"Come, come! Does that seem natural to you? Here I am, taking the part of Livia in your play, and I tell you that it's not natural at all. Because I know Livia better than you do, and I also happen to know that she has a deathly fear of bats. I'm speaking of Livia, mind you, not of myself! You never thought of it, because it never occurred to you that a bat would fly into the room just when she was rebelling against the plans made for her by the cardinal and her mother. But tonight you can be sure that the bat is coming into the room during that scene. And I ask you, for the sake of the reality you are seeking to create, whether it seems natural, when she's so scared of bats that the very idea of touching one makes her scream and wriggle all over, for her to pay no attention when a bat flies into the scene. No, you must be joking! Livia runs away, I'm telling you; she leaves the stage and runs away, or else she ducks under a table and starts shouting like a madwoman. I advise you to think it over. Wouldn't the best thing be to have His Eminence call Giuseppe and repeat the line: 'Giuseppe, turn off the lights!'? Or else . . . wait a minute . . . I've got a better idea. . . . That would mean liberation! . . . He should tell him to fetch a broom, get up on a stool, and . . ."

"Of course, Signorina, of course! Breaking the scene off in the middle and causing the audience to burst into laughter."

"But it would be the most natural thing in the world! Believe me! Your play is sure to benefit. After all, the bat is a part of the scene; whether you like it or not he's forced his way into it. . . . A *real bat*, too. If you don't take him into account, he's bound to seem artificial. That is, if Livia and the other two pay no attention and go on speaking their parts as if nothing had happened. Can't you see?"

Faustino Perres let his arms fall to his sides in despair.

"Good heavens, Signorina . . . If you're joking, that's one thing, but . . ."

"No, no, no! I'm serious, I tell you," Gastina retorted. "Very serious!"

"Then I tell you that you're mad," said Perres, rising to his feet. "If I were to take the bat into account and make my characters pay attention to him, then he would have to be part of the reality which I have created. And in that case he'd be an artificial bat, not a real one. And incidentally, an element of perfectly casual reality can't be allowed to introduce itself into the essential and created reality of a work of art."

"But what if it does introduce itself?"

"But it doesn't! It can't! That bat doesn't get into my play; it simply gets onto the stage where you are reciting it."

"Very good! Where I am reciting your play. Then one of two things must be true. Either your play is alive, or the bat is alive. And the bat is alive, very much so, I can tell you. I've proved that to you because he's so alive Livia and the other characters can't seem natural if they go on with the scene as if he weren't there. So the conclusion is this: either throw out the bat, or throw out the play. If the bat can't be got rid of, then look to God for the salvation of your play. Now I'm going to show you that I know my role and put my whole heart into it. But I'm not responsible for my nerves this evening."

Every true writer, no matter how mediocre he may be, if we look at him at a moment like that through which Faustino Perres was now living, on the first night of his new play, has something touching, or if you like, ridiculous, about him. For he, more than all the others, and perhaps alone in the company, is under the spell of what he has written; he laughs, weeps, and unconsciously mimics the actors' expressions, breathing fast in his anxiety and raising first one hand and then the other, in a gesture of support or defense.

I was with him that evening, among the firemen and the stagehands behind the scenes, and I can promise that during all the first act and part of the second he was so wrapped up in his work that he never did think of the bat. It wasn't just because the bat hadn't yet put in its usual appearance. No. He didn't think of it simply because he couldn't. In fact, when the bat finally appeared, about halfway through the second act, he failed to notice it and had no idea why I was nudging him with my elbow.

"What's the matter?" he asked, looking me wildly in the face.

He began to think about it only when the play took a bad turn. And that was not on account of the bat or its effect upon the actors, but because of some fundamental defect of writing or construction. Already the first act had met with little and feeble applause.

"Good God, there it is . . . !" the poor fellow started to exclaim, breaking out into a cold sweat, raising one shoulder and bending his head first to one side and then to the other, as if the bat were flying around him and he were trying to stave it off. A moment later he wrung his hands and buried his face in them. "Good God, the bat seems to be mad! Any minute now and he'll be flying into Rossi's face. . . ! What can we do? Gastina's just about to come on!"

"For heaven's sake, be quiet," I exhorted him, shaking his arm and trying to lead him away.

But I was quite unable to do so. Gastina made her entrance from the opposite wing and Perres stared at her in fascination, trembling all over.

The bat wheeled about high up in the air, around the eight-branch hanging lamp, and Gastina seemed unaware of its existence. She must have been lulled by the expectant silence with which the audience greeted her appearance upon the stage. The silence continued as the scene went on and was obviously successful. Oh, if only the bat had not been there! But it was there, and very much so! The audience was so attentive to the play that it did not see, but there it was! It seemed to be aiming at Gastina, and just at the moment when she was doing all she could to save the play. With superhuman courage she held out against the growing terror inflicted upon her by the cursed bat's obstinate and disgusting persecution.

All of a sudden Faustino Perres saw an abyss gape before his eyes and covered his face with his hands. Gastina had given an abrupt sharp cry and collapsed into the cardinal's arms. I was ready to drag him away, just as the actors were dragging away the inanimate Gastina.

In the confusion of that first moment no one on the disorderly stage noticed what was going on in the main body of the Arena. There was a faraway, thundering sound, to which no one paid any attention. Thunder? No, it wasn't thunder, it was applause, delirious applause! The audience stood up and applauded for four mintes in succession, calling for the author and actors of the play. The fainting scene had been played so realistically as to convince them that it was an integral part of the whole, and this was the reason for their ovation.

What next? The angry director took Faustino Perres by the shoulders as he stared, perplexed and trembling, around him, and pushed him out from behind the curtains onto the stage. Two more minutes of applause followed, and he took six or seven bows, while the audience went on clapping, this time for Gastina.

"Gastina! Gastina!"

But Gastina was in a state of shattered nerves, and the friends gathered in her dressing room were powerless to help her. The director had to come forward and regretfully tell the audience that she could not come out to thank them. The intensity with which she had acted the scene had made her positively ill, and since she could not go on, the performance had to be interrupted.

Was there anything worse that damned bat could have done, that is, to Faustino Perres? If it had caused the play to fail, there might have been some consolation. But to owe success to the mad fluttering of those filthy wings. . . ! As soon as he had recovered from the first shock, but while he was still more dead than alive, Perres ran to the director, who had so ungraciously pushed him out onto the stage, and said, with his hands tearing at his hair: "What are we going to do about tomorrow evening?"

"What else could I say?" shouted the director furiously. "You wouldn't want me to tell the audience that they should applaud the bat rather than you! Now it's up to you to do something about it, so that tomorrow night's applause will be meant for the author."

"Yes. But do what?" asked Faustino Perres, relapsing into a state of panic.

"What? You're asking me what to do?"

"But that fainting isn't in the play at all; it has nothing to do with it."

"You'll have to fit it in, then, that's all. Didn't you take in the extent of the success? All the newspapers will be talking about it tomorrow. There's no doing without it now. And don't worry. My actors will handle something artificial just as realistically as they unconsciously handled tonight's improvisation."

"That's all very well," said Perres didactically. "But if it came off so well, it's because the play was interrupted. If tomorrow night it has to go on . . ."

"There's just the place where you must find a cure!" the director shouted at him.

Just then Gastina came out, with her heavily ringed hands pushing down a fur hat over her gorgeous hair.

"What's that?" she asked. "Can't you see that it's up to the bat to say something, not to you?"

"Forget about the bat!" shouted the director, advancing threateningly upon her.

"Forget about it? Forget about it yourself!" said Gastina, smiling beatifically because she knew that now she could give the director more trouble than ever. "Just think it out, and you'll see. I could have an artificial fainting spell in the second act, if Signor Perres were to follow your advice and write it in for me. But you'd have to have the bat under control, so that it wouldn't make me do the real thing, say in the first or third act, or right after tonight's scene. I wasn't fooling, I can tell you. When I felt that bird brush my cheek, I fainted dead away. And I'm not playing tomorrow night at all, if you want to know. Nobody in the world can force me to go on the stage with a bat flapping against my face!"

"You can't say that!" said the director, shaking his head. "We'll just see!"

But Faustino Perres was convinced that the success of his play was due entirely to the violent intrusion of a purely casual, extraneous element, which instead of upsetting his artifice completely had miraculously fitted into it and given the audience the illusion of truth. He withdrew it from the boards, and it was never given again.

ITALO SVEVO

This Indolence of Mine

TRANSLATED BY BEN JOHNSON

From neither calendar nor clock can the present really be sought; calendars and clocks are consulted simply to establish one's relationship with the past or in order to move with some semblance of consciousness into the future. I and the things and people surrounding me constitute the true present.

Besides this, the present consists of various stages. Thus there is this very significant and very lengthy present stage: the abandonment of business. It has lasted for eight years. A touching inertia. Then there are some important events that break it up: the marriage of my daughter, for instance, an event long passed and one which is becoming part of the other drawn-out present, undisturbed—or perhaps renewed or, better, rectified—by her husband's death. The birth of my little grandson is distant now as well, because the real present as far as Umberto is concerned is my affection for him and his winning of it. He is not aware of this since he believes it a birthright. (Or, generally speaking, is that wee soul able to believe anything at all?) His present, and mine in relation to him, are actually his short, steady steps interrupted by painful moments of fear and relieved by the company of dolls when he cannot win help from his mother or me, his grandfather. My present is also Augusta (the poor woman!), reduced now to her animals— dogs, cats, and birds—and her eternal petty complaints to which she is not devoting energy enough to recover. She does the little bit prescribed by Dr. Raulli but refuses to listen to me, who by superhuman effort was able to overcome a similar tendency toward heart strain;

nor does she see fit to listen to Carlo, our nephew (Guido's son), who has just finished the University and is therefore acquainted with the most up-to-date medicines.

Unquestionably, a great part of my present has its origins in the pharmacy. I cannot recall exactly when this present began, but every now and then it has been intersected by medicines and new theories. Where is the time when once I believed I was fulfilling all my organism required—every evening gulping down a hearty dose of some compound of powdered licorice or those ordinary powdered or broth bromides? Now, with Carlo's help, I have at my disposal much better means for the struggle against disease. Carlo imparts all he knows; but I am not telling all I surmise because I am afraid that he does not agree with me and might with his objections demolish the castle which I sought with such effort and which gave me a measure of tranquillity, a security people at my age do not normally have. A real castle it is! Carlo believes that it is out of confidence in him that I accept all of his suggestions so readily. Tommyrot! I am quite aware that he knows a great deal; I am trying to pick it up, to put it to use—but with discretion. My arteries are not what they ought to be. About this there is no doubt. Last summer my blood pressure reached two hundred and twenty. I cannot say whether it was due to that or something else; at any rate I was very depressed at the time. The depression ended as soon as generous doses of iodine and another chemical, the name of which I never remember, reduced the pressure to a hundred and sixty, where it has remained till now. . . . (I have just now interrupted my writing for a moment in order to measure it at the machine I keep ever ready on my table. It is exactly a hundred and sixty!) In the past I always used to feel threatened by an apoplectic stroke which I honestly felt was coming on. In the presence of death I did not really become any kinder, because I was unable to stomach all those people who were not threatened by a stroke, and had the disgusting look of safe people who pity, commiserate with, and amuse themselves.

Guided by Carlo, I even cured some organs which in no way required help. It has to be understood that every one of my organs cannot help but feel fagged out after so many years of work, and that they profit from being assisted. I send them unasked-for aid. When disease strikes, the doctor is very apt to sigh: I've been called too late! For that reason it is better to look ahead. I cannot initiate cures for the liver when it shows no sign of malfunction; but even so, I must not lay myself open to an end like that of a son of a friend of mine who, one fine day, at the age of thirty-two and in full health, turned yellow as a melon with a violent attack of jaundice and then died within forty-eight hours. "He had never been sick," his poor father told me, "he was a giant, yet he had to die." Many giants finish badly. I have noticed this and I am quite happy not being a giant. But prudence is a fine thing. So every Monday I donate a pill to my liver, and this protects it from violent and sudden maladies, at least until the following Monday. I watch over my kidneys with periodic analyses, and until now they have shown no sign of malfunction. But I know that they can stand some help. My exclusively milk diet on Tuesdays affords me a certain security for the rest of the week. Wouldn't it be fine, while others— who never give a thought to their kidneys—keep them running merrily along, for me, sacrificing myself to them every week, to be suddenly rewarded by a surprise like that which befell poor Copler!

About five years ago I was disturbed by chronic bronchitis. It interfered with my sleep and from period to period had me jumping out of bed to spend several hours nightly sitting in an easy chair. The doctor did not see fit to tell me, but doubtless a cardiac weakness was involved. Raulli proceeded to prescribe that I give up smoking, that I lose weight, and that I eat very little meat. Inasmuch as giving up smoking was difficult, I sought to fulfill the prescription by renouncing all meat. But not even losing weight was easy. At the time I had a net weight of two hundred and seven pounds. In three years I succeeded in losing four and a half pounds, and at that rate, to reach the weight Raulli wanted, another eighteen years would have been called for. But it was a bit difficult to eat moderately when I was abstaining from meat.

And here I must confess that I really owe my loss of weight to Carlo. It was one of his first curative successes. He proposed that I forego one of my three daily meals; and I resolved to sacrifice supper, which we Triestines take at eight in the evening unlike other Italians who have lunch at noon and dinner at seven. Every day I fast uninterruptedly for eighteen hours.

First of all, I slept better. I felt at once that my heart, no longer assisting in digestive work, could devote every beat to filling the veins, to carrying waste matter from the organism, and above all to nourishing the lungs. I, who had once suffered from terrible periods of insomnia—the great unsettlement of one longing for peace and who for that very reason loses it—I would lie there motionless, calmly awaiting the approach of warmth and sleep—a genuine parenthesis in an exhausting life. Sleep after a sumptuous dinner is entirely something else again: then the heart is occupied with digestion alone and its other duties are dismissed.

In the first place, it proved that I was better adapted to abstinence than to moderation. It was easier not to eat supper at all than to limit the amount of food at lunch and breakfast. At these times there were no limitations. Twice a day I could gorge myself. There was no harm in it because eighteen hours of autophagy followed. At first, the midday meal of *pasta asciutta* and vegetables was topped off with some eggs. Then I even gave these up, not because Raulli or Carlo asked me to, but in accordance with the judicious advice of a philosopher, Herbert Spencer, who discovered some law or other to the effect that organs which develop too fast—through overnourishment—are less strong than those taking a longer time to grow. The law naturally pertained to children, but I am convinced that returning to it is a step forward, that even a seventy-year-old child would do well to starve his organs rather than overnourish them. Carlo, moreover, agreed with my theory, and sometimes wanted others to believe that he himself had formulated it.

In this effort to renounce dinner, smoking was a tremendous boon. The smoker can fast more easily than others. A good smoke numbs whatever appetite there is. It is precisely to smoking that I believe I owe having been able to reduce my net weight to one hundred and seventy-six pounds. It was a great relief to smoke for hygienic reasons. I smoked a little more with this perfectly guiltless conscience. Fundamentally, health is a truly miraculous state. Brought about by the interworking of various organs whose functions we can only know imperfectly (as even Carlo admits, who has grasped the whole science), it derives from the belief that perfect health never exists. Otherwise its termination would be even more miraculous. Moving things ought to be able to move forever. Why not? Isn't this the law in Heaven, the same law as that enforced on earth? But I know that from birth onward diseases are predestined and prepared. From the very beginning some organs start out weaker than others, overexerting themselves and driving related organs to greater effort; and where there is exertion fatigue results, and from it, ultimately, death.

Because of that, and only because of that, a malady followed by death does not reveal any disorders in our constitutions. I am too ignorant to know whether at the end, up there in Heaven, as down here on earth, there exists the possibility of death and reproduction. I only know that some stars and even some planets have less complete movements than others. It must be that a planet which does not rotate on itself is either lame, blind, or humpbacked.

But among our organs there is one that is the center, almost the sun in a solar system. Up until a few years ago this organ was thought to be the heart. At the moment everybody knows that our entire life is dependent upon the genital organs. Carlo turns up his nose at rejuvenation operations, but still he doffs his cap when the genitals are mentioned. He says: If the sexual organs could be rejuvenated they would naturally rejuvenate the whole organism. This was nothing new to me. I would have known that without his telling me. But it will never come to pass. It's impossible. God only knows what the effects of monkey glands are. Maybe a rejuvenated person upon seeing a beautiful woman will be driven to climb the nearest tree. (Even so, this is a pretty juvenile act.)

This I understand: Mother Nature is a maniac. That is to say, she has a mania for reproduction. She maintains life within an organism as long as there is hope of its reproducing itself. Then she kills it off, and does so in the most diverse ways because of her other mania of remaining mysterious. She does not wish to give herself away by always finding recourse in the same malady to do away with old folks—like a malady which might throw light upon our deaths, a little tumor always in the same place, for example.

I have always been very enterprising. Without resorting to an operation, I wanted to hoodwink Mother Nature and make her believe that I was still fit for reproduction; so I took a mistress. This was the least disturbing affair I have ever had in my life: first of all, I considered it neither a lapse of character nor a betrayal of Augusta. I should have felt a bit uneasy, but I regarded taking a mistress a decision equivalent to entering a pharmacy.

Then, of course, matters complicated themselves a little. It ended with my awareness that a whole person cannot be used as a medicine: besides, it is a complex medicine containing a substantial amount of poison. I was still not really old. It was an episode which occurred three years ago, when I was sixty-seven: I was not yet a very old man. Therefore my heart, which was an organ of secondary importance in the adventure and should not have had to enter it, ended by taking part. And it so happened that on some days even Augusta profited from my adventure and was caressed, fondled, and rewarded as she had been when I had had Carla. The curious thing was that it did not surprise her and that she was not even aware of the novelty. She inhabits her great calm and finds it natural that I occupy myself with her less than in the past; still our present inertia does not weaken the bonds between us, which are knotted with caresses and affectionate words. These caresses and affectionate words do not have to be repeated in order to endure, to exist anywhere, to remain always alive and always equally intimate, this bond between us. When, one day, in order to salve my conscience, I placed two fingers underneath her chin and gazed at length into her faithful eyes, she abandoned herself to me, offering up her lips: "You have always remained affectionate." At the moment I was a little taken aback. Then, examining the past, I noticed that in fact I had never been so wanting in affection as to deny her my old love. I had even hugged her (a little distractedly) every evening before closing my eyes in sleep.

It was somewhat difficult to find the woman I sought. There was no one in the house suited to such a role; no more was I eager to sully my home. But I would have done so, since I had to hoodwink Mother Nature into believing that the moment for my final illness had not yet arrived—since there was the grand, the enormous task of finding one who would serve the purposes of an old man engaged in political economy. But, really, that was not the approach. The handsomest woman at home was Augusta herself. There was a little fourteen-year-old girl Augusta made use of for certain household chores. But I knew that if I were to accost this child Mother Nature would not have believed me and would have struck me down at once with one of those thunderbolts she always keeps at her disposal.

It is pointless to relate how I came to find Felicita. Out of sheer devotion to hygiene I used to go every day, to supply myself with cigarettes, some distance beyond Piazza Unità, and this called for a walk of more than a half-hour. The clerk was an old woman, but the owner of the tobacco shop and one who spent occasional hours there supervising was actually Felicita, a girl about twenty-four years old. At the beginning I was of the impression that she had inherited the shop; much later I learned that she had bought it with her own money. It was there that I came to know her. We struck it off well at once. I liked her. She was a blonde who dressed in a variety of colors, in material that did not seem expensive to me but was always new and gaudy. She took pride in that beauty of hers: the small head puffed out at the sides with close-cropped, very curly hair, and the very erect and lovely little body which appeared to contain a staff within it arching a little backwards. It was not long before I came to learn something of her liking for varied colors. At her house this taste was revealed all over the place. From time to time the house was not well heated, and once I took note of the colors she was wearing: she had a red kerchief bound around her head in the style of a peasant woman, a yellow brocaded shawl about her shoulders, a quilted apron in red, yellow and green over her blue skirt, and a pair of multicolored quilted slippers on her feet. She was a real oriental figurine; but her pale face was actually one from our parts, with its eyes that scrutinized things and people to derive from them as much as possible. A monthly allotment was established at the outset and, frankly, it was so high that I could not help comparing it with regret to the much lower allowances given before the war. And as early as the twentieth of the month Felicita (the dear girl) began to talk about the stipend that was falling due, thereby disturbing a good part of the month. She was sincere, transparent. I was less so; and she never learned that I had come to her after having studied medical texts.

But I soon lost sight of that fact. I must say that at the moment I long for that house, so completely rural in aspect except for a single room appointed in the good taste and luxury one would expect at the price, very soberly colored and dimly lighted—a background against which Felicita stood out like a multicolored blossom. She had a brother living in the same house: a good, hard-working electrician whose daily wages were more than enough. He was extremely skinny, but that had nothing to do with his not being married; rather, one could easily see, this was due to his economy. I spoke with him the times Felicita called him in to check the fuses in our room. I discovered that brother and sister were partners, about to make themselves some money. Felicita carried on a very serious life between the tobacconist's shop and the house, Gastone between the house and his workshop. Felicita must have been making more than Gastone but that did not matter, since—as I later learned—she apparently needed her brother's help. It was he who had organized the tobacco-shop business which was proving itself such a sound investment. He was so convinced that he was leading the life of an upright man that he spoke scornfully of the many workers who were frittering their earnings away with never a thought of tomorrow.

All in all we three got along rather well together. The room, so soberly and meticulously kept, smacked of a doctor's consultation chamber. But only because Felicita was a slightly tart medicine that had to be bolted down without the palate's savoring it at its leisure. At the very beginning, somewhat before drawing up terms and in order to encourage me, she threw her arms around me and said: "I give you my word, I don't find you repulsive." It was said nicely enough because said so sweetly, but it gave me pause. I had never really thought of myself as being repulsive. On the contrary, I had believed that I was returning to love, from which I had long abstained through a misinterpretation of hygienic laws, in order to surrender, to offer myself up, to whomever wanted me. This would have been real hygienic practice, which was my aim, and in any other form it would have been incomplete and ineffectual. But notwithstanding the money I paid for the cure I did not dare explain to Felicita how I wanted her to be. And she, very frequently throwing herself at me, would spoil the cure with her complete naïveté: "Isn't it curious! I don't find you repulsive." One day, with the crudeness I can sink to on certain occasions, I murmured gently in her ear: "Isn't it curious! I don't find you repulsive either." This made her giggle so much that the cure was interrupted.

And off and on, in my mind, I even dare boast—to give myself a lift, feel more confident of myself, worthier, loftier, to forget that I have dedicated a part of my life to the task of making myself unrepulsive— I boast that Felicita during brief moments of our long relationship was even in love with me. But when I seek a genuine expression of her affection I find it not in the never-changing sweetness with which she invariably greeted me, nor in the maternal care with which she protected me from drafts, nor in her solicitude once when she covered me with one of her brother's overcoats and lent me an umbrella because a storm had blown up while we were together; but I remember this honest prattle of hers: "Oh, how I loathe you! How I *loathe* you!"

One day when as usual I was talking with Carlo about medicine, he remarked: "What you need is an affectionate girl given to gerontophilia." Who knows? I did not confess to Carlo, but perhaps I had once already found and then lost such a girl. Except that I do not believe that Felicita was a thoroughgoing gerontophile. She took me for too much money for me to think that she really loved me as I was.

She certainly was the most costly woman I have ever known in all my life. She quietly studied me with those cool, tender eyes of hers, often squinting the better to determine the extent to which I would allow myself to be fleeced. In the beginning, and for a long time thereafter, she was completely satisfied with her allowance, because I, not yet a slave of habit, intimated that I would refuse to spend more on her. On several occasions she tried to reach for my money, but withdrew her hand from my pocket in order not to expose herself to the risk of losing me. Once, though, she did bring it off. She got money out of me to buy a rather expensive fur piece, which I never laid eyes on. Another time she got me to pay for an entire Parisian ensemble and then let me see it: but for one even as blind as I was her varicolored clothes were unforgettable and I found that I had seen her in that suit before. She was an economy-minded woman who pretended caprice only because she thought that a man understood caprice in a woman more easily than avarice.

And now this is how against my wishes the relationship was broken off.

I had visited her at set hours twice a week. Then, one Tuesday after I had set out for her house it occurred to me midway there that I would be better off by myself. I returned to my study and quietly devoted myself to a recording of Beethoven's *Ninth Symphony*.

On Wednesday I should not have felt such a strong craving for Felicita, but it was really my avarice that drove me to her. I was paying her a substantial allowance and somehow, not receiving my just due, I finished by paying too much. One must remember that when I take a cure I am very conscientious in its application and resort to the greatest and most scientific exactitude. In the end, only in this way can it be determined whether the cure was good or bad.

As fast as my legs would carry me I was in that room which I believed to be ours. For the moment it belonged to another. Fat old Misceli, a man about my age, was sitting in an easy chair in a corner while Felicita lounged comfortably on the couch, concentrating on the flavor of a long and very choice cigarette—one which was not to be had in her shop. Essentially, it was the very same position in which Felicita and I found ourselves when we were left together, the only difference being that whereas Misceli was not smoking I joined Felicita in it.

"What may I do for you?" Felicita asked icily, studying the fingernails of the hand which was holding the cigarette aloft.

Words failed me. Then it became easier to speak because, to tell the truth, I did not feel the least resentment toward Misceli. This fat man, who was as old as I, looked considerably older because of his tremendous weight. He eyed me warily over the rim of the shiny spectacles he had perched on the tip of his nose. I always feel other old men to be older than I am.

"Oh, Misceli," I said forthrightly, fully resolved not to make a scene, "it's a long time since we've seen each other." And I extended my hand. He laid his ham of a hand in mine without returning my clasp. Still he said nothing. He was indeed showing himself to be older than I.

At that moment, with the objectivity that is precisely a wise man's, I understood perfectly that my position and Misceli's were identical. I felt that because of it we were in no position to resent each other. After all, our meeting here amounted to no more than an ordinary bumping-together on a sidewalk. However painful it may be, one continues on one's way mumbling a word of pardon.

With this thought, the gentleman I have always been reformed within me. I even felt called upon to make Felicita's situation more tolerable. And I said to her: "Signorina, listen: I've got to have a hundred packets of well-selected 'sport' cigarettes because I have to make a gift. Would you see to it that they are soft, please? The tobacco shop is a little too far and I've dropped up here for a moment."

Felicita stopped staring at her nails and her attitude softened. She even rose and walked me to the door. In a low voice, with intense accents of reproach, she managed to say: "Why didn't you come yesterday?" And then, quickly: "And what have you come today for?"

I was offended. It was disgusting to see myself limited to fixed days at the price I was paying. I allowed myself immediate relief by giving vent to my pique: "I've only come here today to let you know that I don't want to see you any more and that we won't see each other again!"

She looked at me astonished, and to see me better stepped off, leaning way back for a moment. Quite frankly, she had struck an odd pose, but it was one that lent her a certain grace, that of a self-assured person capable of maintaining the most difficult equilibrium.

"As you like," she said, shrugging her shoulders. Then, to be sure she had understood me perfectly, just as she was opening the door, she asked me: "Then we don't see any more of each other?" And she searched my face.

"Naturally we don't see any more of each other," said I a little querulously.

I was starting down the stairs when fat old Misceli came bumbling to the door, yelling: "Wait! wait! I'm coming with you too. I've already told the Signorina how many 'sport' cigarettes I need. One hundred. Just like you."

We descended the stair together while Felicita closed the door after a long pause, a pause which gave me a certain amount of delight.

We went down the long slope that leads into Piazza Unità, slowly, careful where we placed our feet. Lumbering along on the slope he certainly appeared older than I. There was even a moment when he stumbled and nearly fell. I helped him right away. He did not thank me. He was panting a little, and we had not yet reached the foot of the slope. Because of that, and only because of that, he did not speak.

This is borne out by the fact that when we reached the level area behind the town hall he loosened up and started talking: "I never smoke 'sports.' But they're preferred as a cigarette. I have to give a present to my carpenter. And then I want to buy the good ones which Signorina Felicita can get." Now that he was talking he could only go step by step. He stopped dead to rummage about in a trousers pocket. He pulled out a gold cigarette case, pressed a little button, and the case flew open: "Would you like one?" he asked. "They're denicotinized." I accepted one and also stopped, in order to light it. He stood there stock-still just to put the case back in his pocket. And I thought, *At least she could have given me a manlier rival.* In fact, I handled myself better than he both on the slope and on the flat area. Compared to him I was really a youngster. He even smoked denicotinized cigarettes, which are entirely flavorless. I was more a man because though I had always tried not to smoke I had never thought of stooping to the cowardice of denicotinized cigarettes.

As God would have it, we arrived at the gate of the Tergesteo, where we had to part. Misceli was now talking about other things: affairs in the Exchange in which he was very adept. He seemed a trifle excited to me, even a little distraught. Actually, it seemed as though he were speaking without listening to himself. I was not listening to him at all either; rather I was studying him, trying to discover exactly what he was *not* saying.

I did not want to break away from him without having tried better to find out what he was thinking. With this in mind I began by giving myself away completely. That is, I burst out with: "Felicita is nothing but a whore." Misceli showed himself in a new light: that of his embarrassment. His fat lower jaw began to move like that of a ruminant. (*Did he do this when he was uncertain as to what to say?*)

Then he said: "She doesn't seem so to me. She's got the best 'sports.'" He wanted to prolong this stupid comedy forever.

I became angry: "Then in other words you intend to continue seeing Signorina Felicita?"

Another pause. His jaw jutted out, swung to the left, returned to the right before fixing itself. Then, for the first time betraying an impulse to laugh, he said: "I'll be going back as soon as I need some 'sports' again."

I laughed too. But I wanted further explanation: "Well, why did you walk out on her today?"

He hesitated, and I detected signs of great sadness in his eyes, fixed darkly on the far end of the street: "I'm a little superstitious. When I'm interrupted in something I believe in recognizing immediately the hand of Providence, and I drop everything I'm doing. Once I was called to Berlin on important business, but I stopped over in Sessana because the train was held up there for several hours for some reason or other. I don't believe in forcing worldly things . . . especially at our age."

That was enough for me and I asked: "You didn't mind when you saw me getting 'sports' from Signorina Felicita too, did you?"

He shot back with such decisiveness that his jaw did not have time to swivel: "What difference should it make to me? Me jealous? Absolutely not! We two are old. We're old! It's all right for us to make love from time to time, but we mustn't become jealous because we are easily made to look ludicrous. We should never get jealous. Listen to me and don't ever let yourself seem jealous, because it would make you look foolish."

His words sounded friendly enough—just as they are written here on paper—but their tone was rather heavily saturated with anger and contempt. His fat face flaming, he approached me; being smaller than I, he looked up at me as though trying to find in my body the weakest point to strike. Why had he become angry with me while declaring that we should not be jealous? What could it have been that I had done to him? Maybe he was angry with me because I had held his train up at Sessana when he should have been arriving in Berlin.

But I was not jealous. I should, however, have liked to know how much he paid Felicita monthly. I felt that if I knew he paid more than I, as I thought he should, I would be satisfied.

But I did not have time to investigate. Suddenly, Misceli became gentler, and addressed himself to my discretion. His gentleness converted itself into a threat when he recalled that we were in each other's hands. I reassured him: I too was married and was aware of the importance of an imprudent word by either one of us.

"Oh," he said with an offhand gesture, "it's not because of my wife that I ask discretion. There are certain things which have not interested her for years. But I know that you too are under Dr. Raulli's care. He threatened to leave me if I didn't follow his prescriptions, if I drank just one glass of wine, if I smoked more than ten, even denicotinized, cigarettes a day, if I didn't give up . . . all the rest. He says that at our age a man's body maintains its equilibrium only because it can't decide what part must collapse. For that reason you shouldn't hint at the part because then the decision would be easy." He went on in a self-pitying mood. "When you come right down to it, it's simple to prescribe things for another person: Don't do this or that or the other. He might just as well say that one had better be resigned to living a few months less than to living like that."

Then he let up for a moment and used the time to extract some information about my own condition. I told him that I had once attained a blood pressure of two hundred and twenty, which pleased him enormously because his had reached only two hundred and ten. With one foot on the step that leads into the Tergesteo, he left with a friendly wave, adding: "Now, please, don't say a thing about it."

I was obsessed for some days by Raulli's fine rhetorical figure of an old man's body that continues to run because it does not know what part should collapse first. Of course when the old doctor spoke of "a part" he meant organ. And "equilibrium" also had its meaning for him. Raulli must have known what he was talking about. With us oldsters, health can only mean a gradual and simultaneous weakening of all organs. Heaven forbid that one of them fall behind, that is, remain too young! I suspect that their interdependence is capable of changing into a struggle and that the weak organs can be beaten up—with magnificent results on the general economy, one can imagine. Misceli's intervention must therefore have been desired by Providence, who guards my life and who even sent word as to how I should behave by way of that mouth with the wandering jaw.

And I returned, pensive, to my gramophone. In the *Ninth Symphony* I again found my organs working together and struggling. Working together during the first movements—the sort of working-together found in the scherzo when even, with two notes, the timpani are allowed to synthesize that which all the instruments are murmuring around them. The joy of the last movement seemed rebellion to me. Crude, with a strength which is violence, with light, brief moments of regret and hesitation. Not for nothing does the human voice, this least sensible of all sounds in nature, enter into the last movement. I admit that on other occasions I had interpreted this symphony otherwise—as the most intense representation of accord between the most divergent of forces, into which finally the human voice is also received and fused. But that day the symphony, played by the same records, appeared as I say.

"Farewell, Felicita," I whispered when the music had faded away. I need not think of you any longer. She was not worth risking a sudden collapse. There were so many medical theories in the world that it was hard to be governed by them. Those rascally doctors' only contribution was toward making life more difficult. The simplest of things are too complicated. To abstain from drinking alcohol is a prescription made from an evident truth. But even so it is known that alcohol at times has curative properties. Then why must I await the intervention of the doctor to offer me the comfort of this potent medicine? There is no doubt that death sometimes results from an organ's occasionally brief and sudden caprice or is the incidental and coincidental product of a variety of weaknesses. I mean that it would be momentary if it were not followed by death. Things must be so managed as to make the coincidence only momentary. So aid has to be at hand, ready even before the onset of cramps from excessive activity or a collapse due to inertia. Why should one wait for the doctor, who comes running merely to scribble out his bill? I alone am able to tell in time when I need something, by a feeling of discomfort. Unfortunately, doctors have not made a study of what can help in a case like that. For that reason, then, I take various things: a purgative with a wine chaser; and then I study myself. I might need something else: a glass of milk—but also a drop of digitalis. And all taken in the most minute quantities, as recommended by the great Hannemann. The mere presence of these minute quantities is enough to produce reactions necessary for the activation of life, just as though an organ, rather than nourished or stimulated, had to be reminded. Seeing a drop of calcium, it exclaims: "Oh, look! I'd forgotten. I've got to work."

This was what I had against Felicita. It was impossible to take her in doses.

In the evening Felicita's brother came over to visit me. On seeing him I was shaken with fear because Augusta herself showed him to my study. Fearing what he had to say to me, I was very happy when Augusta promptly withdrew.

He unknotted a bandanna from which he pulled a package: one hundred boxes of "sport" cigarettes. He broke them down into five stacks, each of twenty boxes; it was easy, therefore, to verify the quantity. Then he had me feel how soft every box was. They had been selected one by one from a large stock. He was sure I would be pleased.

Actually I was tremendously pleased, because after having been so frightened I was feeling completely at ease. I at once paid the hundred and sixty lire I owed him and cheerfully thanked him. Cheerfully, because I really wanted to laugh. A curious woman, Felicita; even though jilted, she was not neglecting her interest in the tobacco shop.

But the pale, lean man, after having jammed the lire he had received into his pocket, still made no move to leave. He did not seem Felicita's brother. I had seen him before, on other occasions, but better dressed. Now he was without a collar, and his clothes, though neat, were absolutely worn out. Strange that he felt he had to have a special hat for workdays: and the one he had was positively filthy and misshapen from long use.

He looked at me intently, hesitating to speak. It seemed that his look was rather dark, and the light that glowed in it, inviting me to guess what was on his mind, off-center. When he finally spoke his look became even more imploring, so imploring that it resulted in seeming to threaten me. Intense supplications border on threats. I can very well understand that certain peasants punish the images of saints they have prayed to by throwing them down beneath their beds.

Finally he said to me in a steady voice: "Felicita says we have reached the tenth of the month."

I looked at the calendar from which I tore away a sheet every day and said: "She's quite right. We have reached the tenth of the month. There's no doubt about it."

"But then," he said hesitantly, "you owe her for all the month."

A second before he spoke I understood why he had led me to look at the calendar. I believe I blushed the moment I discovered that between brother and sister everything was clear and sincere and honest in so far as money was concerned. The only thing that surprised me was the out-and-out request that I pay for the whole month. I even doubted whether I had to pay anything. In my relations with Felicita I had failed to keep very accurate accounts. But hadn't I always paid in advance? and because of that didn't the last payment overlap this fraction of the month? And I sat there with my mouth somewhat agape having to look into those strange eyes, trying to determine whether they were imploring or threatening me. It is precisely the man of vast and long experience like myself who does not know how to behave, because he is aware that by a single word of his, by a single deed, the most unforeseen events are liable to happen. One has only to peruse world history to learn that causes and effects can work themselves into the most peculiar relations with each other. During my hesitation I took out my wallet and also counted and sorted out my money so as not to mistake a hundred-lire note for a five hundred. And when I had the bills counted out I gave them to him. Thus everything I did was done with thought of gaining time through action. And I thought, *I'll pay now and I'll think about it later.*

Felicita's brother himself had ceased to think about it, and his eye, no longer fixed upon me, had lost all of its intensity. He put the money in a different pocket from the one in which he had deposited the hundred and sixty lire. He kept accounts and money separate. He bowed to me: "Good evening, Signor," and left. But he soon returned because he had forgotten another package similar to the one he had given me. By way of excusing himself for having come back he said to me: "This is another hundred boxes of 'sports' I have to deliver to another gentleman."

They were for poor Misceli, of course, who could not stand them either. I smoked all of mine, however, except for some boxes I gave to Fortunato, my chauffeur. When I have paid for something, sooner or later I finish by using it up. It is proof of a sense of thrift that is within me. And everytime I had that taste of straw in my mouth I remembered Felicita and her brother more vividly. By thinking about it over and over I was able to remember with absolute certainty that I had in fact not paid the allowance in advance. After thinking I had been cheated by so much I was relieved to find out that they had been paid for only twenty days extra.

I think I must have returned to see Felicita once again before the twenty days had elapsed only because of my above-mentioned sense of economy: this sense of thrift which had even gotten me into accepting the "sports." I said to myself, *Now that I have paid I'd like to risk once more—for the last time—the danger of tipping off my organism to the part it ought to have collapse. Just once! It'll never know the difference.*

The door to her apartment opened just as I was about to ring. Startled in the darkness, I saw her pale, lovely little face, as though in a visor, clamped in a hat that covered her head back to her ears and the nape of her neck. A solitary blonde curl stole from the hat down her forehead. I knew that at about this hour she was accustomed to go to the tobacco shop to supervise the more complicated part of her money-making enterprises. But I had hoped to induce her to wait for that short while I wanted to have with her.

In the dark she did not immediately recognize me. In a questioning tone she uttered a name, neither mine or Misceli's, which I could not make out. When she did recognize me she extended her hand without a trace of ill feeling, and a little inquisitively. I clasped her cold hand with both of mine and grew bold. She let her hand lie still but drew her head back. Never had that staff within her arched back so far: so much so that I felt like releasing her hand and seizing her by the waist if for no other reason than to steady her.

And that faraway face adorned with the single curl regarded me. Or was it actually looking at me? Wasn't it really looking at a problem which she had brought upon herself and which demanded a ready solution, immediately, there on those steps?

"It's impossible now," she said after a long pause. She was still looking at me. Then every shadow of hesitancy vanished. She stood there, that voluptuous body of hers holding its extremely perilous position, immobile, her little face wan and serious below the yellow ringlet; but slowly, just as though she were acting upon some serious resolution, she withdrew her hand.

"Yes!—it's impossible," she added. It was repeated to convince me that she was still considering the matter to see if perhaps there might be a way to content me, but apart from this repetition there was no other evidence that she was really looking into and thinking about it. She had already made her final decision.

And then she said to me: "You might return on the first of the month, if you wish . . . I'll see . . . I'll think about it."

It is only recently, only since I have set to paper this account of my love affair with Felicita that I have become objective enough to judge her and myself with sufficient justice. I found myself there asserting my rights to those few days due my subscription. She let me know instead that by my renunciation I had lost those rights. I believe that if she had proposed that I immediately enter a new subscription I would have suffered less. I am sure that I would not have run away. At the moment I was bent on love, and to tell the truth, at my age, it very much resembles the crocodile on dry land where, they say, he has to have a great deal of time to change directions. I would have paid for the whole month perhaps, even though resolved to make it the last time.

Instead, this way, she was making me angry. I could not find words; I hardly found air enough to breathe. I said: "Uff!" with the maximum of indignation. I was of the impression that I had said something, and even remained still for an instant, as if I thought that at my "uff," a cry that must have wounded her and given evidence of my deep-seated unhappiness, she would have replied. But neither she nor I had anything else to say. I started down the stairs. A few steps down, I turned to look at her again. Perhaps on her colorless face there was now some sign to belie such hardhearted selfishness, so cold and calculated. I did not see her face. She was completely absorbed in locking up the apartment, which must have remained unvisited for some hours. Once again I said: "Uff," but not so loudly as to be heard by her. I said it to all the world, to society, to our institutions, and to Mother Nature— all that had permitted me to find myself on that staircase, in that position.

It was my last love. Now that the whole adventure has adjusted itself to the past I no longer consider it so worthless, because Felicita—with that flax-colored hair of hers, her pallid face, slender nose, and inscrutable eyes, her disinclination to talk seldom revealing the iciness of her heart—Felicita is not unworthy of being regretted. But after her there was no room for another mistress. She had educated me. Up till then, whenever I happened to be with a woman for more than ten minutes I used to feel hope and desire surging in my heart. Of course I wanted to conceal both, but still my strongest wish was to let them grow so that I might feel more alive and have a sense of participating in life. In order to let hope and desire grow I had to express them in words and let them out. Who knows how many times I was laughed at? To the career of old man to which I am now condemned, it was Felicita who educated me. I can hardly bring myself to realize that now in the field of love I am worth no more than what I pay.

My ugliness is ever before my eyes. This morning upon awakening I studied the position in which I found my mouth the moment I opened my eyes. My lower jaw lolled on the side I was lying on, and my dead and swollen tongue felt out of place.

I thought of Felicita, whom I very often think of with desire and hatred. At that moment I murmured: "She's right."

"Who's right?" demanded Augusta, who was dressing.

And I promptly replied: "A certain Misceli I ran into yesterday, who told me that he doesn't understand why one is born to live and grow old. He's right."

Thus I actually told her everything without compromising myself in the least.

And until now no one has ever taken Felicita's place. Nevertheless I seek to deceive Mother Nature, who is keeping her eye on me so as to liquidate me no sooner than it becomes apparent that I can no longer reproduce. With wise dosages in Hannemann's prescribed quantities I take a little of that medicine every day. I watch women passing by; I follow them with my eyes, seeking to discover in their legs something other than walking apparatus, so that I may again feel a craving to stop and fondle them. In this respect the dosages are becoming more measured than Hannemann or I should like. That is, I have to control my eyes lest they betray what they are looking for, and so it must be understood how rarely the medicine is of service. One may do without the caresses of others in order to attain a complete feeling, but it is impossible to feign indifference without running the risk of chilling one's heart. And having written this I can better understand my adventure with old Signora Dondi. I greeted her to do right by her and to make her aware of her beauty. The fate of old men is gallantry.

Never think that such ephemeral relations, entered into with the intention merely of rescuing oneself from death, do not leave their mark, do not contribute toward the adornment and troubling of one's life, like my affairs with Carla and Felicita. On rare occasions, because of the strong impression received, they reach the point of leaving an indelible memory.

I recall a girl who was seated opposite me in a tram. She left me with a memory. We reached a certain intimacy because I gave her a name: Amphora. She did not have a very striking face, but her eyes, luminous and rather round, stared at everything with great curiosity and something of a little girl's inquisitiveness. She might have been over twenty, but I would not have been surprised if she had playfully jerked the ropelike pigtail of the baby girl sitting next to her. I do not know whether it was because of a rare figure, or because her dress made her appear to have one, but from the waist up her slender body resembled an exquisite amphora placed upon her hips. And I was greatly taken by her breasts. The better to hoodwink Mother Nature, who had her eye on me, I thought, *Naturally I can't die yet because, if this girl wants me to, I've got to stand ready to reproduce.*

My face must have taken on a curious look as I gazed at that amphora. But I dismiss its having been that of a lecher, inasmuch as I was thinking of death. Still, others interpreted it as suppressed lust. As I later noticed, the girl, who must have been of a well-to-do family, was accompanied by a rather old maidservant who got off the tram with her. And it was this old woman who, when she passed by me, looked down and whispered: "Old lecher." She called me old. She was summoning death. I said to her: "You old fool." But she left without replying.

II

FROM FUTURISM TO FASCISM

The second decade of the twentieth century was crucial for Italy's destiny. Between 1910 and 1920 all the contradictions which confronted the country in her newly assumed role of a major European power sharpened considerably. International tension, the Lybian campaign, which marked the beginning of Italy's colonial drive, the upsurge of the nationalistic movement, the grim years of World War I, in 1915–1918, with their alternation of defeats, hopes, and sacrifices, the difficult postwar period with its social unrest and disappointment, and, finally, the rise of Fascism—these and many other, less momentous but significant, events filled the decade with the clamor of arms and the din of discussion.

The perpetual conflict between an idyllic country of poor and colorful peasants and a rapidly progressing urban and industrial civilization continued to divide the Italian imagination and to furnish topics for Italian writers. The wealthy north of plants and mills and the relatively prosperous Tuscany of vineyards and olive plantations looked down on the backward and starving provinces of the south, where outdated husbandry and administrative corruption were buttressed by feudal customs. But the southern ways of life seemed to hold an irresistible attraction for native and particularly foreign readers. For example, the international reputation of Grazia Deledda, the Nobel Prize winner, was largely based on the "exoticism" of her descriptions. Naturalism and regionalism took on a new flavor in her tales of Sardinia, an island of archaic traditions and magic rites. Deledda's Romantic folklore, which had all the dramatic intensity of a medieval pageant, had also that morbid ardor which made her close to d'Annunzio as well as modern in mood. This added a new dimension to her realistic narrative: anxiety and perversion make her heroes and heroines complex and refined under their slovenly and provincially boorish exteriors. The true nature of the southerners is also clear in G. A. Borgese's Sicilian stories, conceived as poetic units with symbolic overtones; yet the author's attitude toward his unfortunate heroes and heroines is more critical and detached.

While Deledda emphasized the romantic and passionate soul of rural Italy, Alfredo Panzini undertook a defense of traditional virtues from the standpoint of a middle-class intellectual. This gentle skeptic and master of transparent, well-constructed prose was a contemplative man, a follower of the ancient classics and a painter of impressions. Like Deledda and the majority of his contemporaries, he favored the short story, and even his novels are little more than loosely knit successions of sketches. He extolled the simplicity and bucolic passivity of the peasants of Emilia, Tuscany, and Romagna, and took issue with the cruelty and pettiness of the machine age, fearing that industrialism threatened to crush both the contemplative peace of the intellectuals and the organic "naturalness" of the farmers. In his struggle against this danger he handled adroitly a paternal, benevolent sort of humor which he used so kindheartedly in "The Mistress and the Master Speak." The humane irony of this nonreligious moralist, though not very deep, had an infectious quality. Panzini's importance lay also in the fact that his ironical manner was typical of many writers of the period, to such an extent that many critics saw it almost as a national trait. It has been remarked that Italian laughter is often a defense mechanism against poverty and misfortune, against the upheavals of both nature and history. It is true that a blasé attitude serves in most cases as self-protection against disillusionment, and Panzini certainly was an embodiment of smiling skepticism and ironic resignation.

The main bent of life and letters on the eve of World War I in great Italian centers was, however, against indulgence and passivity and in any case against that very provincialism which Panzini cherished as the last resort of a crumbling patriarchal civilization. The younger generation, particularly in the north and in the center, was no longer amused by mild irony and evocations of folklore. While the disciples of d'Annunzio arrived at their nationalism through glorification of the past, a strong anti-past literary movement was gathering momentum. Various "modernistic" circles concurred in their rejection of the Academy and of the idols of the day, including d'Annunzio. They refused to be reminded constantly of Dante, Petrarch and Ariosto, or to serve as guardians of that huge museum called Italy.

Whatever their exaggerations and extravagancies, the futurists, as the extremists were called, dreamed of transforming Italy into a modern country dominated by speed and industrialization. They were intoxicated by the revolutionary spirit of triumphant capitalism and aimed at supplanting sleepy villages with roaring towns and old wisdom with a new attitude of struggle and adventure. By 1912–1915 they had become widely popular. Most of them favored war as a proof of strength and talked of a Great Italy carving her place in the sun by force of arms. The ideology of Fascism derived later from some of the principles formulated by those futurists. Other groups of the young avant-garde, however, were less interested in the political and social implication of their rebellion and limited their iconoclastic battles to arts and letters. Some others found an outlet for their impatience in socialist and anarchist movements.

Whatever the political consequences, the impetus of all those young rebels was felt strongly in literature. Most of the writers who became well known under Fascism, such as Bontempelli, Palazzeschi, Papini, and dozens of modern poets and storytellers, served their apprenticeship in the futurist ranks.

What was most typical of the prewar generation, of which Papini is so representative, was the desire for innovation and the feverish search for new forms and "modern" trends in art. Papini first joined the Voce group in Florence which had been founded by Giuseppe Prezzolini and was active in introducing the Parisian impressionists, Ibsen and Gide, Dostoevsky and Debussy, Wagner and Verlaine to his neo-Romantic friends. He studied Croce's philosophy of history and the

French symbolists. He opposed naturalism and materialism and displayed the apostolic zeal of a teacher and a moralist who is extremely critical of his time, his society, and his country's literature. The cerebral, bookish inspiration of this Italian intellectual is obvious in such sophisticated fantasies of his as "The Maker of Clouds" or "The Mask Factory." Although he finally changed from futurism to Catholicism, he remained a wanderer and a seeker rather than a firm believer, and this quality of his made him both popular and representative of a whole segment of Italian thought and art.

The end of World War I and discontent over the Versailles Treaty gave the Italians the feeling of a Pyrrhic victory. Despite all their efforts, which shattered the fragile economy of the country and canceled many achievements of the prewar years, they gained hardly anything from the defeat of the Central Powers and were offended by their own allies, who treated them as a poor relative. While resentment sharpened nationalistic outbursts in the aftermath of the war, the working masses, encouraged by Bolshevism in Russia, started a revolutionary movement. Existing political parties, from socialists to conservatives, wasted time and energy in sterile squabbling. The man in the street, tired of the general confusion and disappointed in democratic slogans, was ready to lend his support to anything which would restore law and order and dispel the ghost of social revolution. The victory of Fascism in 1923, undoubtedly caused by a multiplicity of factors, fulfilled the wishes of a large majority of the middle class and of an important and powerful part of the upper classes. Naturally it provoked a sense of defeat and gloom among liberals, intelligentsia, and large groups of workmen and peasants who retired into their customary passivity. Moravia's first novel, The Time of Indifference, and Borgese's Rube, as well as many other minor novels and novelettes, are documents of this discouragement, and it is interesting to compare them with such depositions of the lost generation in America as the works of F. Scott Fitzgerald or Ernest Hemingway.

Social historians would probably claim that in the atmosphere created by Fascism, the collapse of democratic values and general discontent, many artists subconsciously looked for an escape from the pressures of an unsatisfactory actuality. Literary critics, however, would discover aesthetic reasons for the concentration in literature on purely formal problems, a concentration which avoided direct representation of life or discussion of reality in its social and philosophical aspects. In any case, while verismo seemed to decline, the so-called prosa d'arte became one of the principal literary trends of the twenties. A group called La Ronda, which included many former La Voce members, advocated craftsmanship, artistic discipline, and professional integrity and proclaimed the self-sufficiency of a work of art. Their morality was that of formal perfection, of a "thing well done," and they fought against "corruption of art by political and religious ends," against the pseudo-Romanticism still popular with readers, as well as against the shallow eloquence of the drumbeaters for Fascism.

La Ronda's leader, Emilio Cecchi, a man of wide culture and a specialist in American and English literature, about which he wrote extensively and penetratingly, was a brilliant critic and essayist. A sophisticated and delicate mind, a writer of wit, sometimes given to a mischievous twist, he fully adhered to the saying that one can write in many manners but not without a manner. His seemed a rather complex one: there was always something more than the retelling of an impression or incident in his impressionistic sketches. They usually concealed a hidden point and conveyed an ambiguity, while his jests were generally double-edged.

Cecchi and most of the Rondists shied away from large canvases. "Fragmentism" was one of their favorite artistic methods. There was more to it than the usual Italian penchant for the tale, which Leo Olschi, in his The Genius of Italy, considers symptomatic of Italian interest, taste, and preference. It was definitely a bent toward fragmentary, rather than integrated and conclusive, composition. In some cases, it occasioned literary flourishes, a prose with baroque ornamentation and decadent convolutions.

The reaction it provoked came from La Ronda's own ranks and was most visible in Riccardo Bacchelli. A savant, a lover of history, a versatile and loquacious narrator, he underwent a strict artistic training, from his early participation in the La Ronda group, and worked hard, with an incredible perseverance. The honesty of his effort and the range of his work command the respect of even his enemies—of whom he has no lack in the republic of letters. A protean writer, he left hardly any genre untried and published dozens of different books.

They reveal an amazing amalgam of erudition and exuberant imagination, of scholarly research and verbal virtuosity. He is a born teller of yarns, many of them flowery and full-bodied. The collections of his short stories contain jocose, fantastic, satirical, realistic, and romantic specimens. He is at his best when describing the valley of the Po, which he knows and loves, and its inhabitants in whom civilization has not yet stifled elemental passions; his men and women, drawn against a rich background of nature, all tingle with sensuality and zest for life.

Under Fascism, Bacchelli won the reputation of being one of Italy's leading writers, and his historical novels, particularly The Mill on the Po, a three-volume chronicle, became best sellers. Ill-disposed critics attributed this success to the fact that Bacchelli's skepticism in political matters and his ironical attitude toward humanitarian dreams of freedom and progress flattered vast groups of the general public which neither joined nor rejected the Fascist regime and preferred the noncommittal attitude of historical detachment. Today, however, we can see that Bacchelli's work, as well as that of some other prose writers in the thirties, was symptomatic of certain gradual changes within Italian literature. Along with fragmentism, there began a return to a more comprehensive art concerned with large human and historical issues; and the desire to reconcile the new national and the old universal values was paralleled by the yearning for a closer connection between life and fiction.

GRAZIA DELEDDA

The Sardinian Fox

TRANSLATED BY WILLIAM FENSE WEAVER

The long, warm May days had come back, and Ziu * Tomas again sat as he had the year before—ten years before—in the open courtyard in front of his house, which was the last in a bunch of little, black buildings huddled against the gray slope of a mountain. But in vain spring sent its breath of wild voluptuousness up there: the decrepit old man, motionless between his old black dog and his old yellow cat, seemed as stony and insensible as everything around him.

Only, at night, the smell of the grass reminded him of the pastures where he had spent most of his life; and when the moon rose out of the sea, far off, as huge and golden as the sun, and the coastal mountains, black beneath a silver sky, and all the huge valley and the fantastic semicircle of hills before and to the right of the horizon were covered with shimmering veils and areas of light and shadow, then the old man used to think of childish things, of Lusbé, the devil who leads damned souls to the pasture, after they have been changed into wild boars; and if the moon hid behind a cloud, he thought seriously of the seven calving cows which the planet, at that moment going to supper, devoured calmly in its hiding place.

He almost never spoke; but one evening his granddaughter Zana, when she shook him to tell him it was bedtime, found him so stubbornly silent, erect, and rigid on his stool that she thought he was

* "Zia" and "Ziu" literally mean "aunt" and "uncle" but are sometimes used as complimentary titles for older people of some standing.

57

dead. Frightened, she called Zia Lenarda, her neighbor, and both women succeeded in moving the old man, helping him into the house, where he stretched out on the mat in front of the hearth.

"Zia Lenarda, we have to call a doctor. Grandfather is as cold as a corpse," the girl said, touching the old man.

"Our doctor's gone away. He went to the mainland for two months to study ear diseases, because he says they're all deaf around here when he asks them to pay the rent on his pastures . . . as if he hadn't bought all that land with the people's money, may justice find him! And now, instead of him, we have that foolish snob of a city doctor, who thinks he's the court physician of the king of Spain. Who knows if he'll come or not?"

"Zia Lenarda, he has to come. He charges twenty lire a visit!" Zana said haughtily.

And the woman went off.

The substitute was living in the regular doctor's house, the only habitable one in the whole village. Surrounded by gardens, with terraces and arbors, with a great courtyard covered with grapevines and wistaria, the house was a comfort even to this substitute, who came from a town that, though small, had all the necessities, vices, murderers, loose women, and gambling houses that the larger cities have.

Zia Lenarda found him reading a yellow-backed book in the dining room, which opened onto the courtyard; no doubt a medical work, she thought, judging by the intensity with which he consumed it, his nearsighted eyes stuck to the page, his white fists supporting his dark, rather soft cheeks, his thick lips parted to show his protruding teeth.

The maid had to call him twice before he noticed the woman's presence. He closed the book sharply and, slack and distracted, followed Zia Lenarda. She didn't dare to speak, and went before him as if to show him the way, leaping, agile and silent, down from rock to rock over the rough lanes, struck by the moon.

Below, in the valley's depth, in front of the woman's darkened window, the doctor looked up and saw the mountains' silver peaks. The pure smell of the valley was mixed with the sheepfold odor that came from the hovels, from the forms of shepherds crouched here and there on the steps before their doors: all was sad and magnificent. But in the courtyard of Ziu Tomas the smell of hay and sage dominated; and in front of the low wall by the embankment, with the huge moon and a star almost scraping her head, the doctor saw a woman's form so slender, especially from the waist down, so shrouded, without outlines, that she gave him the impression of a bust set on a narrow pedestal.

Seeing him, she went back to the kitchen, got a light, and knelt down beside her grandfather's mat, while Zia Lenarda ran into the other room to fetch a painted chair for the doctor.

Then the girl raised her head and looked into his eyes, and he felt a sensation that he would never forget. He thought he had never seen a woman's face more lovely and more enigmatic: a broad forehead covered almost to the eyebrows (one higher than the other) by two bands of black, shiny hair; a narrow, prominent chin; smooth cheekbones that cast a little shadow on her cheeks; and white, straight teeth, which gave a suggestion of cruelty to her proud mouth; while her great black eyes were full of sadness and a deep languor.

Seeing herself examined in this way, Zana lowered her eyes and didn't raise them again; but when her grandfather didn't answer the doctor's questions, she murmured: "He's been deaf for twenty years or more."

"You don't say? Well, at least you might prepare a foot bath for him; his feet are frozen."

"A foot bath? Won't that hurt him?" Zia Lenarda asked, consulting Zana. "He hasn't taken his shoes off for eight months."

"Well, then, are you going to leave him here now?"

"Where else can I put him? He's always slept here."

The doctor got up, and after he had written out a prescription, he gave it to Zana and looked around him.

The place was black as a cave; he could make out a passage at the back, with a wooden ladder; everything indicated the direst poverty. He looked with pity at Zana, so white and thin that she reminded him of an asphodel blooming at the mouth of a cavern.

"The old man is undernourished," he said hesitantly, "and you are, too, I believe. You'd both need a more plentiful diet. If you can . . ."

She understood at once. "We can do anything!"

Her expression was so full of scorn that he went away almost intimidated.

Up, from stone to stone, along the sandstone path he went back to his oasis; the moon silvered the arbor, and the wistaria blooms hung like bunches of fantastic grapes whose very perfume was intoxicating. The old maidservant was spinning in the doorway, and with Zana's strange face still before his eyes, he asked: "Do you know Ziu Tomas Acchittu?"

Who didn't know the Acchittu family?

"They're known even in Nuoro, my prize! More than one learned man wants to marry Zana."

"Yes, she's beautiful. I had never seen her before."

"She never goes out. There's no need of that, to be sure. The rose smells sweet even indoors. Foreigners come from everywhere, even from Nuoro, and pass by just to see her."

"What? Has the town crier gone around to announce her beauty?"

"That's not it, my soul! The old man is so rich he doesn't know how much he has. Land as big as all of Spain, and they say he has more than twenty thousand scudi * in a hole somewhere. Only Zana knows the place. That's why she doesn't want even Don Juacchinu, who's noble but not so rich."

"And may I ask where these riches come from?"

"Where do the things of this world come from? They say the old man (on my life, I can't say yes or no about it, myself) had a hand in more than one bandit raid in the good old days when the dragoons weren't as quick as the carabinieri are nowadays. Then, in those days, more than one shepherd came home with one sack full of cheese and the other of gold coins and silver plate. . . ."

The old woman began to relate all this, and it seemed that she drew the stories from her memory like the thread from her distaff; the man listened, in the shadow of the arbor, sprinkled with gold pieces, and now he understood Zana's laugh and her words: "We can do anything!"

The day after the first visit he was back at the house: the old man was sitting on the mat, calmly gumming his barley bread soaked in cold water, the dog on one side of him, the cat on the other. The sun slanted in through the low door, and the May wind bore away the wild, leathery smell of the old man.

"How's it going?"

"Well, as you can see," Zana said, with a hint of scorn in her voice.

* "Scudo"—a former Italian silver coin equivalent to about 97 U.S. cents.

"Yes. I can see. How old are you, Ziu Tomas?"

"Yes, I still can," the old man said, showing the few, blackened teeth he had left.

"He thought you said *chew*. Grandfather—" Zana said, bending over the old man, showing him her hands with all the fingers sticking out except the right thumb, "—like this, isn't that right?"

"Yes, ninety, may God preserve me."

"Good for you. I hope you live to be a hundred—more than a hundred! And you, Zana, you've stayed here with him, alone?"

She told him how all her relatives were dead, her aunts, uncles, cousins, the old, the children; and she spoke calmly of death as of a simple event without importance; but when the doctor turned to the old man, shouting: "Change your way of living! Cleanliness! Roast meat! Good wine! and make Zana enjoy herself a little, Ziu Tomas."

Then the old man asked: "When's he coming back?"

"Who?"

"Oh," Zana said, "it's just that he's waiting for our regular doctor to come back and cure his ears."

"Wonderful! Our doctor's fame is assured then."

The old man, who went on understanding everything in his own way, touched the sleeve of his torn jacket, which was shiny with grease. "Dirty? It's the custom. People who are well off don't have to make a show of it."

As a matter of fact, the doctor observed that the cleanest people in town were the poor; the rich paid no attention to their clothes, scorning appearances, and also finding it convenient perhaps. Here, one day, was Zia Lenarda, waiting for the doctor in the courtyard, dressed like a servant, though she too was a woman of means, with property and flocks, so rich that in spite of her forty-three years she had married a handsome boy of twenty.

"Good morning, doctor, your honor. I'd like to ask a favor of you. My husband Jacu is off on military service: now it's shearing time and I want him to come home on leave. Your honor doesn't know anyone at the Court?"

"No, unfortunately, my good woman."

"I asked our regular doctor about it. Take care of it, I said, if you pass through Rome. But he always says yes, then he forgets. My Jacu is a handsome boy (I'm not boasting just because I'm his wife) and just as good as honey . . . with a little pushing he could get everything. . . ."

She made a gesture of pushing with her spindle, but the doctor went off, sighing.

"It's not enough to be handsome and good in this world to get what we want, my dear lady."

And he went back to his oasis, thinking of Zana and of many things in his past. He was thinking that in his youth he had been handsome and good and yet he had got nothing, not love, or wealth, or even pleasure. True, he had not hunted for them; perhaps he had been waiting for them to offer themselves spontaneously; and as he had waited and waited, time had passed in futility. But in the past few years he had been seized sometimes by fits of mad rebellion; he sold his property and went off to search urgently for love, wealth, pleasure. But one day he realized that these cannot be bought, and when his wallet was empty, he went back to his few patients, joked with them good-naturedly, took long, absent-minded walks, and read yellow-backed French novels.

Zia Lenarda, on her side, convinced that good looks can obtain everything, seeing that the doctor went to the Acchittu's every day even though the old man was well, turned to Zana.

"You tell him, treasure! Everyone's getting ready for the shearing. What can I do, with everything turned over to the hired hands? The doctor looks at you with eyes as big as doorknobs. . . . How can he help it, dear heart? If you tell him to ask for Jacu's leave, he can't say no."

But Zana didn't promise; and when, after the tedium of those long days when the warm wind, the empty blue sky, the bright sun created an ineffable sadness, the doctor went at evening to the courtyard of Ziu Tomas, where he sat astride the painted chair in front of the hedge, full of fireflies and stars, she joked with him and asked him what causes certain diseases, how poisons are made, and she spoke calmly of many things, but she didn't ask the favor her neighbor wanted.

Sometimes Zia Lenarda herself, seated on the low wall, spun in the dark and joined in the conversation. This annoyed the doctor, who wanted to be alone with Zana after he had convinced the old man to go to bed early because the night air was bad for the deaf. The older woman spoke of nothing but the shearing.

"If you could just see the celebration, your honor! Nothing is more fun, not even the feast of San Michele and San Constantino. I'd invite you if Jacu came, but without him the feast would be like a funeral for me."

"Well, my good woman, do you want to know the truth? They'd give Jacu leave only if you were ill, and you're as healthy as a goat."

Then she began to complain; she had had so many aches since Jacu left, and now that shearing time approached, she really was suffering mortally. To convince the doctor more readily, she took to her bed. He was touched. He wrote out the certificate and ordered some medicine. Zana waited on her neighbor, poured out the dosage, looking at it in the reddish light of the oil lantern, and murmured: "It's not poison, is it?"

Then she went back to the courtyard, where the doctor was sitting on the painted chair. It was an evening in early June, warm already and scented. Night of love and memories! And the memories came, sweet and bitter, from the doctor's dark, tortuous past, as from the dark and tortuous valley came the sweet and bitter odor of the oleander. He drew his chair closer to the low wall where Zana was sitting, and they began their usual conversation. Occasionally a shepherd passed in the lane, without too much surprise at hearing the doctor's voice in the courtyard of Ziu Tomas. By now everybody believed that the doctor was regularly courting Zana, and they were sure that Zana would accept him, otherwise she would have kept him at a distance. But the two of them spoke of matters apparently innocent, of grasses, poisonous plants, medicaments.

"Oleander? No, that isn't poisonous, but hemlock is. Do you know what it looks like?"

"Who doesn't?"

"It's called the sardonic plant. It makes people die laughing . . . like you!"

"Let go of my wrist, doctor. I don't have the fever like Zia Lenarda."

"I have the fever, Zana."

"Well, take some quinine. Or is that poison, too?"

"Why do you keep talking about poisons tonight? Are you plan-

ning to kill somebody? If you are, I'll kill him for you at once . . .
but . . ."

"But?"

"But . . ."

He took her wrist again, and she allowed it. It was dark anyway, and
nobody could see from the lane.

"Yes, I do want some poison. For the fox."

"What? She comes this close?"

"She certainly does! Let go of me," she added in a whisper, twisting
threateningly, but he took her other hand and held her fast, as if she
were a thief.

"Give me a kiss, Zana. Just one."

"You can go and kiss a firebrand. Well, all right, if you give me the
poison. That fox even comes and steals our newborn lambs. . . ."

When Jacu's application for leave had been mailed off, along with
the doctor's certificate, Zia Lenarda recovered and went back to mind-
ing her neighbors' business. And without any surprise she realized that
the doctor was aflame like a field of stubble. He went back and forth
in the lane like a boy, and even twice in a day he visited Ziu Tomas,
claiming he would cure the old man's deafness before his colleague
came back from the mainland. Zana seemed impassive; often she
wouldn't make an appearance, but stayed shut in her room, like a
spider in its hole.

On Sundays, the only day she went out—to go to mass—the doctor
waited for her in front of the church.

One after another, the women came up the winding lane, stiff in
their holiday clothes, their hands folded on their embroidered aprons,
or carrying their babies on their arms, in red cloaks marked with a
blue cross. When they reached a certain spot they turned toward
Mount Nuoro, guarded by a statue of the Redeemer, and blessed themselves. The sun gleamed on the gold of their sashes and illuminated
their fine Greek profiles. But the doctor, as if bewitched, looked only
at Zana, and the old gossips thought: "The daughter of Tomas
Acchittu has given him mandrake to drink. . . ."

One day, among the few men who took part in the women's procession, there was Jacu, home on leave. He was really handsome, no two

ways about it: tall, ruddy, clean-shaven, with green eyes so bright that the women lowered theirs when they went by him, even if he were paying no attention to them. Military life had given him the air of a conqueror, but of things far more serious than mere women. As soon as he arrived, he had gone up to the doctor's to thank him, bringing him a young kid and an invitation to the famous shearing. The doctor spoke to him in dialect; he answered in proper Italian. And when the doctor asked, rather pointedly: "Are you inviting many people?" he answered: "Yes, because it's a big family, and a man like me—well, I may have many enemies, but I also have many friends. Besides, I'm broad-minded, and I'm inviting even the relatives of Lenarda's first husband. They can kill me, if I'm lying. And if she had had three husbands, I'd invite the relatives of them all."

"You're a man of the world, I see. Good for you. I suppose you'll invite your neighbors, too."

Being a man of the world, Jacu pretended to know nothing of the doctor's madness over Zana.

"Of course, a neighbor is more than a relative."

The day of the shearing came, and Zana, Zia Lenarda, and the other women took seats in the cart that Jacu drove.

The sheepfold was on the plateau, and the heavy vehicle, drawn by two black steers, scarcely broken, bounced up along the rocky path; but the women weren't afraid, and Zana, her hands clasping her knees, was calmly crouched down as if in front of her own hearth. She seemed sad, but her eyes gleamed with a kind of hidden lightening, like a far-off blaze, shining on a dark night in the heart of a forest.

"Neighbor," Jacu said, good-humoredly, "hang me, but you have a face like a funeral. He'll come, he'll come. He's coming later, with the priest, as soon as mass is over. . . ."

"Cheer up, Zana," the women said then, joking a little maliciously, "I hear a horse now, trotting like the devil himself."

"Cheer up, girl. I can see his watch chain shining."

"What a chain that is! How much would that chain cost? Nine *reali*?" *

Then Zana grew angry. "Evil take you all. Leave me alone. I can't

* One *real*—a former Spanish silver coin—was equal to about 13 U.S. cents.

bear him. The crows can pluck out my eyes if I even look at that man's face today. . . ."

The doctor and the priest arrived a little before noon, welcomed with shouts of joy. In the shade of a cork tree Jacu, the servant, and his friends sheared the sheep, laying them out, carefully bound, on a broad stone that looked like a sacrificial altar. The dogs chased one another through the grass, birds chirped in the oak, an old man who looked like the prophet Elijah gathered the wool into a sack, and all around the asphodel and the wild lilies, bent by the scent-laden wind, seemed to lean forward, curious to see what was happening in the midst of that group of men who stooped down, the shears in their hands. Once they were sheared and released, the sheep jumped up from the heap of wool, as from a foaming wave, and bounded off, shrunken, their muzzles rubbing the earth.

For a while the doctor stood watching, his hands clasped behind him, then he turned to the hut, where the women were cooking, assisted by Jacu's old father, who reserved for himself the honor of roasting a whole kid on the spit. Farther on, the priest, stretched out on the grass in the shade of another cork tree, was telling a Boccaccian tale to a select group of youths. The women nudged Zana and pointed to the doctor; and all at once, with a change of mood, she began to joke with him, asking him to make himself useful at least, by going to get some water at the spring. He went along with her jokes and, taking a cork pail, walked off in the bright sunlight that scorched the grass and the sage and made a perfume that was enough to intoxicate a man.

The group around the priest sent whistles and shouts after the doctor, and the old man roasting the kid caught his thumb in his fingers as a gesture of contempt. A learned man, a grown man, letting himself be made a fool of like this by the women! Then Zana cursed and ran off, holding her kerchief to her head, until she caught up with the doctor and took the pail out of his hand. From a distance, the women saw the man follow her along the path that led to the spring, and Jacu's old father began to spit furiously on the fire, as if he wanted to put it out.

"The granddaughter of Tomas Acchittu—you see her? She wanted to be alone with the man. If she was my daughter, I'd put my foot on her neck."

"Let her be, father-in-law," Zia Lenarda said kindly. Ah, she knew what love was, how it made you mad, like drinking bewitched water.

The doctor, in fact, dazed by the bright sun, followed Zana into the thicket around the spring, and again he tried to take her in his arms. She looked at him with those eyes of hers, like the Queen of Sheba's; but she pushed him away, threatening to pour the pail full of water on his head. Always the same, since the first evening there by the low wall of the courtyard; she led him on and repulsed him, half ingenuous, half treacherous, and asked him always for the same thing: some poison.

"All right, then, Zana, I'll make you happy. Tonight I'll come to your house, and I'll bring one of those little bottles with a skull on it. But be careful you don't end in jail."

"It's for the fox, I tell you. All right, but leave me now. You hear? Someone's coming."

In fact, the thicket around the fountain shook as if a boar were crashing through, then Jacu appeared. His face was overwrought, although he pretended that finding the two of them was a joke.

"Hey! What are you doing there in the dark? It's time to eat, not to be courting. . . ."

"You're not so hungry; you're thirsty," Zana said sarcastically, lifting the pail, "have a drink, handsome. . . ."

But Jacu threw himself full-length on the ground and drank, panting, from the spring.

During the banquet the doctor laughed, while the priest threw bread crumbs at him and hinted maliciously. He laughed, but from time to time he was distracted, struck by a new idea. After the banquet was over he went off to lie down in the shade among the rocks behind the hut; from there he could see without being seen, and he commanded a view of the area down to the oak in whose shade the shepherd went on shearing. The priest and the others, nearer by, had begun a singing contest, and the women were listening, seated in a row, their hands in their laps.

In the intense silence, the voices, the songs, the laughter were dispelled like the thin white clouds in the blue vastness; and the doctor could hear a horse cropping the grass beyond the rocks, a dog gnawing a bone inside the hut, where Jacu came every so often to empty the sheared wool.

All at once Zana, as the song contest grew more lively, got up and came into the hut. The doctor was smoking; he observed the blue thread that rose from his cigar, and a kind of grin raised his upper lip, showing the gold fillings of his teeth.

Finally Jacu arrived, and Zana's choked voice came like a moan through the cracks in the hut.

"I swear . . . May I be eaten by the hawks . . . if he's even touched my hand. I have my own reasons for smiling at him. . . . It's all for our own good. . . . But this suffering will end . . . end. . . ."

The man, intent perhaps on emptying the wool, was silent. She went on, exasperated, her voice filled with hate: "What about me? Am I ever jealous of your wife? The old crow, the fox. But it's going to end . . . soon. . . ."

Then Jacu laughed; and again there was heard the laughter, the singing, the grazing horse.

But the doctor wanted to enjoy himself a little. He leaped to his feet and began to shout: "Hey! a fox! a fox!"

And the two lovers ran out of the hut, amazed, while below, the group stopped their singing, the women looked all around them, and the dogs started to bark as if a fox had really gone past.

ALFREDO PANZINI

The Mistress and the Master Speak

TRANSLATED BY MARIANNE CECCONI

When the mistress of the villa was in good fettle she was as good as bread when bread is good. But she was so rarely in good fettle! If there was no fresh bread in the morning she was immediately in a bad mood. And then little Robert, too, wouldn't drink his milky coffee with stale bread in it.

"And yet he wants to be an explorer!" the master of the villa, who was a scientist, an explorer of the skies, would exclaim.

She was dainty at her eating. My mother used to say she wouldn't board her for a Napoleon a day. She didn't eat much, but she picked a bit at everything. After the fried dish there must be the roast, after the roast some fruit to take away the greasy taste of the roast, after the fruit a little sweet to take away the acid of the fruit, after the sweet the bitter coffee, to take away the sweet of the sweet, after the bitter coffee an apoplectic stroke to finish you off!

That's what my mother used to say.

She liked raw eggs, and my mother would fetch her two or three a day.

"Oh, my dear, my dear," she'd say to the egg. "It's still warm!" and she'd put it against her cheek.

"It's just now come out of the hen," my mother would say.

"That's no way to talk, Marietta! One should say: It's just been born!"

And she'd make a little opening in it with a needle and swallow it like that, which was disgusting to us.

As for cleanliness, she was terrible about it! The new maids were frightened when they saw the huge salon—who was to polish the floor? Who to dust all those little dolls, all those *pretties* set about on the furniture? You would have to start by cleaning the legs of the footstools.

Nobody but my mother could get along with her.

She had such a gracious air, my mother! As soon as the mistress arrived from town on vacation she'd give her such a welcome as ever could be, and she'd say: "Oh, my beautiful! How beautiful she is, my mistress! She's like a rose of May!" And she'd say: "How do you do it, my mistress, becoming more beautiful and fresh every year?" And wasn't the mistress pleased with herself!

When she quarreled with the maids about cleanliness, my mother would say: "Why, yes, of course, cleanliness is something that's proper any place."

"You see! Even she knows that—and she's only a peasant girl," the mistress would say then to the maids.

So that when she'd leave on All Saints' Day she'd empty all the drawers and give everything to my mother.

"Take this! Away with it! Away! Here you are, take it Marietta! All rags, rags, rags!"

But what she wouldn't put up with was the pack of village youngsters. Sometimes there were droves of them that romped and shouted around the villa: the smaller ones, just in shirts, would run behind the bigger ones.

"Why, they're growing every year!" she'd say. "Filthy, dirty, nasty! Oh, oh, oh!"

"Mingon, Zvani, send off that pack of youngsters!" she'd call out to my father and me.

Then when she saw the dirty mess they'd made by the gate, she got furious. My mother'd say: "For you, people should be born without any little asses at all, like the sacramental angels with a head and two wings!"

Once she called me and said as usual: "Send off that pack at the gate."

I went out and one of the bigger boys said to me: "Go tell your mistress she commands inside the gate but outside it's us who command and we do what we please."

So I told her. Did you ever see an earthquake? She ran and told my father.

"Did you hear that? If they talk that way while they're small, what will they say when they're grown up? And where's their respect for us?"

"That's what me too says," my father answered.

"But you, Mingon, are too much like a lamb. Take the whip and beat them!"

"It's easy to say *take the whip*, but afterward they look on you as a tyrant and as soon as they get a chance, they'll spite you, they'll give you a nickname that'll last three generations. They're neighbors, and you've got to get along with neighbors."

That's how my father answered her.

When she'd happen on a woman with a belly out straight, she'd even go so far as to say, "But what have you done, my good woman, where's your common sense?"

One woman answered her back: "But don't you know that's the only fun we've got?"

"Oh, the shameless creature, the shameless creature," she kept saying. "Mingon, did you hear that?"

"What do you want, mistress, peasants are made that way. In winter, soon as they're under the covers and feel a little warm beside the woman, they mount on her. They don't stop to think much."

"What a foul mouth you have, Mingon!"

"Keep quiet, you long-tongue," my mother'd say to my father, "because you don't have education."

"Oh, well said, Marietta!"

So the people looked on the mistress as haughty, and a tyrant, one who wouldn't even let the peasant girls amuse themselves with their men, which is the only just thing the Lord has made, because it's the same for all.

When she was in a good fettle she gave the children candy drops, and bought linen to make little shirts. But what she liked best to give was soap.

"Not for the laundry," she told the women, "but to wash the faces of your urchins, don't you see how snotty their noses are? And all those scabs they have on their heads?"

The women would answer that the filth, the scabs, and the lice on their heads were only healthy; and she'd run off horrified.

One day the master said to her: "My dear, this belief of the peasant women isn't so wrong as you think."

"Come, come! Even your brain is softening with the years!"

Her greatest pride was a white rosebush that grew near the door and climbed in lovely garlands to the window.

She also had an acacia tree and she was more jealous of it than of her husband. One winter the woodcutters chopped it down and she cried from rage all summer long.

She always called her maid "imbecile," and the word had worn itself out from being said over and over again and all that was left of it was: "becile," "becile."

The master would say to her then, "When you've said 'imbecile' once, that's enough."

"When I'm right, I'll say it a hundred thousand times."

"Yes, my dear, you are right," he'd say. "But you're wrong to want to make someone understand who doesn't have the gift of understanding. It's because she's of little intelligence that she's a maid."

"Of little intelligence—that would be you!" the maid said to the master.

He wouldn't answer back. But between maid and mistress it never ended, the mistress would say: "Who'll have the last word? You, perhaps? I've told you to keep quiet, and that's enough."

At table, too, she was always the same. There was too much salt in the spaghetti or too much tomato sauce, or a glass was smudged, or the meat was too tough.

Then she'd say: "Salt, salt, salt! Tomato, tomato, tomato! Bad beef, bad beef, bad beef!"

The master would tell her: "My dear, it's enough to say 'tomato' once, but if you'd have a look in the kitchen before it's served . . ."

Then she'd bark and go bow-wow even at him.

"You direct the stars and the moon where you command, but in the house, I am the queen."

And in many other things, too, they didn't get along.

She liked new red and white furniture, and he was only too happy when he could find those worm-eaten chests in the peasants' houses.

"It's because you don't have a sense of smell," she'd say. "Can't you notice the stench of mice and bedbugs?"

When he came home he'd open everything wide because he wanted to see the sun. But she liked to close everything: everything must be dark, curtain over curtain.

She'd say: "Don't you realize that the sun fades the colors, softens the glue, cracks the veneer, ruins every piece of furniture, and brings in dust, flies, bugs, and beetles?"

My father once said to the master: "You should have tamed her right from the start the way I did with mine."

"My dear Mingon," he answered, "if I'd wasted my time taming my wife, I wouldn't have had any left for study."

I remember the year I was confirmed. I had new shoes, a white shirt, a new suit, and two cakes, one in each hand. My mother had bought me a fine white ribbon. It was the custom to stay dressed up like that all day and to keep the confirmation ribbon on your forehead until night. Their little Robert saw me and called out to the mistress: "Mamma, Mamma, come and see how Zvani looks!"

She came down, saw me, and began to laugh: "Zvani, let me see you. How well-greased you look!"

I started to cry, but I couldn't wipe my eyes because I was holding the cakes, and the mistress laughed even harder.

The master, however, fondled me a lot, and said: "Bravo, bravo, Zvani, you did very well to be confirmed."

And he gave me one of the lovely gold coins they had in those days.

"I want to be confirmed, too," said little Robert.

"Yes, dear, you will be."

But when strangers came to the house, she changed completely. Then, she wanted to show how proud she was to be her husband's wife. How sweet she could make her little voice: "Do you take much or little sugar?"

And when the master had finished his coffee she'd take the little cup away herself or she'd put a little bowl in front of him for his cigarette ashes.

Every time guests came we had grand dinners with a lace tablecloth, with three glasses for each and a green glass for the white wine.

I served at table. She gave me lessons on how to serve at table.

"When we have guests for dinner, you must never talk, Zvani," she'd say to me, "but watch my eyes. Just think you're mute, but never stand there bemused like an imbecile. You must pass the dish around, first serving the mistress, and then the others."

The dirty looks she gave me!

But after I'd served her and turned to the guests, they'd make a polite fuss over it.

"Well, then," she'd say, "serve the Commendatore * next."

"That's right, that's right! First your husband, the great man who discovered the moon!"

After the last course you had to bring the brush right away to take off all the crumbs and pieces of bread, and then, finally, bring in the little cups to wash the finger tips.

It was a matter of importance, like serving the mass.

She had a suit made for me, of fine gray cloth embroidered in front.

In winter the pants came in handy but not the jacket because it had a tail at the back and my friends laughed at me.

"Zvani," they'd say, "they've embroidered you like the lizards."

At noon I had to ring a bell like in church. It was she who started this custom so that everyone would come to table on time.

"Are the spaghetti on to boil?" I'd ask the maid.

"Yes, ring your bell, Zvani."

The peasants would say: "See what a good profession bell ringing is? What are we going to have today? Macaroni? Turkey? Well, we can do without a bell!"

When I brought the spaghetti to table, I had to say out loud: "The mistress is served."

* Commendatore—an honorific title bestowed by the Italian government to out-standing citizens.

But she was hardly ever there, and even with the bell, she'd come when she pleased.

After dinner the master would take a rest, and then she'd start to make herself pretty, and you should have seen her when she came out! Shiny shoes, powder, little curls!

After sunset they'd go calling on others; or others would come to us.

There'd be so many ladies and young girls that it looked like the blossoming of May around the villa. The gentlemen came wearing gloves. "To catch monkeys," my mother'd say.

Then the mistress offered refreshments, which were tea, really a hot drink. But before the people came, she'd say: "Quick, quick, Zvani." And she'd send me out to pick huge bunches of wild flowers: poppies, slippers of the Madonna, sunflowers, and the ones we call the flower of the snake. Even thistles that grow on the beach! Then she'd arrange them in crystal vases and pitchers, like we do with sheaves of corn. When I brought them she'd give me a big welcome.

"See, Zvani, how nice they look. Oh, how wonderful! My whole salon simply drowned in flowers. Do you like them? But how can one help loving flowers?"

Later on, the maid and I would set a little table with lovely embroidered blue and red napkins. The easy chairs, the cushions, the little tables seemed to wait for the guests.

I'd bring in plates with little mountains of biscuits that she'd taught me to put one on top of the other the way we stack hay. Then we'd have to boil water in a big silver kettle, and they'd throw the *tea* in.

"The *tea*, the *tea*. I adore *tea*. Do you take it with rum? You with lemon? Oh, I take it with milk. Delicious. But where do you get this tea?"

It always tasted like camomile to me. Oh, but the biscuits, yes!

"How the biscuits evaporate," the mistress would say. "Oh, that Robert, that Robert!"

"Mamma, it's Zvani," he'd say.

"It must be both of you. I'll really have to lock them up with a key!"

But she always lost the key.

Then there were those crumbly biscuits with chocolate cream inside that I'll remember forever.

They had boxes of chocolate candies, too, with almonds or liqueurs inside. You should have seen how greedy little Robert was! His father, who was very tall, amused himself by making him jump as you do when you give a piece of bread to a beagle.

And the bottles of liqueur evaporated, too.

One day when all the guests were there I began to laugh, and little Robert was laughing along with me. I began to laugh harder, and he laughed harder still. I pointed my finger at Robert and he pointed his finger at me. And how we laughed!

"What's the matter? Can't you stop it, now?"

The mistress was upset at me and the master began to fear for little Robert.

"But don't you see," said a gentleman, "that they're both drunk?"

We had finished, one sip Robert, one sip me, half a bottle of cognac!

When the ladies and the young girls saw the flowers, they'd say: "Oh, but how lovely, how lovely! They're lovelier than garden flowers!" And they'd all walk around the flowers and give them many names.

"But where do you find all these flowers, Signora?"

"Why, in the fields. There are so many. My little helper picks them for me."

Then they'd all look wide-eyed at me, and the ladies would say: "Oh, how very clever!"

"Of course it's I, with my sense of the artistic, who arranges them," the mistress would then say.

"Naturally! Otherwise they wouldn't look so lovely! But how clever you are, Signora!"

And you should have seen how pleased she was. She'd say: "An intelligent woman can do everything."

There were so many lovely young ladies, who talked sedately in mewing tones. There was one lady—and you could look down her fat white bosom! She'd say to Robert: "Come here, let me feel. Oh, this boy has silken hair!" just to find an excuse to hug him against her.

She should have hugged me. That's what she should have done. But Robert would run off to play with the more boyish-looking girls in the garden. Or he'd amuse himself by playing with the dog Dir.

He'd trained Dir so that when he'd say: "Go get the handkerchief," he'd go. And when he'd say: "Oh, poor Dir, how unhappy you are!" he'd start crying. When he'd say: "But now you're very happy!" he'd start yelping with happiness. When he'd say: "Go lie down," he'd walk off sheepishly. And if some of us would say: "No, poor Dir, don't go off," he'd come back all happy again. And he'd always get a biscuit, too.

Every so often Dir, all on his own, would start walking on his hind legs. This was the trick Robert had had the hardest time teaching him. And Dir liked to show off doing it in front of the ladies. He'd walk up to them with his naked little belly and the sealing wax outside.

"Indecent! Get away, Dir! Zvani, take him away!" the mistress would say immediately.

They also threw rings and played guessing games and sometimes they even danced. Then they'd go out the gate for a walk with all those lovely white shoes. They'd talk about their villas and their gardens, and in those days the lowly peasants made way for the *signori* and moved back toward the ditch.

At night they'd play cards; such lovely cards to play "The Merchant at the Fair," and they'd lose so much money! They'd play, too, the foreign kind of *briscola* * they called "poker." And the ladies were the fiercest ones at raising the bets.

The master played a little but he soon got tired of it. Then he'd go out into the garden to look at the moon.

Every now and then a girl would come out on the terrace.

One of them said to him in her little voice: "Is it true, *commendatore*, that you can see a woman in the moon?"

"Undoubtedly. A young woman with wavy hair."

"But I've heard that it was an elderly lady with glasses on."

"Undoubtedly."

"Well, then?"

"Two thousand years ago one saw the head of a young girl who was kissing a young man."

"Oh, dear, dear!"

"And now, instead, one sees a man carrying an enormous burden and a lion coming toward him."

"But is that all possible?"

* *Briscola*—Italian popular card game.

"Certainly. The moon is very capricious."

"Is it true that it's bad luck to let the moon into the room while one's sleeping?"

"Legends of the moon, my child."

Another girl asked him—as if he were a magician—whether he knew her little star.

"Oh, my little star," she said. "My pretty little star; I've lost it! It was white, it was light, it was alone. And I saw it every evening at the same place where the sun rises. But now I look and look over the sea and I can't find it."

"Little star?" he said. "That's Aldebrand."

"Did it die?"

"No, but in summer it rises very much later."

"So then it's difficult to know the stars."

"Papa, I've lost everything," later Robert said. "Give me some money."

"Gambling, you see," said his father, "is the ugliest vice we know of."

"To you, papa, all vices are ugly. But what should I do?"

"What should you do? Don't you know what you should do?"

"No, papa."

"My son, I advise you to make good use of money, not for the money itself, but because using money well means using all things well. Do you understand that, Robert?"

"No, papa."

"Well then, go back and play."

Sometimes in August they'd eat those sugared cucumbers from Faenza that they had first put inside a well to cool. They were as green as snakes on the outside, inside as red as hell's fire.

Before daylight my mother would come to fetch the rinds for the sow, and the master would say: "Marietta's like death, she takes everything away!"

The master didn't even care to talk with all those women. He'd whistle and that meant that my father should join him.

"Come here, Mingon," he'd say, "but you want to drink, of course—" and he'd order something to drink.

He'd be sitting on an easy chair, and my father'd sit close by on the grass.

"Talk to me now."

"What about?"

"Tell me what you think of the stars."

"I say they're a fine sight."

"And if there weren't any?"

"That would be too bad for your kind of work, but for mine, as long as the morning star, the cart, and the hen and chickens mark the hours, and the moon, too, I'd have more than enough."

"But why the moon?"

"To know when to do things."

"What do you mean, Mingon?"

"I mean when to do things like sowing, pruning the vines, spreading manure, you do them when the moon's right."

"When the moon's right?"

"When it's still very small."

The master liked this kind of reasoning and had him repeat it, and then said to himself: *That's what's still left from the days of the patriarchs, Isaac and Jacob, who walked with the stars and with the moon.*

"And don't you marvel how they all turn so precisely, like a merry-go-round?" the master asked.

"They turn because they're supposed to. I'm more surprised they're so shiny. They look like new, and yet it must have been quite some time since they're born."

"Well, Mingon, you must know that a day will come when even the stars go out and the sun also will die bit by bit, and then all men will have to congregate where there's a little patch of sun, and there, like wild animals, they'll battle each other over the last bit of sun that's left. Doesn't that frighten you?"

"The ones that live then will worry about it," said my father.

"So don't you believe the dead live on?"

"What do you mean by that?"

"That they live on in the next world."

"In hell or paradise?"

"Yes—something of the sort."

"I'd say no, my master."

"And why?"

"Because my grandfather who's been dead so many years, and my father, bless his soul, should have sent me news whether one fares well or ill over there. I've waited a long while for them to come and say: 'Mingon, be wise, go to mass, say your prayers for the poor dead.' But nobody's come so far, and I no longer believe they will. The only ghosts I've seen, my master, were in a puppet show. When the puppet Sandrone says: 'Hey, you ghosts, what's it you want? *Speak up!*' But in real life I've never seen them."

"This subject's a little difficult," said the master. "So let's change it."

"It's all the same to me."

"Tell me something else, Mingon, do you believe in great men?"

"And what do you mean by that?"

"Those who study, who write, like me, for example."

"You mean those who sit in a chair and work with the head?"

"Don't you think it's labor working with your head even sitting in a chair?"

"It might be labor, but I wish it were me sitting in a chair! I notice that all those who work with their hands envy those who work with their head and sit in a chair. And I've yet to meet one who's put down the pen to take up a spade!"

"You know, Mingon, you're not quite right about that! If you only knew! But let's drop that subject. Tell me, do you know people of whom you could say they're cleverer than you are?"

"You mean those who can do things I can't do?"

"Oh, yes, bravo, Mingon. Now we understand each other: a doctor, a lawyer, an engineer . . . What? You don't go for doctors, lawyers, engineers?"

"They're all right. But I'm of the opinion that if they'd sent me to schools I could have had these professions, too."

"Who is it, then, you admire, who?"

"Those who sing in the theater, the tenors."

"And who else?"

"Those who make speeches on the square."

"Mountebanks?"

"They may be mountebanks but they have a lot of ability because all the people listen to them."

"And who are they?"

"It's a long story."

"Tell it, Mingon, tell it."

"They're people who've been coming to these parts for the last twenty years. They waited for us on Sundays when we came out of mass. At first we thought they'd come to play-act on the square. One of them had a little organ and another had a monkey. But when they saw they'd got a crowd of us they'd start saying: 'Peasants, it's time to open your eyes! Don't believe what the priest tells you!'

"Then the priest would come out and say: 'Shame on you!' and they'd run off. But the next Sunday they were back again.

" 'Peasants, don't go to mass,' they'd say. 'The priest wants to make you believe there's hell, purgatory, and paradise, like there's first, second, and third class on a train. Meanwhile, *they* eat turkey and you eat corn-meal mush!'

"They were the ones who came to divide up the land among the peasants! We older ones hardly listened to them, but you should have seen how the younger ones stood there with their ears cocked. Now they don't have to look for us in front of the church, but it's the people who go to the square to hear them.

" 'Until now,' they say, 'the laws have been made by your masters, but now you must make them yourselves!' They come out with such strange ideas, we wouldn't have had them in a hundred years. 'Peasants, you're small because you're on your knees!'—'Peasants, you must choke the last king with the guts of the last priest!'

"When the priests saw that the people didn't come to church as they used to, they got worried and started to act like the socialists, with a difference—if the socialists promised us only one paradise, they promised two, one here and one up there, with the difference that they no longer say: *Ora pro nobis*, but they say: *Vota pro nobis!*

"And then there's Christ! The priests say Christ belongs to them. And the socialists say that Christ is the first socialist and so they pull him a little to one side and a little to the other, and the priest doesn't even know any longer who Christ is."

"Christ," said the master, "is one who suffered!"

"That's what those others say: 'Peasants, you've been suffering over two thousand years!' "

"I think that's a little exaggerated."

"They also say something else."

"Speak out, Mingon."

"They say: 'Now it's time for the masters to suffer!' "

"Well, now, that isn't much of a change!"

"I say it's a change, there ought to be a bit for each: till now the hares did the running, now the dogs can do it. But you and I, my master, will always get along!"

"I should say we will!" said the master. "When we go over the accounts, it's always you who gets something from me."

GIOVANNI PAPINI

Strange Stories

TRANSLATED BY ANGUS DAVIDSON

1.

THE MASK FACTORY

I was recently granted permission to visit the International Mask Factory, a powerful industrial concern formed by a joint stock company with a capital of many billions and a staff composed of thousands of specialists.

The I.M.F. is situated on the edge of the sea and—with its laboratories, offices, sheds, warehouses, and yards—covers several acres of ground. Its immense buildings, surmounted by domes of metal, by many-colored towers, by gleaming lanterns and smoky columns, are enclosed in a double circle of thick walls, guarded day and night by men taller than cuirassiers and more heavily armed than brigands.

It is not easy to gain entrance into the I.M.F. establishments. I had to show my four passes, which I had succeeded in obtaining after months of intrigue, at four different guardrooms. But, as our old friend Cervantes wrote, "The greater the trouble, the greater the enjoyment."

I was received with great civility by one of the assistant directors of the "creation" unit, who accompanied me throughout my visit to the famous factory. He was a man of about fifty, long and lean, with a face of an ashy pallor that revealed no feeling, except, perhaps, a melancholy, if repressed, uneasiness. He was, as I at once discovered, by no means talkative. He warned me, however, that I must not, for any reason whatever, reveal to anyone the technical secrets of the processes of manufacture—if by any chance I managed to understand them—and that I must undertake to speak only of the goods ready for sale.

"We do not concern ourselves," added my guide, "only with facial masks of the old type, but with complete disguises, with permanent forms of make-up, with plastic remodeling, and, particularly, with adhesive, invisible, impenetrable masks, which our clients, once they have started using them, can never again take off, even on the day of their death. I can state definitely that this is the most sought-after article. Men nowadays no longer require masks for a few hours' pastime, but for the whole of their lives."

After these preliminary remarks, he led me into the "modeling" department. This consisted of an extremely long glass gallery, furnished with three long, parallel benches before which stood rows of artist-workmen dressed in white like surgeons. I noticed that they were all old men, most of them white-haired or bald, with absorbed, deathly pale faces and slow, careful movements. Each of them had in front of him a kind of reading desk, upon which he had placed a picture— a portrait, in color, of a man or woman—and each one was employed in modeling, in a material unknown to me, like semiliquid silk, a mask corresponding to the painted face before his eyes. The plump, yellowish hands of the old men were lightly stroking the sticky paste, which very gradually began to take on human form beneath their delicate touch. I moved very slowly along the benches and discovered, to my great astonishment, that the masks in process of being made were not in the least clownish, or distorted, or bestial, or monstrous like those of savages, or of the Japanese, or those that were to be seen in our own ancient carnivals; they were ordinary, perfectly ordinary faces such as are to be seen any day in the streets, in the train, in the pit of a theater or a photographer's shop window. There were fleshy faces and lean faces, smooth faces and bearded faces, some of them bitter, some expressionless, some elderly and some young—most of them, indeed, young. But all of them were ordinary and normal to the point of being quite commonplace.

I turned to my guide to ask for an explanation of this mystery, but all he gave me was this simple reply. "We make what we are asked for by our customers, and their name is legion."

I persisted in trying to find out something further.

"People's real faces," my guide answered, "are often frightful, because they reveal, almost always, the innate ferocity or the confused imbecility of their owners' minds. They turn to us, therefore, in very large numbers—and every year there are more—to obtain masks which are not only fixed but endurable to wear, and which do not single them out too much from people who have faces or masks with ordinary features. When men were less bestial they were willing to wear masks of beasts, both for amusement and contrast, and when they were more intelligent they took pleasure in hiding behind masks that were gloomy or idiotic. But nowadays, since the events of this last half century, which has distorted every soul and every face and brought to the surface, in many, their atavistic animal qualities, everything is altered. Real faces have taken on the aspect of ancient, fearsome masks, and we are called upon to provide masks which, in other centuries, would not have looked like masks at all but like natural faces. Hamlet's apostrophe to Ophelia is truer now than it ever was: 'God has given you one face, and you make yourselves another.' "

When we left this building I was taken to the "sampling" department, where the finished products were on view, arranged in rows, for the inspection and choice of clients, on stands covered with soft carpets all along the walls. It looked like an exhibition of exact reproductions of human beings, of well-dressed dummies in all styles and all attitudes, and it reminded me of the Musée Grévin in Paris or Madame Tussaud's in London.

"This one here," said my polite companion, pointing to one of the silent, motionless figures, "is the 'Man of Honor' mask, carried out according to the latest models. Observe the kindliness of the brows, the austerity of the nose, the cordiality of the mouth, the benevolence of the ears, the frankness of the chin. It is a much sought-after model nowadays, especially by businessmen, by captains and leaders of industry, and even by habitual criminals.

"And this other one," went on my mentor, "is the 'Pious Man' model, which sells every day by the gross in all countries where a dominant and recognized religion still exists. You will not, I am sure, fail to notice the ascetic reserve of the cheeks, the chastity of the lips, the modesty of the hair, the humility of the nostrils, the resigned posture of the neck. This model is much sought after by individuals of egotistical, choleric, and sensual character.

"This one here," said my gentle cicerone, pointing toward a clumsy figure of an old man, "is the 'Great Philosopher.' It is a model that is not often asked for, these days, because it is not sufficiently attractive and elegant, but amateurs of it are not lacking, though they become more and more rare. Persons who are dried up and heartless, spiteful and vindictive, desirous of lording it over their equals in the name of abstract ideas, readily acquire this very lifelike model.

"And this," went on the assistant director, showing me a female mask, "is the famous 'Femme du Monde' model—rather cynical, rather sentimental, very stupid but troublesome and arrogant, cold but often adulterous, bold, loquacious. Wives of the newly rich, adventuresses who have made good marriages, provincials hurled suddenly into a great city, hostesses of the fashionable world, these are our best clients for this model.

"We have a good sale for this one, too," my guide resumed, indicating a solemn figure close beside us. "It is, as perhaps you have guessed, the 'Politician'—the legislator, the man who governs nations. We make different types of this model, according to the opinions and position of the client, but in the one we have here before us you will be able to admire the haughtiness of the eye sockets, the geniality of the frontal bumps, the mildness of the cheekbones which offers a fine contrast with the pitiable poverty of the hair and the profound bitterness of the folds at each side of the mouth, in which, as you see, the lips are slightly parted to allow of the impatient ejaculation of remarks.

"And here is one of our most popular models, that of the 'Latest Fashion Artist.' Note the thrown-back hair, the cold but insolent expression of the face, the thinness of the lips, the smallness of the head, the mean shortness of the clipped mustache, the provoking impudence of the sharp chin. Those who have ambition but no talent, charlatans whose features are too coarse, revolutionaries who are lacking in imagination, the seekers of facile adventures and of rapid renown—all these spare no expense to disguise themselves with this type of mask, which we have to touch up, each season, with opportune and ingenious improvements."

I was shown many other figures, of an even more unexpected and bizarre kind; and during that morning I visited many other departments, full of curious secret devices for mass production. But I made a solemn undertaking with that excellent and accomplished assistant director that I would not say more than I have said, that I would not reveal these surprising secrets to any living soul. And I am keeping my promise scrupulously, because I do not wish to have any trouble with that extremely powerful institution, the International Mask Factory.

2.

THE CLOUD MAKER

On the third day, after I had explored the streets and squares and local picture galleries, I asked the innkeeper whether there was any exceptional man in the town whom it might be worth my while to meet. He replied that there was just one, Doctor Nilforss, and promised that he would ask him for an appointment on my behalf. He kept his promise, and Dr. Nilforss invited me to his house next day.

This house was planted on the top of a high hill, quite close to the fiord: a fine, very large building, all made of stone, and dominated by an iron tower. Dr. Nilforss turned out to be far more agreeable than I had expected in a man who had been described to me as solitary and eccentric. He was a handsome old man, thin but large-limbed, entirely bald but with a white, prophetlike beard that covered the whole front of his shirt. He told me at once that for some years he had been a professor of physics but that he had devoted his whole life to the study of the clouds.

"My collection," he said to me, "is unique in the entire world. Come and have a look at it."

He led me into a small room filled with books.

"Here are collected all the works in which mention is made of clouds—works of science and of poetry, too. Here, for instance, are the earliest editions of *The Clouds* of Aristophanes; the famous *Cloud*

Messenger of Kalidasa; Shakespeare's *Hamlet*, in which the mad Prince discovered—perhaps before anybody else—the language figured in the clouds; Shelley's *The Cloud* in every existing translation; Conrad's *Typhoon*; Baudelaire's *Petits Poèmes en Prose*. You remember the confession of the last of the children? '*J'aime les nuages . . . les nuages qui passent là-bas . . . les merveilleux nuages. . . .*' But this is merely the anteroom to my museum. Come this way."

The doctor threw open a door and led me into an immense room, the ceiling of which consisted of a lantern of stained glass. The walls were covered with large photographs of clouds—wonderful clouds over sea and mountains, cirri and cumuli rimmed with light, gloomy sunsets in stormy skies. There were also photographs of famous paintings, but only by artists who had introduced clouds into the backgrounds of their pictures: I recognized, amongst others, Mantegna and Turner.

"These," said the doctor, "are the pictorial archives. But I have not been content merely to collect documentary records of these splendid inhabitants of the sky. I did not wish to be merely an observer, but have sought to be a creator as well. I have succeeded in setting up a laboratory for the production of artificial clouds. Thanks to a process I have invented, I can make clouds rise, at my will, toward the heavens, and—which is more important—in such shapes and appearances as I myself choose, according to my own wishes and tastes. When the air is clear, I send up, at my pleasure, dolphins or whales or ships or castles or human profiles in watery vapor, with such coloring as best suits the form produced—a silvery ash color or a rosy gray, a sooty brown or a funereal sepia. And so I, too, in my way, am a painter, a painter whose palette is of vapors, whose canvas is the sky. Would you like to see a proof of it? You would have to wait here, however, for a short time before going up onto my tower to contemplate my aerial design."

I politely refused his polite offer, but asked him how in the world he had come to choose such a strange and unusual subject of study.

"Clouds," he answered, "are for me the most fantastically and stupendously surprising things in nature. They are as unstable as women, errant as angels, changeable as dreams, delicate as a spell, supple as a youthful body, fragile as beauty itself, fleeting as an apparition, divine as a masterpiece of art. These isles that softly sail from one gulf of the heavens to another, suffused with gold or black as smoke, that now press heavily upon the earth like a suffocating feather bed, now dissolve and break into pieces like the fantasies of the soul—these, for me, are the most exquisite decorations of the universe, the most lovable companions of man, the most exact symbols of our own life. For what are our lives but little clouds, ephemeral, wandering, breaking up, at last, in tears, or dissolving in light? And I must tell you too, so that you may know all about me, I am a Christian, and I cannot therefore forget that Christ, in order to ascend to Heaven, concealed Himself in a cloud; and that when He returns to judge the living and the dead He will be seated—as has been foretold—upon the clouds. If God Himself has chosen the clouds for His garment and His footstool, do you not think that they must be among the most divine of all earthly forms, and worthy, therefore, of study and of admiration?"

I had to admit he was right. I thanked Dr. Nilforss warmly for his kind welcome and went back, a little unwillingly, down the hill. When I was almost at the bottom, I turned around for a moment to give one last look at the cloud museum and laboratory, and my curiosity was rewarded by a joyful surprise. Up in the air, a short distance above the iron tower, swaying gently in the breeze, was a small cloud, all by itself, the only one in a perfectly clear sky. Its color was a deep pink, and it was in the shape of a heart.

3.

MADMEN'S CONGRESS

The Madmen's Congress met secretly, on a wooded plateau on Mount Suma, on the morning of the first of June. All the great asylums —including the criminal lunatic asylums—and all the clinics for the treatment of mental diseases were represented by delegates. The famous paranoiac Gumè, whose case is recorded even in the most widely different manuals of psychiatry, was elected, not without opposition, to the post of President of Congress.

The assembly, contrary to what might be imagined by an outsider, was disciplined and perfectly calm. The absence of hateful doctors and intolerable nurses inspired all those who had come together with a feeling of quiet happiness which was enough to wipe out, or anyhow to conceal, every sign of agitation.

A few faces were distorted, or turned to stone; many eyes flashed fire like the eyes of maniacs; there were bristling, rumpled mops of hair that made you think of clowns at a circus: but, on the whole, the faces of the assembled congress did not look very different from those that you can see any day at the reunions and meetings of sane, serious people. Most of them squatted down on the short, velvety grass on top of the hill; others perched on the bigger branches of the beech trees; a few remained standing, drawn up proudly erect like pieces of monumental sculpture. The President had taken his seat on a high rock that rose up in the middle of the clearing, and he was brandishing, as a mark of authority, a handsome knotty stick which bore, fastened to its top, a bunch of roses. He raised this flowery staff toward the heavens, and this was the signal for work to begin.

In rolling, old-fashioned phrases, Gumè briefly expounded the subject of the discussion which was about to take place. This subject, as all the delegates knew, was the most grave, the most urgent, of all— the reattainment of liberty.

"As you know," said Gumè, "our enemies, in the name of science and of society, hold us cruelly imprisoned in houses of segregation and torture. This detention, in our opinion, is completely and absolutely unjust. Unjust from the scientific point of view because even the doctors themselves admit that our maladies are, in most cases, incurable in spite of their scientific persecutions. Unjust from the point of view of society because the majority of self-styled 'normal' persons, who are not subject to restraint, are almost exactly like us in their thoughts and in their acts and habits. We claim, therefore, our right to equality and freedom. We demand the closing and suppression of all these useless penal establishments that go under the pretentious name of psychotherapeutic hospitals."

All the assembled madmen gave vent to their approval in a clamorous burst of laughter which roused even the shiest woodland birds to flight.

The first to demand the right of speech was Signora Taibon, famous among her companions as "The Bacchante of the South."

"These professorial executioners," she began, "maintain that we provide a spectacle of hysterical crises and attacks of raving fury. But just look at what goes on every day, in every town, *outside* our asylums. Either indoors or in the open air, troops of men and women assemble in order to embrace in couples, to exhaust themselves by leaping around like people bitten by tarantulas, to whirl like dervishes, to writhe and twist themselves indecently, imitating the bestial movements of bears and apes, and all this accompanied by the hiccupings and sobbings, the rumblings and roarings of hellish, barbaric music. Sweating, overheated, excited, in a state bordering on craziness and hallucination, they stop every now and then, but only for a moment, for at once, at the first hint of the renewal of the savage cacophony, they recommence their lascivious, convulsive shudderings, and their demented sarabands continue for hours on end, for entire nights. What do our brilliant alienists think about it all? What do they think of these daily spectacles?"

"Collective psychosis," proclaimed a baritone voice somewhat thickened by catarrh; "a form of raving madness of aphrodisiac type."

Baron Suk, who was celebrated for his philosophical treatise on the *Nonexistence of the Universe*, was the second speaker of the day.

"They accuse us," he said, "of monomania, of mythomania, and of immoral perversions. But do our learned psychologists never notice what goes on every day in every part of the world? Tens of millions of supposedly sane people of both sexes shut themselves up voluntarily in large, dark, evil-smelling rooms in order to watch the imaginary adventures—often bestial or grotesque—of luminous specters projected upon a rectangle of white cloth. The stories of these specters consist, almost always, in an apologia of corruption, of treachery, of fraud, of adultery, of prostitution, of violence, and of murder. And yet these dark halls are crammed to bursting point with husbands and wives, with fathers and mothers and their children, with schoolmasters and magistrates cheek by jowl with girls from the streets, with idle, lustful youths side by side with old men of evil life and disappointed vixens. The thing that they are all seeking there, that they are seeking in those visions where very often sin goes hand in hand with imbecility, is a stupefying drug to counteract the boredom of spiritual emptiness, an escape from real life, and above all a substitute and a compensation for repressed instincts of a shameful kind. What do our friends the psychiatrists think of it, what do they think of this morbid but universal mania?"

"Collective psychosis," repeated the same voice; "a search for stimuli and antisocial emotions."

The President next gave the right of speech to Doctor Saurocthonus, who had been imprisoned by the specialists under the accusation of cyclically recurrent madness.

"There is one even more serious phenomenon," began the doctor in a booming voice, "—the one that can be observed every Sunday, in every city on earth, in those vast open-air arenas where tens of thousands of apparently normal beings collect in order to watch the famous game of pushing and kicking. The game, in itself, has nothing particularly wonderful about it; it seems, to all appearance, to be merely a matter of driving a leather ball into a certain place, without using one's hands. But what is astonishing and disconcerting to a rational observer is the uncontrolled and growing frenzy of the multitudes who watch this orgy of kicking and leaping. These thousands of spectators appear to be possessed, all at once, by an hysterical or epileptic fury: they become agitated, they writhe, they lean forward, they wrangle, they raise arms and voices to encourage or insult the players, they become elated or despairing just as though their own fate and the honor of their country depended upon the result of these childish contests. There rises from these arenas an immense chorus of howling and screeching, of threats and blasphemies and imprecations, of joyful trumpetings, furious roars and fearful bellowings, so that anyone might think they contained a tormented army of maniacs instead of a crowd of sane and worthy citizens. Kindly tell me what they think of that, our astute mental specialists?"

"Collective psychosis," answered the baritone voice; "attacks of spasmodic cerebral fever."

The next delegate who rose to speak was the elderly accountant Fatilu, who was affected (so rumor said) by a dangerous form of megalomania.

"They keep me shut up," said the accountant, "under the pretext of megalomania, because I assert that I am the emperor of the world. I recognize that there is something premature about such an announcement, since a real emperor of the world would not have allowed himself to be shut up in a vulgar lunatic asylum. I should like to point out, however, that in the society of so-called rational beings there are innumerable cases very similar to mine. One encounters, at every turn, little chatterboxes who believe themselves to be great politicians, shabby businessmen who present themselves as kings of the world's exchanges and markets, mediocre daubers who are under the illusion that they are supreme artists, vague, muddleheaded weavers of riddles who give themselves the airs of profound philosophers. . . ."

But the implacable Fatilu was unable to finish his speech. The plateau had been silently encircled. Starting up and running out from every direction came robust, white-clad young men, armed with handcuffs and strait jackets, who lost no time in mingling with the crowd of fugitives and urging them, one and all, with shouts and gestures, to follow them. The loquacious rebels, now dumb and confused, made no resistance. The whole crowd of them went off, docile and obedient, behind their keepers. Thus ended, with exemplary orderliness, the first session of the Madmen's Congress.

GIUSEPPE ANTONIO BORGESE

Tales of Sicily

1.

THE SIRACUSAN

TRANSLATED BY UGUCCIONE RANIERI

In Megara there are still carnations on the balconies, and women wear their skirts long, so that if an ankle is bared you still literally can see the young men tremble. But this happens rarely, for women go forth cautious and well guarded; and they guard themselves; and, when it rains, they prefer to come home with the hems of their gowns mud-splashed rather than have their stockings bitten by glances hotter than kisses. And anyway there are few women to be seen in the streets; except for the servant girls, and the women of the working class who still—to this day—go to the fountain with the tall water jars on their heads.

Yes, all this still exists: the little cobbled streets are still there, climbing from the water front to the Castello, so narrow that no woman can get through without being jostled by the crowding men (and that is why they keep to their homes), so steep that people going up on one side seem to be helped by the weight of those coming down on the other like the cabs of a funicular. And always there is a crowd, as if it were an everlasting market day: a dark crowd, darkly dressed even in the month of the "Lion sun." The streets are narrow, and the houses high, their façades often leaning forward against improvised props, and the sun gets no chance of entering them. Steps are slow, yet resolute; they echo on the cobbles. Here and there people cluster like flies still further slowing up the traffic. Voices are either excited or mysterious; greetings exchanged across the street resound like challenges.

I can recall the clang of the big front doors as they open and shut; I can recall the bells of the goats as they come down of a morning with their udders so swollen that they stumble, brushing their horns against the knees of the passer-by. Even the crack of Maestro Angelo's match still pierces my ear, as he lights his last black cigar when returning late at night to his house opposite ours.

Toward evening, halfway up the Strada Lunga, the rotting smell of the day's fish catch clashes with the perfume of orange blossoms, thin and bitter like that of the lily of the valley; the breath of the sea is lost in the dust of the Red Lands borne on the south wind—lands that are red like the pelt of a lion—where the vines give a wine that is fire.

It is then that the women come to the doors of their *bassi*, their basement homes level with the street, and open their eyes as if on the point of awakening. Their eyelids open like sliding doors upon eyes which are dolorous and indolent, full of darkness, of yellow flame, of undecipherable dreams, like the eyes of animals. If someone calls them from within, they turn their heads and answer with a singsong voice. Higher up, meanwhile, balconies are opening; the "ladies" appear greeting each other from balcony to balcony, resuming their monotonous and unending gossip. But, when they lean their elbows on the rail, they are careful to keep their bodies well back; and if one should sit down, she immediately adjusts her skirts around her high shoes for fear a passer-by might raise his eyes. Above all, the ladies whose balconies have bow railings must be careful; it never happens that one of them, absent-mindedly, places a foot on the rail.

The women of Megara live in this hour between sunset and nightfall; like flowers that blossom at dusk. Then night wraps them in.

It is night. Lullabies in the *bassi*; or the sound of a quarrel; but the voice of the woman is soon stilled; and not long after, the voice of the man drops likewise into silence. From the houses of the gentry never a sound, for they have walls like prisons.

I was born in those parts; not in Megara itself, but farther up in a village three miles from the castle. My people were from Siracusa, but my father had left it, and not long after he settled in Megara when I was still a child.

For how many years had I not set foot there! When Galliani decided to visit the place to study the Sicilian *quattrocento*, I suddenly felt the urge to go with him. As it turned out, Galliani, upon arrival, fell in love with the seventeenth century, the *seicento*, with its monasteries as formidable as fortresses and its churches overflowing with music and gold, where the saints appear to be engaged in an endless dance.

So it happened. Without knowing where I was going, almost against my will, I turned with my friend from the Strada Lunga into a side street wide and deserted, cut short after a hundred paces by hanging gardens. It was a June day which would not die. At the end of the street, a dark fringe of sea.

Here I found again the footsteps of my childhood along the high mysterious wall of an orchard. In front of me rose a strange façade, orange melting into yellow, and high up a lonely balcony with a black iron railing so monstrously swollen outward that one might think it had throbbed for centuries to the sound of secret serenades.

"This," I said with a shiver, "is the balcony of Aunt Clementina; the balcony of 'the Siracusan.' "

And I leaned on my friend.

For a long time, as long as I can remember, it was called the balcony of the Siracusan.

Though she was my father's sister, to all of us she was known as "the Siracusan," as if she hailed from some remote place, while, in truth, from her city, Megara can be reached in three hours by sea. She came to it to marry my father's partner, Nicola Laudisi.

He was an enormous, corpulent man, with arms like tree trunks which he was obliged to hold slightly akimbo and fleshy, shiny wrists like those of a newborn giant. When he dozed he kept his hands on his belly. I saw him thus a couple of times and was frightened. He resembled the Ogre. He was also very tall and you felt that without a stool no one could reach his face. His gray mustache could hardly be distinguished on his tired fat features. His breath was asthmatic, like the working of bellows.

Being rich, he wanted children, to leave them "the things"; for this he sought a wife. For this they brought him Aunt Clementina.

She reached Megara no longer in her first youth, though not yet near thirty. She came from a family of orphans; and she was silent.

I loved her, before ever I knew what love was. Almost daily I would find myself there under the balcony of the Siracusan at the hour when she opened it to step forward like a queen. But there was no crowd in the street to whom she could appear; no one but me. There were not even other balconies next to or opposite hers, with other women to whom she could talk, as all the ladies of Megara did at that hour. She could see only gardens and a rim of sea.

She never had children. I heard a rumor about some ailment. Often she suffered from headaches and then she would become pale like a sleepwalker.

Naturally she paid no attention to me. To attract her notice I would climb the smooth wall of the orchard and display my daring. Sometimes, for fear that I might hurt myself, she would call "Alberto!" and her voice hurt me. So I would get down and approach the house. Aunt Clementina then withdrew from the railing and adjusted her gown around her high shoes.

I do not believe I have ever looked upon a woman more beautiful. You could see nothing of her except her face. The women of that time were not like those of our day who resemble naked fruit seen through the foliage. They were concealed in a maze of lace and embroidery with their underskirts white and starched like the ornate paper that was used for wrapping flowers, and over these a great flowery gown with bows, as majestic as a pagoda, and on their breasts a corset, armored and impregnable.

But from her fingers, from her wrists, one could gather that she was slim and lithe, of the color of dark amber. She carried no perfume other than that of the lavender in which she kept her linen, and of the Macassar oil that she used on her black hair.

And her face was peerless: the nose straight, the lips pure, the eyes something between a quiet blue and the gray of cinders over a hidden fire.

At the first breath of evening the balcony would close. The darkness was transparent, like a veil in which the light of dawn were already atremble. Sometimes, on a summer night, the white flower of a cactus would open, and its delirious perfume spill over like a stream.

But when I returned to Megara and again found myself stepping along the wall of the orchard, there were no longer any clustered carnations or cactus plants on the balcony of Aunt Clementina. The irons which once had held the flowerpots were bent like old daggers, red with a rust which looked like ancient blood.

I saw her the last time on a Sunday, at the hour of high mass. She lay, dead, in the street; clothed to her feet in her beautiful dress of white satin embroidered with rose-colored flowers. One could hear no goat bells from the Strada Lunga; and one could hear—and it seemed never to end—the tinkle of the mass bell.

I was the first to see her there. Every Sunday morning I used to place myself in front of her door to watch her exit. When she went out to mass—and it wasn't easy to see her in the street at any other time during the week—a canopy seemed to stretch, invisible, over her head.

I kept reaching for my voice at the bottom of my chest, and finally I shrieked. Then the husband came down and, after him, the servant, Zulicchia; almost immediately my mother, too, arrived, I know not how, from the neighboring street. We stood there near the body. She had thrown herself, head foremost, from the balcony.

Later, much later—when Nicola Laudisi died of a stroke—I learned something. The day before, Aunt Clementina, opening a door, had seen her husband caressing the servant girl, Zulicchia. I who was thirteen at the time and read Byron in translations used to call her Zuleika to myself. She too was beautiful and strangely resembled her mistress; except that her nose, too thin and cutting, gave her a wicked look. I can remember her at the fountain straightening up after placing the jar on the ground; the tightly twisted cloth worn around her forehead to hold the weight of the jar would stand out like a towered crown on her lovely slave face.

I can almost see him in the darkened room, Nicola Laudisi, enormous, gigantic, breathing deeply but without bending or exertion—caressing the head of the servant as one strokes a dog.

Thus did his wife see him; and because she had nothing in life—not even neighbors with whom to chat from the balcony at evening—she decided to die. She confided in no one; she wrote nothing (she hardly knew how to write).

On the Sunday morning she dressed for mass and opened the balcony. Because it was a bow railing and might have been difficult to climb, or because she feared, on account of the not excessive height, to maim herself without dying, she saw no alternative but to let herself go head down. But, first, honor must be saved.

At that time safety pins were still unknown. She chose a rather long dark pin, one of those pins with a round head the color of a grape. She pierced her skirt at opposite ends and bent the pin to hold it fast. But she pricked a finger hard, and cried out.

Zulicchia appeared at the door: "What has your excellency done?"

"I have pricked myself and I bleed," she said. "It is nothing." Then she was alone.

Little step by little step—for the skirt was in her way—she reached the railing. She leaned forward; she must, for sure, have made a strong effort with her elbows—managed at last to get over—and fell. The road was deserted.

The pin never moved. The flowered gown uncovered just a bit of an ankle. My mother bent down to adjust it.

My mother said: "She was to have gone to mass; she has gone to the Lord instead."

Nicola Laudisi rocked as if he were about to crumble. Zulicchia and my mother, who barely reached his shoulders, were holding him up on both sides.

"Kneel down, Alberto," said my mother.

I knelt near the head of Aunt Clementina. I had never hoped to be so near her.

On the tip of her index finger a drop of dark blood stood out. A trickle of lighter blood was running down now from her skull toward an eyebrow. I took out the freshly laundered handkerchief that my mother had placed in my pocket and dried her forehead. Then people began to arrive.

2.

THE BOY

TRANSLATED BY PETER B. WARREN

Cannot forward cargo to Messina. Buona Fortuna seriously damaged by storm and held up in Genoa for repair. Three-month delay. The telegram he half read aloud, half quoted from memory, holding it at a distance from his eyes as he would look at the watermark of a bank note, to see if it were false or genuine.

"And they call that tub the *Good Fortune*; what an unseaworthy barge! 'We await your decision on forwarding perishable goods.' What kind of decision do they expect me to make?"

Not one in the family dared breathe a suggestion.

"Holy Mary!" he exploded, striking his palms together. "If I don't go to Genoa to make the arrangements myself, I'm ruined, the whole company is ruined."

"But how can you make a trip like that?" gasped his wife.

For three days he had been lying back in his easy chair, his gouty leg resting on a stool in front of him and so racked with pain that he could not rest in his own bed. Suddenly he felt miraculously cured by the urgency of the business. He unwrapped his knee, which appeared shiny and swollen. In spite of the heavy weight in his head, he determined to make the effort. He pulled himself upright, leaning on the stout cane which he had kept within arm's reach—only to fall back, choking a groan of desperation, his mouth gaping like a Tragic Mask. Trembling, his wife ran to his side to seat him comfortably again.

A while later he called to her. "Consolata!" This tone of voice the two little girls and the boy, who was older, understood immediately. They obeyed it at once, filing out of the room one after the other. "Could the boy go to Genoa? Would he know what to do?" he asked when they were alone.

His wife assured him: "He's worth his weight in gold."

That was how they decided that Nicolangelo should start off on the fabulous journey; their Nicolangelo who in all his nineteen years had never left Messina, who, after his third year of high school, had left the house only to go to the obscure warehouse along the docks. Hearing the news, his two little sisters stared at him up and down from head to foot, as if he were a god. In spite of his pale, olive skin, he really was a boy who was worth his weight in gold. His heavy shock of hair, black without a fleck of color, was slightly curly. In his whole life, he had never knowingly committed any sin more terrible than the occasional furtive smoking of a cigarette. His mother was the only woman who had ever praised his appearance. Life had kept him away from other women, but he was close to his mother. His father was older, actually old enough to have been his grandfather. The boy addressed him as "sir," and kissed his hand. As he listened to his father hurling detailed instructions to him, he nodded obediently, or at most answered, "Yes, sir," or "Certainly, sir." He changed to his best black suit, knotting a huge black string tie. From his father he received the necessary money for expenses, with a warning to account for every lira. His father also wrote for him diffuse introductory letters to agents of the company, to customs officials, and even to the manager of a small third-class hotel remembered from a visit fifteen years before. His mother gave him a little pocket money and a medallion of Our Lady of the Letter.

So equipped, Nicolangelo departed from Messina, still hearing the sound of the weeping of his mother and his sisters. Propped up on his pillows, his father could watch him only as far as the head of the stairs. Then, during a confusing night and a day, the boy saw mountains and tunnels, the shore and the waves of the open sea dancing before his eyes. For fear of thieves, he kept his cloth bag locked and fastened to the baggage rack above his head.

He found that the manager of the Pilot's Hotel in Genoa had long forgotten the gentleman from Messina who had spent the night beneath his roof fifteen years previously. Reading the oddly solemn phrases of the letter, so like a formal letter of introduction, he pursed his lips and shook his head from side to side.

"A great many people have stayed here in fifteen years," he stated finally. Handing the letter back to the boy, he sent him to a room on the second floor, the only one remaining vacant. The cold reception by the innkeeper and the high price of the room gave the boy a feeling of being abandoned and alone. He looked around suspiciously, as if wary of ambush from all sides. With nothing to do until evening, he stayed in his room, guarding his cloth bag and considering how he might take care of his father's affairs quickly enough the next day so that he could leave immediately for Messina.

When he went to the hotel restaurant, he had no thought in mind except to study the menu attentively enough to choose the least expensive dinner. It was a drab and poorly lighted room, and not all of the tablecloths were as clean as they might be. Tourists from abroad were staying wherever they could find a room in Genoa that spring, waiting until reservations were available along the Riviera. At the table adjoining his, Nicolangelo beheld people of another race, born beneath another sky. The two men were tall and blond. They laughed heartily and aloud, moving their arms in casual but sweeping gestures. They wore large pearls in the buttonholes of their white shirts. Between them sat a woman who was also tall and blond. Her throat and shoulders were bare, half veiled with misty silk, violet like haze on a distant mountain in the morning sunshine. Marvelous to his eyes, she bore the divinity of a princess, yet so near, he could have reached to touch her. Clearly wealthy, they were "Americans," "millionaires," strong and alive with the joy of existence. Probably they were laughing together at their adventure. Here they were, hidden away in such a den, daring to order omelet from such a kitchen. After finishing the main course, they peeled a banana and sliced a pineapple they had brought wrapped in wax paper for dessert. They filled goblets of champagne for each other, and their laughter was mingled with delightful, exotic mouthfuls of heady wine. The boy knew nothing of the thoughts that passed through their minds and understood none of the words they spoke. He knew only that every other minute, the woman looked at him sharply. He wondered why—was he so completely foolish and outlandish? Did she have the desire to pay for his supper so that his father would not think that he had spent his money carelessly? His thoughts disturbed him so much that he returned to his room to study his face and profile in the mirror on the chest of drawers. He tied his necktie with greater care and tugged at the hem of his jacket to make it fit better at his waist. Suddenly and without warning the awareness of his own beauty burst into his breast, stifling him with its splendor; he saw his exact nose, his eyes of velvet, his thick hair, as luxuriant and curly as the brow of a statue of antiquity. With this realization, he mused that this was what his goddess had seen, and seeing it, loved him for it. The blood had almost ceased to move in his veins, but a passionate, piercing glance from her golden lashes met him as he once more crossed the threshold of the restaurant. Unnoticed by her companions, she touched a goblet to her lips and drank its champagne to him. By the time he had found a seat, they were rising to leave the place. Letting the others go ahead of her, she brushed next to him, and as she passed, murmured a word as fragrant and wanton as a white blossom falling from a flowering tree.

He shut the door of his room and waited for her, his heart beating in his throat. It was after midnight when there were steps in the corridor and he knew that they had come back. A door closed and lights were turned off. When he looked out, the woman was waiting for him, framed in the open door of her own room. The way she looked at him was the only signal. Going toward her, he could only say, "Did you call me?" Making him be silent, she drew him into her room.

Sometimes, during the passing hours, he wanted to shout aloud, but always she placed her hand, with its perfume stronger than incense, on his lips.

"What is your name?" he asked her twice. In answer, she shook her head and laughed. For this laugh, he felt the desire to kill her. When at last he had to leave her, he felt himself to be her master and said firmly, "Tomorrow!"

"To-mor-row?" she repeated after him, pronouncing each syllable by itself, and she held him back while she turned the pages of a small red dictionary. When she understood the word, she whispered, "No tomorrow." She led him to the door, still gently caressing his hair.

He could not sleep at all, and when the first light of dawn appeared, even before the hotel had opened its doors, he began to wait for her, sitting in a wicker chair before the desk of the clerk. The porter was still sweeping. They looked at him suspiciously, without his noticing. He waited for her for hours.

As soon as the woman appeared, he rose to meet her. She moved as if winged. She was not startled by seeing him, but looked away and continued toward the door. When he blocked her way, she turned her back and walked toward the stairs. Much later, she descended again, now accompanied by the men who looked enough like her to be her brothers. Once again, Nicolangelo rose to his feet and approached her as if to speak. For a moment, they were speechless. The woman seemed to be shielded by one of the men, while the other, behind her, said bruskly, "Get out of the way." Saying this, he caught up with the others, and the three of them filled the width of the narrow vestibule as they went out to the street.

Trembling, he stood without moving a step. His whole body shook. Only his voice refused to tremble when he spoke to the manager, who had seen everything from the corner where he was standing.

"Who were they? What was their name?"

For answer, the man said only, "Take away your baggage before noon. Your room is reserved for tonight."

After that, he went out into the street. In a stupor of grief he found himself at the shop of a gunsmith. Had he been asked, he would have roused himself from the daze in which he moved to say that he was going to kill himself. He remembered, when he thought about it later, that he had hesitated in his choice of revolvers so as to buy one that was good but inexpensive. He felt obliged to record the cost in the expense book he had brought along to show his father. When the gun was in his pocket, he returned to pace the sidewalk in the bright sunshine. As the three of them entered the hotel, he ran after them and stood before them, barring their way.

"She is my wife!"

As he uttered these words, he accompanied them with an absurd gesture of his hand, touching the hand of the woman. She shrank back.

"Beat it, you ridiculous . . . ," said one of the men, not finishing his sentence. He turned to the porter. "Get rid of this beggar." The porter was quick to reach the boy and tried to lay hands on him, but the boy sprang away from him. He drew the revolver and fired at the woman, crying as he did so, "Your sister is a whore!"

He was absolved by the jury, but it would have mattered little if he had been imprisoned for a number of years. During the trial, his father died of a heart attack. In Messina now, passers-by look at the boy who "was worth his weight in gold" just a few years ago. During the long summer evenings, he comes to the door of the warehouse to catch a breath of air in the twilight. He is still thin and dressed in black, and he is as pale as he was when he caught the attention of the beautiful visitor from abroad and cost her her life. But now he has a few early wisps of gray to spoil the perfection of his black hair. He is even more quiet than he was in those days. There is nothing that he has to say to anyone.

EMILIO CECCHI

Two Sketches

TRANSLATED BY ANGUS DAVIDSON

1.

AQUARIUM

The water in the tanks was not distinguishable except where its level had sunk somewhat. Then, looking up from below, you could see, mirrored in its surface, the bottom of the tank, with its pebbles and shells, seaweed and sleeping fish. The liquid in the tank was also visible at the point where the fresh water flows in, in a tiny jet, for here it is made iridescent by little shining, frothy bubbles. But everywhere else it was invisible; and one forgot that it was water. The fish moved round like minute airships in a glass case at a fair; there were some little snakelike ones that looked like flames or streamers; and the jellyfish, hovering in mid-air, were like small parachutes thrown out by an airman in distress.

The rhythmic movements of these tiny creatures had something surprising and artificial about them, as though they were playing a game of shuttlecock. When they touched bottom for an instant, the fish rebounded like India rubber balls and rose up again at a vertiginous speed—so much so that sometimes, inadvertently, they broke through the skin of the surface with fin or tail. Then the whole mass of the water would be suddenly thrown into confusion by silvery lightning flashes, and you could see big pieces of light, like pieces of tin foil, sink oscillating downward.

At such moments some marine recollection, drawn from bygone readings of the South Seas or dimmed memories of *Twenty Thousand Leagues under the Sea*, would mingle with the narrow submarine landscape and its arrangement of coral sprays, spongelike stones, and curled pink plumes. A few yellowish stars were stuck onto the glass walls of the tanks, just as though on the skylight of Captain Nemo's cabin. But the majority of the fish did not waste their time upon such games, nor upon making a combined effect; they sought, warily, to concentrate the attention of visitors upon themselves, by acting in a demanding, determined fashion.

One, the color of verdigris, and another, with orange stripes and fringes of the most brilliant blue, surveyed themselves out of the corner of their eyes, like mannequins, as they swam round and round. A third, big-nosed and almost black, had taken up its position, motionless and in profile, behind the glass, so as to let itself be looked at; and the alarming thing about it was the human quality of its wrinkled face. Nature, leaving few signs of her work, had changed the face of an old aunt into the face of a fish.

Bored and full of complicated disorders, a green-spotted tench dozed the livelong day, half-hidden among the stones. But a huge lobster, whose claws had been bound with wire so that it could do no real damage, came swaying and slithering along and gave it a gentle prod. Gliding away between its feet, the patient little fish went off to seek refuge at a distance. And the big lobster went after it. When it arrived, the fish had gone to sleep again, and it gave it another touch. Disturbed again, again the tench fled, returning to its former tiny grotto; and so on *ad infinitum*. Similar jokes of neighborly life were repeated among the crowd of hermit crabs, which looked like a heap of chestnuts with a faint movement running through it. There were certain spiteful little hunchbacked fish which amused themselves by passing in a troop among the hermits and knocking them down in rows of three or four.

And while the time passed in comedies of this kind amid the treelike growths on the bottom, amid the tufted filaments and the Murano glassware, in the clear spaces of the water above, on the other hand, hundreds of little diaphanous fish with large eyes were leaping in jubilation like swarms of angels above the Holy Manger. Like a perfectly ordered *corps de ballet* they would hurl themselves, poised on their fins, from the enchanted distances to the front of the stage, and then, with a pirouette, fly away back again to their positions. On one side, great submerged glass tubes formed a translucent, quieter harbor where embryonic jellyfish, as yet barely congealed into shape, were dimly outlined, like drops of anise essence, in a bluish cloud. Rose-colored disks swayed gently halfway down in the water; in them the only sign of life was a slight undulation, a silvery curl at their edges—the same thing that can be seen when water sputters imperceptibly around some kind of salt as it melts. A slimy abortion, in shape like an elephant but without feet, was in the act of digesting a piece of coarse, black fish. And the weight of the putrefaction that was being accomplished inside its tiny stomach, transparent as a pane of glass, kept it down, anchored to the bottom.

In general, however, the spectacle might have become a little monotonous, if the sea eels had not introduced a note of horror into it. Their pool should rather have been termed a cage, from the way they circled round and round it, like little wild beasts, elegant and in a raging hurry. Interminably they twisted and twined and untwined, in bundles of five or six; moving with extreme rapidity, glutinous, formidable, they were like creatures of the same sex seeking each other in a sterile embrace, releasing each other and immediately intertwining again, all the more lustful for their disappointment. One of them, a veritable boa constrictor and, instead of tawny, quite black, held away from the others, slowly lashing the water; it looked like a plump matron presiding over the incestuous couplings of a monstrous gynaeceum. Their snouts were like the snouts of weasels, with little black, angry eyes; and it looked as though the insides of their mouths were hairy. The finless frill that fluctuated on their backs as they swam cut as sharply as a razor blade into one's flesh as one looked at them.

But, next door to the sea eels, the ichthyologist had placed, by way of contrast, the tank—dimmer and, one might even say, more silent— in which, as though in the cell of a criminal lunatic asylum, lived the octopuses.

The small octopus, as it sat there, looked like a rabbit; and the inside of one of its tentacles looked like the pink lobe of an ear, as one sometimes sees it in a rabbit, dangling and folded inside out. The big octopus, on the other hand—the midwife—clung to the winding intricacies of the wall, displaying purple, vaginalike suckers; and it touched itself and stroked itself continually with its tentacles, with the caressing, hand-washing gesture that lunatics make use of, while its eye remained fixed and stony, turned up toward the skylight from which a glimmer of light fell like rain.

It gave one the idea of a slow delirium of matter gone mad upon itself; of an accursed form of life in which that embryonic motion, that touching and stroking, exhausted all possibility of imagination and desire. Even God, one could not help thinking, indulges in some queer amusements! And, in front of that paralyzed damnation, it was a comfort to be able to believe that death, perhaps, exists.

2.

VISITORS

A little time ago my home was the scene of a small drama, bloodless indeed but so sinister that even the atmosphere and the furnishings of the place seemed to remain, as a result of it, shocked and desecrated for quite a considerable period.

About three o'clock one rainy night a man, with the intention of stealing, forced his way through the door of a balcony, one which is easily reached from the roof. At the sudden gleam of a lamp turned on in the adjoining room, a little girl woke up and caught a glimpse of him—bearded, his hat pulled down over his eyes—as he appeared in the doorway and vanished again. Then, immediately, we also awoke; and, even before we had taken in what the child was saying, caught sight of the wet footmarks of the thief, crisscross, enormous, in the light shining on the floor.

It was then noticed that the door leading to the staircase was also not closed. And, leaning over the banisters, I could see the wretched man, down on the floor below, in the act of trying to escape. He was dressed in brown and was soaked with the rain; he was shoeless and was wearing a black bandage as a mask: it was this bandage, obviously, that the little girl, in the half light, had mistaken for a beard.

Huddling himself together, he stared at me through the holes in his mask with a nasty, but imploring, look. I retained, more than anything, an impression of sheer nastiness from those few seconds that we stood gazing at each other in this way. Against the blank wall he looked like some gigantic bug, some nonhuman larva. It was a revelation of an unbelievable shape of horror, all the more evil because it had crept right into our intimate seclusion, close to the bed of innocence.

I had seized my revolver and now pointed it at him, so that he did not venture to emerge from the kind of hiding place he had found under the arch of the stairway; in fact he looked as though he were trying to sink back into the wall. And—so unnatural are such situations —I was acutely conscious of my own coolness as I took careful aim at him, with the deliberate intention of killing him. Twice the trigger clicked, to no purpose. Quick to take advantage of his luck, the man hurled himself downstairs. I can still see his back, immensely elongated as he leaped down the stairs, four at a time; and, before I could think of chasing him, he had vanished. In actual fact, if it had not been for the providential, almost comic, misfiring of my revolver, I could have killed him a thousand times. But to touch him with my hands would have been quite impossible—like putting one's hands into a heap of snakes. This is not a confession of courage.

Then I turned back into the apartment, into a group of terrified people. Ears were strained to catch strange rustling noises which made one think of a possible accomplice escaping up over the roofs; there lay the housebreaking tools beside the door the man had forced; the neighborhood had been roused. Then the visit of the police to the spot, followed by that of the Inspector, who looked like a dentist. The event was entering upon a mechanical, external existence on its own account, with the depressing obligation, for me, of going and consulting with the police and having to pass in front of the cells, amid tubs of excrement. Then there was the unforgettable feeling that the house had been profaned. And the thought of having wished to kill; the thought, too, that not even the fact of being poor is enough to save one from such experiences.

There were yet other results. I was often compelled to sit up late over some piece of work, and in intervals of weariness it would happen that my mind would go back to this episode. (Sane people, in fact, have always contrived to do their work in the daytime; and one of the causes of modern imperfection is that too many things have to be fitted in at night.) When the others went off to bed and I began to prepare myself for hard work, each door would be carefully inspected and the apartment made secure as a fortress. The hours would pass, until at last imagination would find itself caught in the toils of fear. Each shudder and start inside the building, the creaking sound of shrinking wood, the cavernous symphonies of water gurgling in tanks, a dog scratching itself on the open ground near by—all these assumed a fearful lyrical clearness, creating a poem of terror.

Nothing can be more irrefutable than the warm, shining wall that separates one's room from the rest of the world. But place your ear close against it; you will hear it vibrate with bursts of dull sound, trickle with the slow dripping of mysterious veins, tremble with deep-buried reverberations. The footstep of a passer-by makes it toll like a bell. The indulgence of such impressions was enough to drive one out of one's mind. Night, which seems so still, so solid, was changed into a subdued dialogue of resonant anxieties, within which the house lost all quality of human possession, until it dissolved and reverted to its pristine formlessness.

It was no longer a question of re-evoking the thief's intrusion. Nor yet of the picturesque terrors one has as a child, when doorways are filled with flamelike writhings, or the blank, closed door seems to be yielding to some irresistible pressure, to be moving very, very slowly, in a way that prolongs fear to an infinite extent. It was something airy and vague, physically explainable, yet terrifying. As though an uncoiling of unconscious life, and the disorder, the ravings, the ghastly inhabitants of the world of crime and of dreams, were strangling the soul; as though one perceived the crawling fermentation and decay of created things; and also, in a kind of internal pulsation like the very thump of the blood, the vital, murderous heartbeat of time.

Finally, during one of these night watches, another visitor got in, notwithstanding all the bolts and locks—a small millepede, attracted, perhaps, by the line of light under the shutter; or by a thin thread of warmth, for, outside, spring was under vehement attack from wind and ice and rain. A small millepede, tender, only just out of its shell, too young to have formed scales or to have felt the sun; and of a washed-out color like the scorpions that are found under stones in damp places.

I caught sight of it out of the tail of my eye; and at first it was like a whitish mote moving on the lens of my glasses. When I turned, I saw it circling on the floor, which seemed, in comparison, boundless; it was going round and round in broad circles, with an infinite rippling movement of all its joints and legs. Then, all of a sudden, it stopped right in the middle of the floor; and so it remained motionless, interminably, without the slightest inflection of its limbs or the faintest quiver of its minutely delicate horns.

Night seemed suspended in this utter immobility. The evidence of that other savage warning, changed now into a more secret alarm, rushed back into the mind. How acutely conscious one was of the reality of the nocturnal obsessions that terrified the old Christian poets, and of the ghosts that probed and pried like moles; and how far away it seemed, how eagerly longed for—the morning cockcrow!

That tiny monster, so easy to crush, in actual fact nothing, nothing would ever succeed in crushing it! And one felt that there is nothing that can save us from terror, unless God takes pity upon us and upon our nights.

RICCARDO BACCHELLI

An Etruscan Harvest

TRANSLATED BY FRANCES KEENE

The fertile plain curves inward in an easy arc from the pontifical lantern of white Civitavecchia to the fragile crook of Monte Argentario, silhouetted like a dark cloud between the sky and the Tyrrhenian Sea. This coastal plain is a land all of sun and golden grain.

On the first levels of the cloistered hills crowned by the walled town of Montalto di Castro and from which the towers of Corneto Tarquinia look toward the sea, the sun-bleached pallor of the olives gleams, and the trees consecrated to desperate acts, start up sheer from the gray, lichen-scored stone.

Colts and young bulls are raised on the gentle slopes and in the little valleys of these fields, and one can see scattered flocks of sheep, and the round corrals ready for the inspection, branding, and castration of the animals. Farther down on the level stretch between hills and sea, nothing breaks the great burning flame of the sky, scorching earth and sea alike. Old, scowling, the fortress of Porto Clementino watches over the deserted coast line and the salt mines of the convicts.

When the mowing is done, stubble, lumpy earth, and meadows are all one and the same burned yellow. The rows of wheat sheaves gleam and shine in the sun in the midst of the fields as they await the thresher.

The green, rich rivers of the Marta, the Arrone, the Fiora, which come down from the high Amiata, flow lazily through the dry countryside, their fresh banks gaining but a narrow margin over the dryness of the earth.

113

Slender water arcs snake their way seaward between the gurgling rivers and their dry banks. Scorched ilexes and some few wretched cork oaks break the sun's blaze with their meager shade, and horses, milch cows, and oxen group about their trunks, heads lowered, unable to find a blade of grass to graze, yet freed of the yoke for their hour's rest.

No farm cottages are to be seen and, in fact, the field work is let out to groups of migrants hired by contractors who bid for the jobs. Many tales were told in time gone by about the contractors and how they managed the troops of men and women they recruited from the poverty-stricken mountainside. But little by little they have softened up, even Griffoleschi, scion of a line of contractors who were hardened to all the rules of the game.

Certainly it was no easy life to try to manage bands of people in whose hands the sickle or the hoe was ever present, when it was not indeed a knife. And it was easy enough to deal a blow in the dark without anyone's being the wiser, when all were asleep at night in the ditches as snugly as in a sheepfold. No, it was no easy task, and if one went a little heavy on acts of meanness or brutality over pay or women, the migrants were swift and sure in retribution. Thus each act was balanced out in the end by another, and our milder, less violent customs of today have everywhere bred up a lesser cast of men.

During the reign of Braschi or Mastai popes *, the women knew what was expected of them aside from work if they hired out under a Griffoleschi. Nor were women recruits, and handsome ones at that, lacking on this account. And proud of their robust, agile bodies, they boasted that it was not necessity alone which made them look for work.

Out of a love of fair play and to avoid jealousies, contractors of the period honored the plain and even the ugly ones as well as the beauties, provided, of course, that they weren't downright hideous. But their descendant was not of this ilk. Having grown more civilized and enjoying far less absolute power over his squads of threshers and hoers, he had made up for this by being more choosy about his women.

After his discharge from the army, young Griffoleschi had returned to the job of his forebears, the only one that meant anything to him.

---

* Pope Pius VI (1717–1799) was of the Braschi family, and Pope Pius IX (1792–1878) of the Mastai family.

He would be thirty-two on Saint Mary's Day, August, 1926. He was
a fine, up-and-coming man, bold and enterprising, with a carrying
voice, proud glance, and springing stride. His medium-sized body,
slender and fine-boned, could give no idea to one who had not tested it,
of the great strength at the command of this dark young man with the
ready fists. A sure winner, people said, a bonny boy, as in the love songs!
He was a fine horseman and generally wore the habit of a trainer:
waist-hugging short jacket, trousers tapered at the calf like cavalry
britches, and high-polished boots. Decked out thus, he could have
been taken for a young fop when he went to the inn of a Sunday.
And jealous of their professional prerogatives, their service under
Roman princes, their work on stud farms of the Maremma, a group
of veteran trainers mumbled: "Why doesn't this bumpkin dress like
other peasants, as his father and grandfather did before him? Or if he
wants to let the world know he can sit a horse, why doesn't he wear
shepherd's clothes?"

Irritation finally mounted to such a pitch that, one Sunday, when
they were all dismounting before the crowded inn, one of the trainers
gravely went up to him and presented him with a stave such as the
mounted shepherds used to prod on and discipline their flocks. The
trainer sarcastically invited him to trade his crop, which Griffoleschi
had in his hand, for the shepherd's staff.

There in the middle of the street at the very inn door Griffoleschi
gave proof once and for all of the stuff he was made of. His adversary
was a head and a half taller and, with bulging muscles flexed, seemed
his double in bulk. The trainer poured heavy, thudding blows on Griffoleschi's back and shoulders, while the lighter man stayed in close to
protect his chest and ribs, punching from the ground with well-placed,
telling, all-but-noiseless uppercuts at the jaw and chest of his opponent.

All those gathered around had expected to see Griffoleschi get his
come-uppance. Instead, they now watched the big fellow pale, flail
the air with his arms, and collapse under the last, perfectly timed blow
to the jaw. He lost three teeth plus his pride and had reaped a couple
of weeks in bed, for Griffoleschi's knuckles left more telling blows
within than were visible on the surface.

The winner went to have hot poultices of oil and soothing herbs applied by the skilled hands of the mistress of the inn, a rich, hand-some woman who was kindness itself as far as he was concerned.

But during the fall planting of 1926, Griffoleschi lost all taste for women when his fancy was caught by a youngster just like an olive tree. Her limbs were slender and smooth, her eyes black and shining as the ripe olive, her skin fair, of a pallor that even the sun on the fields did not manage to darken. And her hair, a golden blond, gleamed in the light like oil when it is poured in a thin stream past a steady flame. But this neat little girl, who could even have been called fas-tidious, considering her station in life, always kept her hair caught up and bound by her kerchief. She was just losing the last raw looks of adolescence when Griffoleschi saw her hoeing the rows and breaking up the clods of autumn earth.

Whether it was because of her headstrong age or native pride, she repulsed him then and for the rest of the winter, holding him off with rough, sarcastic taunts. When spring came, he began to notice that his yearning for this girl had taken away all enjoyment, even his taste for his daily bread. Prayers and presents had gotten him no further than had boasting and masterful ways. And later, as if to challenge him, she had come straight to him to ask to be taken on as hired hand for the mowing—just as he had given up all hope of winning her.

This little girl had managed to check his petulance and pride as a contractor and lady-killer, perhaps in part because she was defenseless and alone, quite without fear, the child of unknown parents, who had been raised out of charity. No one would come to her aid, and Griffo-leschi had, to a degree he would have hated to admit, the instincts of a gentleman. There were even moments when he confessed he would have married her! And he bit his lip in rage. He had even told her so, though in such general terms, that he could not be pinned down . . . and the jade had answered that, in order to get married, two people must want each other. She had said that to him!

She was called La Sighignola * and, as a child, had been called Mousy because she was so neat and quick, but now that she was grown up, she no longer permitted the nickname and demanded re-spect.

She felt fear for only one thing, the tarantula which nests among

* Sighignola—snippet.

the clods of earth in the fields and bites the bare feet of the reapers. The ugly, hairy spider caused her convulsive terror. If one was pointed out to her, she fainted. She believed all the strange and frightening tales of the effect of its bites: she believed in the wild dances, the delirium, the spasmodic and lethal fits of laughter. When she heard some girl friend who had been bitten by the fearful spider begin the light and wailing delirium that often affects those stung by the tarantula, La Sighignola got up trembling, covered her ears, and fled the maddened girl. She was worse off, in fact, than the one who had been poisoned, since, in our part of the world, the harmful effects of the tarantula's bite lie more in the mind than in the body. This should not be taken to mean that it does little physical damage: quite the contrary.

At the end of a day when the sun had burned down pitilessly on the reapers' backs, the early dusk softened fields and labor, men's spirit and the day's late hour. The girls had been elbowing and teasing La Sighignola because the contractor never stayed far from her tucked up skirts. He turned about her as do little birds, afraid to wander far from the nest in their first flight. He could no longer even speak to her, found no peace either near or far from her and felt timid and infuriated. This was La Sighignola's triumph: she was near yielding, but far indeed from suspecting it.

It was because of the tarantula that came out as dusk drew on, just as work was about to end for the day. Griffoleschi had worked his hand into the clods of earth for some reason or other, and the tarantula bit him. He managed to grab the spider before, quick as it was, it had time to regain its lair, and he raised it in the air, cursing it, but quietly like a man who could not be affected by pain, poison, imagination, or fear. During the incident, he had been near La Sighignola, who, first out of horror then admiration, stood rooted to the spot. She was unable to take her eyes from Griffoleschi's face, which now seemed to her godlike. Motionless, intent, stunned, she was scarcely breathing and hung on his every word.

The contractor threw the spider down hard on the ground, then crushed it. Timidly, as if awakening from a dream, La Sighignola asked: "Aren't you going to die?"

Griffoleschi laughed off the remark, gently, a laugh that seemed to her superhuman.

"But doesn't it hurt?" she insisted, worried, admiring, deeply moved as a woman by his plight.

"When I look at you, it doesn't hurt. Only you can cause me pain, and you could, if you chose, cure me." He said this with a kind of dark, voluptuous despair.

Griffoleschi's threshers slept in the fields under a clear sky pulsating with stars. It was in late June. The contractor had stretched out in a narrow ditch, his "bed," still warm from the sun, and could not sleep because of the swollen hand bitten by the tarantula. His sleeplessness made the lovesick yearning in him more bitter than ever. He looked sadly at the sky and shivered every now and then with fever. Hearing the grass rustle, he believed a light evening breeze had risen over the plain, blown seaward from the fertile valley of the Marta, and hoped that it would cool him. When the rustling ceased, he glanced up, disappointed. There stood La Sighignola; she had come to find him.

"Does your hand hurt much?" she asked hurriedly, frightened as soon as she saw him looking at her in the clear night.

"You pity me for ills that cure themselves," he answered, "but for those you alone can cure you have no pity."

Then the girl knelt down beside him and tried to suck the poisoned flesh. Griffoleschi swore he felt no pain and would let the tarantula bite him every day from then on. Thus La Sighignola began to go to the contractor every night to tell him how brave and strong he had seemed to her when he faced the tarantula, and to hear, in return, how he yearned for her beautiful, unyielding self. Nor did the mowing end before the two young lovers knew together the sharp fragrance of mint, intermingled with kisses, which rose from their scented bed, and they learned the ways the warm earth at night yields comfort for the tremors of love.

From the moment he became La Sighignola's lover, Griffoleschi allowed no one to outdo him in any enterprise. Thus, a month later, at the end of July, he wanted to win the bid for transporting and threshing the wheat on a great farm on the plains. He paid no attention to the bids of his competitors who, upon losing, told him that he was ruining the market, nor to the advice of his friends who told him that he would ruin himself. He wanted the job and he got it. Then he busied himself with renting wagons and engaged the thresher and bailer. It was no small job. Several tons of wheat were involved, scattered over rough fields poorly serviced by run-down roads; Griffoleschi's team must negotiate a ford awkward enough to be dangerous and time consuming, and the distances were considerable. The job was to gather up the sheaves, carry them to the thresher, cart the sacks of grain to the granaries in the village and the hay, baled and tied by machine, directly to the railroad station. In short, the task called for intensive work and quickness of mind, limb, and eye, if one were not to derive a greater loss than profit from it. Never had Griffoleschi lacked on any of these qualities, much less now, when to love of self he added love of a woman. The job had to be completed well and on time, had to bring profit to him and discomfiture to his friends and competitors, in payment of envy and good advice alike.

He had never spoken again of marrying La Sighignola; he had not even suggested setting up housekeeping in the village and thus making her, as they say, his "columbine." She was not a woman for that sort of thing, and he, he could not have said why, found the idea repugnant. However, she continued to work with his teams, but Griffoleschi, in addition to expensive gifts he timidly offered her, was careful to have her do as light work as possible. For these shy attentions La Sighignola was very grateful and she thought and asked for nothing more than his love, which she now returned with all her heart.

A certain Sannaccio, a professional scrounger who had dropped in from heaven knows where and established himself these many years in those villages where manners are both cordial and openhanded and where the well-to-do love to spend money and amuse themselves by supporting parasites in order to make fun of them, this same Sannaccio, then, busied himself by giving Griffoleschi a quantity of unsolicited advice. He hung around the young man a great deal, flattering him, and the day the contract was let, he kept volunteering suggestions as long as the bidding lasted. Griffoleschi called him a buffoon and told him to get on his way. He turned up again at the inn, where he vaunted the courage and skill of Griffoleschi, who gave him a plate of roast kid, cooked to a turn with sweet herbs, with these words: "Eat, fool, and then at least you'll keep still."

"He talks like that out of friendship," explained Sannaccio, a great one for face-saving, "I don't know what I wouldn't do for friendship's sake."

The tables loaded with odorous dishes and bottles of strong, full-bodied white wine shook at the young men's laughter. Griffoleschi, whose successful bid gave him more appetite than usual, bent with a will over the goat's head, roasted in the oven with pungent sage and the good oil of those very hills, which now stared sadly at him with its herb-seasoned eyes.

A few days later ten wagons with thirty pairs of oxen, more than fifty hands of both sexes, a great thresher, two presses, and a good tractor engine worked in the fields under his direction. He had set La Sighignola to a job requiring little physical effort but great trustworthiness: she was to watch over the bales as they issued from the thresher's many mouths. The work progressed in a happy, orderly fashion. A brisk northwest wind swept over the threshing floor, clearing the early morning air of dust and smoke. The shiny belt linking motor and thresher spun gaily. The girls sang:

> Flower of the mulberry,
> The wind rushes by and flows, flows over the sea,
> Searching, forever searching, the most beautiful thing of all.

> Flower of love,
> The wind sees you, it longs to tarry,
> But neither on land nor over the sea can it stay.

Sensibly directed and fairly paid, the group worked quickly and well; Griffoleschi was worth ten men, and everything went smoothly until, on the third day, the hay, tightly baled and secured by wires, had to be carted to the station. The road, and especially the ford, turned out to be more difficult than he had expected; in taking on the job, the contractor had calculated that he could complete ten trips within a certain time, but it soon became apparent that at least fifteen would be needed. The idle clown, Sannaccio, who up to that point had wandered about interfering with the workers, giving La Sighignola a wide berth, however, and singing the praises of the wonderful Griffoleschi, now began with pasty-faced foreboding to study the difficulties at the ford, shaking his head with the air of a man who says: "I knew as much."

Griffoleschi had not lost heart, but his industry had become tinged with a certain agitation and he persisted in wanting to cross the river with loads that were too heavy. The sounder the objections of the drivers, the more they infuriated him, as if they were proposing that he surrender to an enemy when they advised him to lighten the loads.

"This river will eat up Griffoleschi's profit," Sannaccio began to remark sententiously. And he looked at Griffoleschi in the distance, standing upright on top of a big wagon piled with bales of hay. He was shouting at the dismayed drivers that he would get that load across himself, since no one of them had nerve enough to do it. And when, balanced on the top bales, he caught sight of Sannaccio's yellow face by the river bank, he called him out for a clown, a scrounge, a hex, until he made everyone laugh. Partly from bravado and partly to hearten the drivers, he refused to leave the wagon at the ford. He seemed possessed by devils. Sannaccio came up and counseled caution, prudence, and that was all that was needed! The drivers spurred on their oxen and shouted encouragement to them so that the wagon, moving resolutely down and into the water, might pass over some rocks which had considerably slowed the earlier wagons. Griffoleschi was screaming like a hawk, and the wagon, jerking heavily, rolled down the bank. Perhaps it was due to a lurch of the wagon, a dizzy spell, a touch of sunstroke, or loss of breath from his shouting and straining, but Griffoleschi lost his balance, fell headfirst from the top of the hay and under the wheels of the wagon which could have missed him only by a miracle for which there was no time to pray. A long and mournful blast from the tractor near by interrupted the work in the field, and La Sighignola ran wordlessly toward the ford, her eyes glassy with terror, as she used to flee from the tarantula. The wagon was standing in the middle of the ford, the water was gurgling through the wheels and around the legs of the oxen. Griffoleschi was lying on the narrow river bank.

How much blood the healthy body of a young man can pour forth! At the sight of her maimed lover, La Sighignola's heart shrank within her. She pushed aside the ineffectual onlookers and Sannaccio first of all, for she surprised him as he was shouting that desperate men come to a bad end, and she cut his insolence short with a violent blow. Then she raised Griffoleschi's head and laid it on her lap, opened his shirt, and with dry, courageous eyes, more grief-stricken than had they been filled with tears, tried to stanch the blood which ran tepid from the body of the wounded man over her knees. When she saw that she could do nothing, she began to call for an ambulance, which had already been summoned, and to beg help of the Madonna.

Meanwhile, Griffoleschi came to and he was giving orders as if he still stood on the wagon. "Death," he shouted. "Death, you don't scare me! I want to meet you in my own way!" He was already delirious and from time to time he vomited blood.

When the ambulance arrived, La Sighignola watched them lift the wounded man from her knees; she rose and seized him by the arm, but he could no longer recognize her. He kept on shouting that he wanted to meet Death in his own way. When the stretcher had gone, the women turned to console her, but, heedless of them all, she struck out on foot along the sun-drenched road. The thought that he might die had not even dawned on her.

When she stood before the gate of the city on the hill she saw she was covered with dust and blood and ran home to change her skirt, afraid that she would not be allowed in the hospital.

Griffoleschi was calling for her. She was brought in. At first the young man had continued his defiance of Death; then, when his brain had been cleared by the great loss of blood, he turned to the doctor: "Doctor, save me. I'm thirty years old, only thirty, Doctor!" As he was speaking La Sighignola entered the room and, wordless, threw herself on her knees before the doctor. He answered the injured man with a few words which the young woman sensed were encouraging lies.

"Give me time to marry her," Griffoleschi begged the doctor, and these were his last rational words. Soon he began to rave about the wagon, hay, blood that must be stopped. "I'm going," he kept saying. "I'm going if you don't stanch it."

A priest was called in, but could no longer confess him and absolved him *in articulo mortis*.

At the foot of those ancient Etruscan hills, the larks, startled by the passing trains, whirred through the air in mad, frantic flight. A few vultures, slow of wing, searched the ground from on high, seeking out a field mouse or a little grass snake in the damp fields by the river. A motionless tractor smoked lazily in the midst of a field where people were talking about Griffoleschi's accident and their own fear of having to remain without jobs at the very height of the working season.

Griffoleschi did not last until night.

In the great drought of this time of year when a few hours of sunlight make all the fields alike, the plowed and the unplowed, the new graves, too, were no different in color from the old. Not many days had passed before La Sighignola, dressed in her best clothes and with a black veil over her golden hair, went to the cemetery and placed her lips close to the parched earth under which Griffoleschi lay to tell her lover, with grave sweetness, that a son of his blood was to be born.

III

LITERATURE UNDER MUSSOLINI

Fascism ruled Italy for twenty years, from 1923 to 1943, and its domination did bring many changes to Italian life—yet they were neither quick, rapid, nor deep.

From the seizure of power in 1923 to the assassination of the socialist leader Matteotti in 1924, there was a period of struggle and uncertainty. It was not until the late twenties that one-party government evolved into an outright dictatorship; and then in the thirties came the totalitarian regime with its inevitable consequences of mass parades, propaganda, police state, and official ideology. The latter, however, seemed to be the weakest point of Fascism. Despite its various intellectual borrowings from syndicalism, old nationalism, and modern theories of violence, Italian Fascism had an empirical rather than a theoretical character. It cherished imitation and oratorical commonplace much more than dogmatic principle and, as far as philosophy was concerned, relied on grandiloquent slogans: "The state is morality in action"; "To believe, to obey, to fight—is the highest virtue"; "The class struggle is wrong, but the struggle of proletarian nations [i.e., Italy] against capitalist nations [i.e., England, France] is a necessity."

It is true that Italian Fascism was eager to acquire a more consistent system of ideas—and in the last years of its existence it did make attempts to forge some kind of state religion—but on the whole it was not too doctrinaire and therefore did not impose such definite and rigid dogma upon literature as did other totalitarian regimes, particularly Nazism and Communism. Mussolini and his aides, however, fully understood the importance of propaganda and official control over all the media of mass communication, hence the series of practical measures which spread censorship over all fields of art, literature, radio, and book publication. By 1930 no free press was left in Italy, and all newspapers, magazines, or publishing houses were being run by the Black Shirts or their stooges. Persecution of suspects and dissenters, various forms of loyalty oaths, the curtailing of academic freedom—these and other similar actions aimed at consolidating the hold of Fascism over Italy's cultural life.

Although Fascist leaders did not adopt an official artistic policy or a clear-cut literary program, they did try to suffuse literature with their slogans and with the "Fascist spirit." The manifestations of the latter included antidemocratic preaching and official optimism: "Italy is the best country in the world, Italians are great and happy, everything is healthy and is going to be even better." At one time the censors banned the figure of the suicide from all works of fiction. Nobody had the right to take his own life in the land of Mussolini. An atmosphere of false respectability coexisted with the utter corruption of Fascist officialdom. The length of women's bathing suits was regulated and bordellos were closed. (The pervasive crudity and sexuality in fiction after World War II was, in part, a reaction against Fascist restrictions.) Then there were the fanfares of aggressive nationalism, the bragging and the shouting, the reviling of other nations, the attacks on "pernicious cosmopolitanism"—all the adjuncts of a dictatorial three-ring circus which by the end of the thirties showed signs of disintegration. Fascism promoted grandiloquence and verbosity in letters, and Mussolini's pompous processions and stage effects, which appealed to a certain histrionic streak in the Italian character, were echoed in literature by the resurrection of d'Annunzio's lavish eloquence and by shallow but vociferous works of prose and poetry.

Despite all the efforts made by the government to support Fascist poets and novelists, the direct impress of Fascism on the arts was rather negligible, while its indirect effects were limited. Of course, writers were often compelled to remain silent or to watch their step. Certain topics were tabu, and any elaboration on contemporary issues was extremely dangerous. Government subsidies and control of the press distorted the general picture and in many cases pushed forward literary misfits and ambitious morons, while all sorts of nincompoops climbed to key posts in various cultural organizations. But only a small minority of writers actually adhered to Fascism and seriously propounded it. One can easily find scores of novels of the period which repeated antidemocratic slogans and apparently adopted Fascist terminology, but even such influence was only skin deep. The majority of Italian writers under Mussolini wore a cloak of indifference or of passive acceptance.

This explains the fact that many writers contributed superficially to the government press without believing profoundly in its slogans. But hundreds of others rejected the regime ideologically, morally, or politically, and often on all three grounds. Despite—or because of— this, they developed a technique for avoiding reality, for seeking shelter in purely formal, aesthetic attainments. In many literary circles there prevailed a peculiar spirit of detachment, an attitude of "business as usual." Literature tried to ignore social reality and to keep aloof from it; fiction seemed to exist independently, outside of any political context. The leading articles of this periodical or that would repeat Fascist maxims; literary forums would be opened by the chairman shouting, "Evviva il Duce"; but the stories in the magazine or the talks at the meeting would have absolutely nothing to do with "living dangerously," or with colonial expansion, the corporative state, or nationalism.

A survey of literary production between 1923 and 1943 would reveal a curious absence, not only of Fascist ideas, but also of Fascist reality. One could claim that Fascism had no deep effect on Italian letters, and that behind its façade the organic development of various artistic schools and tendencies followed its natural course. In a subdued or roundabout way, writers continued along the lines of development laid down in the early twenties. This explains the unflagging popularity of such writers as Papini, Panzini, Pirandello, or Svevo. Outside influences grew considerably. Italians, always avid readers of foreign literature, now saw it as a relief from Fascist pressure. A great variety of trends were linked with Proust's psychological slow motion, with the dreamlike sequences of French surrealism, with Freud's sexual determinism, and with the terse and full-blooded naturalism of the Ameri-

cans, who were strangely in vogue in the late thirties. Of course, besides the innovators and modernists, there was an important, eclectic,
academic current which kept on flowing and often flooding. There
are even more professors writing fiction in Italy than there are teachers
producing poetry in the United States.

Some of the most talented futurists turned toward surrealism. Such
was the case of Massimo Bontempelli, one of the leading writers of the
period. He combined a penchant for avant-garde experimentalism with
a scholarly background; in a way he forms a counterpart of Papini.
While the latter underwent many intellectual changes, Bontempelli
passed through artistic adventures of extreme variety. This member of
the Italian Academy, a former Senator and a left-wing sympathizer, assumed many attitudes during his long career. He wrote novels, poems,
symbolic tales, social allegories, poetic novelettes, and paradoxical
sketches, quite closely connected with those of Pirandello, yet in a
more definitely surrealistic disguise. A great number of short stories by
this elusive and important writer, such as "Linaria" or "The Sleeping
Beauty," are delightful fantasies with symbolic and ironic overtones.
In general, the "lucid delirium" of his prose is a deliberate mélange of
lyrical outbursts, jests, meditations, paradoxical statements, and studies
of character and environment. Faithful to his futurist youth but de-
void of nationalistic dreams, he opposed Curzio Malaparte's Strapaese
(super-country)—a nationalistic interpretation of the rural and regional virtues of Italy—with Stracittà—an international vision of the
super-city.

Aldo Palazzeschi, another refugee from futurism, evolved from the
eccentricities of his youth and settled down as an entertaining and
ironic storyteller who delights in the incongruities of life. He is as much
fascinated by the bizarre as Bontempelli is by the fantastic. A Florentine, Palazzeschi revived the arch and jocular techniques of great Tuscan masters. His stressing of realistic details leads to a certain long-
windedness, but it is offset by his feeling for the baroque. His chuckle
is amusing, and mischievous, even though in some stories, such as
"Love Letters," he conveys a strange sense of madness and treads on
the verge of the dramatic. There are psychopathic traits in many of his
heroes and heroines, and Palazzeschi is obviously interested in the dis-

tortions of the human mind. The modern Tuscan school, led by Pratolini, owes a great deal to this bizarre and fascinating author.

More conservative trends were represented by one group of writers
who, without belonging to the regional or prosa d'arte movements,
tried to develop the domestic literary tradition, mainly the craft of the
short story. Giovanni Comisso, although he refuses to be identified
with any specific coterie, fits into this category. His work is so strongly
attached to the soil and to classical models that even those foreigners
who know Italian well fail to appreciate Comisso's true stature. The
lyrical, almost musical, quality of his verbal rhythms in a harmonious
stylistic whole, his anti-intellectualism, his extraordinary feel for life
and sensations and for this world, are couched in deceptively simple,
transparent prose. Although he has written several novels, it is in the
short story that he expresses best the freshness of his vision of life and
that sense of rapture and discovery which makes so enchanting his
"reports on men and things." He is too overwhelmed by the plenitude
and joy of existence to pay attention to plots and involved constructions. He prefers to describe impressions and fragments of his reality.
This puts him close to the Rondists, although their stylistic fragmentism was more distinctly psychological. It was strongly felt in the kin-
dred group of Solaria, which included such representatives of the
psychological school as Carlo Gadda, Arturo Loria, Alessandro Bon-
santi, and Gianna Manzini. Manzini's subtle intelligence, rare sensitivity, and lightness of touch made critics call her the Italian Virginia
Woolf. Although she lacks the depth and the tragic intensity of her
English counterpart, she is an excellent writer, endowed with a sort of
clairvoyance. She transmutes descriptions of bodily reactions into
spiritualized images, sublimating the trivia of experience through a
platonic, poetic comprehension.

The stories of Bonaventura Tecchi, a highly civilized and honest
writer and a good craftsman, are also inclined toward the psychological.
His analysis of emotions, usually of sad, crepuscular moods, fits into
an atmosphere conveyed in an impressionistic fashion: landscape is
fused with state of mind, as in "Departure," a fine story in which
Tecchi's main preoccupation—the attraction of evil—is delicately projected against the background of Venice.

Toward the end of Fascism, Alberto Moravia emerged as the leader of the psychological trend. He gained recognition rapidly abroad and was widely read and discussed at home. While Tecchi and the purists pointed at his faulty style, his morbidity, his almost pornographic eroticism, and his errors of taste, others claimed that Moravia's uneven work was intensely powerful and revealed a strong artistic personality. His polemically bitter fugue, his incessant exploration of sexual perversity as well as of all the other complexities in modern man, fully compensated, in their opinion, for his aesthetic shortcomings. His first novel, The Time of Indifference, written in 1929, ranked among the most significant Italian novels of the period, and since that time Moravia's literary stature has continued to grow.

While his contemporary, Silone, is a moralist who stresses social reality, Moravia is a moralist who stresses primarily psychological reality. His weak and unstable heroes, who reflect so well the confusion and anxiety of our era, are often impelled toward crime and self-destruction, and the problem of evil, which was only sketched in Tecchi, is presented in all its magnitude in Moravia's tales. Some of them, such as "The Unfortunate Lover," are so effective in evoking the atmosphere of a place and the aura of a human being, so penetrating in their analysis of all the tortuous threads of amorous relationship, that they certainly equal the best of the Italian novella, even though they bear the imprint of various domestic and foreign influences. A mordant, cold, and often cruel observer of the nocturnal, sinful side of human nature, an experimenter who, like Pirandello, places his cerebrally conceived characters in strange situations, Moravia connects the new Italian literature with its European and American counterparts.

Moravia's manner is certainly far distant from what is called today neorealism. The only thing he has in common with the latter is his desire to face reality, to represent the existing state of things without reticence and hypocrisy. He does it in a nervous, occasionally clinical, "anti-literary," but always eminently modern, way; and here he obeys one imperative demand of his times.

Even under Fascism, verismo and the realistic tradition had been a living force, and the popularity of such authors as Alvaro or Bernari indicated that a new and rebellious generation was gathering its forces in the totalitarian prison. Verismo was a point of departure for Corrado

Alvaro, a highly talented Calabrian who went from a direct and most illuminating depiction of his native region to a poetic transformation of life from an intensely personal angle. Some critics may wonder whether he has achieved harmony between lyric aspiration and straight narrative, but what counts is his deliberate attempt to avoid fragmentism, to turn toward large moral issues and to cover the totality of life-experience. Alvaro, by the way, was a consistent anti-Fascist and a democratic liberal, and had exposed communist totalitarianism in one of his novels. He was highly conscious of the problems of our age and tried to reach that direct "facing of reality" which the censorship and the corruption of the regime banished from Italian literature.

It is obvious that until 1943 such tendencies could be manifested only indirectly, in a devious way. Only the expatriates could speak up straightforwardly and write fearlessly. A whole body of exile literature developed in France, Switzerland, England, and America; and along with historians and political writers, such as Guglielmo Ferrero, Gaetano Salvemini, Emilio Lussu, G. Borgese; art critics, such as Lionello Venturi; or poets, such as Lauro de Bosis, there were prominent storytellers and novelists—G. Borgese and Ignazio Silone.

Alvaro was primarily an artist, and his interest in ideas was genuine but secondary. Silone emerged as a man of faith and action, a moralist and a combatant, and a spokesman for the Italians whom Fascism reduced to silence. He stood for the full novel of large scope and moral significance, the modern problem novel which the regime made impossible at home. All Silone's merits and defects stem from his deep concern with man's social conduct, and he put all his undeniable talent at the service of a cause. What saves him from producing fictionalized essays on revolution, democracy, religion, and Fascism is his sincere interest in people, his mild humor, and his profound, almost mystical, sense of higher values and of the dignity of man among the indignities of life. In his short stories, just as in those larger works which brought him international fame, there are always a hope and a warmth which make so attractive such pieces as "Return to Fontamara," a wonderful specimen of his simple, "heart-to-heart" prose. The authenticity of his quest, the spontaneity of his humanism, the moral integrity of the man and the writer, have endeared him to millions of readers. In both Europe and America, Silone has been for

years a significant figure. As a political fighter and an exile, he personi-
fied in the late thirties the resistance to Fascism and the hope for the
new Italy. It is true that while his popularity was very great all over
the free world, he hardly exerted any strong influence within his own
country; and even after his return home in 1944, his works did not find
too warm a welcome in Italy. Aside from political reasons, the critics
explained this paradoxical situation by the fact that Silone was a bookish fellow of old-fashioned literary patterns. New trends in contemporary letters apparently did not have much effect on him, and he
remained an outsider in the aesthetic debates of modern Italian authors. They wanted to depict reality freely but in a new way, and when
the collapse of Fascism allowed them freedom to speak out, they all
attempted to renovate the realistic tradition—and thus promoted its
modern brand, which became known in the post-Mussolini era as
neorealism.

BONAVENTURA TECCHI

A Day in Venice

TRANSLATED BY ANGUS DAVIDSON

The boy had come from a town in Emilia. Gloomy, angry, his hair standing thick like a brush on his narrow, pale head, his whole body like a cane, still green, still sensitive, in the grip of sorrow's furious hand, he had accomplished the first part of his journey in a third-class carriage, huddled in a corner, an enemy both to himself and to those near him, with a feeling of hostility and ill-humor even toward his own suitcases and bundles which reminded him of the town, of the things, among which he had grown up.

At Mestre he had tumbled out of the train. He did not want to go straight on to Udine and the frontier. He wanted to see Venice. By a sudden resolve he had thrown out his belongings, taken another train, and found himself, almost automatically, still with that sensation of painful dullness that pressed upon his heart like a cloak of lead, in the midst of other people, on the boat, in Venice.

So far it had been as though he had not seen his fellow passengers. Young or old, men or women, he had looked at nobody; but if he chanced to do so, the women had given him a feeling of disgust—the faces of young women of which he had caught a fleeting glimpse in the train or at some station or other. Now, sitting in the boat, in a world wholly new to him, he had, quite close to him, just in front of him, a man and a woman. And, although he had no wish to leave the prickly shell of solitude in which he had taken refuge, he could not help looking at them. Whenever his eyes traveled ahead of him, drawn, instinctively, by the novel aspect of the things they saw, they

133

could not but dwell, for a second, upon this couple. A man and a woman, no longer young; but one look was enough to show what sort of a chain it was that bound them together. The woman's body, as though not content to be close to the man's, owing to the narrowing of the seats toward the bow of the boat, had drawn even closer, leaning sideways toward him, while her ankles entwined themselves with her companion's feet. One of her legs, uncovered almost up to the knee, gave an indication of what her body was like: no longer young, already well versed in love, but still full of eager desires.

The boy withdrew his eyes, pierced by a yet sharper stab of pain. The thing which brought joy to others, which in him, at his age, with senses already awakened and a precocious intelligence, should have aroused pleasure or at least interest, brought nothing but pain to him.

His story was both crude and simple. A few months earlier his father, head designer in a factory in that town in Emilia, had driven his mother out of the house, after a noisy scene, having caught her red-handed in a guilty passion, of which the boy had become aware, secretly and tremblingly, some time before. And now he was running away, summoned by an uncle who lived in a foreign country, to take up a job which he did not like, leaving his mother whom he could not bring himself to hate, deserting his father whom he felt to be weak and alien to him—or perhaps merely unhappy—and whom he yet could not love.

The boy withdrew his eyes and switched his glance to the water, as though he were looking for help in the novel and unusual aspect of the things that surrounded him. If, previously, possessed by gloomy melancholy and by a violent hatred for everything and everybody, he had refused to look at anything at all, now he realized confusedly that what he wanted was a sudden and wonderful sight, to distract him for a few moments. Without being conscious of it, without thinking about it, perhaps it was precisely for this that he had decided to spend a few hours in Venice.

It was a Sunday afternoon, dull and cloudy, toward the end of October. In the silence that hung over its gloomy, deserted waters—the small volume of traffic on working days, already slackened by the ending of the season, was reduced to almost nothing on a Sunday afternoon—the Grand Canal made a singular impression upon the boy.

The palaces were gray and deserted, too, and even the whiteness of their marble, darkened by the great clouds, looked as though it wished to doze a little, after so much splendor; deserted, also, were the mooring posts for gondolas in front of the palaces, and against them the boat, as it went slowly past, sent its languid, sinuous wash, water within livid water. What a strange invitation to the pleasures of the senses came from that water, from that silence! Even the wail of the siren, which, as the boat approached the landing places (they too almost always deserted), would suddenly discover some lonely, undecided pair of lovers on the top of a little bridge or at the opening of a side canal, seemed, on that slow Sunday afternoon, to be repeating the invitation with its hoarse, prolonged cry, full of some strange suggestiveness: an invitation to make haste, to brook no delay in the pleasures of love, to take refuge in some discreet corner, in some solitary house.

The boy withdrew his eyes from the things he saw all around him and brought them back to the two people. It might be, perhaps, that he had been mistaken. Perhaps it was just a case of a married couple, on their honeymoon journey. He looked for the ring, on her hand and on his. Her hands were covered by gloves, upon his there were no rings. He seemed younger than she, thin and vigorous in figure, with a suggestion of the sportsman in his clothes and his movements, as he sat with his face held up to the air in the bows of the boat, his features vigorous and clear-cut now that he was seen in profile. But, as soon as he turned his eyes toward the other passengers, the boy, who was examining him, noticed in them a troubled light, unmistakable. There was something irregular, something sinful between those two. And, although they were so different in appearance—she plump, he thin and bony—the desire that bound them together was so impatient that they yet seemed, at moments, to resemble each other. The boy hoped that they were foreigners, people from outside Italy. From a word of hers, however, carried to him suddenly by the wind— the woman had been leaning forward all the time, her face turned toward the bows—he realized that they were Italians, from a town not far away. And when, at last, he saw her eyes, her mouth, and the unexpected gray streak in the midst of her raven-black hair, the painful, terrible remembrance of his mother, whom he had so often examined and understood during the moments when she was awaiting her lover, struck him so violently that he bit his lip to prevent himself from crying out.

She, too, his own mother, had a streak of gray hair above a youthful brow.... The boy took refuge at the opposite end of the boat, in the stern, which was filled with people.

St. Mark's, the Doges' Palace went by almost without his noticing them: such was the grayness in the atmosphere, such the great grief in his heart, that everything had turned pale and dead.

It was only when the boat had turned toward Veneta Marina, and there were few people left on board, that he made up his mind to land. But he found himself in an almost deserted place, with his two heavy suitcases and no porters or hotels in the neighborhood. When a gondolier approached him and suggested taking him back toward St. Mark's, he refused his offer. He wanted to be alone. He started wandering around, carrying the two suitcases and the bundles, with that same gloomy, furious melancholy in his heart. ... At one point he noticed that, at a little distance, in the direction of an open space beyond which there was a glimpse of greenness, there were people at work. He was surprised, because it was Sunday. Workmen were carrying wooden hoardings, others were building a kind of altar or pulpit. Evidently some festival was about to take place, but he could not quite understand the purpose of all these preparations. In the midst of the workmen was a man with a white paper cap on his head such as is worn by decorators; he was drawing on a big piece of cardboard.... The boy went closer to him, filled with curiosity. He had a passion for drawing: son of a head designer in a factory, he had attended an evening school, in his Emilian town, and his dream had been to be able, some day, to enter the Academy. Whereas the work which was awaiting him, in that faraway, unknown town to which he was going, was so very different! Selling fruit, probably, on a stall; or staying shut up all day in a warehouse. At this idea he suffered a renewed pang of grief, an impulse of revolt. ... In contrast, how lightly, how joyfully did the designer's fingers run over his piece of cardboard! He sketched in a horse, and intended, perhaps, to place upon it an archangel or a saint.... The boy remembered how his own drawing master—the only person, according to him, who understood him, who was really fond of him, and to whom he felt himself deeply attached—had told him, more than once, before he left, that, when he went through Venice, he must not forget to see the famous horse at—yes, he remembered the name of the place perfectly well: San Zanipòlo. Now he came to a sudden decision. He looked around for the gondolier, who was still not far off, and told him to take him and his two suitcases to the Hospital of SS. Giovanni e Paolo.

The gondola moved slowly away toward St. Mark's, whence came a distant sound of crowds and a fair; but, before reaching it, turned off to the right into a narrow canal and passed under a bridge.

"The Bridge of Sighs," explained the gondolier, a sprightly, talkative little old man, pointing to the bridge to make the boy look at it. The latter raised his eyes.... Then the old man began his tale. He talked, in his gossipy Venetian way, about the Italian patriots, those who had been prisoners, those who were dead, those others who had passed over that bridge on their way to die or to suffer in other, yet darker, prisons, far away from Italy. The boy's attention was caught for a moment; but then he thought, with a kind of envy, how much more exalted and beautiful, in spite of everything, had been the suffering of the Italian patriots, in comparison with his own.... Ah, if only he could have had a sorrow as exalted, as great as theirs! His own was but a poor, a despairing sorrow: a sorrow that could not be confessed.

The gondola continued on its way and was now passing through one of the poorest parts of Venice, where even the names of the little canals seemed to have been given in order deliberately to create an impression of abandonment and death. "The Rio of the Beggars"—he read on a peeling wall, in large, rustic characters; and the name echoed for a long time in his head, as he looked. There were old crumbling, tumble-down buildings; windows barred by gratings, behind which you could see, now and then, a dozing cat; rusty shutters, half off their hinges. The boy reflected that they might be either old monasteries, deserted and silent for centuries, or else perhaps houses of ill repute. Everywhere there was a sense of weary indifference, of silent decay. These old buildings seemed to have been abandoned even by the waters, which, having fallen to a lower level at low tide, had left, all along the walls, shamelessly uncovered, large areas of sticky, thickly crusted dampness, upon which you might expect to see, at any moment, a few crabs or rats dancing; and from these greenish, slimy walls there stuck out, unexpectedly, short disconnected flights of stairs, after the manner of bridges; and in the walls were half-dark caves and wide, hollowed-out doorways. "Is Venice always like this?" he asked, with a sudden rush of indignation. The old gondolier related that there had been no foreign visitors that year, that there was no money anywhere, that the season was dead—as though these facts, for him, contained everything.

The gondola came to a stop in front of the Colleoni statue,* and the boy got out. Following the instructions of his drawing master, he wished to have a good look at it, both at the horse and at Colleoni's face. But twilight had come rapidly down; in the gray evening, a kind of thin mist, just in that particular small square and at that particular moment, enveloped the horse and, higher up, obscured the face of the war lord. The boy made a gesture of annoyance; then, as he lowered his eyes again, found close to him the burning eyes of a woman staring at him.

The gondola moved in the direction of the Arsenal, and he was again enveloped in that deceitful silence, in that atmosphere of deadness, from which, however, there emanated a strange kind of suggestiveness. "Which way is the sea?" the boy demanded eagerly. The gondolier explained, with a slight smile, that one could not go to the sea in a gondola, that the sea was over there (he pointed toward it) at the Lido. . . . The boy asked to be taken to a small hotel where he might spend the night, and the gondola penetrated again into a network of larger and smaller canals, of bridges and embankments of piles, as evening swiftly fell. The boy lost all sense of direction and no longer had any idea where the gondola was taking him. When the gondolier put him down in front of a small house with a sign outside it, he thought he recognized it. Had he not already passed this way, a short time before, in the gondola, in front of those two little bridges

* This colossal bronze statue of the Venetian general Colleoni is by Andrea del Verrocchio.

that were bunched so closely together that they seemed almost to be trying to embrace? No, after all, he did not know the house. But as soon as he was inside, on a landing between two flights of stairs, he at once realized what kind of an hotel he was in. Couples were coming furtively down the other staircase, at the end of this Sunday afternoon, while he was arranging with the proprietor for a room; a couple of young people, scarcely grown up, parted company even before they reached the landing, the young man going straight downstairs, with a false air of self-possession, while the girl stood waiting, her face turned away into the shadow, until he had gone out. . . . In the room allotted to the boy, the bed was still unmade. He had to wait outside while the manservant came and went two or three times, changing the linen, before he could go in. When he did at last go in and the noise of suitcases being put down and of his own footsteps had ceased, he began to hear certain words, certain intimate sounds that he knew well, coming through the thin walls from the adjoining room. . . . It was the sad experience of his own life that was speaking to him. Then he was seized by an impulse of sensuality and of rage, by one of those brutal onslaughts that blinded him, that seemed suddenly to trans- form him, extinguishing utterly in him the light of his delicate sensi- tiveness.

There was a strange mingling of emotions within him—rebellious- ness and cunning, sensuality and ingenuousness. His intelligence, sharpened by suffering (and by that particular sort of suffering), knew everything, had discovered everything, had become extremely shrewd; and yet he had never touched a woman. In relation to women he felt contempt, rage, and a kind of bitterness; and at the same time he was filled with a strange, boundless timidity. How furiously angry this timidity made him! Ah, but that very evening he would tear it out, would trample it underfoot like a rag. . . .

The moment he had put down his belongings, he rushed downstairs and out again into the little deserted square, and started off along canals and through byways.

"Me?" inquired the clear, laughing voice of the girl to whom he had spoken, at the entrance to a shadow-filled lane. "Me?!"—and her eyes sparkled with quick intelligence and impudence, with fearless curiosity. "You must be crazy! Where on earth d'you come from—the North Pole?"

She was not frightened. Small and slim, with a delicate, jaunty figure, wearing a black velvet bodice that enclosed her like a little piece of armor, she had something childish, and at the same time alert, soldierly, about her; but on her breast, close to her neck, hung a little necklace, white and slender, and it was like a cry of joy.

The boy became flustered.

"I was asking for a café. . . . Excuse me, you must have misunderstood me," he stammered, red in the face with shame and astonishment.

"Ah, you were looking for a café?"—and she gave another laugh, fresh and clear as though bubbling from a mountain spring. Her eyes, her mouth, her neck, her fluttering necklace—everything about her was laughing. "In that case you've come to the right place. . . . We own a café, just here. . . . Come along, then!"

The boy, suspicious, had for a moment the idea that he had guessed rightly at first and had then made a mistake in thinking her to be so distant and unapproachable. . . . He followed her, his blood still boiling with blind, arrogant desire.

It was one of those pleasant little Venetian cafés with a number of separate rooms, all of them small and low, with a staircase leading to the rooms above, and down below, a couple of people looking out, in a bored manner, from behind the windowpanes, or playing chess. That day, being Sunday, the café was exceptionally full.

Finding himself in the midst of this buzz of voices, this warmth, this assembly of staring people, the boy had the impression that it was all a joke. He made an instinctive movement of retreat, feeling he wanted to escape. There was a little table still unoccupied under the stairs, so he placed himself at it, as though to hide himself; he also felt obliged to order something from the waiter. . . . The girl had vanished up the stairs; perhaps she did not intend to appear again.

Nevertheless she did reappear at the top of the staircase: she was no longer wearing the velvet bodice, but had replaced it by an orange jumper. She came down with her legs close together, her little heels tapping on the wooden steps, almost above his head. She was the proprietor's daughter, obviously; you could tell that from a thousand different signs. Everyone greeted her, everyone smiled at her in the good-natured Venetian manner, with the admiring confidence that the Venetians show toward women, but also with a feeling of respect. The boy stared at her with wide-open eyes. She went over to her father, who was behind the counter, at the cash desk; and from there, as though from a platform, she looked brightly all around. She sought him with her eyes and discovered him at once, at the table under the stairs; and then gaily made her way straight toward him as if he were a friend. The boy felt a thrill of delight and invited her to sit down beside him, to have a drink, not really quite knowing what he was saying or doing, his face flaming; then he was all at once paralyzed by a rush of shyness. . . . As for her, she made a pretense of not understanding; she did not accept his invitation, but stood leaning on the back of a chair, laughing and remote. Then he was seized with a desire to say something disagreeable to her, to unload onto her a little of the black melancholy that he had inside him. He told her that he did not like Venice, that it had been a great disappointment to him, with its grayness, its feeling of deadness. . . .

"No, it's not true!" she said loudly, almost shouting; and into that cry of protest, clear, laughing, silvery, there seemed to flow all the color, all the joy of Venice that he had not known.

The boy was conscious of this in a confused way, but he would not give in; and he went on repeating, detail by detail, fearlessly and with a kind of cruel pleasure—perhaps exaggerating a little—all the impressions that he had received.

"No, no, it's not true, it's not true!" she kept saying, and all the time she was laughing and laughing, as though the obvious truth of the argument, and the enormity of what the boy was saying, amused her.

There was, however, in the girl's expression, a look of intelligence and of readiness to understand, perhaps even to pity, as though she were listening to a sick man and wanted to heal him. He was not accustomed to pity, to kindness from other people, and he did not understand. And, as he continued his tale, he hinted at something mysterious, something that he "knew," that he had "seen": he did not say now whether it was at Venice, or somewhere else, or in his earlier life. Then, suddenly, he went on to say, with great assurance, that he knew "all about women, yes, all kinds of women; and very nice, too. . . ."

"No, it's not true," she said; and she drew herself up in front of him with the same defiant movement as before, in the deserted lane, and with something so lively, so sane, so unassailable in her voice and in her eyes that her companion was compelled to be silent.

At that moment more people came into the café, and her father called the girl back to the counter.

"It's not true! It's not true!" He heard the beautiful voice again during the night, as he slept in the little hotel; he heard it in the midst of an agitated sleep. He was in a strange state, between waking and sleeping, that night. He seemed to see a black fish close to his bed; and while, at the extreme edge of sleep, he was trying to break its barriers with a cry, this same fish darted swiftly into some dark, muddy water, and the bed was like a gondola going slowly along between houses utterly black and reeking with dampness; but from far off, beyond the canals and the little squares, he heard that silvery voice: "No, it's not true!" He awoke, and it seemed to him that the voice had come from the room next door; but suddenly he remembered that that was the room in which he had heard those suspicious, secret sounds, and he sank again into his nightmare-ridden sleep. . . . Now he saw a great crowd of people in a café, and under the tables there was nothing but legs, crossed legs pressing each other, seeking each other. But was it a café? Was it not a boat? Yes, it was a boat; and there was a woman, on a bench, embracing a man, and the face of a woman, with a streak of gray hair, that gave him great pain and looked like . . . "No, it's not true!" cried the voice, from the other end of the boat.

He awoke completely. "If only the whole of my life wasn't true!" he said to himself. "If only the woman with the streak of gray hair on her forehead had never existed except in a dream. . . ."

For a moment he lay there, bewildered. Then he reflected that it must already be late, and he dressed in a great hurry and rushed downstairs. He knew there was a train that left early in the morning, for the frontier.

He left the little hotel. It was not late: day had scarcely broken.

No sooner was he outside than he had the impression that something had changed. He could not quite understand how, nor what it was. When he came to a small canal, it seemed to him that the water, though still black in the dim light of dawn, was not so low, and indeed that the whole town had risen up, after the manner of a ship. And how strange the town was at that hour! With its narrow lanes and canals even more deserted than before, with its veiled lamps and its odd feeling of freshness! Toiling along with his suitcases and bundles, he found himself beside a big canal, near an enormous bridge. Even this, massive as it was, seemed to be rising lightly into the air. A shivering ray of dawn touched the bridge lightly, high up, as though it were in some different region; then a faint whiteness, veined with shadow and streaked with blue, started to tremble on the surface of the stone and to melt into the air, reaching out toward the full light of day. The city was coming to birth beneath this symbol of white and blue.

The boy could not believe his eyes, and he stopped several times, mistrustful. As if to escape from a dream, he plunged again into the narrow lanes in the neighborhood of the Mercerie. Here, too, there was a sense of things rising up into the air. He could not quite make out what it was: the smell of plants growing in distant vegetable gardens, or just the smell of bread being taken out of ovens in some bakery near by? But was it possible that there could be gardens in that neighborhood, when houses and roofs clustered thicker and thicker together? And was it possible that there could be, in that solitude of stone, a man with a gun on his shoulder, with clattering, nailed boots and a dog at his heels? They had popped out suddenly, from a turning, the man and the dog, the sole inhabitants of the city; the man with a gun on his shoulder, a gamebag at his side, and a light spring in his walk, the dog running back and forth in the deserted lanes, sniffing in all directions. They both moved with great assurance, as though toward an opening and a wide space, and no doubt toward some boat lying waiting for them; and the dog stopped every now and then, nose in air, as though sniffing the blueness of the sky and the smell of the distant countryside beyond the mass of roofs and walls.

The boy followed them; and when he stood beyond the clock tower, in the famous Piazza, the impression made upon him was so strong that, instinctively, he closed his eyes. He had a desire to weep. He shook himself violently, trying to hold back the tears. The whole of his sorrow, the whole of his past life, came floating back into his mind in face of that loveliness of color and form. Color and freshness and joy, such as he had heard, confusedly, in the voice of the girl, came to birth there, beneath that blueness, in the great Piazza. He stood still for a long time, wanting to touch every piece of marble, to impress thoroughly upon his mind every detail, every aspect of the scene. When the sunshine struck upon the façade of the Basilica, reaching it together with an airy band of pigeons that seemed to be carrying it as they flew; when a stronger vibration of light, a more intense brightness blazed upon the marbles and the colors, the boy closed his eyes again so as not to see it. He was resting his hand, at that moment, on a block of marble; and the sun was already making it warm and gentle beneath his fingers, which seemed to throb in harmony with it. How beautiful it was, this country of his, which he was about to leave!

He shook himself again, thinking that he must have missed the train. But now there was a source of joy within him, a first renewal of calm. It was tenuous, fragile, but—for a few hours, at least—it would afford him help. . . . He caught the boat, put down his suitcases, and went straight to the bow, his eyes sharp and intent, to look at everything around him. The Grand Canal, the palaces, the churches passed before him, clothed now with an air of freshness and lightness, with a touch of early-morning rawness in it, yet linking their shapes together, laying bare the beauty of their marble, awakening even the sleepiest corners. And now the boy thought of nothing except looking, and looking again; of gathering light to his eyes and strength to his heart, so that he might never forget. He took note of the market, coming gaily back to life in the early morning; he caught sight of a little church near the station and felt that the station itself, also, that morning, was animated and wide awake.

As the train moved away and his eyes took their last look at the lagoon and at the lights growing more and more distant over the water, he believed that he had so much strength in himself that he would be able to hold fast to an illusion. To the illusion that he could go with a fairly tranquil heart, or at least with a gloomy, desperate strength, toward the gray lands that awaited him, toward a new and difficult life.

GIANNA MANZINI

An Indiscreet Madrigal

TRANSLATED BY WILLIAM FENSE WEAVER

Their hostess poured the tea, holding out her index finger, on which a white bandage was prominent. With her hand and arm nearly erased by the room's shadows, that patch of white stood out, alone, tracing a pattern that was enchantment: without meaning, yet completely natural. It had a touch of elegance, and it aroused a tender anxiety.

"These little hurts. It isn't so easy to heal them, because today's medicines have an endless capacity for destruction."

In the room's atmosphere, in the voices that were mingled with a slightly affected gaiety, and—above all—in the sunset's light which poured into the room along with the garden's smells through the open windows, there crept now a shadow of alarm, the effect perhaps of that "endless" or that "capacity for destruction," so ambiguous, so out of keeping with the light intimacy of the gathering and that childish, almost coy bandage around a lacquered fingernail.

The bound finger went on moving, pointed now toward the last cup, set on a little table in front of the youngest guest, a girl entirely bent on controlling, mortifying herself. Her fearful reserve removed everything from her eyes: warmth, meaning, even direction, leaving them vague, in spite of the limpid, clearly outlined irises; her body, as a result, had a touching composure. Still her every action showed her fervid, sinuous in a hidden way, revealed her, betrayed her.

This deep, splendid eagerness to live, revealed earlier, terminated with her and radiated from her. And so between the garden, poured into the room on waves of perfume with an immeasurably happy and rapid breath, and the twilight diffused about the table, something lovely and consuming was woven that recalled the youth of the world and attracted the youth in the room.

"Sugar?"

The girl raised her eyes and put out her hand; but when she had lifted the tongs an inch from the sugar bowl, she let the white cube fall back again.

"Thank you, I don't take sugar." The sentence failed to scratch the conversation. It was noticed only by the young man who had spoken of destructive power, because he divined that the sacrifice of sugar was a reducing diet's rule, and now his eyes contracted in a faintly frowning surprise, which she answered with a mute, questioning glance, pursing her lips in involuntary annoyance.

"September is the loveliest month in the country."

"The end of September," an overdressed old gentleman couldn't help adding, in a foolishly joyous voice.

"Especially because of the light. These sudden sunsets have a charm all their own."

"Sudden, very sudden," the young man said with strange resentment.

The girl caught his inexplicable bitterness and lowered her glance to her plate, where she detached an almond from a cake. Her wrist rested on the table, and thus, with a graceful gesture, her whole arm was exposed, round, tanned by the sun, bare almost to her shoulder. With odd, impersonal anxiety the young man looked at it.

"What about these swallows? Don't their cries seem impatient to you—as if they had a mad desire to devour the light altogether?"

The girl also looked at her own arm and, embarrassed, placed her left hand over it, covering it a little, above the elbow.

He was thinking of the reducing diet: tiny, constant sacrifices, medicines, food watched over, weighed, selected; and he imagined the disorder all this produced in the infinitesimal but distinct life that determined the roundness of those arms, the single softness of that throat, that breast. White, active, innocent cells, each with its tiny heart, lively as an eye. And one fine day, without any declaration, without any of those events that presage change, the massacre begins. Whole ranks fall on the frontier of that perfect arm; others come forward, call for more help, then die. It is like a dance, all this swift and desperate traffic. Farther away, a rumor circulates, a grief-stricken questioning. Panic. And it might well be visible, transparent under the skin, at the bend of the elbow, at the wrist, the temple. Active until a short while ago, certain of a future that was worth all their happy toil (see, what a beautiful girl); now grief disorganizes them; perhaps they even feel guilty.

"But what am I doing?" the young man asked himself. "Instead of speculating on the body of this dazzling, closed girl, I'm like the worm in an apple, working beneath her skin. And if it were in order to reach her heart . . . Surely there are forbidden things. Irresistible. Underneath. Like a gallery."

He imagined among the dead cells of that firm, almost gleaming epidermis a kind of arcade in which he, a stranger, advanced, terrified. There was the sort of light dust that falls when a word is erased on a blackboard.

"Is this your only daughter?" the elderly gentleman asked the lady beside him.

"Yes, she's all alone." And the sentence echoed from mouth to mouth, growing more precious, amplified into a discussion of only children and their difficult distinction.

"And I am traveling all alone," the young man said with tremulous pride, as without breathing he went forward in that aridness that was clear and sad, like ruins. But the word "alone" made him ambitious in a new way. Having stripped the girl, he left her standing before him, at some distance, wearing only the reflection from the window, a greenish light, all alive with imperceptible shimmering. Naked, with a great feathered hat on her head and a gold ornament at her throat. Her hand rests on a tree trunk. "It is a picture. A masterpiece that I recognize. To recognize: what damnation and what solace. But, in this journey of mine, I must recognize nothing."

"She's done very well in her studies. Now she's preparing her thesis."

"The young people of today . . ."

"But is there any real difference between young people today and those of yesterday?"

Ascending her arm then, through that stratum of slaughtered hosts, he followed the outline of her shoulders, the collarbone. The subterranean passage of extinct cells began, toward her breast, to glow slightly.

"Yes, I recognize one thing. I recognize death." And death was revealed to him: a lunar silence suspended between two heartbeats. "The ineffable silence of beauty, the same that governs her body's superior harmony and the life beyond it; and the blood's silence, precise, as if it marked and recorded an interval; and both seduce me, engulf me, breathe in my substance. So that, obeying a kind of repugnance or—I don't know—a strange voluptuousness, I resist desperately instead of remaining suspended, a restless relic on the derisive boundary of her nothingness!"

"I'm almost cold," the girl said in a light voice, alien to her imposing body, whose innocence had the air of a glorious punishment.

For an instant she could be seen standing, between the extended arms of the old gentleman, who gallantly held out his coat. She leaned against the purple color that brought into relief her skin's whiteness and the black of her hair.

"The hours of sunlight, at this time of year, grow less every day."

"Consequently they become more desirable."

"Like everything that is fleeting."

No doubt, love would be spoken of. He felt an inner movement of defense. What did it mean—his hesitation about her life? He tried to imagine her naked again, this time with a twisted, shining sash. An unconscious nude, as if removed into a higher distraction. Her head, inclined to one side, showed a gentle melancholy; and again it was a picture he recalled; and it was reticence, almost passing indifference, that he had read in her blood when he paused to question its pulse, then drawing back at once: for in that fugitive lassitude he seemed to understand the sign of an inviting laziness, a bait.

"I walk among numberless tombs," he recited, attempting the slightly amused emotion of before. "Tombs hedged in by the last, trembling, wasted cells." Extremely pale, they were still extremely alive, even electric. "They will go so far as to promise themselves another life. They deserve it, they receive it." Already he sensed it, he recognized it in the air with her scent, the scent of her skin. An august presence, the corpse that she nourished within was thus revealed and, exhaling it thus, she escaped death, indicating an element of immortality. All this, with that minimum of decision it implied, seemed extraordinary to him, something whose value and meaning were surely lost on the girl. "She should be warned, protected," and meanwhile his wandering about her body became an embrace, more tender and timid than voluptuous. Disappointed and almost surprised by such unexpected lack of pleasure, he murmured, winking to himself, "Now I'll go farther, much farther." And he urged himself on, hidden behind a bluish veil, the epidermis, to descend along her thigh. Suddenly a fearful vacuum attracted him. He felt that his blood had left him. Never could he return from such distance; nothing, no one could succeed in recalling him.

He leaned back in his chair, half-closing his eyes; but instead, he was at her feet. It was impossible to begin with the first words or to say anything else: "How much I love you, you attract me, I want to live at your side." Leaning forward a little, he looked boldly into her eyes: "What a strange route my emotion has taken. In your freshness I have discovered a miniature death; in your impassiveness, a confusion that has nothing to do with you, but is yours; in your twenty years, I have seen you at fifty; in the soft fertility of your flesh, the barren drought that scarcely touches it. I'm in love, and I don't know if it's with you or with my game. But beyond all doubt, loving you, I would settle down in a term of years, not fearing corruption or death. For now, what I would like is to be able to tell you the most absurd, the most outspoken things—and to hear you saying the same things to me."

The servant poured more hot water into the pot. Separated by that fugitive steam, she smiled at him.

In the darker air, the little white bandage around the painted fingernail made its usual, extravagant voyage.

"Allow me to help you," the young man said to the hostess, getting up with an air of ability. And to the girl, he added:

"A little sugar?"

"Yes," she said, confused. She felt she was agreeing to something that went beyond the white cube that gleamed, held in silver tongs.

ALDO PALAZZESCHI

Love Letters

TRANSLATED BY ANGUS DAVIDSON

Michele, Michelino . . . Lumachino;
that was how the name started. Lumachino . . . the little slug. Michele,
already rather a soft kind of a name, was not enough, and even its
diminutive was not quite enough; so they had recourse to the brute
creation, to the molluscs, in fact; and possibly they might have gone
even a little further than that. He was the ugliest man in the village:
and not all villages have the privilege of possessing an inhabitant so
excessively ugly. He was the postmaster, having inherited this position
when left an orphan by the early deaths of both father and mother, the
former from consumption, the latter as the result of a malignant tumor:
he was, therefore, the product of two horrible diseases. The movements
of his arms, of his thin, crooked body, were apelike, sluggish; his face
was emaciated, greenish yellow in hue; he was shortsighted to the point
of being ridiculous, absurd, with eyes like a toad behind thick lenses attached by a thin black cord; while his mouth—yet another horror—was
a mere slit, indecent both in its color, its softness, and its expression.

He liked women. All the men in that village liked women, as they do,
of course, in many other villages too; but no one liked them quite to the
extent that he did, nor with less return, for he had never succeeded in
getting possession of a single one. If he had been content to put up with
some hideous, dried-up, disregarded old maid, as yellow and green in
the face as himself, one of those who would keep her eyes tight shut in
order to maintain a position of dignity, he might have had a wife; but
not at all—Lumachino loved beautiful women, the very beautiful ones,

the most beautiful of all. Even Signora Rondoni, the exuberantly ripe widow, universally pleasing and desired by young men and old, left him indifferent; and she was the woman who was known all over the countryside for her beauty, her elegance, and a life which, in a discreet, domestic manner, was not at all respectable—for an important personage, one with the title of "honorable," came, from time to time, to stay for brief periods at her villa. Not even this lady would have made him satisfied and contented; beneath her beauty and elegance there was a suggestion of indifference, of calculation, of worldy wisdom, whereas what Lumachino wanted was true love, the love that bursts forth in early youth, that came bursting forth in himself every day, to no purpose, like a broken spring, the love that makes its victims lose their heads and commit acts of folly.

When he heard a report that a beautiful young girl was officially betrothed, or was carrying on a secret love affair—which gave him infinitely greater pleasure—his melon-colored blood would leap up beneath his greenish skin; and if she happened to come to the pigeonhole in his office—and sooner or later they all came there, bent on some post office business—he would stick out his head, leaning forward right under her nose as if he were trying to read an address there, laughing with his mouth wide open and melting with pleasure as he laughed.

Then the girls would burst into fits of laughter too, and screams of laughter would fill the room; for they either laughed or teased him mercilessly. He was quite content to be teased by the girls, and they asked nothing better than to satisfy him in this way; for he derived immense pleasure from their cruel, indecorous guffaws, and they required no pressing to oblige him ungrudgingly.

There are ugly men in this world whose ugliness is of a virile kind that can be very pleasing to women and can exercise a power over them greater than the power of beauty itself; this is what the English call "sex appeal" (a happy expression which they must have invented on their travels abroad). But this poor little man possessed, not sex appeal, but the quality of sex repulsion. There are also some who are ugly and unattractive, without any appeal, but who do not arouse mirth in others. And others again, ugly, unattractive, and ridiculous, but at least not actually repugnant: Lumachino was repugnant as well.

Those were the girls that Lumachino wanted, the ones who despised him; and above all Argìa, the most exuberant, the freshest of all, the most beautiful, a rosebud scarcely opened, overflowing with health and vigor, and the one who mocked at him most mercilessly. She was in love with Giotto, the biggest scamp in the village; and these two wretches had come to an understanding and sworn to love each other in spite of their families and the world in general; they were burning with passion for each other. Giotto was a big, strong, handsome young man, rather arrogant, who had never worked seriously for his living; gambling, amusements, shooting, riding a motor bicycle, love-making—these were his chief passions, to the considerable discomfort of his modestly placed family. Oh, to be Giotto! That was the passionate desire of Lumachino: Oh, to be Giotto! But not the Giotto who put a stop to Cimabue's boasting, who painted St. Francis with such heavenly skill—not at all! He did not even think of him; it was Giotto the scamp, the despair of his family, the scandal of the village, the betrothed of Argìa in spite of all the world.

Argìa . . . In that harsh, sweet name Lumachino tasted the savor of all the fruits of the earth, the perfume of all its flowers, that were like the flames of redness glowing in her full cheeks, where skin and flesh were one. With such a treasure in his heart he would have felt himself a god; yet Giotto carried it about everywhere with perfect self-possession.

No one else could have given a woman so much devotion, so much tenderness, so much passion; and yet the women, on their side, did not know what to do with all these fine things, for slugs, alas! cannot enter into the temple of love and must be content to creep by, with bursting hearts, leaving a little slime at the doors: for if they enter, the sacristan will kick them out at once. Or crush them beneath gentle feet. Gentle for him, of course, not for the slugs.

He had passed the age of thirty, and even though, in his apparent idiocy, he might appear not to suffer from being the butt of everyone, Lumachino, beneath his slimy laugh, was aware of a stone growing hard within his breast.

All around him there was love, and in the warm days of spring he saw nothing but embracing couples, heard nothing but the twittering of kisses. The young people went off together along discreet lanes bordered by flowering hedges: even the branches clung together or stretched out their arms to each other; and there was singing and whispering, caresses, vows (oh, such vows!), smiles, perfumes. . . . Ugly as he was, he yearned for beauty and for love.

All the girls arrived, sooner or later, at the pigeonhole in his office to buy stamps or to entrust him with jealous, urgent letters; to fetch them away jealously, too, or to find out, with unbearable impatience, whether there was anything for them. Then off they would go, empty-handed and depressed, or else trembling, with the letter scorching their fingers.

Leaning upon the well-worn counter, alone, deep in thought, he would start at the sound of letters falling into the letter box; he would recognize the different handwritings, would speculate vainly upon their contents; he would postmark them and still hold them in his hand before sealing them up inside the bag; finally, with a long sigh, he would make up his mind to dispatch them to their fate, following them, mentally, right into the hands of the person to whom they were addressed. He himself had never received a love letter.

When Giotto went to Rome to do his military service as a grenadier, Lumachino kept a careful lookout for his letters and those of Argìa, and always recognized them. Argìa would go into the post office to fetch the letters and bring her own, prepared to face a struggle. Before he put that particular letter into the bag, he would rub his nose against it a hundred times and then press it to his heart. One of these letters he kept for two days; he could not bear to part with it. And one he did not send at all; he opened it and kept it altogether.

Lumachino came thus to know the language of the heart, the tender words, the burning phrases, the vows (oh, such vows!), the confidences, the intimate revelations, the requests and promises that drove him to madness, the power that overcomes obstacles in spite of everybody and in opposition to everybody. The letter ended like this: ". . . no one shall tear me away from you! I shall be yours, yours, yours, until the grave." He was intoxicated, just as though these remarks belonged to him personally, and kept repeating: "yours, yours, yours, until the grave!" He kept other letters, too, letters from Argìa, from Giotto, from other girls and other young men, and, in a kind of delirium, in an ecstasy, opened all those which seemed to smell of love; he was in heaven, now, unmindful of the world.

The village began to show signs of ill-humor, of doubt, to make claims for undelivered letters; people began to be suspicious, there were scenes inside the post office, scenes which increased in violence. Lumachino laughed, and by laughing fomented this violence with his irritating composure; he laughed, rejoicing in the steadily growing tumult of which he felt himself to be the center, the protagonist. He laughed, with an idiotic, happy smile on his face which was as good as a confession; and as he answered the complainants he almost died with happiness at the sight of their scowling faces.

Suspicions were consolidated and he was accused, and, at a first interview with the Superintendent of Police, he said at once: "Yes, yes, yes, yes, sir." Yes, he had taken the letters and read them; yes, he had them, they were his, he asserted impenitently. Declared to be under arrest, he was transferred in a public vehicle to a detention cell at the prison in the near-by town; he was accompanied by the Superintendent and two police constables, who had great difficulty in saving him from the fury of the crowd, which demanded the right of taking justice into its own hands. And the girls screamed and hurled imprecations behind the carriage which took him away, following it to the last bend in the road, flourishing their fists and their nails at Lumachino. "Coward! Cad! Shameless brute!" In the midst of the group Argìa stood out, taller and stronger than the rest, blazing with anger. "To prison with you! You cad!" In her passionate rage, she was even more beautiful. And Lumachino, wriggling and writhing between the two policemen who prevented him from seeing her, kept on saying, as he slipped his face in between their arms: "Yours, yours, yours, until the grave!" And he was laughing. Not even the policemen could manage to keep serious; they laughed at the infuriated girls. "To prison with you! You cad!" They laughed at Lumachino. "Yours! yours! yours! . . ." They laughed at the unusualness of the case.

When placed in the lockup he looked all around, drew hastily to one side, and sought to avoid his companions who were watching him, trying to see what sort of a person the new recruit was, weighing him up, and deciding, at once, that he was an imbecile. Sitting down on one corner of the pallet that had been assigned to him, he drew out some papers from his breast pocket, put his spectacles on his nose, and started reading them, shaking his head and swaying his body and smiling as if he were getting ready to sing or to fly suddenly away. "He's here because of women," said someone. "Ha! ha! ha!" They laughed and shrugged their shoulders unconcernedly. "He's an idiot," added another, and that was the end of it. Disqualified even from being a criminal, Lumachino raised his head, stared at them, and understood. "So even they knew all about it, everyone knew about it, the whole world knew his secret, his love story. . . ." Delighted beyond measure, he started to read again.

In front of the magistrate, as previously in front of the Superintendent of Police, he did not hesitate for an instant, but kept on answering: "Yes, sir, yes, sir." Yes, he had taken them.

"How many of them?"

"All."

"In order to read them?"

"Yes, sir, yes, sir."

"Only love letters?"

"Yes, sir, yes, sir."

And he laughed as he looked at his judges, who, themselves, were unable to keep serious faces. The presiding magistrate laughed, too, the policemen laughed. . . . There was general laughter.

He was found not guilty because of congenital idiocy and placed under disciplinary control. Stripped of his position and rank, he was appointed, with the job of porter, to the central post office in the neighboring town.

When he presented himself, according to orders, at the post office building, he was at once conducted to the lavatories. "Here you are," said the employee who accompanied him. "This is your place, and here are the jobs you have to do." He showed him the dressing rooms, the lavatories, the washrooms, the passages, the stairs, and a courtyard. "You must be careful to keep all these places clean; from now on they come under your direct responsibility. Mind you do your duty. . . ."

He pointed out a small cupboard. "Here you will find dusters and brooms and brushes and all you need for cleaning and polishing: you can begin now." And he left him.

Lumachino took up a broom, went into a lavatory and began sweeping; but after a few strokes he clutched the broom handle tightly under his arm and, taking a piece of paper from his bosom, put on his spectacles. "No one shall tear me away from you! I shall be yours, yours, yours, until the grave!" He trembled, and was happy.

MASSIMO BONTEMPELLI

Curious Tales

TRANSLATED BY ELISABETH ABBOTT

1.

LINARIA *

Ⓘn a moving train a woman, still young, and a boy of eleven sat facing each other. They did not know each other. They did not even glance at each other. The woman did not look at the boy because her mind was filled with worrisome thoughts: the boy did not look at her because he was ashamed of not yet being a man.

Instead they both gazed out at the countryside and the long row of poplars as they slipped swiftly by. The windows were open and over the fields the air quivered and danced with light. Far in the distance Marcello saw horses appearing and disappearing and he even saw a big bull now and then. That sight distracted him a little from a great anxiety that had been tormenting him ever since the train left the station. He amused himself by looking for the ditches that cut through the grass and were lost in it. He would have liked to kneel on the seat to be able to see better, but he remembered that only babies behaved that way in trains. He heard the woman stirring and unconsciously he turned his head toward her and saw that she had risen to her feet.

She was wearing a veil over her face and this seemed important to Marcello. But she immediately turned her back, pushed aside her lug-

* "Linaria" or "honesty" is a plant (of the mustard family) with pale purple flowers and semitransparent pods.

gage on the rack, took down a small suitcase, and tossed a book and an illustrated magazine on the seat. Alongside of the suitcase were a bag, a fur, and a package wrapped in tissue paper. The young woman opened and closed the bag two or three times, picked up the package and promptly put it back where it had been before. Marcello liked to see her with her arms uplifted. When she had finished, she stood with one knee leaning lightly on the edge of the seat and stared out of the window again. Marcello admired the pose. He would have given anything to kneel in that way, but he should have thought of it before she did. The young woman stared so intently at the passing scene that Marcello leaned forward to see if something new had appeared there. But no, there was nothing in sight.

Marcello felt depressed. He drew into his shell, shrank back in his corner, and lowering his eyes, began to think about his troubles.

I do not know whether you have ever seen certain strange leaves called lunaria annua, linaria, or honesty. In some places they are known locally as Pope's pence, in others, as night violets. Once upon a time ladies used to keep bunches of them in vases in their drawing rooms. I said leaves, but they are not leaves. They are a sort of skeleton of the pod after the fleshy part has withered. They have slender stalks covered with those delicate florets that look like thin sheets of parchment, diaphanous as membrane and of a pale, truly lunar color. Each floret ends in a heart-shaped point at the tip of which a minute fibril sticks up as straight as those little tufts of hair on babies only a few months old.

In the drawing room at Marcello's home there was a cabinet in which his mother kept many priceless objects and, on top of the cabinet, photographs. In front of one of the photographs stood a large vase that held one branch, one only, of linaria. Marcello had often examined it. The little branches were divided into two forks, and each fork into a few stems, each stem bearing its own leaf—five leaves in all. One day the branch fell down and the old dried leaves crumbled.

For some unknown and pathetic reason Marcello's mother had been in despair at the loss of her branch of linaria. She longed passionately for a new one, but there were none to be had in the town, and for four months she had been lamenting her loss.

When, at the beginning of vacation, Marcello was sent for eight days to visit with the family of friends in the big city, he had promised solemnly to look for a branch of the precious plant and bring it home to his mother. But in that week he had been so busy going here and there, having a good time, that he forgot all about his promise. He remembered it suddenly only when he was seated in the train homeward bound and the train was pulling out of the station and the handkerchiefs his friends were waving were almost lost to sight.

Marcello almost fainted from shame and remorse. He raged inwardly with tremendous anger at himself, then sank into the depths of despair. Gone was every happy memory. The past week seemed to him a troubled abyss of guilt. He remembered his mother's sighs as she gazed at the empty vase, her instructions when he left, and he felt that his soul was a black monster. At a certain point, exhausted by that helpless rage, he became almost resigned. He might as well distract his thoughts by looking at the scenery and at that signora opposite him who had got on the train God knows when. The next moment he was overwhelmed again by his awful humiliation.

The young woman sat down again, picked up the book, and read a few pages. Marcello would have liked to see the title. Every now and then she raised the book a little and Marcello caught the flash of red and black signs on the cover, but he could not make out the words. She put the book down without closing it, stood up, pulled down the bag and placed it beside her, took out a cigarette case and a box of matches, and, finally, selected a cigarette. Then she placed the cigarette, the case, and the matchbox on the open book. Why didn't she smoke? Now, slowly, using both hands, she raised her veil from the chin up to the line of her cheekbones. Pushed up that way the edge of the veil made a black line across her face, cutting it strangely in half. Marcello waited for her to light her cigarette. Instead the lady stood up again, took down from the rack the package wrapped in tissue paper, and laid it between the bag and the book. She sat down again, put the illustrated magazine on her knees, opened it, but did not look at it. Marcello was fascinated. This was as good as being at a cinema.

Every now and then, realizing that he was staring too obviously, he came to himself with a start. The lady, however, was apparently unaware of his interest. Her glance roved unseeing over the landscape and her thoughts were obviously far away. The sun, now high in the sky, poured waves of drowsy heat over the land. Two or three times Marcello nodded and his chin rested on his chest. He closed his eyes and he thought he was standing at the window and could see the whole countryside abloom with linaria. A slight noise roused him and, raising his head, he saw that the signora had picked up the paper parcel and had begun to unwrap it. Slowly she removed the last vestige of paper, and there appeared a large bunch of linaria.

The boy almost cried out in surprised delight. For perhaps a second he thought he was still dreaming. But no, he was not dreaming. They were linaria and how many there were! Perhaps thirty, perhaps fifty branches! More than one could count! His heart began to beat violently. He had just had a wonderful idea: I must ask the signora to give me one of those branches. Then his heart quieted because the idea had become resolve, and when one has something to do, the most important thing of all is to keep calm.

The young woman held up the large bundle and shook it gently. To the boy it seemed that a hundred bells were ringing and the train was transformed into a ballroom. Now, holding the bouquet in one hand, in the other the tissue paper, she leaned back against the seat and raised her eyes to the distant sky. She had obviously forgotten all about the paper and the flowers.

All this time Marcello had been wondering how he could open the conversation. For example: "Signora . . . ," and then quickly, not to give her time to answer, he would tell her the whole story, confess everything, finally ask her for one, just one, little branch to take home to Mamma. Surely she would give it to him—of this there could be no doubt. The difficult thing was to know when, at what moment, to approach her. When the right moment comes, thought Marcello, the first word will be enough: "Signora . . . ," and she will turn her head toward me and will listen to what I have to say. On the other hand, perhaps I'd better wait till she turns around this way, till she is through looking out of the window. What is she looking at, anyway?

As if in answer to his unspoken query, the young woman lowered her eyes. If she should turn them in Marcello's direction for even a single moment, the thing was as good as done. After all, it did not matter. The moment was almost at hand. But now the scene changes a little. The lady opens her hands, tosses the bunch of flowers on one side of the seat and the paper on the other. Why doesn't she smoke her cigarette? Not at all. Marcello begins to stare at the linaria. He keeps his eyes glued on them as though, if he were to look away for one second, they might disappear. And again, as before, he is afraid of staring too shamelessly; but the next moment he tells himself that now it is a different matter. On the contrary, it is much better if she does notice that he is staring at the flowers. Perhaps then she will offer him one of her own accord. Oh! that would be the simplest way. (What, Marcello, are you passing up the certainty of action?) Just be patient a little longer. Perhaps she intends to put the flowers in the bag or in that valise up there. But there are too many! They would not all go in. When she starts to put them in, I will offer very politely to help her, and a few of them will be left outside.

"Keep those to remember me by," she will say.

"Thank you, Signora," I will reply.

Marcello was extremely pleased with this solution. He had to make an effort to realize that it was all in his imagination. He now felt as if he were floating in the clouds.

Suddenly the young woman roused herself, took out a match, and picked up the poor cigarette that had been waiting such a long time. Oh, if only Marcello had some matches in his pockets! Under similar circumstances grownups always made haste to offer a light.

The lady lit her own cigarette. Perhaps this was the moment. The puff of blue smoke that almost struck Marcello in the face was like a breath of paradise. Yes, it is the moment. Marcello opens his mouth: "Signora . . ." Did he speak the word or did he only think it? He cannot be sure. Perhaps his voice was too weak. Well, let's try a little louder: "Sign . . . ," but at that moment the lady suddenly snatches the cigarette from her lips and flings it violently out of the window. So swift and abrupt is her gesture that Marcello is startled. Whatever is the matter with that woman? She is certainly in a bad mood. Lucky for me I did not speak.

The signora raised her hands to her face, took off her veil, and dropped it on the seat beside her with a great sigh.

No, not the moment after all!

On the contrary, she picks up the flowers and looks at them. Of course she likes those flowers, thinks Marcello, but one, just one, she would gladly give him. All he has to do is to speak. The signora looks up. Perhaps she will speak first.

Then, just as suddenly and violently as she threw away the cigarette, the signora flings the whole bunch of linaria out of the window.

Many years later when Marcello related this youthful drama, he had to confess that as he recalled that absurd moment he knew what it was to turn to stone. He did not know how many minutes he sat there like a statue.

The next moment he leaped to his feet and a burning rage from deep within him rose to his throat and burst forth in a few high-pitched sobs.

Then, for the first time, the signora became aware of Marcello's presence. She leaned toward the panting boy, touched him gently on the shoulder.

"What is the matter with you? Why are you crying?"

Marcello suddenly left off crying. He was silent a moment, then, stepping back a pace, exclaimed dramatically: "That you will never know!" so mysteriously and so forcefully that she turned pale and looked completely dumbfounded. Nor did she recover until she realized that the train had stopped, the door had been opened, and the little boy was getting out to be clasped in the arms of a man who greeted him happily: "Marcello, Marcello!"

2.

THE SLEEPING BEAUTY

One night when a high wind was blowing, I stepped into a café that was blue with smoke. Holding my hands before me, I cut my way through and, thrusting the smoke first to one side, then to the other, I moved forward as though I were pushing through a thicket of canes. Coils of grayish vapor rose in thick clouds from the mouths and tankards of beer drinkers, floated down over the marble-topped tables, caught at my feet, and swirled around on the floor, writhing like angry snakes. Every seat appeared to be taken. I caught the gleam of a waiter's white shirt front and signaled to it. From either side of that shirt two black sleeves pointed heavenward like the bifurcating branches of a tree stripped of its green, and on top of those straight sleeves two trays, laden with bright-colored foods and liquids, opened like a fan spread out flat.

As he hurried away, the waiter motioned—I don't know how! Perhaps with a third, invisible hand—to an empty place at a small table. The other occupant, a woman, was asleep, with her head propped on one hand. I turned discreetly to the right to get a better look at the lady—and I recognized the Sleeping Beauty in the Woods. I should like to have spoken to her. Then the waiter came back and I saw that his face shone like his shirt front with a noble light. He set down a cup before me and, holding the pot high, poured out the steaming liquid with the classic gesture of Temperance, that temporal virtue; then he vanished into air like an arrow shot into a cloud.

I caught sight of a friend who was making his way with difficulty through the room. He saw me and started toward me. Then, noticing the lady at my side and obviously thinking she was with me, he nodded, looked away in embarrassment, and passed on. All this made me feel very uncomfortable. I wanted to leave, but first I had to finish that drink. I suspected that it might be poisoned, yet I could not go away without drinking it, for fear of offending the waiter.

Two couples got up from the table opposite and began to dance in the narrow space between their table and mine. At the same moment I realized that there was a sound of music in that dense, smoky atmosphere—dance music, an old-fashioned dance, a slow, plaintive tune accompanied by pizzicato chords and, on the even beat, a light roll of drums, over which the music seemed to float suspended in air. The drums ceased and the melody faltered as if it were about to break down; but immediately the drums came in again at a quickened tempo and kept control.

One of the two couples bumped into the edge of my table. I turned and glanced quickly at the Sleeping Beauty, fearing that she might have been awakened. No, indeed! All she did was to spread her hand a little wider under her cheek and go right on sleeping. But now a soft and sibilant hiss began to issue from her half-opened lips. At first I was annoyed, and I was about to wake her myself when I thought of several good reasons for not doing so.

"If I wake her, she will no longer be the Sleeping Beauty in the Woods. Who knows whom she might turn out to be, and that would be a mess! And, in any case, let's not forget that only Prince Charming can waken the Sleeping Beauty. If, therefore, I wake her and she does not change, I will change, because that will mean I am Prince Charming and I did not know it (so many times, because of the usual family mysteries, a man does not know what he is!) and that would be a nuisance. I have several engagements tomorrow morning—this may change a lot of things in my life for which I am not prepared. In short, it is better to keep quiet and let the girl hiss."

While I was meditating thus intently, the hiss had lengthened and modulated in perfect harmony with the music. It came in just where the drums left off as if to lend a hand by carrying the tune till the drums took over again. Then the hiss stopped and the Sleeping Beauty drew a long breath in preparation for the next one. That hiss even gained in volume; it broadened or, rather, thickened and changed in quality. It became a gurgling, grew louder and louder, deep and at the same time well-placed, steady; in short, the Sleeping Beauty snored!

Never in my wildest dreams would I have imagined that the Sleeping Beauty snored. This seemed to me both admirable and important. I looked around to see whether the occupants of this smoke-filled café were equally as impressed and fascinated as I was. Instead, they were all intent upon their own affairs. Obviously, the occupants of the smoke-filled café had never formed any clear conception of the way the Sleeping Beauty in the Woods slept. Oh! how careless and vague man is in his knowledge, how gross and unheeding when confronted with the spectacle of Truth! And how inexperienced most of us are in the art of the divine faculty of wonder! The Sleeping Beauty in the Woods snored. By now the noise of her snoring had drowned out the music; it rose and fell against the room like clouds erupting from a volcano; it enveloped people and objects. At moments it attained the full thunder of a storm, punctuated here and there by a sort of battle neigh; but soon it came to rest on a broad and serene note that filled the air with a noble throbbing.

Out of the corner of my eye shapes began to emerge again: men and women, tables, bottles, heads of hair, trains of dresses, froth from the beer. And now only did the room have a soul, and the life in it a meaning; that noise gave them substance and reality, an organic power and a form, a reason for being.

The snoring rose and swelled as if it were reaching toward richer, purer, higher climes, toward heaven.

I turned gratefully to the Sleeping Beauty in the Woods.

Her neck had now drooped lower till it formed a right angle to her body. One cheek was hidden, pressed flat on the palm of her hand so that her head was bent horizontally above it as if on a platter. A high-relief medallion in profile. Half of her face seen thus outlined in the light was suffused by a blessed hebetude which, starting at the outer edge—at the line of her forehead just where the hair began and the profile of her fat, impassive chin—was intensified toward the vital center, her mouth, half opened, below nostrils that curled slightly with every emission of that measured and powerful trumpeting.

I was sure, absolutely sure, that there was no danger—the Sleeping Beauty in the Woods would not awaken for ages and ages.

Full of pride and joy, I rose, made her a magnificent bow and in-vited her to dance. Then without waiting for her consent, I pulled her to her feet.

Wildly we danced around and around among the tables, urged on and pursued by the rhythm of the music. She danced as lightly as a feather, one hand resting on my shoulder, the other still engaged in supporting her sleeping head, and as she danced she snored. Shouts of wonder and delight greeted the miracle from all sides of the smoke-filled café. Tables were pushed back to give us room, and we two danced alone to the applause of the assembled guests. Intoxicated by the general excitement (to hell with my appointments for to-morrow!) I danced and danced, and as I danced I shouted:

"Allow me to present my Lady, for now and forever. Prepare the nuptial feast."

At that the café rang with shouts of laughter. The joy of those men and women burst open the ceiling and flung down the walls. The smoke in the smoke-filled café sailed off gaily toward the distant hori-zon to announce the marriage of the Sleeping Beauty in the Woods.

Cheering multitudes, triumphal marches, a great rejoicing that suddenly burst forth and spread in the night like an enchanted forest over all the land. And as they looked down from on high at this spectacle, the constellations shook their great black heads and opened their eyes wide in astonishment.

GIOVANNI COMISSO

Mario and Fortune

TRANSLATED BY WILLIAM FENSE WEAVER

Life, in the little city of fishermen, had the same seasons as the sea. If there were days when gentle breezes played on the water and promised good fishing, then the shops were filled with people who bought things, and the taverns were filled with other people who drank and gambled. And when there were storms, the *scirocco*,* when the sea was deserted and the fishing boats were crowded together in the canal, the town lived through days of desolation, its inhabitants huddled in their houses around the fire, living off *polenta* † and potatoes. Life alternated between these extremes of abundance and starvation, and people's spirits were always ready to sink into gloom or soar in joy, according to which wind was blowing. Life was precarious, dependent on these very winds; but its precariousness was a matter of centuries, and this alternation had become a natural process.

Mario's mother, too, lived like the sea, with her spells of good humor and her violent storms: abandoned by her first husband, who had wandered off leaving her with two children, she had settled down with a widower, who ran a tavern and needed a woman to help in the kitchen. Then Mario was born. The inn functioned when the fishing was good, and was empty when the boats lay in the canal. Poverty and well-being: this was the law of the place. Mario, who early in life began helping his mother in the inn, knew he was poor; but he

---

* *Scirocco* or *sirocco*—a hot, dry, dust-laden southeast wind.
† *Polenta*—a thick mush of corn meal much used in Italy.

was convinced he would not be so for his whole life. At least for a season he would have a taste of wealth, a season, like a series of days of good fishing. And his boy's eyes were greedy in anticipation. He saw the young girls his age, sitting on low chairs in front of their houses, bent over their looms to make lace that brought them a few lire per yard; they too were waiting for their season of wealth; and if a stranger passed them, they began to sing, looking out of the corners of their eyes to see if he turned to glance back; and as he went on his way, one of the girls always sighed, grief-stricken: "If only somebody would come and take me away."

Mario had better luck. One day a gentleman came to eat in the tavern; and seeing how quick Mario was, how careful to give good service, the gentleman asked if the boy would like to come and be his servant. Mario's mother, who had heard, exclaimed: "I hope to God he means what he says. He can have the boy—for nothing, even."

This gentleman had a villa and needed a boy to take care of the garden, to wash the automobile, and also serve at table. Mario's heart beat faster at the thought; he laughed and cried at the same time. He ran off to put on his good suit, and he left that same evening.

Mario enjoyed himself in the gentleman's service. He was given new clothes and two pairs of shoes, a fine room to sleep in, and his pay, which he spent for cigarettes and candy. And when there were guests at the villa, they always tipped Mario generously. His work was light, and he always had free time in which to do nothing except lie on his bed or go out riding a bicycle. After a while he learned to drive the car, and when his employer was going off on some trip and didn't want to drive, he turned the wheel over to Mario. Driving the car, he was convinced that he had achieved more than he had ever expected. He felt like his master, and in the dust behind him he left the wretched memories of his childhood.

Sometimes his master gave him leave to visit his home; then, elegantly dressed, he enjoyed his position in life, comparing it with that of his former companions, who stood around, ragged and barefoot still, waiting for a boat to arrive so they could carry some suitcases. But his mother was not so pleased with him. "I brought you up," she said, "I wore myself out to feed you. And look at the way I still have to work, old as I am. Why don't you ever send me a little money so I could buy some new shoes, too?"

Mario was upset by what his mother said, especially because his wealth was only apparent: in reality he hadn't saved anything at all. He had everything he needed, but he didn't have money in the bank like his master. He realized that he was only a servant—well paid, well dressed, but nevertheless a servant; and none of this had anything to do with true wealth. So his position, which until then had seemed enviable, began to annoy him.

During the summer his master decided to go to the mountains. They traveled by car. There his master knew some beautiful ladies with whom he made little excursions, where they played cards, smoked, listened to the phonograph, ate, and ran off to amuse themselves, like children, by hiding from one another in the shrubbery. Mario and the ladies' maids, who followed the party to carry the provisions, did the same things. One of the ladies had a local girl for her maid, who welcomed the tricks Mario played on her, imitating his master's behavior with the girl's mistress. She always hid a little farther off than the others; and when Mario found her, they would crouch among the huckleberry bushes and stay there a long time, deaf to the other maids' shouts that echoed in the woods.

When the vacation was over, Mario was satisfied with this new experience, but after a few weeks he had already forgotten the girl. Five months later he was calmly stretched out on his bed, watching his cigarette's smoke drift up toward the ceiling, when he heard an automobile stop at the gate. He went down at once, thinking it was some friend of his master's, and found a fat, red-faced man with graying hair and a timid and confused expression. The man asked at once if this were Mario and held out his hand, inquiring if the master were at home.

From the man's accent Mario could tell he came from the village where they had spent the summer. He asked who was calling. The man, after some hesitation, gave his name and said he had to see the master on an urgent matter. He was shown in, and Mario, suspicious and curious, stayed in the next room to listen. In a pathetic voice the man introduced himself as the father of the girl Mario had known in the mountains, and almost in tears, he told how his daughter had been sad and thoughtful for some time until they had forced her to confess she was pregnant by Mario. At this point Mario didn't want to hear any more, so he ran off to hide in the garden. Thus he didn't hear the father explain that he was a man of standing in his town, the owner of a hotel, of numerous tracts of woodland, that he had worked in America as a young man and had saved money which, wisely invested, brought him in a good income. Still, he said, they lived simply at home and he had sent his daughters into service to teach them to support themselves, as he had done when a boy. Now that his family honor was threatened by this misfortune, he was ready to make any sacrifice. Mario would have to marry the girl, and he would set them up well; he would buy another hotel that was for sale, and he would let Mario operate it. He would give the shirt off his back, he insisted, to keep them in the lap of luxury; and the tears began to run down his purple cheeks.

At first Mario's master had been slightly amused, then he grew bored. Above all he was annoyed at having to find a new servant. He said he had no influence over the boy: the man would have to speak to Mario's mother. He showed the visitor into the next room, sent for Mario, and when he arrived all pale and trembling, said happily: "Smile, Mario. We've been talking of your good fortune."

Mario was close to fainting. "This gentleman is the father of my friend's maid," the master went on, "and the girl is in trouble because of you, but her father has money and he's going to set you up with a hotel and give you whatever you want, provided you marry her. Take him to your mother now and come to some agreement. The only thing I have to say to you is this: Don't trust these mountaineers too far. You people of the sea are too easygoing. So if you want to marry her, if you're sure the child is yours, make them give you everything first, in writing, and then get married. You understand? Because once you're married, you stay married."

His master was right. Mountaineers are a race apart, people with a single season: winter. In that bitter climate their land is made for ice and snow; ice and snow are the true expression of their earth. And when it appears, the green of the grass is like the bed of a dry stream. To struggle against this climate, to overcome it, mountaineers—men and women alike—from their earliest childhood prepare to work tenaciously. First of all, they dream of having a house, clean and well protected, then their piece of ground, their bit of woodland for fuel, and their stock for milk and wool. And if the family is too large, they emigrate, ready to do the hardest work so long as they put a little money aside which can be invested in house, ground, woodland, and stock. There are no periods of storm and fair weather with them. The storm is always there, and they have to be strong to conquer it, or else they are lost. They overcome all their difficulties with the same strength that they use, in the first place, to overcome life itself. When they have accumulated wealth, they commit no excesses, and they go on living as they did when they were poor.

So this girl's father had trained her and her sisters to work as maids in the hotel or in private families, and when there was no work for them at home they had to go out on the mountain for the haying; they had to be always ready to work, for in the mountain nature is harsh. And when the girl's father found out about her condition, he didn't lose heart for a moment; he shut himself in his room with his wife and decided at once how to remedy the situation.

Her mother asked the girl with whom she had been love-making. To tell the truth, her parents hadn't realized she had ever made love with anyone; she was the youngest of the daughters, the one who was always interested only in haying, and this year for the first time she had gone into that lady's service, her parents thinking it would brighten her up a little. For her, love was something belonging to the woods; up high, on the mountain, when she was cutting the hay, all by herself, she heard the men on the other slopes, calling one another, and those shouts pierced her heart with a desire to be caught and thrown to the ground on the sweet-smelling hay. When she went into service, she saw the other girls, who unabashedly made love with the clerks in the local stores; and her meeting with Mario—who had the strangeness of someone from another part of the country—was decisive. He gave her the pleasure of being caught and thrown on the ground among the huckleberry bushes, as she had always dreamed. But when he went away, slowly she forgot him. There were other boys whose glance met hers; and other men, too, from other parts of the country often passed through her town and stopped at the hotel.

She gave her mother Mario's name because he had been the first to give her that pleasure. Her father decided to write to his daughter's former mistress for the address of Mario's master. Meanwhile the girl had to be kept out of sight, so she was sent to an aunt in a near-by town. They would hunt up the boy, and by fair means or foul, they would convince him to marry her. But her older sister got her to confess that, about two months after she had seen Mario, she had yielded to another man, passing through town with a truck, who had stopped at the hotel to eat; the girl herself didn't know who he was, and none of them could remember him. He was a tall man, she met him in the garden behind the house; it was a lightning affair, and not even the girl herself could explain it. First the mother, then the sister, then the father along with them tried to extract a further explanation. To look at her, no one would have suspected anything. If she went to the midwife, the news would be spread all over town. They asked her a number of questions, but the girl—simple mountain creature that she was—didn't know what to answer. And her father couldn't understand all the calculations his wife made with her fingers, naming the months, those months they had spent in ignorance of the disaster that was being prepared under their roof. At any rate Mario was the only one they could track down, and besides he had been the first.

At night they had trouble getting to sleep, thinking what would happen if the little town learned of it—with all the envious people there were—and their hotel where so many families came for the summer with their sons and their young daughters. Both their honor and their income were at stake. All their labor, their sacrifices, might prove to have been in vain. The father couldn't sleep; and his wife, hearing his sighs, remained sleepless, too. Once in a while they spoke. "We could . . . and if he can't be forced to . . .," one of them would say, then be unable to finish the sentence. Finally one morning at dawn he saw the light and said at once to his wife: "With money, we can do what we want. We'll have to make some sacrifice—the smallest necessary—but he'll come and eat out of our hands. Leave it to me."

Proudly then, full of strength and the same enthusiasm he had felt the day he sailed for America, he got out of bed and dressed. That very day the letter came with the address; and without wasting time on trains, he hired an automobile and came to the villa of Mario's

master. He was so determined to overcome this sudden obstacle life
had set in front of him, and so prepared by his mountaineer's life, that
it was easy for him to assume that timid, confused appearance as soon
as Mario met him at the gate, and to make himself seem tearful and
whining when he had to tell the story of his misfortune.

When they got into the automobile to go to Mario's mother, the
older man had Mario take the place of honor as if the boy were his
favorite relative, for whom he was ready to do anything. Mario didn't
refuse; when the car started off, he felt he was going toward a new life
that gave him a hotel, a wife, money, wealth—what he had been waiting for always. The girl's father observed him out of the corner of his
eye and tried to figure out what kind of boy he was. Meanwhile he
ascertained that he was healthy, presentable; and from the look of enchantment in Mario's great eyes, the man judged him gullible as well.
To break the ice he asked if Mario had any cigarettes. He didn't. At
the next tobacconist's the man stopped the car, got out himself to buy
them, and put three packs in Mario's hands. "I smoked all the time
myself when I was young. Because of the air. I was working in America, building a road through the swamps."

As they were going through a town, he asked Mario if he wanted to
drink something, and they stopped at a bar. He ordered an expensive
liqueur, a plate of cakes, and insisted that Mario eat all he wanted.
Mario was happy. Gradually, the man began to learn about the boy's
family. Mario explained that his mother had always been unlucky,
that he had a lot of brothers, that they had a tavern and in their town
there were times when they earned plenty and other times when they
starved—according to how the fishing went at sea.

"Fine. Your mother already knows how to run a tavern, so she could
come up with you and take over the hotel I'm going to open for you,"
he said, feeling that he was gaining ground all the time. They're poor
people, he thought, and with a little money I can get what I want.
I'll have to dazzle them with big promises and hurry up the wedding.
And he touched his wallet, which he had filled with money before
leaving home.

As soon as they arrived, Mario's mother realized something extraordinary had happened. "*Madonna mia*," she cried, "Mario, what have
you done?" And her eyes filled with tears.

"Nothing serious, Signora," the girl's father said, "I'm here to make everything all right." And when he had explained what had happened, he repeated the business of the hotel and how they would live in the lap of luxury. "You must come up, too, to run the hotel. We do a wonderful business up there with the summer people, vacationers who spend plenty if you can give them what they want."

Mario's father, who was a good-natured sort of man, came forward to say that all he knew about was the cellar, but he would come up, too.

"Naturally," the girl's father said, "the wine cellar is the hotel's most sensitive point. It's a wonderful hotel—you'll see—and since mine is the only hotel in my town, we won't compete in prices. Between ourselves we'll have the hotel business of the whole area in the palm of our hand."

They had to decide at once, however, because the hotel had already been put up for sale, some inquiries had been made already, and they might lose a good thing.

"This is all fine, sir, but it's happened so suddenly. . . . We'll have to think about it for a moment, because we have some obligations, too," Mario's mother said, drying her tears.

"Don't worry about a thing. I'll take care of everything. If you have any debts outstanding, tell me," the mountaineer said, reaching for his wallet.

"We'll have to think about it," Mario's father said, self-importantly.

And Mario, who was feeling as if he had wings on his feet, said: "I have an idea of my own, and I have to talk it over with my mother and father."

The girl's father agreed that Mario had every right to an idea of his own, since after all he was marrying into the family, and everything should be arranged in the best interest of the two of them. He added that he would leave them alone while he took a walk around the city.

When he had gone out, they all sat down at a table and Mario exclaimed at once: "You see? You always said I wouldn't amount to anything. A hotel all our own. We'll be millionaires."

His mother could only repeat "*Madonna mia!*" and tears fell on her apron.

Mario's idea was that there was no point in their becoming rich if they couldn't display their wealth in this town, where they had always been oppressed by debts. He wanted their hotel to be here, where vacationers also came in the summer to bathe; they could earn plenty and forget about the fishermen, who only came around when the price of fish had gone up.

"We ought to live like gentlemen right here," he said forcefully, "to show all the people who've always looked down on us."

His father agreed with him; his mother was afraid the girl's father wouldn't agree and they might lose everything. "The Madonna has given us this blessing, and we're throwing it out the window." She sighed.

Mario had the advantage, and he ran off into the town, looking for the other man. He found him standing in front of a shopwindow which displayed an elegant bedroom suite, including a shiny blue silk coverlet on the huge double bed.

"Would this suit the two of you?" the girl's father asked. "I've inquired about the price, and it's not too expensive."

Mario's eyes widened, and his mouth fell open in amazement. He hadn't imagined that in addition to the hotel and the money there would also be a fine bed for his love-making.

When they were all reassembled, Mario revealed his idea. The girl's father felt immediately that the situation was more in his favor than ever. He was, as a matter of fact, really willing to buy the hotel in the mountains; but now that they wanted it here . . . better still. He wouldn't have to pay out any money right away, and he could gain time with one excuse or another. The important thing was to arrange for the wedding. "I agree with you entirely. I understand completely. You've always lived here; you're used to the place. So we'll look around; when the first good opportunity comes . . . Do you already have your eye on anything in particular?"

They said that they would look around.

And he quickly took out his wallet, gave a roll of thousand-lire notes to Mario, and said: "This is for your wedding suit and the rest of your clothes. If your mother can come with me now, we'll go and buy that bedroom furniture right away."

Mario looked at the money, took it, and brought out his wallet, which was almost empty. At first he couldn't fit all the bills into it; finally he folded them, got up abruptly, while his parents looked at him in silent envy. "I'm going straight to the tailor's. You can take care of the furniture." And he hurried out along the main street, convinced that everyone would be aware of his good luck. He passed without a word a ragged former companion, who murmured: "Aren't you proud, now that you have shoes on?"

Mario turned and waved, shouting: "I'm marrying a real lady. I'm going to open a hotel." And when his old friend came up to ask for a cigarette, Mario handed him a whole pack and ran on. When he came back home, he found that they had already bought the furniture, ordered mattresses and sheets, and the rest. They had even been to the town hall to post the banns.

Before evening the future father-in-law said that, if they had no objection, the wedding could take place in two weeks. They would be on the lookout for a hotel, and in the meantime the newlyweds could stay temporarily in Mario's mother's house; his daughter would help out in the tavern, since she was already experienced; and he would take care of everything. He spoke with the greatest simplicity and humility, as if he were ashamed to have so much money in his wallet. They couldn't speak; they would have liked to thank him—and the Madonna too—for the miracle. Meanwhile Mario was to go back with him to see the girl again. And when they had left, his mother could only repeat: "Like winning the lottery. What can I say? It never happened to me in all the years I've been playing it, and this time my number has really come out!" And the women who had come to learn the news said that really she should play the number that this event called for, but the mother shunned temptation: "To ask for anything more would be a crime."

When he arrived in the mountain village, Mario was welcomed lovingly by his fiancée, though he was a little shy about facing her, since he was responsible for her condition. The whole family received him like a hero, and finally he began to play the part himself. They waited on him hand and foot: they brushed his suit, shined his shoes, sent the barber to his room. He asked for a bath, and they prepared a nice, hot one for him. He wanted tea, and they served it with bread, butter, and jam. Finally, the girl, instructed by her sister to renew the pleasures of the past, came to his room to embrace him, when the others were asleep, and she spent the whole night with him.

After several blissful days Mario went back home to get the room ready and to see about his new clothes; he was given more money. The shops seemed open only for him; he came out of one and went into another. He remembered from his ex-master's example what was necessary to cut a fine figure: a handsome overcoat, silk handkerchiefs, toilet articles, gloves, a silk umbrella, ties, shirts, scarves, a light suit (in addition to the one for the wedding), numerous pairs of stockings. Meanwhile he didn't wait for the wedding to show everything off; and for him these were sublime days, days of real wealth, for which he had always waited; and he knew that this was still just the beginning. Later would come the opening of the hotel, where he would be master with servants under him and, the next season, the foreigners, who would increase his wealth still further. The girl's father wrote to ask if he had found a hotel for sale, if they needed more money for the preparations; he also said he would come with an automobile two days before the wedding to pick up Mario and his parents.

So far no hotels had turned up for sale. Mario asked for a little more money so that his parents could be dressed properly for the ceremony. The sum was telegraphed to him immediately. His mother spent whole days just sitting, her heart overflowing with happiness. Mario wanted her to buy a hat and gloves, but she wouldn't hear of it. The thought of making a long motor trip for the first time in her life troubled her and delighted her at once.

The wedding day came. The girl pleased Mario's mother, and when she saw them approach the altar, she was proud of her son, who looked so handsome in the elegance of his new clothes. Despite the unusual circumstances, the wedding was performed among a great assembly of relatives, because the bride, who was plump anyway, didn't betray her condition. At the wedding feast there seemed to be a law that they should drink as much wine as possible; in fact, they began to serve it in the morning, with a snack of cheese and salami, so soon they were all feeling happy, and before long their happiness had become bliss. But while they were at table Mario twice happened to spill salt on the cloth; the first time he paid no attention, but when it happened again, he paled at the bad omen and put his hand on his cheek in alarm. His mother noticed and called to him. His father-in-law immediately asked him, worried, "What's wrong, Mario?"

The bride's sister hastened to brush away the salt.

"What foolishness! Strong men like you shouldn't pay any attention to this business," his father-in-law added, and he broke the silence which was beginning to spread among the guests with the pop of the first bottle of champagne. So they all began to laugh and make noise again. That afternoon the newlyweds and Mario's parents went back home in the car; that night the beautiful silk-covered bed was inaugurated, and Mario wore some scarlet pajamas he had bought because they were exactly like his former master's.

Several days after the wedding, his mother, as if she had risen from a blissful, refreshing sleep after all the years of poverty and insecurity, said to him: "I think you've wasted enough time now taking your wife around to show her off and staying in bed until noon to enjoy the new furniture. You'd better lend a hand and look for that hotel, and you can also write your father-in-law to send you some money, because I'm the one who's supporting you and your wife, and that wasn't part of the bargain. And besides—you know what I think? I've had plenty of children and I know what it means, and I could swear on the Bible that girl is nowhere near six months gone."

Mario was shocked. He had spent wonderful days with his wife, with his fine clothes that everybody admired, with his beautiful bedroom, the dreams that his father-in-law had aroused for the future; and now this was for him, too, an awakening. He wrote off at once asking for the money to provide for them while they waited to find the hotel. And when the answer came he was surprised to find only enough money for cigarettes and a few cold words saying that their writer was busy and apologized for being brief.

A few weeks later Mario's mother said again that he should write to his father-in-law because the bride was eating for two now, and instead of helping out in the tavern she stayed in their room or else sat at the table, as if she expected to be waited on. Also a hotel was for sale, on the sea but near the city, so they would have work in the winter as well as during the swimming season. Mario wrote to his father-in-law about both matters, but his reply consisted in even less money than last time and, as for the hotel, he said they would have to let it go for the moment because he was busy with some work being done on his own hotel. When Mario finished reading, he couldn't believe that was all;

he turned the sheet over to see if there was more writing on it. His mother and father read the letter, too, and were silent. His mother recovered herself first: "I knew there was something behind all this. He made too many fine promises before. So you were going to live in the lap of luxury? Now that you've married her, he's going back on the whole thing. Two hundred lire. How can I keep you? And there won't be any hotel, and besides, that girl is *not* seven months gone, either."

Mario was stunned. At last he said: "All right, she's not seven months gone. What of it?"

"What of it?" his mother repeated. "Don't you understand that if she isn't in the seventh month then it isn't your baby?"

"So much the better," Mario answered. "If it isn't mine, then he'll have to give me even more than he promised." And he went out, thoroughly upset.

The bride felt that Mario's mother was looking at her in a different way, and Mario seemed annoyed, too. He told her what her father had written, but it made no difference to her. Mario's mother spoke to the midwife, who came to examine the girl and found that she was barely five months along. Mario's mother spoke of it privately with the bride, who said she didn't know anything about it and they would have to wait and see when the baby came, she only loved Mario.

Mario was told the news; the earth seemed to give way under his feet. He went out immediately to see a lawyer, who told him there was nothing to be done, he had married her and now he would have to keep her, he should have thought of it before; even if the child wasn't his, it would have his name, so he would just have to wait until it was born. The lawyer was smiling, and Mario felt better. Certainly they would have to agree about the hotel now, and his father-in-law would have to give them an allowance of so much a month. He wrote again, inviting him to come down. The father-in-law answered that he was busy, and he sent a little more money. Meanwhile, nine months had gone by, and the bride showed no signs of giving birth. Mario wrote again to his father-in-law, saying that he absolutely had to come down because of an urgent matter. This time he came. He appeared as timid and confused as the first time, and they all avoided talking.

Mario's mother was crying. "Look what you've brought us to," she said finally, "we're on a sinking ship, that's what."

Mario himself was more explicit. "Take your daughter and take her away from here. The baby isn't mine—and what about all your promises? Where is this lap of luxury we were going to live in?"

He apologized, saying that he had been deceived as much as they had been, but he was ready to do whatever he could to make things right. For a while nobody said anything, they all sighed, then the man looked up. They all waited attentively, expecting more fabulous promises. Indicating the room they were in, he said: "Couldn't we fix this tavern up a little? I'll pay the rent; you can take care of the rest."

Mario's mother said right away that there was the electricity to think of, and the wood for the kitchen, and they needed money to buy the wine; they would have to agree on a figure.

"Name it, name it," he said humbly.

They couldn't arrive at it right away; they would have to do some figuring. He contradicted them, begging, because he had to leave. He suggested he give them five thousand lire a month.

Mario leaped up abruptly. "Ten thousand," he said.

His father-in-law glanced at him and murmured, "I don't have any legal obligation. I shouldn't even give you that much. It's just so you won't think I'm a cheat that I'm willing to make this sacrifice and give you the five thousand, but I can't give a lira more." He took the money from his wallet and held it out to Mario, who wouldn't take it; then he put the bills on the table. He wrote out a receipt and asked Mario to sign it, adding: "This is for the rest of this month. So you see I'm not counting the days."

Mario walked up and down, he couldn't think, he didn't know what to decide; he looked again at the five thousand lire on the table, and all at once he thought that five thousand was certainly better than nothing. He took the money and asked where he should sign. When his father-in-law had gone, his mother wanted the money because it was for the tavern. Mario shouted that the money was his and ran off; he had already made up his mind. He went down to the harbor, and after talking to the captain of a fishing schooner, he signed on for the voyage. His good season was over; now the fog and the storms were beginning. Wealth had come to him, but its season had been brief. He knew he could stand no longer his friends' asking him if he was going to take the hotel by the sea. His mother was happy at his decision; after all, this was the destiny of her sons. And when he was at sea, under the great sails, open to the favoring wind, he thought back to the days when his pockets were full of thousand-lire notes, and he said to himself: "At least I have lived like a rich man." And he knew that he still had his elegant suits, his silk handkerchiefs, his ties, and his huge bed—more beautiful than the beds of all the other sailors—and his wife.

When his wife finally had the baby, his mother wrote him: it was a boy, and his mother was happy, because when he grew up he could find a berth at sea like his father. And Mario was happy, too.

CORRADO ALVARO

The Wedding Journey

TRANSLATED BY FRANCES FRENAYE

I was going home for the first time in many years, and as I drew nearer and nearer, childhood memories crowded upon me. I remembered even the holes in the walls, those holes where the stone is eaten away by the wind and the southern sun, where women hide combings of their hair and their children's first teeth, safe from bad luck, holes that were my storehouse for buttons and nails which I had picked up off the rain-washed road, or my garden, where I watched a pale sheaf of wheat grow from a seed that had fallen upon a wind-swept pile of dirt. Any number of things like this came into my mind. But the most vivid memory awaited me just inside the house, when I saw the high chest in one corner of my father's room, whose top drawer used to hang like a canopy over my little head and where my father kept such very mysterious possessions. There it was, just as I used to see it, with the slender black columns at either side that made it the temple of my dreams, and I remembered a wasp which once made its home there, in a hole filled with soft, golden dust. I waited, now that I was taller, for my father to pull open some of the drawers and let me look in. A familiar odor spun about my head, and I was intoxicated by the smell that still came out of a drop of tar, distilled from the wood one summer long ago.

"This is your mother's dress, the one she wore on her wedding journey. And here are her boots."

I felt the silk of the dress in my fingers. Faille, I remembered hearing my mother call it, a light-brown silk with an odor of faded flowers, which rustled now in my hands. A high collar, puffed sleeves, and a delicate ladder of lace running up the front. And the high, yellow shoes, barely scratched on the soles or wrinkled at the instep, after their too-short walk on the Neapolitan pavements.

For it was to Naples that my mother and father went on their wedding journey. No sooner had my grandfather given his daughter to this thirty-year-old man than he was sorry. The dinner was hardly finished before he shut himself gloomily up in his room and refused even to say good-by. "The bandit!" he muttered over and over. My grandmother, in her bare feet, sighed beside the dying kitchen fire, while her other daughters sat huddled in one corner, like so many bundles. Meanwhile, the bride, in her rustling silk dress, with a tiny straw hat perched on her knot of hair, rode away on horseback down the road leading to the sea. And my father's shadow rode beside her, along the stream beds, where occasional pools of water, not yet dried up by the summer heat, gleamed stilly in the sun.

The bridegroom had the same big wallet that I remembered seeing him carry. He kept it in an inside pocket which he had fastened with a pin. Aboard the train he did not relax his vigilance for a moment. Every now and then he laid his hand on the suitcase to make sure it was still there, and he watched everyone that got on or off at the stations. The bride was happy to be with a man so reliable, in this new great world where the Lord had made no two faces alike. Her straw hat, placed now in the net over the seat, still danced in her brain. The great world, filled with all the voices to be heard on the train, seemed to knit the two of them closer together. She was glad to have chosen a man she knew, who spoke her dialect, and was, in short, a friend. They searched, both of them, for the humblest figure of those seated in the compartment and their eyes fastened upon a woman dressed in black with a baby, who seemed like an answer to their prayer.

"Is his father dead?" asked the bride, looking at the baby, and this was the beginning of their conversation. Her guess was correct, and she proceeded to ask about the dead man, speaking with all the reverent timidity to which he was entitled. Then they fell silent, because they had nothing more to say, except when they pointed out the growing things in the fields on either side of the track. But they looked at one another in friendly fashion, because simplehearted people are naturally drawn together by sorrow.

They arrived in Naples toward evening. The wide streets were frightening, and everyone seemed to have something to tell them: cabbies, small boys, and men who stepped virtually out of the walls in order to recommend a certain furnished room in the house of respectable people. The bridegroom had buttoned up his jacket and he carried the heavy suitcase in both hands, dangling in front of him, so that he could feel the stiff corner of the wallet in his pocket with one thumb. The bride was tempted to answer a polite no to all the solicitations shot at them by perfect strangers, but he warned her with his eyes and walked straight ahead as if they were not talking to him at all. She was afraid and held onto his arm, with her feet tired from the pavement, which was as stony and hard as the floor of the church in their native village. The houses seemed to lean over her on either side, with their dizzily high balconies and out-of-sight, secret windows, which gave her a hitherto inexperienced feeling of panic. She admired her man, who knew what it was all about and walked proudly ahead, and she resolved to be worthy of him.

"We shan't go to a hotel," he was saying. "Those schemers aren't going to take our money!" He had pronounced himself in the same way before they left, as if he were baring a plan to defraud a whole city, which lay in wait for him at its peril. Now they took heart again whenever they crossed people in dark suits, old men and women, or couples with their children around them. What mystified them was the number of isolated individuals who poured out onto the street and stood there, looking uncertainly around, pacing up and down the long sidewalks and pausing at a street corner as if in expectation. Were they waiting for them?

The bridegroom meant to take her to a safe place, to the house of some friends he had made ten years before when he was doing his military service. These friends would provide a room for a few days, and one where he could feel at ease. But now the city seemed new and strange and he didn't know where he was. They came to a halt in an enormous square, with their eyes on a luminous clock that suddenly flashed on, in spite of the fact that there was still sun in the sky. The shops were lit up like churches, and in front of the smaller ones the owners sat taking the air. The bride and groom searched the passing crowd for someone of whom to inquire about the street for which they were looking. They were unwilling to confide their predicament to just anyone, for the human race, as they saw it around them, had faces such as they had never seen before; all these people were involved in trades and passions that were unknown and hence vaguely terrifying. Finally they spotted a man who looked as if he might have come from their part of the world. They asked their question in a low voice, listened attentively to the answer, and followed with their eyes the motions of the man's hand. But afterward they hesitated before starting out and watched their informant walk away.

The house was in a poor street, teeming with loaded pushcarts and loud voices, except where silent lines stood in front of the pawnshops. Here they took courage and felt at home. The little women straggling across the street, the cripples sticking out here and there like evidences of fate, the fat, bejeweled shopkeepers who were having their hair curled out in the open, the children crawling over the sidewalks, and the merchants who opened their mouths shamelessly wide in strident praise of the wares they were selling, all these seemed familiar and put them in a good humor. The bridegroom pointed out the wealth of fruit, vegetables, and other goods set out on the street, with no fear of their being stolen. "Just think, you can get grapes here the whole year around, and other fruits, too, even out of season!" he said to startle her.

They came to the house, and he rushed in with all the impetuousness of ten years before, trying to recapture the same words and tone of voice that he had had then. But he was met by an old woman who hardly remembered him. She thought and thought, and finally muttered: "Yes, yes," staring at him all the while. Her husband was dead and her sons were all married and had trades of their own. Her daughter was married too, and when she said this she raised her eyes to look at him. The bride bent her head and blushed. But the bridegroom broke the silence with his loudest and gayest voice, the voice in which he had spoken in days gone by. "Here we are in Naples," he said, "and of course we wanted to come to you. You're as young and beautiful as ever!" And he went on to say other things, to which she listened with a remote smile. She opened up her big bedroom with the faded red, gold-flowered paper on the wall and the photographs draped in black for mourning and also for protection from the flies. Then she brought a kerosene lamp and accepted the two lire which it was agreed she should charge them for the night.

The clamor of the city outside made the windowpanes rattle. The bridegroom locked the door and leaned a chair against it, while the bride sat down on a chair beside the chest of drawers, where a statuette of the Madonna under a glass bell was clothed in a torn blue dress and a crown that was all askew. The kerosene lamp made a sputtering sound, and when the bridegroom sat down at the table, solitude fell upon them. "Now we must have something to eat," he said in a low voice. "I've taken care of that, you'll see." He opened the suitcase and took out two parcels, one of which he set aside, saying: "That's for tomorrow."

They didn't say it, but the same thought was in both their minds, a thought of those that were to come, the children that would one day be theirs. The bride's hands, so accustomed to work and so ill at ease being idle, lay folded in her lap, while the bridegroom cut a piece of the chicken he had set out on a newspaper. Then he poured the wine and held the glass up to the light. He made an effort to laugh and said in a low voice: "Draw up your chair, and let's eat some of the good things from our own village. They don't have anything like this here. In fact, if the old lady could see what we have, she'd surely want some for herself. Just taste the goodness of it! We're not wasting our money in the hotels! What do you say if tomorrow we go buy a cradle, with a pink embroidered lining? Pink or blue?"

My mother had put her arm on the table and was silently weeping.

IGNAZIO SILONE

Return to Fontamara

TRANSLATED BY DARINA SILONE

The moment I received the parish priest's letter, I decided to go. And for reasons of my own, I chose the night train. A friend who was in my confidence offered to drive me there; but I refused, murmuring pretexts and vague, halfhearted excuses.

In the end, to silence him, I said: "You know, when I left the place, twenty-five years ago, I took the train. So you ought to understand—"

"But the line has been badly damaged by the war," he insisted. "The bridges are mostly makeshift wooden affairs; the train crawls at a snail's pace; you'll be traveling all night."

"That suits me," I said, somewhat annoyed.

All night long I kept my face close to the window of the railway carriage. Through it I saw opening up before me a landscape stamped indelibly on my memory, stony little fields and dark barren mountains with no trace of human habitation. I saw deserted little stations appear and disappear, barred doors and shuttered windows, tumble-down houses, crumbling walls, ruins everywhere. From the acrid smell of the men and women huddled near me in the darkness of the railway carriage, their bundles, suitcases, boxes, and sacks crammed with purchases made in the town, I could guess their peasant origin. Some had a deathlike pallor, as they slept in the early dawn; others had the terrified look of thieves caught red-handed; others again were haggard, as though guilty of an incestuous love or the murder of a parent or wife. But the ticket collector's tone of authority roused them; they shook

187

themselves and quickly resumed the mask of impenetrable reserve habitual to their waking hours.

Someone called me as I was trying to pick my way between the prostrate forms of my fellow travelers and the barricade of sacks in the corridor.

"Hello there," he shouted. "What the devil are you doing on this train? Going back to your Fontamara?"

"The same as everyone else;" I answered with some irritation. "I'm traveling."

The voice drew nearer. "But where is it exactly, this Fontamara of yours?" he insisted in a conspiratorial tone. "Which of our villages is it, in your imagination? Aielli? Ortona? Lecce?"

"That's my secret," said I, jumping out at the next stop.

"Where's your bag?" shouted the other from the window. "Have you forgotten it?"

"Haven't got one," I answered. "You can go to hell." I had brought no luggage. It would, I felt, have been really absurd for me to arrive there with suitcases, like a tourist or a commercial traveler. It was twenty-five years since I had set off from this station, and I had carried no suitcases that time either. I had left like a thief, by night, never dreaming that so many years would pass before I could return. Lazzaro the frog catcher had insisted on seeing me off. He was an old Socialist and a native of the place.

"Don't come," I had told him. "The *carabinieri* might recognize you and hold it against you. Don't give me cause for remorse."

"I'll pretend I just happened to be at the station," he answered. "You'll see, I'll not as much as say a word to you."

And so, with his daughter and his donkey, he came down the valley and over to the station. But of course we ended up by talking to each other.

"Go far away and forget this land of sorrow," he told me. "It's well for you that you're only a boy and have time to forget."

"Lazzaro," I answered, "I swear to you that I'll never forget."

"You'll forget," he repeated vehemently. "You'll finish your studies, you'll get on in the world, and of course you'll forget. You'll see how easy it will be."

"Lazzaro," I answered, "why quarrel just at the moment of parting? I swear to you, Lazzaro, I'll never forget."

"I don't want to quarrel," he assured me. "That's the last thing I'd want. But you'll see, that's how it will be. You too will get on in the world and you'll forget. Believe me, I'm old—I could be your grandfather—and I know life better than you."

I went on protesting, with tears in my eyes, trying hard not to burst into sobs; and even Laurina, Lazzaro's daughter, begged her father to stop it, or talk of something else.

"Maybe it's the last time you'll ever have a word with each other," said Laurina. "Maybe you'll never see each other again, and yet you're quarreling."

"I don't want to quarrel," said the old man, humbly and apologetically. "That's the last thing I'd want, especially just now, when we have to part. What I was saying is only natural, and after all, what's natural is right. You'll settle down, I was saying, you'll get on in the world, and you'll forget."

His daughter Laurina turned to me in distress.

"You've got to understand him," she said. "The fact is, he has a great love for you. You have no idea how much he loves you. You have no idea of the way he talks about you when you're not there. He has a greater love for you than he has for me, his daughter."

"Maybe that's so," said the old man, nodding assent to her, "indeed, that's how it is. But what am I? A poor peasant. And what is he? A person of learning. And so, like all learned persons, he'll get on in the world and forget us and this unfortunate land."

My journey took me farther than I had then imagined it would, and my absence lasted longer. Some years later, in 1930, ill and disheartened, I took refuge in a Swiss mountain village. Thinking I had not much longer to live, I began to write a tale which I called "Fontamara." I built myself a village with the stuff of my memories and my dreams, and then I began to inhabit it. The result was a plain and simple tale, but its readers in many countries found it moving because of the nostalgia that pervaded it. Later on I heard that this same name of Fontamara, which I had invented, already belonged to several vil-

lages in southern Italy, and that the events told by me in the story
had actually occurred shortly before in various places, although not in
the same order as in the book, and with differences of detail. Still,
there is clearly no reason why these numerous coincidences should
lessen the importance or the significance of this testimony of mine; I
rather think that, if anything, they increase it. Names like Mary, John,
Francis, Louis, and so on, are common to a great many people; and
the really important events of life—birth, love, suffering, death—are
common to all living beings; and yet people never grow tired of talking
about them.

Alas, it is not easy, when one has grown to maturity, to return to the
places where one spent one's childhood, if one's thoughts have never
left them during all the years of absence, if one has continued, even at
a distance, to live through their imagined events. It can even be a risky
undertaking.

And so I was painfully embarrassed when, a few days after the newspapers and radio had announced my return to Italy, a queer deputation
composed of village authorities and leaders of local political groups
came to see me in Rome, proposing a program of ceremonies to be held
in honor of my return to my native district. I was unable, at a moment's
notice, to improvise the sort of little speech that would have used a
screen of conventional arguments to hide from these good people the
shudders of horror that I felt at the mere idea of returning, amid a lot
of fuss and speechmaking, to those places laden, for me, with memories of unspeakable sadness. The deputation consequently departed
in bewilderment, and as I heard later, uncertain whether to attribute
my discourteous refusal to extreme political intransigence or to morbid misanthropy. At any rate, fortunately for me, the matter rested
there.

Then I got the parish priest's letter, and at first glance it seemed the
usual letter, asking me to use my influence with some government
department to obtain a subsidy for an old ex-convict who had lately
returned to the village; the sort of letter, in fact, that I was used to
getting. But the name of the ex-convict stirred an echo in me that the
parish priest could not have suspected. "You can't possibly know the
poor fellow," he had written, "because he went to jail, for a criminal

offense, the very year you were born." It was the truth, but not the whole truth.

In the square outside the station, I looked in vain for the bus that used once to pass up the valley as far as B——. It had been discontinued a few years back, they told me.

"Wait here," the post-office clerk suggested. "Maybe some cart or buggy will be along. You're a native of these parts yourself, aren't you?"

In the middle of the square there was a large fountain, with women crowding around it. I went closer. Their traditional way of speaking, their traditional gestures, as in some ancient ritual, fell like drops of honey on my heart. The young women wore their kerchiefs knotted at the nape of the neck, the old women wore them knotted under the chin. When one woman had filled her water jar, another would help her to lift it and set it straight on the pad which protected her head. Even the old women would hold their heads high under the weight and walk erect, so as not to spill the water. Farther off, in the shade of a tree, a mother was rocking her baby; the cradle was formed like a tiny ship, and it had a slow undulating movement. Then some peasants arrived at the station, dressed in their Sunday clothes, weighed down with cumbersome baggage, and looking like refugees or vagabonds.

"Did the war pass this way?" I asked the post-office clerk, as I looked around me. "Somehow one wouldn't think so."

"This village has been persecuted by fate," he explained. "Not even the earthquake passed it by. Here there's no rebuilding, no subsidies, no help at all. Nothing but misery."

Suddenly I decided to go ahead on foot; in fact, I thought I'd even like it better.

"You'll be a couple of hours on the road," the clerk warned me. "You don't know that road; it's dusty and stony."

"I'll take the short cut," I answered in dialect.

"Ah, so you really are from these parts!" he exclaimed.

In the valley, the green and yellow mosaic of the vines soon gave way to a barer landscape. The gloomy hills had as their sole adornment a few sickly cypresses and almond trees, and a few crucifixes that looked almost as though made of cardboard. The idea came to me that adolescence was an experience defined not only by time but also by space.

How, I wondered, can people at a certain age cross the boundary into a new country, if physically they go on living in the old country all the time? It is easier, simpler, more natural, perhaps also more honest, when you reach a certain age, to go away. But when you come to think of it, what does it really mean, "going away?" How many of those who stayed here always, and are now buried here, spent their lives in sighing for foreign countries, while it is an ancient truth that homesickness is the malady of emigrants? This land—had I myself ever forgotten it? Had my imagination ever dreamed of anything that did not have here its beginning and its end? As I walked along, I tried to link up one year with another, to retrace my life's pattern; and in vain I asked myself if it had any meaning.

I met a country policeman with a gun slung across his shoulder and a string of skinned frogs threaded on a willow branch in his hand.

"There used to be a frog catcher in B——," I said to him, "a man called Lazzaro. Did you ever know him? What became of him?"

"Poor fellow, he had nothing but trouble as long as he lived," answered the policeman. "But it was his own fault, believe you me, he was really mad; not bad, but just mad."

"What sort of trouble?" I asked.

"All sorts," he answered. "But I must say he brought them on himself. The fact is, he simply couldn't mind his own business; that was his way of being mad."

"He had a daughter called Laurina, hadn't he?" I asked. "What became of her? Where is she now?"

The policeman, with a vague gesture, answered that he did not know.

At a certain point the valley narrowed and became warmer, hoarding the heat as though in a hothouse. The path began to run alongside the stream and soon brought me to the point where the water falls from a wall of rock to form a clear and limpid pool. As a boy I often came there and sat on the bank, dangling my feet in the icy current, and watching it flow by; after a little while the bank would begin to move, and I with the bank.

In this same place I now found an old woman resting on the grass, with a basket of walnuts beside her. In her abandoned exhaustion and weariness, she seemed a drowned thing stretched out there on the grass to dry. The moment she noticed me she sat up and smoothed her clothes. She had been to the weekly market at P——, she told me, trying to sell the walnuts, but no one wanted to buy them. This was the third time she had brought them to market.

"But even if you did sell them," I said, "how much would you get for them? Would it make up to you for all your labor?"

"Labor?" she answered. "A woman like me, the mother of a family, can I stop to think about the labor?"

She told me that she had a sick daughter at home, and that a doctor had prescribed pills for her; and pills cost money. So she was trying to sell what she could, in order to buy the pills. She had been trying for three weeks, unsuccessfully. If meanwhile her daughter died, what would people say? They would say: It's her mother's fault.

The old woman coughed, and after groping about a bit, struggled awkwardly to her feet in order to resume her wandering. I walked beside her for a while, carrying the basket.

"I mustn't rest for long," she said. "If I were to rest for long, all the weariness would come to the surface, and I'd never get to my feet again; what little strength I have would take the opportunity of leaving me for ever. Even at night I have to get up two or three times, because I bake all the bread for our village. So I haven't got time to be ill."

After a short distance our ways parted, because the woman lived in the neighborhood of O——.

"Did you ever happen to know an old peasant of B——?" I asked her. "Lazzaro was his name, and they called him the frog catcher."

"Indeed I did know him," she answered. "Poor soul, what a hard life they gave him. He was a saint, no one could say a bad word about him, he never harmed a living creature; but he didn't know the meaning of resignation, he couldn't keep his head bowed."

"No one should resign himself to contempt," said I. "No one should resign himself to injustice."

The woman stopped and looked at me pityingly.

"Poor fellow," she said. "So you too are one of those? But, my poor boy, what good does it do, tell me, what good does it do, not being resigned?"

"And being resigned, what good does that do?" I answered. "What about you, old mother? Did it do you any good?"

"Indeed it didn't," she said. "But if it's all one whether we hold our heads high or low, we might just as well hold them low. For the salvation of our souls."

"Lazzaro had a daughter," I said. "Laurina, they called her. Is she still alive?"

"She's still alive," answered the woman. "She lives like me, as a poor woman should, with bowed head. We're neighbors, as it happens." Then she added: "I'll tell her I met you: she'll be pleased. What was your father's name?"

"The name doesn't matter."

There was B——, on the hilltop. The village had not changed since the day I left it; you could still see, amid the black huddle of houses, the ruined spaces left by the earthquake of thirty years before. At the entrance to the village I was seized by a sudden, unaccountable hesitation; I wanted to turn back, to run away. But my hesitation must have come just at the moment when the bread was being taken out of the oven, and a puff of wind brought me the fragrance of fresh bread. That softened and won me, and I continued on my way.

An old man, a stranger to me, looking like a beggar, was walking ahead, dragging his feet after him and spitting to his right at intervals of about ten paces.

"Old man," I said, "where does the parish priest live?"

He stopped and looked suspiciously at me.

"Can you give me a match?" he asked.

I gave him a match.

"Give me another," he said.

I gave him several others. Then he promptly turned his back on me and went off down a lane without answering the question. But I found him again at the sacristy door.

"It must be the fellow for the taxes," he was saying to the priest. "Hurry up and hide yourself."

The parish priest did not recognize me at first and invited me into the sacristy with an embarrassed gesture and a timid smile calculated to inspire pity, a sickly-sweet smile, like the honey of bees that feed in cemeteries. But on hearing my first words he sighed with relief, flushed with excitement, began gesticulating wildly, and wanted to go out and tell the news to the mayor and the villagers. He must have been about my age, because we had been to high school together, but he looked much older.

"I'm just here by accident," I said. "I'm only passing through. I'm off again tonight or tomorrow."

"Did no one recognize you on the road?" he asked.

"Twenty-five years have passed," I said.

"You mean twenty-five centuries," he corrected. "Exactly twenty-five centuries."

"I'd be glad if no one recognized me," I said. "I've lost my taste for fuss and commotion. And the few people I'd have liked to see again are no longer alive."

"The village suffered greatly during the war," he told me. "The Germans killed or carried off all the cattle. You ought to talk to the mayor. You could help us a lot."

"It's just by sheer accident that I've come this time," I said. "I happened to be passing this way, and thought I'd stop here for a few hours, that's all. So I'd be grateful if you wouldn't give me away to anyone. But since I am here, there is that thing you wrote to me about. Could I have a word with the man himself?"

"I'll call him right away," he said, rising to his feet. "There he is, outside the door; the very one that was telling me of your arrival."

The priest went to the door to call the man; he called him a couple of times, but the man refused to come in.

"Leave me alone with him," I said then.

The man was squatting on the trunk of an elm tree that lay against the sacristy wall. He was leaning with his back against the wall and he looked like any old beggar.

"I have a story to tell you," said I.

"First give me a match," he answered.

I gave him a match and sat down beside him. I saw that instead of shoes he had wrappings of rags on his feet; his gray hair was still thick and unruly; his hands and face were of an earthy brown color and cracked all over. But what struck me most in him were his eyes, of a strange rare green, which gave him a look of shrewd wariness.

"At home," said I, "when I was still a child, we had as a servant a village woman whom you could see, by her appearance and manner, to be of a better family than the usual run of servants in our part of the country."

"Are you from these parts?" he asked. "What was your father's name?"

"You'll soon guess," said I. "I never could understand why that woman had been obliged to become a servant in other people's houses. Throughout my childhood, this remained one of the many questions to which I could get only evasive answers. 'She's had a great misfortune in her family,' my mother would tell me. 'She's had to spend every penny on lawyers' fees. Be good to her.' In her bearing and manner she was, as I said, in no way different from us; misfortune had not curbed her pride. And her eyes were green, like yours. You know, I've traveled far, but nowhere else have I seen such eyes."

The man rose abruptly to his feet and signed to me to follow him. Someone called to him from a distance, but he made no reply. Down deserted lanes he led me to an old church that had been half destroyed by the earthquake and never rebuilt. Among other fragments there remained standing—you could see it from a distance—part of the dome, painted on the inside a blue sky with hosts of the blessed carrying garlands of roses and the inscription GLORIA. A corner of the building remained intact and had been walled off and roofed. This was now allotted by the parish as a refuge to the ex-convict. There were just four bare walls, with the joinings of the stones clearly visible. A lantern hung by a piece of wire from a beam in the roof; in one corner stood a cot, and beside it a table with a loaf of bread, an onion, and a few walnuts. From a deep niche hollowed out of the wall, the man took a bottle and a glass and silently offered me a drink, with the solemnity and reverence of a deacon pouring the wine into the chalice of the celebrant.

We sat down on the cot and I pursued my story.

"It was only," I said, "after the long period of solitary confinement —the first part of your life sentence—was ended that your mother began to get letters from you. But as you know, although intelligent and the daughter of well-to-do farmers, she could neither read nor write. Such cases were, as you remember, frequent in our part of the country; in those days, for a girl to be taught reading and writing was still considered, by country people, if not a sin, at least frivolous or extravagant. I hadn't yet left elementary school and couldn't understand why, with so many trustworthy people who could have read her your letters and answered them for her, your mother should have singled me out. You know the unvarying theme of all your letters and of all our replies, and if you remember how young I was then, you won't be surprised if I tell you now that, without exaggeration, it was the first great event of my life. My whole future was determined by it and by other more or less similar experiences that later followed it.

"One of the things that used to amaze me at first was the fact that such a scrupulously honest woman as your mother should use me for so serious a correspondence without telling my parents anything. Finally I asked her why. 'Now that you've read my son's letters,' she said, 'do you believe in his innocence?' 'Oh, I'm sure of it,' I answered. 'I know he wasn't the murderer.' 'Well,' said your mother, 'the others, all the others, are convinced of his guilt. That's why I don't want to turn to them.'

" 'But,' I asked your mother, 'how can it possibly matter to you what I think? I'm still a child.' 'That's the very reason,' your mother explained, 'just because you are still innocent.'

"From that moment, however, I must confess that I began to doubt my own innocence and the innocence of the world. It was a new and deeply troubling thought for me that I could not share my certainty of your innocence with my parents, nor with the schoolmaster, nor with the parish priest; and that everything I did in consequence of that secret certainty of mine had therefore also to be done in secret. So there was a forbidden good? In short, I felt myself drawn into a real conspiracy with a convict and his mother, a conspiracy against injustice; and the state and public opinion had ranged themselves on the other side. In every letter you used to repeat the arguments for your innocence. You never despaired, but kept on refuting the circumstantial evidence on which, without proof, you had been convicted of homicide. Those letters caused me sleepless nights, and when I did sleep I was haunted by terrible nightmares. And the letters I wrote in reply? Remember I had never been away from home and had never before had occasion to write to anyone. As you can easily imagine, my schoolwork soon took a secondary place in my thoughts, compared with this secret duty. Each reply used to absorb me entirely for several days. It was not easy for a child of my age to find the appropriate expression for all the things your mother used to tell me, about herself, the lawyers, the false witnesses, the debts to be paid, the petitions to be sent to the King, the Queen Mother, the Crown Prince, the Duke of the Abruzzi, the Pope, and General Garibaldi's granddaughter. All this, as you know, lasted for several years; and during all those years it was my adventure, my romance, my conspiracy, until your mother died of heart failure, when she became convinced that there could be no reopening of your case.

"There, I've told you all this only to explain why, yesterday, the moment I got a letter from the parish priest mentioning your name, I took the train and came at once."

By now the man's face was buried in his hands.

"Maybe I've talked too much about myself," said I. "But I had to win your confidence."

"Were you convinced of my innocence from the first?" asked the man. "From the very first?"

"Of course," I said. "I knew straightaway."

"How?" he insisted. "What made you think it?"

"It was quite simple," I answered. "I just knew."

The man stood up.

"I don't know if you like green peppers?" he asked. "You must excuse me if I've got nothing else to offer you."

He went out by a little door opening onto what was formerly the enclosure of the church, now cluttered with rubble. A tripod for cooking stood among some blackened stones. I followed him.

"There's one thing I'd like to ask you," said I.

"You want to know if I am really innocent of the murder for which I spent forty-five years in jail?"

"No," I said. "Not at all. I only want to know why you would never explain, neither to your lawyer nor to your mother nor to the jury, where you spent your time the night of the murder. As you know, you were convicted mainly because of your silence on that essential point."

"Listen," he said, "please believe me, I'm very sorry, but I can't tell that even to you."

He took some peppers out of a basket, opened them, carefully removed the seeds, and arranged them in a frying pan on the tripod.

"I don't know," he said, "if you like green peppers. But please excuse me, it's all I have to offer you."

ALBERTO MORAVIA

The Unfortunate Lover

TRANSLATED BY BERNARD WALL

After he had quarreled and broken with his mistress, Sandro could no longer endure the city in which they had been living together, so he left for an island not far from the coast. It was June and not yet too hot, and as the bathing season began only in July he knew that he would not find many visitors on the island. Everything went well on the day of his arrival. For the sake of greater solitude he did not go to a hotel but to furnished rooms let out by a woman. These rooms were arranged side by side and opened out onto a wide balcony enclosed by a colonnade—and this was all that had survived of an ancient convent. Three sides of the original cloister had disappeared, and the row of rooms backed onto the precipitous cliff of the island. The rooms looked out over a shady, well-stocked garden, then a slope scattered with white villas, prickly pears, and olive trees, and then the faraway sea, calm and sparkling like glass in the indentations of the rocky coast.

At the time of his arrival all the rooms except the one next to Sandro's were untenanted; and the first time he went out onto the wide balcony he immediately saw the occupant of that one. It was a young and beautiful girl with magnificent fair hair and a face that bore a close resemblance to a little pig. She greeted Sandro and he returned her greeting. She asked him whether he bathed and he answered that he did so sometimes, and then he went back into his room. From that day onward he was unable to go out onto the terrace even for a moment without the shutters of the next room bursting open and the girl com-

200

ing out to talk to him. She was obstinate and not put off by Sandro's brusque replies. She talked to him with both hands resting on the balustrade, her deep-set and inexpressive little eyes falling alternately on the sea and on him. In the end Sandro took care not to appear beneath the colonnade.

He began leading a very regular life. Early every morning he went down to the sea, undressed and lay on the beach until the sun grew hot enough to allow of bathing. Then he waded into the water, gazing at his white feet shimmering on the rough pebbles. The water would mount slowly and with delicious eagerness, first to his stomach, then to his chest and then up to his chin. As soon as he felt his feet were off the ground, with a thrust he swam out around the rocks or from point to point along the coast. He noticed that he never thought of anything when swimming, and he liked that. Sometimes he lay on his back with arms outstretched and closed his eyes, letting the slight pull of the current bear him over the calm sea to a chance landing. He would stay a long time this way in the water, his eyes shut, his ears caressed by the waves; then reopen his eyes and in the powerful light see the great red rock of the island weighing down on him out of the blazing sky. Bathing was the pleasantest event of the day, for it distracted him almost completely. After his swim he would climb up to the village again, eat alone in an inn, then go back to his room and try to get a couple of hours' sleep. As long as he had something definite to do such as swimming or eating or sun-bathing he was fairly successful at keeping his mind off his mistress and the pain of his separation from her. But during the languid and empty hours of the afternoon he was attacked by the bitterness of boredom and wild desire, as if in expectation of something that he knew would never come to pass. By the evening, and after his unavailing efforts to distract himself, he had reached the end of his tether and was in a frenzy.

Two weeks of this life had already passed when he received a post card of greeting from his mistress from somewhere not far away. The post card gave her address and was obviously an invitation to begin a correspondence. Sandro wrote a rather longer card and two days later received a note telling him about her health, the weather, and other similar matters. Encouraged, he now sent off an eight-page letter in which he asked to see her even if only for a day. He knew from his experience of her character that she was incapable of love except out of contrariness. And as it turned out he received no answer. Two more weeks passed and Sandro had given up hope; and then he received a telegram announcing that she was arriving the following day.

The next morning he awoke with a start, afraid that he had over-slept. But on looking at his watch he saw that he had still more than an hour before the arrival of the boat. He went out onto the terrace to examine the sea; it was calm, there was no danger of a storm pre-venting the boat from reaching the jetty. As usual his next-door neigh-bor immediately appeared on the terrace and very hurriedly, as though she was afraid he might escape, told him that it was a fine day. Sandro answered that the day couldn't be finer and went back to his room. In his mind's eye he still pictured the girl standing upright facing the sea, her hands on the balustrade and a silly disconcerted expression on her face.

He finished dressing and made his way unhurriedly down to the square. The early morning had that peculiar fresh, clear light that in places such as this seems to come less from the sky than the sea. The square was deserted and the tables at the two or three cafés were empty. A few local inhabitants were squatting on the steps of the church enjoying the early sun. The shopkeepers were opening their shops, pulling up the blinds. Occasionally a half-naked woman, an early riser, with sunglasses on her nose and a large canvas bag under her arm, would hurriedly cross the square and make for the short cut down to the sea. For a while Sandro paced up and down the square and then he went to the belvedere.

From up there he could see the whole stretch of the sea, smooth and calm with a few lazy and scattered white tracks—the great wander-ing crystal serpents of the currents, drifting deadly this way and that. The boat which must contain his mistress was already visible in the narrow channel separating the island from the hills of the mainland. It was moving slowly, leaving a long bright wake on the transparent and luminous sea. Now and again sky and sea seemed to turn to vapor and mingle together and then the boat seemed to be sailing in an undefined zone that was no longer water and not yet air. Sandro lowered his gaze to the precipice beneath the belvedere. The black wheel tracks of the funicular descended on their bed and disappeared in the green of the hillside: soon the red carriage, bringing up his mistress, would emerge slowly from among the branches and leaves of the lush vines. He left the belvedere and went and sat down in a café, placing himself so that he could keep an eye on the exit of the funicular.

He was pleased to observe that he was feeling calm and clear-headed. After some time a trickle of people began to arrive, their town clothes noticeable in a place where everyone wore sandals and linen trousers. But the first carriage emptied with no sign of his mistress. In a sudden fit of impatience he got up from the café and took his place near the entrance to the funicular.

He waited for some ten minutes, telling himself that there were no grounds for fear, that his mistress had wired that she was coming, and that she must therefore have come. The second carriage arrived and the passengers got out one after another, and his mistress still failed to make an appearance. Sandro went to buy a pack of cigarettes and waited for the third carriage. He smoked the cigarettes halfway down, or perhaps two-thirds, and then threw them away.

Now came the third carriage. As he had observed from the belvedere, the boat was not very crowded. This time only three or four passengers got out—no more—and a crowd of hotel porters. His mistress was not there.

Mechanically, not knowing what to do, and stunned by his disappointment as if by sunstroke, he set out along the road leading to the jetty. Halfway down he spotted a horse and trap coming toward him. The driver had to go to the very edge of the road to avoid a lorry loaded with vegetables stationed in front of a shop. Then Sandro saw his mistress.

He waited until the trap was on a level with him and then called out her name in a clear voice. She turned, and he could see that she was exactly the same. Severely, and as if their meeting displeased her, she said, "There you are," and ordered the driver to stop.

"I was waiting for you at the funicular," Sandro said, walking toward the trap but not getting in.

"So I imagined," she answered in a cross tone of voice, "but there was such a crowd. . . . I preferred to take a trap."

They measured each other with their eyes.

"Why are you standing there?" she asked in her usual hard yet flattering voice; "why don't you get in? I shall have to go to the hotel first."

Sandro got in and the horse started up at a trot.

"I've booked a room for you," he said as he sat down.

"Thanks," she answered absently. She looked around with satisfied curiosity, then said: "It's not a bad place, you know."

"It's famous," answered Sandro, smiling; but he immediately regretted his phrase—it sounded stupid—and added: "Are you staying long?"

"I don't know," she answered in an undecided voice. "It depends."

Sandro regretted this question too, for it occurred to him that she might think that her stay on the island mattered to him. And he concluded: "If you like it you'll stay . . . otherwise you'll go away?"

"Exactly," she said with a hard laugh. "You're being original today."

Sandro bit his lips till they bled and said nothing more until they reached the square. In the square they got out and Sandro asked the driver how much he wanted. The driver asked for thirty lire. Sandro knew that the proper charge was half as much and answered unthinking: "It's a great deal."

"Come along. . . . What a long discussion," she said, glancing around and feigning embarrassment. Sandro bit his lips again and paid.

They crossed the square, passed under a narrow archway, and began climbing a little street embedded between the tall and serried white houses. Sandro carried the suitcase, and his mistress kept a step ahead of him looking at every object with her characteristic expression of mingled satisfaction and surprise. Every now and again she stopped to gaze up at the summit of the island and contemplate its peculiar architectural formation. Amid the terraces and escarpments far above their heads the blue sky was resplendent. The path twisted, turned into a flight of steps, entered a dark passageway, and then went on mounting. After the houses came long white walls sprouting greenery, and on top of the walls, tangled with the plants, were half-naked girls and infants who watched them as they passed.

"It really is a pretty place," she said emphatically, "like a dream."

She talked like this, Sandro thought, because she was not very intelligent and so expressed herself in terms of clichés. But for all that her conventional expressions had far more weight than his more penetrating and subtle ones.

He tried to say something on her level and answered: "Yes, a dream . . . but a dream for two."

She appeared not to hear and asked: "Is there still far to go?"

"We're there," said Sandro.

He put down the suitcase, took the big iron key from his pocket and inserted it into the keyhole of the old decayed greenish door of the former convent. They entered the dark cool corridor.

"What thick walls," she said, glancing at the lantern holds embedded in the thickness of the vault.

"It was a convent," Sandro said. He went to the end of the corridor, opened the door and added: "I booked you a room next door to mine . . . but meanwhile you can come in here."

Without answering she went straight to the looking glass hanging over the washbasin. Sandro sat on the edge of the bed with his eyes on her. He could see her grave and attentive in the mirror. He was glad to watch her now, for on the way up he had not even dared to glance at her for fear of revealing his real feelings. She had large almond-shaped eyes of a bright, almost furious, blue that seemed to consume her forehead beneath her fair curly hair. The slightness of her forehead and her huge eyes made one think of some animal. And her sharp chiseled nose, her thin cheeks that seemed to find their outlet in her wide full mouth, confirmed this impression of animality. It was a face that suggested to one's mind the muzzle of a goat, a tame goat, mad and a trifle obscene. She was thin and ardent, with a long sensitive neck, bony shoulders, and a very slim waist; but her hips were rounded, and beneath her flanks her thin listless legs emerged from her wide skirt with an air of dancing, malicious joy; one expected to see them, with her big feet shod in narrow sandals, uplifted to beat time in a satyr's dance. There was no doubt about her fear of looking tired after the journey; but when she looked at her face she must have been satisfied, for all of a sudden she gave it an oblique glance over her shoulder and began to hum. It was the only tune she knew by heart, and Sandro knew it well, for he had often heard her singing it when they were in love. She used to sing it with picturesque irony, parodying the clumsy and provocative gestures and the awkward voices of low music-hall artists. For a moment she went on humming and looking at herself in the mirror; then she turned, put her hands on her hips, and intoned the song in a loud voice, shaking her haunches and throwing her feet about in the narrow space between the bed and the washbasin. As she faced Sandro she kept her eyes down, but whenever she turned her back on him she turned her face so as to give him a look over her shoulder. Her large red mouth was wide open and he could see the motion of her thick swift tongue as she sang. She realized that her coquetry was irresistible; indeed, when she came within range Sandro could not resist trying to seize her. She immediately stopped singing and shimmying and said: "We must be serious."

"Do you want to see your room?" asked Sandro, angry. She nodded, and Sandro led the way out onto the terrace. Immediately the neighboring shutters opened and the fair girl appeared. She was just on the point of speaking, and already had her mouth open, when she caught sight of the other woman. Hurriedly she took a bathing costume that had been spread out on the railing and retired to her own room.

"Who is that?" his mistress asked.

"I don't know."

"Come off it, you know perfectly well. I bet you've already spoken with her, if not worse. . . ." Her tone was mocking and had no trace of jealousy.

"No, no," Sandro said, laughing, flattered by the thought that she could suspect him of disloyalty to her. Then, realizing that he had made the usual mistake of betraying his feelings, he became grave again.

"This is your room."

It was a room exactly like Sandro's. The woman sat on the bed and said: "But I don't yet know whether I'll be staying the night or going off this afternoon."

"Do whatever you want," said Sandro in a fury.

She glanced at him and went up to him gaily, provocatively, and stroked his face.

"Are you cross?"

"No," Sandro said and tried to put his arm around her waist. But she immediately drew away.

"It's too early. . . . At least give me time to get used . . . Anyway, I'm really not sure that I'll stay."

"What about having a bathe?"

"Let's."

She deposited her suitcase on the bed, took out all her toilet things, and arranged them one by one on the washing shelf. Then she took a canvas bag into which she put her bathing costume, her rubber cap, a handkerchief, and a bottle of sun oil, and said she was ready. They set out. Sandro walked a little behind her because he wanted to look at her without her noticing. But when they reached the square she calmly said: "Let's walk side by side. . . . I can't endure having you behind with your eyes fixed on me. . . ."

"I wasn't looking at you," said Sandro.

"Rubbish."

They crossed the square and took the short cut down to the sea. For some way the path twisted through bushy gardens whose trees only occasionally permitted a glimpse of blackened fronts of old villas in Moorish or Pompeian style. This was the oldest district on the island, Sandro explained, and those villas all dated back some fifty years. Then the path disappeared between two great rocks, and then they could see the sea at the bottom of a declivity scattered with enormous crags. The short cut zigzagged down between these crags. Its whitewashed parapet gave it the appearance of a gray hem, white-edged, that had fallen from the sky and gently deposited itself between the rocks.

"Where's the bathing place?" Sandro's mistress asked, stopping and looking over the edge.

"Down there," Sandro said, pointing to some faraway green huts ranged between the rocks along the water's edge at the bottom of the perpendicular island wall.

They began slowly descending the steep little cement road, then she increased her pace, quicker and quicker, and began running headlong, turning back laughingly now and again to glance at Sandro. They were breathless when they arrived and they made their way in silence along the earth footpath between the yellow, dry grass in the sun that burned their ears. Now the sea was near and was visibly calm. Gently, foamlessly, the water flowed irregularly over the stones of the shore, unrolling slowly like a carpet. The sucking ebb, fresh and sonorous, was audible on the rocks.

As they reached the sea they saw that there were only a few people there, occasional bathers, spread face downward on the beach, a towel under their heads, or else standing on the shore so that the languid fluctuations of the placid sea could flow over their feet. Sandro led his mistress to the bathing hut; she said she would undress immediately and locked the door. She emerged shortly afterward in a rust-colored bathing suit, pulling it up around her thighs and glancing about through her sunglasses. In his turn Sandro went into the hut, hastily undressed, and, leaving his trousers on the floor, emerged in his trunks. But she was nowhere to be seen on the terrace. Instead, as though Sandro had never existed, she was on her way down the steps that led from the bathing huts to the beach.

He ran after her and they walked side by side along the narrow beach consisting exclusively of big stones. The stones burned the soles of Sandro's feet so that he had to perform a kind of dance; whereas his mistress proceeded safely in her rubber-soled slippers. She looked for a quiet nook and as soon as she was seated handed Sandro the bottle of sun oil.

"Rub it on me."

Sandro took the bottle, uncorked it, poured a little oil into the palm of his hand, and began rubbing in on the woman's back. Her back was slim, and as she bent forward he could feel her spine under the skin which the oil made shiny and brown. When he had finished her back, she spread the oil on her arms and front; then she laid a towel on the rocks, reclined on her front, undid her shoulder straps, and pulled them down. In this position he could see her slight pale breasts crushed between her armpits and the ground. Her body, which skipped around gracelessly when she moved, revealed its harmony now that she was lying still. Her back had wide shoulders and grew narrower down to the slim waist. Her haunches were the only part of her that was fleshy and rounded. Her legs were straight from thigh to heel but they were well jointed and had no blemish. Her thighs displayed a slackening of the skin below her bathing suit; this was the only evidence which recalled that she was no longer young.

Sandro was also lying on his stomach, though he found the position uncomfortable. Approaching his face to hers, he asked: "What are you thinking about?"

"Nothing." She made no movement, her face was concealed behind her huge dark glasses, her elbows were on the rocks, and her head dug into her shoulders. Her hands hung languidly in front of her. They were fleshless, hard, nervous, with slim fingers separated and oddly folded and outstretched as if deformed. A big heavy ring with her family crest on the stone hung loosely around her thin forefinger.

Sandro was tempted by her hands, and the heat of the sun burning his back seemed like temptation too. At last he stretched out a hand and seized hers. She did not move.

"Your sweet hand," he said, breathing deeply.

The woman said nothing, but a slight quiver of the nostrils warned Sandro that she was annoyed. Her sharp nostrils always quivered like that, suggesting a dog that was going to bite. He had a feeling of panic and hurriedly sought for a more rational reason for seizing her hand.

"Where does this ring come from?"

"You must have seen it a thousand times," she said dryly. And with a rough gesture she pulled the ring off her finger and dropped it on the rocks.

"You're right. I've already seen it," said Sandro, returning it.

Someone walked past them, but all they could see was the long feet, soft and white, put down, then contracting and curling up on the burning stones.

"I didn't expect to see you again," began Sandro after a pause. "I'd made up my mind that if you wrote to me I wouldn't even answer." She made no reply.

"You've treated me abominably," Sandro went on, with the confused feeling that he was saying the very thing he ought to avoid, "and I know why it happened."

"Why?"

"Because I let on too soon that I was in love with you . . . and told you too often."

She got her bag, opened it, took out her case, and lit a cigarette. Then she offered the case to Sandro, who refused.

"I'm sleepy," she said. "Let me sleep for a bit." She lay her head between her arms and closed her eyes.

"How can you manage to sleep and smoke at the same time?" asked Sandro, trying to make his voice cheerful and self-possessed.

"I'll smoke for a while and then go to sleep," she murmured, the cigarette between her lips.

"It's impossible to do both."

"Why do you talk so much?" she asked rudely. "It's so pleasant in the sun if there's silence."

Sandro bit his lip and gazed around. By now the tiny beach was becoming crowded. Men and women lay on the burning rocks, some on their stomachs, some on their backs, as motionless as the dead. On the terrace of the bathing establishment which stretched among the rocks like a ship's deck one could see the naked backs of a row of bathers on the railing laughing and chatting with others lying in the deck chairs.

"I'm going to take a dip," he announced, getting up.

She said nothing. Sandro, disgruntled, walked away over the burning rocks. He passed beneath the bathing establishment and went in the direction of a rock which jutted into the sea like a promontory, thereby forming a little inlet where bathers crowded like wavelets at the height of the season. High up on this rock was a cement diving platform. Sandro disliked diving and wasn't good at it, but he hoped that once he had left his mistress she would stop dozing and watch him. He would then spring from the high platform, and when she saw him perform this deed of valor she might feel some revival of her love for him.

He scrambled over the rock, which was all holes and sharp points that cut his feet. The rock was white with salt and at the bottom of the holes between one hump and another lay green stagnant pools full of refuse and old paper. So, stepping from hump to hump, Sandro reached the platform. He mounted it and stood upright, thinking that his body must make a fine picture against the background of the sky. Then he looked down. Some four yards below him the green water with its bluish and white reflections hurried shimmering by, sparkling in the sun. It looked a long way away and made him feel dizzy. He wondered whether he should call his mistress's attention to the dive he was about to make and decided against doing so. But at the last moment an unknown impulse made him wave his arms and shout her name. He couldn't see where she was or whether she was looking. He shut his eyes, clasped his hands above his head, and cast himself in headfirst.

His fall seemed long and clumsy, like that of a rock or any other heavy, shapeless object. Then his head pierced the water and the rest of his body followed. He opened his eyes in a dense green light, struggled to free himself, and felt himself rising again. It seemed to him that he had traveled a long way, but as he emerged from the water he noticed that he was still beneath the rock from which he had jumped. With trepidation and exultation he struck out for the shore.

He found his mistress beside a basket full of sea urchins and an untidy-haired boy who was crouching beside her and opening the sea urchins with a knife and squeezing drops of lemon on them.

"Did you see me?" he asked, panting as he climbed toward her over the burning stones. "I dived from the top platform. . . ."

"You did do a belly flop," she observed. The boy offered her a sea urchin, split open and flavored; she cautiously took the black husk with its bristling spikes between two fingers and fastidiously ate the deep orange sediment with a spoon.

"Shall we go out in a boat?" Sandro proposed, for despite her caustic comments he still felt much heartened by his heroic dive.

"Let's."

Sandro ran to the water's edge and clapped his hands to summon the bathing attendant. He and the attendant pushed the boat into the sea. Then they each offered an arm to help his mistress in. She chose the attendant's arm and with a quick jump went to sit in the poop. Sandro leaped nimbly after her, took up the oars, and with a few pulls drew the boat out of the inlet. For a short while he rowed energetically, pulling toward the open sea. He wanted to round a promontory formed by a single upright sharp cliff. He knew that behind that rock there were no bathers or bathing beaches, nothing but the sea and the rocks. Meanwhile the woman sat in the poop with her back to him looking at the steep cliffs of the island.

The promontory was farther away than appeared at first sight. As they came below the cliff they saw that it was entirely surrounded by rocky banks half submerged and crawling with weeds over which the sea flowed to and fro, covering and uncovering them with the movement of the ebb. Sandro gave these banks a wide berth and reached the other side of the promontory. Here they found an inlet much narrower than where the bathing establishments were. The escarpments of the island looked like a castle at this point, with towers, balconies, and walls, and beneath the precipitous cliffs the calm water sparkled hazily in the sun, darkened by the seaweed beneath its surface, and filled with majestic solitude. In the depth of the cove, backed by the wall of the island, there was a little white pebbly beach. Sandro turned the boat toward this beach. The boat spun over the water, and the prow hit the gravel. Then he leaped ashore and offered his hand to his mistress, who also got out.

"Why have we come here?" she asked, looking around.

"Because . . ." Sandro said in a choked voice. "Well, so as to be more alone."

She looked at him attentively and then asked: "What time is it?"

Sandro glanced at his wrist watch and told her the time.

"It's late," she said. "We'll have to go back. . . . We'll have to eat early because I have to catch the steamer."

As she said this she made a determined move and stumbled over the rocks toward the boat. Sandro hurried after her, and just as she was putting her hand on the prow of the boat he threw an arm around her waist. She turned around with a questioning look. Without a word, Sandro put his lips against hers and kissed her. At first, as if by instinct, she returned his kiss; then Sandro felt her trying to withdraw and pull her lips away. Whereupon he put his hand behind her neck and held her head, which she was trying to free.

In the end they drew apart. Hastily, with her eyes downcast, she leaped into the boat, threw herself on the oars, and began unevenly pulling out to sea. Seeing her intention, Sandro leaped into the boat after her, snatched the oars from her hands, and gave her a push that made her fall into the poop.

"We must go back," she said in a dry, panting voice. "I've already told you often enough that this behavior doesn't work with me. . . ."

If at first I may have thought of staying here tonight . . . now I've decided . . . you couldn't have found a better way of making me leave."

"Liar. You'd already made up your mind to go. . . . From the minute you arrived you've done nothing but talk about leaving."

"Yes, I know, but perhaps I might have stayed. But as it is, it's finished."

"Yet you returned my kiss at one moment," he said with rancor.

"It's not true. You held my head and I couldn't get free."

A long silence followed. The woman had a faraway look and remained stiff and outraged while Sandro rowed. He kept close to the walls of the island. On the red rock at water level every slight backwash of the sea revealed the dripping beard of the brown and green seaweed under a white line of dried salt. Every time the water ebbed, the sea made a pleasant, gentle noise against the rock that sounded like a kiss. Beyond, the sun sparkled brightly on every ripple.

"All right, you're going," Sandro said suddenly with an effort. "But there's no need to stay in a bad temper for the couple of hours we've still got together. At one time you used to enjoy bathing from a boat. Let's let bygones be bygones; you have your swim and then I'll take you ashore."

Her glance showed him she was tempted.

"All right . . . provided you don't try anything else."

"But it was I who made the suggestion."

Sandro stopped the boat and the woman stood up in the poop. She put on her rubber bathing cap, pushing in the unruly curls. Then she tied it under her chin and looked at the sea. When her head was enclosed in the bathing cap she looked warlike, with her protuberant lips and irritated almond eyes. She stepped to the edge, lifted her arms, and joined her hands above her head.

"Please don't jerk the boat."

She bent her legs slightly, as though to try out their strength, and leaped. She fell faultlessly, headfirst, body following, and Sandro's last view of her was of her brown thighs—the rather slackened thighs of a woman approaching middle age—tightly pressed together, penetrating the water amid white foam. In the translucent water he saw her turn and swim away like a green and bubbling shadow. Then, as though thrust up by a spring, her head holed the surface of the sea at some distance from the boat. She was a good diver and swimmer and could stay a long time under water.

Sandro watched her shaking her head and swimming with spirit and energy, yet unhurriedly, toward the boat. When she reached it she gripped the edge with both hands and said, puffing a little: "It's cold."

"Do you want to dive again?" asked Sandro.

"No."

"Then I will."

He crossed the oars inside the boat, mounted the poop, and, without bothering to take precautions, for he had lost all hope of being admired by now, he plunged in headfirst. He fell badly, obliquely, and felt a pain in his side. He quickly broke the surface and blew his nose, looking around to get his bearings.

"What a belly flop," she said, unmoved.

"I know," Sandro answered, "but I don't care."

"If you don't take the trouble you'll never learn."

Sandro felt tempted to swim out to the open sea and leave her thoroughly in the lurch; she would possibly get into the boat and hurry after him. But instead he found himself, to his surprise, swimming toward her. When he reached her side he too caught hold of the boat. As he trod water to keep afloat, his legs touched hers, and gradually their legs became friendlily entangled.

"If I wanted," he said, looking at her, "I could take you by the shoulders and hold you under the water until you drowned. . . . No one could come to your rescue."

Returning his gaze, she answered: "Don't be funny. . . . I can't endure being funny in the sea."

"You call it being funny, do you?"

His mistress made no reply and Sandro, gripping the edge of the boat, leaped in and sat down between the oars.

"Listen," she said, "I'm going to swim slowly toward the bathing huts. . . . You follow me in the boat."

"All right."

She left the boat and began to swim toward the promontory.

In that dark, lonely inlet, shadowed by the rocks, her slow, vigorous strokes sent a sparkle of light below and around her, as when a school of fish swarms just beneath the surface of the water. She swam well and evenly, without crabbing a single stroke. Sandro grasped the oars and began rowing slowly. He felt at last that what she did no longer really mattered to him. He would keep his word, take her to lunch at a good inn and do everything he had to do, and then would accompany her to the funicular. Absorbed in these thoughts, he rowed on, dawdling. By now the sun had tired him; he bent down, took the cigarette case from his mistress's bag, and lit a cigarette. She was a good way away and looked tiny and lost beneath the high cliffs; yet the whole place, with its rock castles and lonely ebb and flow seemed like a theater backcloth for her swim. Then Sandro saw her stop and wave an arm as if to summon him. He began rowing briskly, and a few pulls brought him alongside her.

"I've had enough," she said as she gripped the boat. "I haven't got the stamina I used to have. I must be getting old. Help me. . . ."

Sandro dropped the oars and gripped her under the armpits. She struggled into the boat, took off her bathing cap, and shook out her flattened hair. Her muscles were still tense and quivering under the skin of her slim body, and the water did not stick to her skin but divided into great scattered drops.

"As a matter of fact, it's quite lovely here," she said after a pause, glancing at the deserted inlet glistening beneath the high walls.

"Why don't you stay?" Sandro asked, and as soon as he had said the words he was astonished at himself. "You could stay the night, bathe again tomorrow, and leave in the afternoon."

He was afraid that she would say no and thought: *If she answers grumpily I'll unhook an oar and crack her over the head.* But quite unexpectedly and to his great surprise, she beckoned and said: "Come here."

Sandro obeyed and went and sat beside her. She immediately turned, took his face between the palms of her hands, and kissed him on the mouth. Sandro had a fleeting glimpse of the tallest of the cliffs above their heads and then closed his eyes. For the first time in ages he experienced the savor of her mouth, the intoxicating wine of time gone by, so like herself, and he almost fainted at its sweetness. The moment he had so longed for had come at last.

When they broke apart he asked as if in anger: "Why did you do that?"

"Just because," she answered, smiling at him, "I suddenly felt a strong desire to do so."

Sandro said nothing but took up the oars again. He was in a state of great gladness yet great fear; gladness owing to the hope of renewing his much-regretted relations with his mistress, and fear lest he should take a false step and make a mistake that would once and for all jeopardize the rebirth of their love. It was like hunting some swift, nervous, evasive creature, such as a firefly or moth or bird, with the knowledge that the slightest sound would cause the prey to vanish. He must not make any more mistakes, he thought again; his behavior must be perfect. His mind concentrated on this subject, he went on rowing.

Meanwhile they had rounded the promontory and the row of bathing huts lining the inlet among the irregular rocks was again in sight. The beach was crawling with people. Many bathers were to be seen in the water, some in groups, some alone. A few white pedalboats were scattered over the open water.

"So you really want to leave today?" asked Sandro.

"I'll see . . . how I feel after lunch."

Sandro started rowing again and his mistress turned and fixed her gaze on the horizon. Sandro would have preferred not to look at her, but his eyes were inevitably drawn to where she was sitting. She had crossed her thin muscular legs and was smoking thoughtfully. Out of the blue and as if following a train of thought of her own she said: "I don't like the room you found me. . . . There's no running water."

"I thought you were only staying for one day," Sandro said, delighted, "but if you stayed longer you could go to a hotel; there are plenty."

"And are there good walks?" She loved walking; that and swimming were her favorite pastimes.

"As many as you like."

They had by now entered the inlet and were among the bathers laughing and splashing in the shallow water. Sandro took the boat ashore and the attendant ran up and helped them to get out. It was already late. Many of the bathers were getting out of the water, which had a hot, used look under the blazing sun; others, already dressed, were slowly making their way up the steep steps from the huts to the road. Sandro dressed first, then his mistress went into the hut. After a short while she emerged dressed, with her bag in one hand and the dripping costume in the other.

"Why not leave it here?" suggested Sandro, pointing to the costume. "The attendant will look after it."

"And if I leave?"

"Do just what you wish," said Sandro and began climbing the steps, turning his back on her. That was the right method, he thought—give her no importance, don't go pressing her and bothering her. When they were in the trap which conveyed them slowly up the steep road, he felt almost certain that his mistress would stay and that their love affair would begin all over again. The trap mounted slowly between luxuriant gardens and shady trees. His mistress talked to the driver, asking for information about the villas they espied through the clumps of trees, and the driver, half turning, answered in dialect. It was extremely hot, and no trace of tension and ill-humor remained. She was wearing an aquamarine dress, and against that color her warm brown arms were lovely to look at.

At one point Sandro began wondering whether or not he should take her arm. He remembered that in the early days they were together every time he took hold of her arm she squeezed his hand tightly against her side and gave him long silent glances with loving eyes.

The driver stopped talking, and now that they had reached the level he put the horse to a trot.

"How marvelous to have you here," Sandro said, taking her arm.

She didn't answer but straightened her sunglasses with her free hand, frowning.

"Elena," Sandro whispered.

"You haven't changed," she said, not with ill-will but as if making an undeniable observation.

"What do you mean?"

"This is neither the time nor the place for emotions."

A trap with a white horse that was younger and stronger than theirs drew level and overtook them. In it were sitting a man and a woman. They were holding hands, and the woman's head was resting on her companion's shoulder.

Sandro pointed to the carriage as it drew ahead and said: "The time and place are all right for them."

She shrugged her shoulders and said no more. The trap now began bowling between the houses of the village over large detached flagstones. People scattered in front of them as they went noisily forward. The driver cracked his whip, and the cracks made a cool echo against the houses.

They got out in the square. As Sandro was paying the driver, the woman purposefully went to the little funicular station.

"It looks as if I'll have to spend the night here," she said as they made their way together across the square.

"Do you want to go to a hotel?" Sandro asked crossly.

"Don't be stupid."

From the square they mounted a stairway leading to a covered gallery that ran like a corridor through the village behind the row of houses facing the sea. The gallery was completely whitewashed—with round white roofing, crooked white walls, white pillars—and it looked exactly like a tunnel dug through a solid block of salt or marble. Now and again one of the arcades opened, and then, in the bright light, they could discern the sea sparkling and blue as far as the horizon.

"I know a restaurant with a pergola overlooking the sea," Sandro said.

"I just want to eat, I don't care where. I'm dropping with hunger."

The terrace under the early green leaves and grape clusters of the pergola was deserted except for a couple of middle-aged foreigners lunching in a corner.

"There's some first-class wine here," said Sandro, sitting down contentedly. He knew his mistress liked drinking and became more affectionate when a little tight.

"This is another lovely place," she said, gazing at the sea through the flower vases on the terrace parapet.

"I told you so. Once you come here you never want to go away." He felt desirous of making some display of cheerfulness and self-possession. "I'll go and see what they've got in the kitchen," he went on and, without waiting for an answer, got up from the table.

The kitchen had a window with wide-open shutters giving onto the terrace, and he stood at the window and looked in. The short, plump proprietress was working the bellows for the stoves. Under the blackened hood of the fireplace stood a variety of earthenware pots, frying pans and saucepans. On a marble-topped table were heaps of fruit, bunches of greenstuff, and fishes of all shapes and sizes.

"What have you got to eat?"

"We've *polpi*," * the woman answered in a singsong voice without looking around, "we've potato pie, *melanzane*,† peppers and meat balls.... The meat balls are very good." She lifted the lid off a saucepan to show them.

"Give me two portions of *melanzane*," said Sandro. He wanted to give his mistress a surprise and take the dishes himself. The woman uncovered another saucepan and with only two ladlefuls filled two plates to the brim. Sandro took the plates through the window, asked for two pieces of bread, which he put under his arms, and went back to the table.

"What is it?"

"Melanzane. . . . It's very nourishing."

There was a pause.

"Now she's going to say she doesn't like it," Sandro thought. He felt a fool and thoroughly dissatisfied by his idea of going to get the plates from the kitchen. But to his great surprise, after tasting a little fastidiously on the end of her fork, she said: "It's very nice," and began eating with a will.

One of the little girls came and put a full flask of wine on the table. The bottle was big-bellied and of rough, thick glass made to look like the film of moisture on an iced vessel when it comes into contact with the warm air, and it had an orangeade label on it. Sandro poured out the wine in the glasses and drank; it was light and cool and welcomely thirst-quenching in the burning heat.

"It's good, isn't it?" he asked, putting his glass back on the table.

"Yes, very good," she said with feeling.

After the *melanzane* they ate *polpi*, followed by a tomato salad. Sandro imagined he was pressing her to drink, but it was really himself who was drinking. Drunkenness removed his timidity and the fear of losing his mistress. He almost began to feel that she didn't matter

---

* *Polpi*—a species of small polypus eaten fried.
† *Melanzane*—eggplant.

to him in the slightest; and yet he realized at the same time that he had never before cared so much about her and her love. The meal over, they sat facing each other in silence. His mistress opened her handbag, took out her powder compact, and began touching up her face. Her face looked cold and hostile. Sandro suddenly felt afraid she might feel bored and, remembering that in the old days she used to enjoy his funny stories, he said with a smile:

"I'd like to tell you a story . . . but I don't know whether you'd like to hear it."

"Go ahead."

"A certain lady had a lover. . . ." Sandro hated funny stories but he knew she liked them and he put plenty of gusto into the telling. When he came to the end she laughed in a provocative and flattering way; and with this encouragement he told a second, much spicier one. She laughed again, this time with real abandon, holding one hand on her chest and shutting her eyes. At this Sandro told a third story, but this one was so spicy that she laughed with reserve as if afraid of being compromised; yet there was more complicity in her guarded laugh than in the unbridled laughter of before.

"Now I'll show you a trick," said Sandro. He got up from his place and sat down beside her; and showed her the trick, one with match-sticks. This trick, too, had an obscene meaning, and she made him repeat it twice over so as to learn it.

"It's very easy," she said, surprised. They were now side by side and the terrace was deserted, for the foreigners had paid and gone.

"Do you love me?" Sandro suddenly asked and, bending forward, he brushed her neck with his lips. He could feel her neck trembling and stiffening beneath his lips and he thought it was a shiver of pleasure. She made no response. Her face was bowed toward the table and she held her cigarette between her fingers.

Heartened, Sandro took her by the arm, high, near the armpit, and squeezed. Then she turned on him in unexpected fury, her eyes flaming with dogged resentment, and gave his hand a blow.

"Don't touch me. Please don't touch me."

So violent was her behavior and her eyes so lit up with fury that Sandro was dumbfounded. His hand was smarting from the large signet ring on her finger. He got up, went around the table, and sat down in his original place.

"All right, I won't touch you," he said, "but as for you, you're incapable of love." He was racking his brains for something unpleasant to say.

"I can't bear to have hands touching me."

"Your heart has become arid . . . you're no longer young . . . you'll never be able to love again . . . worse, you have never been in love."

She suddenly blushed all over her face—with her a sign of mortification and pain. Sandro was astonished to see her blue eyes fill with tears.

"Let's go away," she said, getting up.

Sandro called the proprietress and paid. All the time this was taking place she stood beside him, her face turned obstinately toward the sea. It was perfectly plain that her eyes were full of tears and that she couldn't see the sea, sky, or anything else. The minute Sandro finished paying she set out hurriedly, leaving the restaurant ahead of him.

The streets were sun-drenched and deserted, the shutters of all the houses tightly closed, and in one of the cafés a loud-speaker was bellowing to empty tables. They crossed the square and began climbing the path to the convent.

For a while they walked in silence, and then Sandro said: "Had I known it would upset you so much I wouldn't have said that."

She answered at once without looking at him: "It doesn't matter. I'm nervous, that's all," and Sandro's heart rose again. There was no undertone of hatred in her voice.

When they reached the convent, Sandro felt in his pocket for the key, and she waited meekly for the door to open with the air of a woman who has already given her consent and knows that once indoors there will be no alternative but to make love. Yes, Sandro thought, they would now go to the bedroom, they would have a long embrace, and they would relax on the bed together. He felt a pungently pleasant sensation of security and impatience exactly as in the days of their first happy meetings.

When he had closed the door and they were in the corridor, he said: "This house may have many disadvantages, but it's extremely quiet. . . . It's ideal for resting."

"I'll go and sleep at once," she said. "I feel very tired."

They entered the room and Sandro shut the door. She went straight to the washbasin mirror and looked at herself carefully, lifting her lips back from her teeth.

Sandro would have liked to keep well away from her, but—he had no idea why—he suddenly found himself standing just behind her.

"Are you furious with me?" he asked.

"No," she said absently, still looking into the mirror.

"I thought you hated me."

She went on looking at herself and made no answer. Through the open window the glistening sea stretched as far as the eye could reach. From the garden below in the silence of the sun came the crowing of a cock. "Now I'll go to sleep," she said decidedly and went and lay down on the bed.

"What do you want me to do?" Sandro asked, standing in the middle of the room. "If you like, I'll go . . . but if it's all the same to you, I'll stay."

"It's all right. Stay." She was lying on her back one arm shielding her eyes. Her other hand went to her dress, which had slipped up above her knees as she was getting onto the bed, and pulled it down.

He ought not to take advantage of her unwilling invitation, Sandro thought, but should retire to the room next door. She would fall asleep, it might well be true that her nerves were a bit frayed, what with the journey, and once she had slept all would go well. But however convinced he was of the wisdom of these plans, he was unable to put them into practice. Instead, he drew near the bed and, taking care to make no noise or disturb the mattress, he sat down beside his mistress. She neither spoke nor moved. Her arm over her eyes, she seemed to be drowsing. Still taking care to be as quiet as possible, Sandro drew up his legs and lay down. It was nice to go to sleep side by side.

The woman took a deep breath that sounded like a sigh and made a half-turn toward the wall. But Sandro was already feeling incapable of staying stretched out motionless beside the woman he loved. He drew himself up into a sitting position on his elbow and, bending over her, he gazed at her.

She made no movement. Probably she was asleep and had not noticed him. For some while Sandro gazed at the arm which covered the woman's face and at the small part of her face that was still visible. Her arm was tough and strong, almost a man's arm, but her wrist was slim and she had delicate blue veins under the skin. Her eyes were covered by her arm and the only part of her face that showed was her lips, red and full and as if offering themselves. Sandro hesitated for a moment and then he slowly bent down and put his lips gently toward hers. He did not touch her lips but could feel the breath from her nostrils and smell the scent of her lipstick. He fully realized that, by behaving in this way, he was making yet another of the mistakes he had sworn to avoid; but he was unable to resist. He now bent over and put his lips against hers. He remembered occasions when their kisses in the torpor of the afternoon used to stretch on lazily and develop into silent and ardent embraces.

But scarcely had their lips met than she leaped up to a sitting position with a look of exasperation.

"So that's it. One can't have a moment's peace."

"I was looking at you and I couldn't help kissing you."

"But I want to go to sleep ... I'm tired ... so please leave me alone."

"But I love you."

"Can you possibly think I don't know it? You've told me often enough."

"I want to tell you as often as I like."

"And I want to be left in peace. Can you understand?"

By now they were both shouting, face to face. Sandro lifted his hand and slapped the woman on the cheek.

It was the first time he had hit her; and probably the first time in her life that she had ever been hit; she had always maintained that her lovers revered her. Sandro saw her eyes open wide with anger and astonishment.

"Now I'm going. . . . What a fool I was to come."

She lifted her feet off the bed and began making for the door. Sandro forestalled her, shut the door, and put the key in his pocket. Then, with a violent push, he threw her onto the bed. She fell in a sitting posture and cracked her head hard against the wall.

"Please understand that you won't stir from here."

"Help!" she shouted in a loud voice.

Sandro glanced at the wide-open window, thinking that someone might overhear their quarrel. So he went to the window and closed it. But the shutters closed together with the window and plunged the room into darkness. "Help!" He heard her shout again in the gloom. Her voice was now terrified and it was obvious she was afraid that Sandro wanted to kill her.

This idea infuriated him and he threw himself on the bed and seized her by the throat. "You'll stay here, do you understand?" He squeezed the thin, nervous neck tightly, but as soon as she began gesticulating and coughing in her suffocation he let go. Not really knowing what to do next, he went to the window and flung it open again. She was kneeling on the bed and clinging with one hand to the bedstead; the other she held to her throat in a fit of coughing.

"Get out," said Sandro, opening the door. "Go away if that's what you want. I'm not stopping you."

Still coughing she eyed him incredulously, and Sandro had a moment's hope that she would realize that she would not be in the slightest danger if she stayed. Then he saw her looking longingly toward the open door and realized that she was only hesitating to leave for fear of being held back again. "Get out," he repeated in agony. This time she did not wait for a second invitation but leaped off the bed and disappeared into the corridor. Sandro heard her going into the next room and locking the door.

"Now," he thought, sitting down on the bed before the still-open door, "she'll pack and rush to catch the boat." He hoped it was not true, but the noise from the next room—a noise of hurried footsteps and moving furniture—confirmed his supposition. He kept wondering whether he ought to go and beg her forgiveness; but each time the thought occurred he dismissed it, for he knew it would be useless. At last he heard the subdued creaking of the door of the next room being very slowly unlocked; his mistress was going, and making use of every subterfuge to conceal the fact from him. Her precautions seemed like an act of final and irremediable hostility and renewed his pain. He would have liked to tell her that she was free to leave openly and he would not move a finger to detain her; but he remained where he was. He heard her tiptoeing over the brick paving of the corridor. The front door closed so gently that for a moment he wondered whether

he had misheard. Then he looked out of his room and saw the door
of the next room wide open and the empty corridor and the general
desertedness.

He went back to his own room and without thinking began sadly
to smooth the crumpled bedcovers. Then he went out onto the terrace.

Between the tall red cliffs topped with vegetation, the sea was
dazzling in the sunlight. In the stillness of the garden even the hens
were silent. All that could be heard was the buzzing of the insects
taking advantage of the dog hours, nestling in the burned grass and
in the cracks of the arid earth. Sandro rested his hands on the balustrade and gazed at the sea. The shutters of the near-by room burst
open and the fair girl appeared on the terrace.

She set her short, pudgy hands on the balustrade and began gazing
at the sea too, out of her little inexpressive eyes. She really had magnificent fair hair, Sandro thought, but her rounded body looked
ridiculous in her brief doll's skirt. He noticed that, far from wilting
under his gaze, she betrayed her awareness of it by large and provocative
quivers through her muscular thighs and loins like a horse under his
master's touch. Her beautiful body formed a warm dark shadow beneath her transparent dress.

For a while she continued to gaze at the sea with all her flanks and
leg muscles quivering; then she turned to Sandro and asked: "Aren't
you going bathing?"

"I went this morning."

"I go in the afternoon as well."

"This afternoon I'll be going."

"Do you know . . .," and she named a locality on the island. "I always bathe there. I'll be setting out soon."

"We can go there together, then," Sandro said.

She looked at him questioningly as though she had not understood.
"You're going to bathe with me?"

"Yes."

"I'll go and get ready," she said, delighted, and she disappeared back
into her room. "I'll be ready in a minute," she added, appearing for a
moment at the window, and then disappeared again.

"All right," Sandro answered. Hands on the balustrade, he resumed his gazing at the sea. At that moment the church clock in the village began striking. Sandro counted the strokes, thinking of the steamer that would be leaving. It was three o'clock in the afternoon. He re-entered his room and went and sat on the bed.

IV

THE NEW ERA

The collapse of Fascism in 1943 opened one of the most tragic and thrilling chapters of modern Italian history. It was tragic because German, American, and British troops waged war on Italian soil, and air raids, combats, and artillery duels destroyed towns, particularly in the south, killing, wounding, or making homeless thousands of people. Not less disheartening was the civil war between the anti-Fascists and Fascists whose last entrenchment—the republic of Salò led by Mussolini and Graziani—did not fall until the spring of 1945. But all these momentous events seemed to heighten the general feeling of life, and the country was pulsating with new fervor. Committees for liberation united national forces and cemented the struggle for freedom with the blood of partisans who, in twenty months of fighting, suffered twenty thousand dead and forty thousand wounded. Great hopes sprang up despite ruin and starvation, and in a period of acute material and physical distress the air was filled with aspiration and spiritual expectancy. The true rebirth of Italy started during those fateful days of 1943 and 1944.

Then, in 1945, the war was over and Italy found herself with her towns bombed out, her power plants destroyed, her bridges blown up, her agriculture shattered, her economy ruined, a defeated country full

227

of roofless and unemployed people, where the prisoners of war, returning from all parts of the world, found only misery and hunger.

The Fascist and Nazi military might was broken, but the social con-
trasts and problems which had originally generated totalitarian domination were not yet solved; and Italy, the home of Saint Francis of
Assisi, the poet of poverty, was poorer than ever and still had a yearly
surplus of half a million men and women eager to emigrate overseas.
Political passions, suppressed or hidden under the dictatorship, burst
now into the open with redoubled violence. Despite the military
occupation by the Allies, who controlled both the administration and
economic life, and continued to treat Italy as a former enemy, dozens
of parties, from Communists to Christian Democrats, entered into the
arena and began a bitter struggle for power and control over the
masses. The referendum of the summer of 1945, which ruled out the
Savoy monarchy and established a republic by a margin of two million
votes, did not soothe the contradictions, and it took several years before Italy could reach a precarious political equilibrium within the
framework of a democratic regime. By that time a certain psychological
letdown replaced the former enthusiasm. A more sober and critical
attitude prevailed among the intellectuals. International tension, the
hardships of reconstruction, economic and social uncertainties, the
rise of Communism, and the reappearance of Fascism under a new
disguise, contributed to the killing of many optimistic illusions. It did
not, however, prevent the Italians from working hard and from displaying more vitality than any other people in Western Europe. In
fact, the liberation from Fascism seems to have awakened new forces
and rejuvenated the country. Italy emerges today alive and promising
in all fields of human endeavor, much more so than France, and it
would be easy to predict that her role in Europe is going to grow
rapidly in the future.

This comeback was particularly spectacular in literature and the
arts. Writers as well as other artists were working after the war in an
atmosphere of excitement and revolutionary ardor. Even in the early
fifties when general conditions were not too bright, the literary scene
in Italy appeared more alert and dynamic than in any other country
in Europe. And the amount of good writing and the number of talented young authors were amazing.

Many factors contributed to this literary renaissance. First of all, the liberation brought the end of government pressures and consequently an expansion of subject matter. It became possible to describe the days of Mussolini's regime and the horrors of war with complete frankness: young writers, such as Berto, Levi, Pratolini, Brancati, and scores of others did just this in numerous tales and novels. Secondly, a general re-evaluation of prewar writers in an atmosphere of free and unhampered discussion meant that some of them, such as Bacchelli, Palazzeschi, Svevo—the last to a more limited extent—acquired new and greater significance. Writers like Alvaro and Moravia, particularly the latter, seemed to find some release. They could express freely their spirit of revolt and anxiety. Escape into aestheticism and Aesopian language was no longer necessary. Soldati, Pratolini, Bernari, Vittorini, and many others attained the full measure of their strength only after 1943, and although their careers had started earlier, they were definitely part of the postwar revival. And then came the younger generation with Pavese, Jovine, Calvino, Marotta, Guareschi, Berto, and many others, altogether a whole company of literary debutants. Now a "facing of reality" was possible—and it took the form of a neorealistic approach, often in the spirit of the verismo and regionalism of Verga's type. This trend was coupled with the stylistic renovation which had started under Fascism. A relaxation or "unblocking" of the language made it more idiomatic, colloquial, and informal. The Americans, by the way, contributed greatly to this movement. Their naturalism had its effect also on several neorealistic storytellers.

The writer who most clearly indicated the passage from one era to another was certainly Carlo Levi, whose book Christ Stopped at Eboli was a typical example of a populist and regionalist narration couched in a neorealistic manner. Of course, it was written by a political exile and foe of the regime who could at last speak openly about all its evils. But even more significant was the fact that Levi was in a position to do what the Fascist generation has been compelled to avoid: he talked about people and events in a direct manner, discarding all verbosity, sentimentality, and preciosity. Instead of arguing and pleading, he drew and demonstrated. A painter by vocation, his words evoked concrete visual images which added new dimension to his descriptions. And since he received a medical education, he regarded the ills and follies of mankind with a clinical eye and never shied away from depicting filth, disease, and death, as clearly shown in his "The Massacre of Valucciole," a piece which also brings out his sense of contrast, his warm humanity, his love of freedom, and his simple and terse style. One might object that his works are journalistic reports rather than fiction, but this is typical of many neorealists: in their devotion to life material they turned out "first-hand" informative descriptions. Incidentally, this tendency was reinforced by the revival of journalism, which had always been an important part of Italian literature and was greatly bolstered by the liberation. One should not forget that the third page of almost every newspaper in Italy is devoted to stories, essays, and sketches or letters from foreign correspondents—in short, it forms a daily magazine, and it is often of high quality. Well-known journalists, such as Piovene, Monelli, Longanesi, and Montanelli, are also prominent short-story tellers. Montanelli's "His Excellency," a story built on a newspaper item as well as on personal experience, is an example of this kind of prose which aims at presenting the truth, however unpleasant, and accepts human nature as a blend of good and evil, of sin and virtue.

The younger artists assumed a certain challenging attitude partial to close-ups of misery, despair, and filth—a reaction against the genteel sugar-coated writings of Fascism or its pseudo-virile bombastic posturing. One could say that the slice of life became again the goal of representational writers—with this difference, however, that all of them remembered André Gide's remark that "the way an author looks at a thing is often more important than the very thing he looks at." Therefore, unlike their predecessors, they displayed a great variety of literary methods and devices. Some of them were attracted by studies of environment in the Flemish "still-life" manner. This is the case of two Neapolitans, Domenico Rea and Giuseppe Marotta: they both write in a light, humorous vein. Marotta indulges in anecdotes which offer him an opportunity to bring out the local color of his native city, and there is a sensuous quality in the fullness and freshness of his brush. Rea is more dramatic and socially conscious. There is a note of protest and bitterness in such superficially hilarious stories of his as "Piedidifico." He loves the picturesque and the grotesque, yet refuses to see Romanticism in misery and artistic beauty in beggary. Next to the rich oils

of Marotta and aqua fortis etchings of Rea come the benevolent carica-
tures of Guareschi, who poked fun at the very political strife which
created so much disillusionment. Don Camillo, Guareschi's chief character, the ebullient and kindhearted priest who opposes Peppone, the
communist mayor of a small village in northern Italy, has become
known throughout the world. In general, the humorous bent is very
strong in the new Italian literature. Dictatorships usually are harsh and
hostile to laughter, and Fascism did not make an exception—no wonder that Italy wants now to have a good laugh.

Among neorealists who had more ambitious aims, Francesco Jovine
emerges as a mature chronicler of the south, aware of its problems and
evils. In novels and vigorous tales, such as "The Flight to France," he
transcends regionalism by his understanding of large social issues and
his subtle treatment of characters and their confusion and frustration.
He refuses to idealize his heroes, and his critical directness and psychological incisiveness have an almost astringent quality.

Another prominent "regionalist" with populist leanings is Vasco
Pratolini. His early work depicted a section of Florence inhabited by
workmen, artisans, hoodlums, and prostitutes. His tales, written under
the double influence of Gorki and Verga, are often the disguised autobiography of a man who made good the hard way but has remained
attached to the poor folk of his youth. A strong resentment against
social injustice colors his novels and stories in a more obvious way than
those of Jovine. His depiction of environment and of social groups is
even more successful than his individual character studies, although in
one of his later pieces, "The Mistress of Twenty," he achieves two
striking portrayals: those of a little whore from a Florentine suburb,
and of her middle-class, baffled protector—who, by the way, is reminis-
cent of a Svevo hero. An expert storyteller, Pratolini adroitly mixes
humor with straight, almost detached, observation, and his stories are
as entertaining as they are revealing.

The neorealistic tendency found a highly personal and artistic ex-
pression in the works of Cesare Pavese, the excellent translator of
Faulkner and Dos Passos, Sherwood Anderson and Steinbeck, Walt
Whitman and Edgar Lee Masters. He wrote about the peasants of
Piedmont and the working girls and students of Turin in a sharply
realistic fashion, but he achieved that transmutation of life material

into a poetic whole which is the mark of true artistic creativity. His short stories, such as the delicately drawn "The Leather Jacket," depict situations and characters by inferences and hints, and he extracts an illuminating reality of imagination from the coarse surface of fact. The effects of Pavese's lyrical narration are not unlike those produced by Chekhov. Pavese avoided the crudity and sharpness of those who deliberately emphasized the physically shocking, down-to-earth details of everyday life.

Neorealism found its fullest expression in Italian movies; Open City, Paisan, The Bandit, Shoe Shine, Bitter Rice, The Bicycle Thief, and other popular pictures made by a score of talented directors were transcripts of life as it unfolded itself in postwar days. Although literature also strove to register the flux of events and to give a complete and true rendition of this changing reality, it simply could not compete with the cinema in immediacy of presentation, and it also lacked the unity and singleness of purpose of the camera. Some influential Italian critics claimed that neorealism was much more successful in the movies than in novels or short stories, and that after the death of Jovine and Pavese, the two most talented exponents of the populist and radical brand of the movement, neorealism lost its momentum. It is true that in the late forties and early fifties there was a close collaboration between writers and the screen, since neorealists became leading script writers.

In any case, the balance of neorealism is far from being drawn, and it would be altogether erroneous to write it off as a literary school. It is very much alive, and it continues to inspire and to exert strong influence. But it would also be a mistake to assume it as the totality of Italian modern literature, for the latter includes other currents as significant and as important as neorealism. Besides, it is next to impossible to put labels on living authors and fit them in tight compartments of critical classification. Their artistic evolution often takes them away from their initial positions, and although writers such as Bernari, Brancati, Berto, and many others are usually pigeonholed as neorealists, their latest works are written in a different and new mood. Carlo Bernari, for instance, was considered one of the senior neorealists—just as Corrado Alvaro was—and the recent reprint of his novel Three Workmen, originally published in 1934, seemed quite timely at a moment when critics were discussing the roots of neorealism. But while some of his stories are cruelly naturalistic, with an almost perverse pathological stress on disgusting physical and sexual details, others, such as "It's a Question of Degree," are whimsical grotesques with symbolic hints and psychological twists, presented almost as dream sequences.

The same transition from realistic narrative to the grotesque is even more obvious in Vitaliano Brancati, the author of "Bel Antonio," a story about an impotent seducer portrayed against the background of Fascist disintegration. Brancati's war stories, such as "The Cavaliere," blend gruesome factual detail, pungent irony, and trivial episode in their multidimensional implications. Their grotesquery resembles those monstrous shadows which the most innocuous objects often cast on a wall.

Another example of this change from direct representation to interpretation from some oblique and bizarre angle is Guiseppe Berto. At one time he portrayed the corruption and banditry of the postwar era amidst the ruins of a bombed city where teen-age streetwalkers and juvenile delinquents indulged in sex and sentimentality. Now, instead of resorting to crude naturalism, he writes in an ironic vein, as in "Aunt Bess, In Memoriam," that grotesque with a surprise ending which reminds one of O. Henry and also of some cinema techniques. It is noteworthy that Berto is also known as a scenarist of several neo-realist films.

Other writers connected with the cinema refused to be influenced by the naturalistic vogue and continued in the wake of what the French called "magic realism." In their stories, realistically treated situations and characters float in a vague, mysterious atmosphere. Such is the art of Mario Soldati, a successful film producer and art critic who began publishing his tales in the thirties but attained his true stature as a brilliant storyteller only after the liberation. His prose is both earthy and elusive, elegant in its precision and almost fantastic in its exploration of the complexities of the human mind. Some of his stories, such as "Nora," lack a real ending and leave the reader in suspense, with a strange feeling of premonition and foreboding.

This bent toward the fantastic is fairly prevalent in a whole section of Italian postwar literature, and one can easily see in it a sequel to the old "anti-reality" trend which had its roots in aesthetic experimentation as well as in a fear of modern complexities. It differs, however, from the surrealism of a Bontempelli. In the lyrical pieces of such writers as G. B. Angioletti, who is acutely conscious of Europe's cultural unity and sensitive to French influence, the fantastic assumes moral overtones and turns into a parable. Others, such as the pessimistic Dino Buzzati, have felt for more than a decade the impress of Kafka's metaphysical dreams and philosophical allegories. The disembodied men of Buzzati's "Strange New Friends" dwells in an artificial hell not unlike the heroes of Sartre's No Exit. Existentialist characters are projected against Kafkian lunar landscapes in many works by the younger authors as well. The next decade will show whether this will evolve into an important trend toward an abstract and highly symbolic art. It is difficult to believe, however, that Italian prose, so strongly entrenched in its traditions of concreteness and humanism, would take this direction. It is highly indicative that in the works of those Italians who refuse to follow the beaten path of neorealism, the fantastic is more often combined with the idyllic. This is, for example, the key to Italo Calvino's "This Afternoon, Adam . . . ," an eerie tale of charming cross-purposes, of humor and freshness. Its author, by the way, conveys in his other stories much more of the dramatic and of the grotesque.

Most of the writers who display interest in a symbolic interpretation of life are, at the same time, deeply interested in elaborate verbal compositions. While neorealists, with the exception of Pavese, use a colloquial, idiomatic style, the psychological, fantastic, and symbolic writers are interested in poetic experimentation and the devices and contrivances of the literary craft, and can therefore be related to the "prosa d'arte" tradition. The best representative of this complex prose with allegorical intent is, undoubtedly, Elio Vittorini. He, too, has contributed to the promotion of American letters in Italy and has been greatly influenced by them. The symbolic structure of his works reminds one of Faulkner. An author of varied interests and a man of intellectual enthusiasms, he had a turbulent career and went from sympathy toward Communism to a sort of Jungian mysticism, which applied the notion of archetypal patterns to Italian, and particularly, Sicilian lore and mores. "Uncle Agrippa Takes a Train" is an example of his rhythmic (and almost untranslatable) prose, in which humorous character sketches alternate with allusive images and which remains, despite occasional obscurity and preciosity, alive, emotional, and convincing.

All the authors I have mentioned and many others whose names I had—to my regret—to omit lest these explanatory notes become too long—make contemporary Italian literature rich, varied, and exciting. Whatever the differences in artistic credos among these writers, whether they are realists or symbolists, pursuers of fantastic dreams or of palpable realities, bent on social awareness or aesthetic isolation, they all display an emotional warmth which seems to have disappeared of late from most modern works on the Continent and in America.

The general dehumanization of the arts has hardly affected Italy. Italian writers are humane and compassionate, they sympathize with man's sorrows, with his plight on this earth, they rejoice in his brief and humble pleasures, and although they accept his fate with graceful wisdom and irony learned from the experience of centuries, they do not despair over the ultimate victory of kindliness and reason, and remain faithful to humanistic values. Their works make one confident about Italy; for there is great hope in the future for a country which over the last decades, despite all her trials and ordeals, has been able to produce such striking proof of vitality, imagination, and artistic vigor.

CARLO LEVI

The Massacre of Vallucciole

TRANSLATED BY BEN JOHNSON

I knew Giovanni Bardi in the early spring of 1944; we met at the home of friends of mine, the Nerinis, in a charming little villa set back among the hills of Florence. The Germans at that time were after me, I had to keep changing residence, and for a few days I had taken refuge there, with my friends. We spent the daylight hours, Nerini and I, in his garden hoeing to stay warm, whenever we were not with the womenfolk behind fast-closed doors tuned to the radio. Nerini is half English; a flower fancier, a lover of nature and the violin; he was educated at Oxford, and the lorn, melancholy greenswards of England have remained a part of him, a landscape in his soul, yearned for the more in those days of sterile citizen savagery.

That evening, we were near the radio, drinking tea and smoking our pipes, an uncured tobacco, a kind of smelly weed really, but the only thing available then.

And when the war was over, what . . . ?

Nerini dreamed of retiring into the mountains. There was an especially beautiful spot he knew of. A mountain, near the top a broad meadow, a wood, a spring, a grove of centenarian chestnut trees, shadowed places, splashing streams. He had determined to buy a piece of land up there and to build a little house and live, in peace, forever, with his wife and children and friends. And I was to join him there myself.

Didn't I know the Casentino? —Truly, the loveliest, most kindly, coolest place on earth: a secluded verdant paradise.

Indeed, there, among the chestnuts he had set his heart upon, was the source of our celebrated river, the Arno; yet no less celebrated was the fresh, lucent beauty of those springs, rising among the woodland trees. I must certainly have remembered Dante—

> The mountain brooks that sparkle through the grass
> Flowing down to Arno from the Casentin
> And freshening all the soft earth where they pass . . . *

Those mountain brooks, recollection of which so dolorously befits the damned in fevered thirst, were the very ones among which we were all to go to live.

The people up there are kind and gentle folk, far, far removed from the world and full of ancient wisdom. Nerini knew them all, the inhabitants of that valley which he visited every year and where he dreamed of returning for life. His housekeeper, in fact, huge, maternal, faithful Teresa, was one of them herself, a native of Vallucciole, above the mill of Bucchio, from that secluded green valley which runs from Stia to the top of Mount Falterona, the heights capped with fir trees and vagrant clouds. I had taken an especial liking to Teresa; with the simplicity of manner common to Italian women of that period, in a thousand little ways she did what she could to console me in my troubles: preparing for me from the few foodstuffs at her disposal the best dishes, or, in the evening, taking the chill from my lavender-scented sheets with a warming pan; and providing everyone with evidence and instance of patient, courageous serenity, of an equilibrium undisturbed by the hysterical, blood-freighted gale roaring across the plains of Europe and the souls of men. Amid the unrelenting lunacy of the day, how comforting, how simple were the women, how truly motherly, with their bearing of tender, resigned naturalness! Like inscrutable ancient goddesses, they were able to conceal from us even the throb of their hearts. Teresa, for one, must have been torn with worry; she was, in fact; and I knew it; but never did she permit it to appear, serving us tea with bread and marmalade attractively arranged on the tray, always with a broad, affectionate smile on her round peasant-mother's face. She must have been very worried, because Giovanni Bardi, her husband, was days overdue. He had left for the

---

* *Divine Comedy*, translated by Laurence Binyon. London: The Macmillan Company, 1952.

village, for Vallucciole, as he often did, to do some hunting and to take a look at the four chestnut trees on their farmplace, to see if he could bring back a little something to eat from the countryside. He had planned to stay away for no more than two or three days, but now a week had gone by; and only God knew what had happened to him, with the roads infested with Germans, the marauding, and bombs crashing down from the sky.

Nerini said that when the war was over, that's where he was going— up there, up into the woods. He'd have a fine white cow, a few sheep, a trusty dog. . . .

At that point the door opened and Bardi walked in.

There was something strange about him, something strange in his look, in his manner, his gestures. He was a man of forty or so, slender, gaunt, swift, with small darting black eyes and the springy step of the hunter or the smuggler. The clothes he was wearing were too large for him, swimming all about him: obviously, they were not his. And Nerini, who knew him better than I, remarked it at once.

They had been lent to him by the barber in Stia. His were gone. Then, too, he hadn't wished to be recognized. A terrible thing had happened.

And Giovanni Bardi began his story:

I left here last Wednesday, you know, after spending Easter with Teresa. It was very nearly our last one together. It's only a miracle that I'm here now.

The trip up went all right, without incident. But in Stia, when I arrived, everybody was down in the mouth and looked worried: something had happened. And the landlady of the inn, when she heard that I planned to go up to the house, warned me I'd better be careful. In fact, she said, if I had come the day before, she would have told me to turn right around and go back. But the danger was over then. Just that morning, they had burned down the mill of Bucchio and the settlement around it. Now that that was over, it was all right to go up: the Germans had left. But I had better keep my eyes peeled, even so. Of course, then I wanted to go up to the house more than ever, I was anxious to see if they had touched anything at our place. And there was that little bit of salami left to pick up, and chestnuts and tobacco to get. Then, too, I wanted to see exactly what had happened at the mill. So instead of spending the night in Stia, I headed straight for the mountain.

Just around the bend, I ran into some peasant friends of mine who were returning home. They had all left on Easter Sunday and had been hiding in the country. But now, since the worst was over, they could go home. They told me what had happened.

You know, there are partisans on the Falterona, up on top in the woods; sometimes they come down this way, into Tuscany, and sometimes they go down the other side, toward Emilia. Their headquarters must be in Castagno. Anyway, all of us in Vallucciole know them well. They're always coming down to get food from us; we share our chestnuts with them, and every so often, whenever we've slaughtered any livestock, our meat. In fact, I—those other times I've gone back to the house—I used to hike up to the woods to take food to them myself. They're a good sort. And they pay for everything they take. The miller of Bucchio—you know him, Signor Nerini: the one with only one eye, and he wears a black patch—he always used to take them flour. They've got hide-outs in the woods, and we know where they all are. We've always been smugglers in our town, they say: and there are no informers. Not even Fascists. So anybody was safe with the partisans, and there was nothing to worry about. Besides, who would ever go chasing up the mountain after them? Nobody. It was a fine place to hide the English. Which is why they sent them there from Florence. There were lots of them with the partisans, and some hidden in peasant homes. Up there, they had nothing to worry about. They'd never be looked for up there, they figured.

But a week ago Saturday—on Holy Saturday—the morning of April the eighth—up came an automobile. It had been quite a spell since they'd appeared in the valley. The car went all the way up to the mill, practically to where the road ends. But on the mill bridge there were some partisans who had brought down some wheat to be ground. They had heard the car coming up, while it was still a long way off; so they got on both sides of the bridge, and when it arrived they surrounded it with submachine guns and made it stop.

Who was inside?

Besides the driver, there were two others—two foreigners—in civilian clothes. They were trying to pass as English, but it was clear soon enough what they were—*Wehrmacht* officers. Also, the car was full of guns and military papers. They had come up to reconnoiter before making a raid. After they had given themselves away, they tried to escape; they tried to put up a fight, and the partisans fired and left them there, lying on the ground, the two Germans. But in the confusion the driver managed to escape and get back to Stia.

They let the Germans lie there. Then the partisans went back to their headquarters, and the peasants came outside and stood around in the road looking and all wondering what to do. They must have expected something terrible to follow. The Germans would be back. . . . In fact, a little while later the partisans came down again and went to every house alerting the people. They had learned from the papers taken out of the car that the Germans were planning a full-scale raid. The partisans themselves, since they were not armed well enough really to give battle, had decided to evacuate the area, and they were warning all the peasant men to go into hiding till things blew over. So the peasants decided to do this: the women and children would stay at home to look after the animals (after all, they were innocent and had nothing to fear), while the men hid themselves. And that's how they spent Easter Sunday: all the men like hunted animals in the woods, and the women by themselves at home.

The next day went by, and Tuesday also. Then, Wednesday morning, finally, the Germans, armed to the teeth, began rolling up by the truckload. Actually, they were Austrians, they said. They went up as far as the bridge and got out. They made the women come outside, and then they set fire to all the houses, drenching everything with gasoline. The mill of Bucchio and the four or five houses around it, and everything inside, were completely burned. There was nothing—they didn't let them take anything with them, not even a mattress. And everything that didn't burn, they smashed to pieces. The two dead Germans— nobody had dared touch them—: the soldiers presented arms and put the bodies in a truck. After they had destroyed everything, they told the women that they had been spared so that they could look and cry over the ruins: justice had been done, the reprisals were over; but the partisans would get it even worse, they said, when they were caught; the houses had been burned as an object lesson. Then they piled back into their trucks and drove away.

This had all happened in the morning; and along toward sundown, as I was going up the valley, the men were coming out of their hiding places and returning home. I went home too, which is up beyond the mill, a little out of the way. Everything was all right. But for some reason, I don't know, I didn't want to stay there alone; and I decided to go down to Vanni's, back toward Stia, and to spend the night with him. Which is what I did: we all ate supper together—me, Vanni and his wife, and their three baby girls. Vanni's wife fixed me a fine place to sleep and I turned in early because I was tired, and Vanni had done a lot of walking too.

Next morning—it was not even daylight—we were awakened by banging on the door and gunfire outside the house. We didn't have time to get out of bed before the door was smashed in and the house was full of German soldiers. I was half asleep. It must have been about five in the morning. One German, like a wild dog, snatched me by the arm and slung me out of bed, yelling: "*Raus!*" I tried to get dressed but he wouldn't let me. I just had time to get into my pants, but he wouldn't let me put on my shoes. He shoved and kicked me through the door; they did the same to Vanni too. I found him outside standing against the front wall of his house. There were already some others, from other houses around—all men. Vanni's house is one of the first in the dip coming from Stia. There were cases of hand grenades and ammunition stacked on the ground—and they were damned heavy; they made each of us put one on our shoulders and line up out in front of the house. We all had a German guard near us, with a burp gun leveled at our belly. We had to stand rigid. I had Vanni next to me, and we stood looking at the house. The place was still filled with Germans.

Vanni's wife and the girls—where were they?

They were still in the house. We could hear them screaming. The Germans were shooting inside and out. Then the soldiers came out and locked the door. We couldn't hear the children any more, but the flames—we could see flames, through the windows.

Then they shouted at us to form a file and march. Each of us had a German behind him. Vanni was in front of me, with his case on his shoulder, and he kept turning to look back at his house; but every time he did, his German stabbed him in the face with his iron pike; and me, whenever I slowed down, even a little—it was still dark and the path was stony—I could feel the jab of a baton point in my kidneys, and I could hear my German swearing in that falsetto voice he had. My German was small and blond, with a pale complexion and white eyes; he was dressed all in green and, with his helmet which was too large for him, he looked like a mushroom—a toadstool, I mean. God, what a monster!

Well, we walked. We walked for hours. Up the valley. At every house we came to, we stopped, and every time it was the same story. The Germans went inside: they threw the men out and gave them all an ammo case to carry: the line grew longer and longer. The women and children were butchered outright, in the houses. And the livestock too, in the stables. Then they burned everything down. The only thing that changed, sometimes, was the method: at one place they would use gasoline, at another incendiary grenades. And they killed with everything; they had a whole wagonload of an arsenal, and they used everything—grenades, rifles, burp guns, bludgeons, trench knives: everything! And we would wait until they had finished, and then the climb would begin again; on we went with our cases.

When the sun came up over the mountain, there was smoke trailing up all around us, and all the length of the valley we could hear screams: the crying and shrieking of women and animals being slaughtered, and firing and explosions, and up near the meadow on the Falterona, even cannon fire.

Our backs were aching, but we were careful not to stop and not to stumble. One old man, seventy years old—Lucherini—couldn't stay on his feet, and when he started to stagger, the German behind him emptied his magazine into his head.

They dragged the Orai brothers out of their house. You knew them, Signor Nerini—they were all born blind: there were three of them, all blind. They tried, they did try to carry the cases: but I ask you, how could they? And they said they were blind, but the Germans jabbed them with their pikes. And when first one, then another, and then the third tripped and fell with his case, they shot them in the head and left them, dead and bleeding on the trail.

All the way, I had that monster behind me, digging me with his pike. My blood was boiling. I didn't seem to be myself any more, but something else. I don't know what. Every time I felt that point in my back, I wanted to turn around and spit in his face. That little toadstool! But I kept on walking.

Along about eight o'clock we arrived in front of the Becherucci house. There, there's a little clearing in front and just beyond it a deep ravine thick with trees. We stopped while the Germans invaded the house. But here, what a riot there was! The house was large, and the family was large too; there were a lot of women, besides the families of refugees who had come up to get away from the bombing in the city. And the burning, with all the screaming, was something fearsome—awful! The Germans seemed crazed; they were like madmen on a rampage. Before killing the women, they beat them up. In the house there was also some good wine for the taking, which they took. At a certain point, my German—my guardian angel—who had stuck with me from the very beginning, wanted to join in the orgy himself. I saw him unhook an incendiary grenade from his belt and run to the corner window and throw it inside. Me—without stopping to think what I was doing—I made the Sign of the Cross, and before I realized it, I had dumped the case and was rolling through the bushes down the side of the ravine. I know those parts like the back of my hand: I was born there, and I've hunted in those woods all my life. When I had stopped rolling, the thought came to me not to go too far away because they might see me; I should stay right there, at the foot of the slope; then, too, there was a rock I knew of that I could hide under. A second later, I had reached it. I scrambled underneath and covered up with dry leaves and lay motionless, without breathing.

Two or three minutes went by, and then the Germans, up at the top of the ravine, opened up with burp guns, blasting away at the bottom, and throwing hand grenades over the side. I could hear bullets and shrapnel glancing off the rock. I was scared out of my wits. But I didn't move.

After a while, they stopped shooting. And then I could hear the fire crackling as the house burned, and later the crash the roof made when it caved in, and over and over a dog, a wounded dog howling somewhere. By then, I thought, the Germans must have left. From my little burrow under the rock, all I could see was a small patch of sky up above the edge of the ravine, and the branches of some trees near the top; I lay perfectly still, looking. Next thing, up on the edge, profiled against my little white patch of sky, I saw the green pants legs of a German, walking back and forth like a mechanical toy. Then I knew: they had left a guard to see if they could get me. I couldn't take my eyes off his legs; they were like the hands of a clock marking off the hours of my life.

How long had it been since daybreak?

It seemed like centuries. From under the rock I could hear screams and shooting, but all of it deadened by the distance, as if coming up from underground. I was aching all over, terrified, and I had lain there tensed for a long time. The legs went back and forth, back and forth, and after a while went away. At least, I couldn't see them. Only a tree trunk hacking my patch of sky in two.

Had the German left?

Actually, I thought maybe he was off to one side, out of sight—maybe even looking at me!

I lay there for an hour, waiting. Two hours. I can't say how long. Then, some time later, I heard something, like loose gravel sliding. I couldn't tell if it was the sound of the woods or the German again. My back and my arms and legs were knotted with pain; I couldn't stand it, under those leaves lying stock-still. I stared as hard as I could at the sky again; and at one point I saw some birds perched in the top branches of a tree just below the edge of the ravine, unconcerned and peaceful. They were two thrushes: I felt delivered. If thrushes weren't afraid to light there, it meant, then, that the German had gone. But had he really gone or just walked off a little? Maybe he was stealing up on me from behind and I wasn't able to see him because the rock cut off my view! Some more time passed. It seemed like hours. And then I saw a hawk come down and go swooping off to the left. If the man was still anywhere around, the bird wouldn't have dared approach. I decided to stick my head out. Then I slid out altogether and stood up. The house was still burning, but there was no sound of life near by. I stretched, and I moved about a little, without making any noise. I felt as if I had risen from the dead. But where could I go? That was the question. In the distance, all around me, I could hear sounds of the massacre: it was like a gigantic hunt with all the game at bay. And like a hunted animal myself, I crawled back into my shelter and covered up with leaves again.

I stayed there till sundown, with nothing to eat, waiting for night to come to be able to move under cover of darkness. My farmplace was not very far away and I wanted to go to see what had happened there. I didn't take the trail, but detoured through the woods. Standing back in the trees, I looked at the house and listened for sounds. Silence. I got up courage and went over and entered. The roof had collapsed, the room was a shambles, piled with rubble and burned crossbeams. In the corner, the wardrobe hadn't been touched, but everything inside was gone. I could see, first they had looted and then they'd set the place on fire. But under the wardrobe I did find a pair of old shoes. They came in handy, because I had decided to leave the valley that night, not to wait till the next day.

And I left. I set off through the woods toward Castagno. I didn't see anyone on the way: only fires burning everywhere in the night, and now and then I could still hear gunfire, in the distance. I came to a dairy farm where I met several friends of mine who live in Castagno. We didn't dare stay there, in the farmhouse. Instead, we went and hid in a shed out in the fields. The others stayed awake all that night; but I couldn't, I was too tired.

We stayed there, in the shed, for another two days: Friday and Saturday. Shooting was still going on and we knew what was happening. The worse day had been the first, but the hunt continued through Friday and Saturday too. And Saturday evening the Germans came down from the mountain and entered Stia.

As the sun set we could tell that the massacre had ended. The shooting stopped and a great silence settled over the woods. I took the mountain route back to Vallucciole. There was not a living soul to be found anywhere: all the houses were gutted shells. Everybody— everybody in my valley was dead. The carcasses of animals lay strewn in the fields and the open spaces. There was a smell of death, of putrefaction, and burned-out fires. I didn't dare go into any of the houses for fear of seeing too much death.

While I was walking down the footpath toward the mill, I came upon Masini. I found him sitting on a log in front of his house. He had escaped because he had had to get up early Thursday morning for something or other and had been able to hide. His women were all slaughtered in the house, and his baby daughter, only a year old—you must have seen her last summer, Signor Nerini, taking milk from her mother—they hacked her to pieces, for the fun of it, I don't know, and stuffed the pieces into a cardboard box: a shoe box. Believe me, Signor Nerini, I saw what was left of her myself, with my very eyes!

Masini told me more. The men, the ones I had been with, carrying the ammo cases—they were led from house to house all day long, while the Germans butchered and burned. Lots of the men were killed along the way, trying to escape or just faltering on the trail with their cases. Thursday evening, the ones who were left were taken out into that big field beside the Arno. Then they were lined up along the bank of the brook and mowed down by machine guns set up in a half-moon around the field. Only four, in all the confusion, and because it was already dark, were able to jump into the water and make it to the other side. The others all died there in the meadow. On Friday and Saturday, the Germans went back to a number of places, completing the destruction and looting the stables; after that, they went over to the next valley and started in again. There was less killing, but they raped the women, in front of their husbands and children; and they burned and looted; and in the evening they built bonfires and celebrated around them and sang their sentimental songs.

Then they came down to Stia.

I spent Sunday in Vallucciole. I didn't dare come out yet. I scared up a little something to eat. But I was too sick at heart to stay there long, and Monday I found courage and walked into Stia. The Germans had already left. The barber gave me these clothes I'm wearing. On the wall in the piazza the Fascist authority had posted a bill deploring the partisans' actions which had made reprisals "by our great German allies" what was called "a duty and a necessity." I went to the landlady of the inn and picked up my bicycle, which I had left with her before going up on Wednesday. That way, from her, I heard how it had all happened.

The troops responsible for the massacre were from the Hermann Goering Division: Germans and Austrians. Great numbers of them had arrived Wednesday night. They conducted a regular military operation. They split into three columns. One—the one I met—went up the middle of the valley house by house, while the other two, which had left some hours earlier, during the night, went up the mountain, along the two facing ridges, toward the Falterona. That way, they surrounded the whole valley and blocked all escape routes. At the head of the valley, near the top of the mountain, there's that big open field. All the peasants living in the upper end, hearing the shooting approaching from below, who had time to take that one way out, ran for their lives, hoping to hide in the woods on the Falterona. But in the night the Germans had already set up machine gun and mortar positions. They let the peasants reach the middle of the field and then, for sport, picked them off, one by one, like snipes on the wing.

In all the valley only eighteen persons survived: the four that got across the Arno, Masini, the miller of Bucchio, myself, and a handful of others. But four went out of their minds; they had to be taken to the asylum in Arezzo.

The slaughter went on for three days, and then—this is what the landlady told me—"They returned to Stia. But the very day they got back, nineteen young boys arrived in town. Who knows who they were? Workmen, maybe, looking for jobs, or perhaps young fellows who wanted to join the partisans. They were unarmed and didn't have identity cards. They were walking up the road to the mountain when the Germans picked them up and brought them all back here. Then they took them to the graveyard and shot them. Maybe we'll never know who they were.

"The Germans," the landlady said, "acted as if they had just left a party. They drank up everything in town, and when the wine and beer and liqueur, which they ransacked all the houses and shops for, were gone, they gorged themselves on everything they could lay hands on, like swine. In the shop next door there was nothing left but some substitute of lemon concentrate, called 'limonene.' I saw one German fill a carafe with the powder and pour some beer in over it—the concoction was almost solid—and then drink the stuff with bright, shiny eyes and happy satisfaction.

"The officers came here to the inn to eat. I was terribly frightened; I tried to give them good, quick service: God knows, I didn't want anything to happen to me! There was a baby-faced blond, a commandant, who ordered me to make him an omelet with thirty eggs! 'Thirty?'—I couldn't help but repeat it. 'You mean thirty?' The German looked at me and said: 'That's right, thirty—and be quick about it!' And he took a hand grenade out of his haversack and swung it by the cord in front of my nose. I ran back to the kitchen and made him his monstrous omelet. And he ate it too."

This was Giovanni Bardi's story. Some days later a number of partisan friends of mine, led by Faliero Pucci, came down and I had a chance to talk with them: they were of the group that had killed the two Germans. Bardi's story was true from beginning to end. And shortly after the liberation I went up to Stia myself, and I met the barber and the landlady of the inn, and, in the graveyard, stood at the tomb of the nineteen unknown youths. It was summertime, and down through the deserted valley of Vallucciole a cool breeze from the mountain swayed the fir fronds over the mountain brooks that sparkle through the grass. . . .

INDRO MONTANELLI

His Excellency

TRANSLATED BY UGUCCIONE RANIERI

There it is, lined up with the other sixty-four from the Fossoli concentration camp, and the crowd has sprinkled it, like the others, with flowers. Among all these people gathered here in the silence of the Milan cathedral, surely I am not the only one to know. Yet there has been no protest. Truly, men are as lenient to the dead as they are harsh with the living. The coffin will now pass like the others between the reverent throngs, like the others it will be buried and, on June 22 of each year, will receive its quota of rhetoric spilled over the common grave. Fair enough. . . . Who are we to judge?

His Excellency, General Della Rovere, army corps commander, intimate friend of Badoglio's and "technical adviser" to General Alexander, was locked up by the Germans in the San Vittore prison of Milan in the spring of 1944 when the Allied armies were still fighting their slow way up the Italian peninsula. He had been captured near Genoa while trying to land at night from an Allied submarine to take command of the resistance movement in the north. A soldier to his finger tips, he had impressed even Franz, the German warder, who would stand at attention when addressing him and had gone so far as to have a cot placed in his cell. So the Italian guard, Ceraso, informed me as he passed my spy hole with a rose in a glass, picked expressly for His Excellency. Later Ceraso returned to say that the General wished to see me, and, letting me out, escorted me to his cell.

"Cavalry officer" was written all over those arched legs, that slight build, and aristocratic profile. Tight-corseted, he wore a monocle and false teeth, and the thought struck me of how convincing, after all, is our racial destiny. What else could a man like that become if not a general? With steely grace he could give an order and make it sound like a plea, and even now, weeks after his capture, his cheeks were cleanshaven, his trousers miraculously pressed, while one could almost detect on his polished shoes a pair of invisible spurs.

"Montanelli, I presume?" he said with a slight drawl, polishing his monocle without giving me his hand. "I already knew of your presence here before landing. Badoglio in person had informed me. His Majesty's Government is following your case with the utmost sympathy. Let it be understood, however, that the day you face the firing squad you will have done no more than your duty. Please stand at ease." Only at these last words did I realize that I was standing heels joined, thumbs touching the seams of my trousers just as the drill book says. "We are all on temporary duty here, right?" he continued, cleaning the nail of one little finger with the nail of the other. "An officer is at all times merely on temporary duty, he is a *novio de la muerte*, as the Spaniards say, a bridegroom of death." He smiled at me, paced leisurely up and down the cell flexing his slim, arched legs; then, stopping again before me, cleaned and replaced his monocle. "We two are very near our wedding day," he continued. "My sentence has already been pronounced. And yours?"

"Not yet, sir," I answered almost mortified.

"It will be," he went on. "You will have the honor of being shot in the chest, I hear. Splendid. There is no better proof of your conduct under interrogation. The Germans are rough in obtaining confessions but chivalrous toward those who abstain. Good. Your orders are to continue. In case of torture, if you feel you must utter a name—I cast no doubt on your spiritual endurance, but there is a limit to the physical—utter mine. I have nothing to lose. Actually, I had nothing to hide even from my old friend, Marshal Kesselring, when he questioned me. I did, however, explain that I hardly expected the British submarine captain to be such a fool as to answer the decoy signals of a German patrol boat. 'You trust the English?' Kesselring smiled. 'Why not? We even trusted the Germans once,' I smiled back. 'Sorry!' he said, 'I have no choice but to shoot you.' 'No hard feelings,' I concluded.

But to come back to your case: when you are up for questioning again, stick to your line. After all, we have such a simple duty left: to die like gentlemen. What is your indictment?"

I explained my case fully. His Excellency listened with his eyes to the ground like a confessor, nodding approbation from time to time.

"A clear case," he concluded. "Captured in the performance of duty. It's a soldier's death. They absolutely must shoot you in the chest. It's strictly regulations. Let me know how things develop. You can go now."

That was the first day in all the six months since my arrest that I did not think of my wife locked in her cell in another wing of the building. Toward evening I begged Ceraso to sign me up for the barber the next day and in the meanwhile to bring me a comb. And that night, braving the cold, I took my trousers off before lying on my plank and hung them on the window bars hoping they would regain their shape.

On the following days, through my spy hole, I was able to observe His Excellency in his cell just across from mine. One by one, all the prisoners were called to report to him, and all came. In theory, our wing, the dreaded Fifth, was for "solitaries" and so it had been up till that time, but the prestige of His Excellency was obviously so great that the Italian warders felt they could stretch a point. On entering, his guests would stand at attention, even the Communists, and bow stiffly. Later, on leaving, they would walk with a prouder carriage. Number 215, who so often sobbed for his wife and children, after talking with the General fell silent, and even when caught smoking by Franz took his lashes without a whimper. Ceraso told me that almost all, after their talk, had asked, like me, for the barber, a comb, and a little soap. Even the warders now wore their caps straight and tried to speak correct Italian. The wing had never been so quiet, and when Müller came on inspection he praised the new discipline. For the first time he omitted calling us "anti-Fascist dogs" and "dirty Badoglian traitors," confining himself to an allusion to the "felonious King," at which we all looked at the ceiling pretending not to hear, while His Excellency, who was standing a little forward as befitted his rank, turned deliberately on his heels and re-entered his cell. Müller snorted, but said nothing.

One morning Colonel P. and Colonel F. were taken. Asked if they had a last wish, they mentioned the General, who received them on his threshold, and that was the only time I ever saw him shake hands. Then, caressing with a slow gesture his silvery hair and adjusting his monocle, he smiled and said something to the two officers—something cordial and tender, I am sure. Suddenly, snapping to attention and fixing them coldly in the eyes, he gave them the military salute. P. and F. were pale as chalk, but smiling, and never had they looked so much like colonels as when they moved off, erect, with firm step, between the S.S. men. We heard later that they had both cried, "Long live the King" as they fell.

That same afternoon I was taken down for questioning, and Müller warned me that this was my last chance and that if I did not speak up, etc. . . . But I hardly heard, nor, though I kept my eyes glued to his, saw him. All I could see were the two pale faces of P. and F. and the marblelike face of His Excellency, and all I could hear was his drawling soft voice . . . "novio de la muerte" . . . performance of duty . . . death on the field. . . ." Müller gave me up without torture after two hours. Even if he had tortured me, I believe I would not have uttered a word, not even the name of His Excellency, in front of whose cell, on my return, I begged Ceraso to let me stop.

Della Rovere was sitting on the edge of his cot. Putting down his book, he stared at me at length while I stood at attention. Then he said slowly: "Yes, indeed. I expected as much of you," and dismissed me with a gesture. But on the threshold he called me back. "Just a second!" and he rose to his feet. "There is a thing I still wish to say. A—uhm—difficult thing. I am, I wish to say, extremely satisfied with your conduct, Captain Montanelli. And I wish this good warder to listen well, for he will be our only surviving witness. Very, very satisfied. . . . A jolly good show, sir!" And that night, for the first time, I felt alone in the world, joyously alone with my beautiful bride, Death, forgetful of my wife and my mother, and for once my Country seemed to me a real and an important thing.

I never saw him again, but after the liberation I gathered the details of his end from one of the survivors of Fossoli.

His Excellency appeared very put out when suddenly, together with a crowd of other San Vittore inmates, he was packed into a boxcar train and shipped to the Fossoli Lager. During the journey he sat on

the kit packs which his fellow prisoners had laid down as a seat for him and refused to rise even when Schultze came in for inspection. Schultze struck him, shrieking: *"Du bist ein Schwein, Bertoni!"* *
But the General found it superfluous to explain that he was not Bertoni, but Della Rovere, a corps commander, friend of Badoglio's and technical adviser to Alexander. Without a twitch he picked up his monocle, luckily unbroken, replaced it, and remained seated. Schultze went out cursing.

At Fossoli, His Excellency no longer enjoyed the little favors he was used to. He was placed in a common shed and put to work. His companions took turns in sparing him the more humiliating tasks like latrine duty, but never, of his own initiative, did he shirk a job, even though manual labor weighed heavily on him, for he was no longer young. Digging, or carrying bricks, often with a grimace of pain, he would keep a sharp eye open to see that no one gave a poor show, and at day's end he would reprimand those who needed it. To him, they were all officers and gentlemen, and such did they continue to feel under the flash of his monocle and the lash of his words. Desperately, heroically, he struggled to keep his nails spotless and his cheeks shaven. He never complained.

Neither then, nor later, was the motive for the June 22 massacre ever made clear. The order came from Milan, some said as a reprisal for something which had happened in Genoa. Lieutenant Dickermann read out the sixty-five names drawn by lot from those of the four hundred inmates lined up in a square. Among the first was the name Bertoni. No one stepped forward. "Bertoni!" roared Dickermann. "Ber-to-ni!" and he stared at the point where Della Rovere stood. Did Dickermann understand, or did he merely choose to humor a dying man? *"Gut, gut,"* he chuckled. *"Della Rovere, wie Sie wollen. . . ."* †
All held their breath as they watched His Excellency slip his monocle into place and take three slow steps forward. "General Della Rovere, please!" he corrected, taking his place by the other doomed men. With the nail of his right forefinger he began to clean the nail of his left—both marvelously steady.

The sixty-five were manacled, blindfolded, and pushed against the

---

* "You are a pig, Bertoni!"
† "Well, well, Della Rovere, if you want it."

wall. Only His Excellency refused to have his eyes covered and was humored. Then the machine guns were set. His Excellency took a step forward. "Hold it! Stop!" cried Dickermann reaching for his revolver. His Excellency took another step. "Gentlemen!" he cried with a voice like a bugle. "In this supreme moment let our thoughts rise . . ." But Dickermann's "Fire!" and the opening crash of the guns cut him short. They all went down. But the General was the only one who did not squirm on the ground, and his monocle remained miraculously in its place. It was still on when they dropped him into the common trench, and he is still wearing it, I assume, there in his coffin.

That coffin which today, June 22, anniversary of the massacre, stands before me in the Milan cathedral, does not contain the body of the imaginary General Della Rovere—true enough! Merely the remains of the former jailbird Bertoni, a Genoese, by profession cardsharp and thief, who, when arrested by the Germans for some petty crime, offered to spy for them in prison by impersonating a non-existent general, and succeeded only too well. . . .

Does it really matter? Surely the Cardinal Archbishop did no wrong in blessing this body together with the others?

For, after all, Bertoni, the cardsharp, the thief, the spy, was indeed a general at the hour of death, and undoubtedly he died convinced that he was the friend of Badoglio's and "technical adviser" to Alexander. But for him, I would never have felt a hero for one night in my cell. . . . And P. and F. would not have walked to the firing squad as colonels should. . . . Because of him, those who lacked courage found it, and Number 215 stopped whimpering for his wife and children. . . .

Peace to his twisted soul.

GIOVANNI GUARESCHI

The Petition

TRANSLATED BY FRANCES FRENAYE

Don Camillo was walking quietly along the Low Road toward the village, smoking his usual cigar, when, just around a curve, he came upon Peppone's gang. There were five of them, and Smilzo was in charge. Don Camillo looked at them with frank curiosity.

"Are you planning to bump me off?" he asked them. "Or have you some better place in mind?"

"Don't you dare incite us to violence!" said Smilzo, taking a sheet of paper out of an envelope and unfolding it before him.

"Is this for the last wishes of the condemned man?"

"It's for everyone that wants peace to sign," said Smilzo. "If you don't sign, then you don't want peace. From now on, honest men and warmongers are going to be clearly divided."

Don Camillo examined the dove printed at the top of the paper.

"I'm an honest man," he said, "but I'm not signing. A man that wants peace doesn't have to testify to it with his signature."

Smilzo turned to Gigo, who was standing beside him.

"He thinks this is a political move," he said. "According to him, everything we do is tied up with politics."

"Look, there's no politics in this," put in Gigo. "It's just a question of preserving peace. Peace is good for all political parties. It will take a lot of signatures to get us out of the Atlantic Pact, and if we don't get out, it's going to get us into a war, as sure as shooting."

Don Camillo shook the ashes off the end of his cigar.

"You'd better get going," he said. "If I'm not mistaken, you haven't even started."

"Of course not. We wanted you to have the honor of being the first name on the list. That's only natural. When peace is at stake, the clergy ought to take the lead."

Don Camillo threw out his arms. "It can be taken for granted that the clergy's in favor of peace, so it's just as if my signature were there."

"Then you are not going to sign?"

Don Camillo shook his head and walked away.

"If we're saddled with a clergy of this kind, then we'll have to fight not one war but two," Smilzo said bitterly, putting the paper back in the envelope.

A little later Peppone arrived at the rectory door.

"No politics involved," he declared. "I'm here in the capacities of mayor, citizen, father of a family, Christian, and honest man."

"Too many people!" exclaimed Don Camillo. "Too big a crowd! Come in just as Peppone, and leave the rest outside."

Peppone came in and sat down.

"We've come to the ragged edge," he began. "If honest men don't stick together, the world's headed for a smashup."

"Sorry to hear it," Don Camillo answered seriously. "Is there anything new?"

"Only that if we don't safeguard peace, everything's going to pieces. Let's leave politics and parties out of it and all get together."

Don Camillo nodded. "That's the way I like to hear you talk," he said. "It's about time you cut loose from that brood of Satan."

"I said we'd leave politics out of it," retorted Peppone. "This is a time for thinking in world-wide terms."

Don Camillo looked at him with astonishment, for he had never heard him mouth such big words.

"Do you want peace or don't you?" asked Peppone. "Are you with Jesus Christ or against Him?"

"You know the answer."

Out of his pocket Peppone took the envelope and paper Don Camillo had seen earlier in the day.

"When it comes to fighting for peace, the clergy must be in the front line," he asserted.

Don Camillo shook his head. "You're changing the rules of the game. Didn't you say politics wasn't in it?"

"I'm here as a plain citizen," Peppone insisted.

"Very well, then, as one citizen to another, I tell you I'm not biting." And as Peppone started to rise excitedly to his feet, he added: "You know very well that if I sign your paper, a lot of other signatures will follow. Without me, you can only hope for those of your own people, and a lot of them can't write their own names. Since you see that I'm not to be taken in, put that pigeon back in your pocket and hand me two glasses from the sideboard. Otherwise, you and your pigeon and your cause of peace may as well go back where you came from."

Peppone tucked the paper away.

"Since you're giving yourself such airs," he said proudly, "I'll show you that I can get all the signatures I want without yours as an attraction."

Smilzo and the rest of the "peace gang" were waiting outside.

"Start making the rounds," said Peppone. "But go to our people last. Everyone's got to sign. Peace must be defended with blows if necessary."

"Chief, if I go to jail, what will happen?" Smilzo asked him.

"Nothing will happen. A man can serve the cause perfectly well in jail."

These words were not exactly comforting. But Smilzo set out, with the gang at his heels, strengthened by some reinforcements from the People's Palace.

Now, when people have haystacks and vineyards and fields, it's almost impossible for them to say no to a fellow who asks them to sign up for peace and swears politics doesn't enter into it. And in a village the first five or six signatures are what count. It took several evenings to cover the whole area. But there were no arguments, except from Tonini, who shook his head when they showed him the paper.

"Don't you want peace?"

"No," said Tonini, who was a fellow with hands as big as shovels. "I happen to like war. It kills off a lot of rascals and clears the air."

Here Smilzo made a very sensible observation.

"But you know, of course, that more honest men are killed off than rascals?"

"But I care even less for honest men."

"And what if you get killed yourself?"

"I'd rather be killed than sign a paper. At least, when you die, you know where you're going."

The gang started to come forward, but Tonini picked up his shotgun, and Smilzo said he needn't bother.

Everything else went smoothly, and when Peppone saw the sheets full of signatures, he was so happy that he brought his fist down on the table hard enough to make the People's Palace tremble. He compared the peace list with the village census and found that they tallied. The mayors of the neighboring villages complained that they couldn't get people to sign because the reactionaries obstructed them. There had been shooting at Castellina and fisticuffs at Fossa for a whole day. And to think that Smilzo, after taking an hour to persuade each of the first five or six signatures, had won over the rest without a murmur.

"It's the prestige I enjoy as mayor," said Peppone, and he gathered together the papers and went to savor his triumph.

Don Camillo was reading a book when Peppone appeared before him.

"The power of the clergy is on the decline!" Peppone announced to him. "I thank you in the name of world's democracies for not having signed. Your signature wouldn't have brought in half as many others. It's too bad for the Pope, that's all." And he added, spreading his papers out on the table, "America's done for! The Atlantic Pact is no good, because we have a totality of votes against it. And everywhere else it's going to be the same way."

Don Camillo scrutinized the lists carefully. Then he threw out his arms. "I'm sorry to tell you, but one signature is missing. Tonini's. So you can't claim a 'totality.'"

Peppone laughed.

"I have all the rest," he said. "What is one against eight hundred?"

Don Camillo opened the drawer, took out some papers, and scattered them in front of Peppone.

"You have signatures against the Pact and I have signatures in its favor."

Peppone opened his eyes wide.

"Russia's done for," said Don Camillo. "Because I have Tonini's signature along with the rest."

Peppone scratched his head.

"There's nothing so remarkable about it," Don Camillo pointed out. "I worked by day, and your men went around by night, when people were already softened up. As a matter of fact, they were glad to sign for you, because that canceled their signing for me. The only one who didn't like it was Tonini, because I had to knock his head against a wall. But I advise you not to go after him, because he says that before he'll sign another petition he'll shoot to kill."

Peppone took his papers away. And so it was that in Don Camillo's village, America triumphed by one to zero, all on account of Tonini.

FRANCESCO JOVINE

The Flight to France

TRANSLATED BY ANGUS DAVIDSON

1.

For five generations the Milone family of masons and bricklayers had been responsible for repairs at the Caramanicos' house; and for two generations they had been receiving baptism and confirmation at the hands of that lordly family. The last of the Milones had been named Alberto because his young godmother was called Albertina. Signorina Albertina had renounced Satan on his behalf; she had held him tightly in her youthful arms and had said laughingly, "He doesn't like salt," when the priest had placed the salt of wisdom upon the baby's little lips.

From time to time Signorina Albertina used to recount this amusing episode to her godson when she gave him her plump hand, smelling of lilies of the valley, to kiss.

Now that Alberto had been working for a month in the Casa Caramanico he used often to kiss Don Ferdinando's hand, too, and the latter would say to him, with a kind of melancholy apprehension, "Go easy with those bricks!"

And so Alberto went easy, with the bricks.

They had given him the job of repairing the floors in some rooms in the right wing of the house, which had been uninhabited for many years and was now to become the private apartment of the lawyer Michele, son of Don Ferdinando, who had vague projects of marriage and of living an independent life.

Alberto would go to the rooms that had to be put in order and would fling open the windows that looked out over the open country. It was the month of May, and the sun rose vigorously and swiftly in the clear heavens. At that hour the peasants were already scattered over the fields, and around the house that rose, decrepit but proud, among a heap of gray huts, lay a gentle silence.

Alberto would remove the broken bricks that no longer adhered to the floor and would spread the hole with mortar; then he would adorn the new brick with an edging as white as curdled milk and put it in its place, striking it slowly with light taps from his mallet.

He worked slowly, scarcely bending his muscular body; it looked as if he were taking pains to restrain the energy of his big frame while accomplishing so light a task.

He had a bony jaw, a wide, thin mouth, and his low forehead was crowned with violent, bristling hair.

2.

When the sun reached him he raised his head and waited for something to come to him out of the air. And he did, in fact, hear a church bell calling the faithful to the second mass. The bricklayer smiled. After a few moments Maria Vincenza, the old servant who opened the door to him in the mornings, came into the room. She entered in a circumspect manner, as if she were just going to perform some forbidden act. She kept one hand hidden under her apron, from the sides of which came two little puffs of steam. It looked as though her aged lap must contain some secret fountain of heat.

Looking cautiously around her, she went over to the bricklayer and pulled out a coffeepot full of coffee and a big slice of bread. "Here's something for you, my boy," she said; and then she stood looking at him with her hands on her hips.

Alberto gulped it down voraciously, not so much because he was hungry as because he was in a hurry. Old Don Ferdinando might make his appearance at any moment and discover this midmorning attention, which did not form part of their agreement.

"D'you feel better now?" asked the old woman when she saw that Alberto had finished. "You're big and tall and you must eat." And she gazed at him with a rather troubled maternal tenderness, comparing her own figure—small and slight and dried up as it was—with the massive vigor of the young man's body, which seemed very large and flourishing in the dazzling light of the May morning.

All of a sudden she thought she heard a noise; she turned anxiously, for a moment, toward the door and hid the coffeepot in the inside pocket of her skirt. "I must be going."

But the noise died away and the old woman remained.

She liked to keep Alberto informed about the goings on of the house. She had a snappy, allusive, detailed, knowing way of retailing her gossip. She went on now. "They both of them want to get hold of the master's money. But he—you know what *he* says: Chickens are plucked *after* they're dead. Besides, he'll live to be a hundred."

Alberto said slowly: "And so Signorina Albertina doesn't get marrried?"

The old woman made a vague gesture, half contemptuous and half regretful, with both hands, and then continued: "Get married? But that needs money, lots of money. Everyone knows that Don Ferdinando has plenty of money; but when they discover that he'll only give a little, practically nothing, in fact—why then it's good-by to Donna Albertina."

The bricklayer repeated, with his usual, somewhat stolid air: "Good-by to Donna Albertina; so much money and no husband. . . ."

Then he went on: "But don't they know where the old man keeps his money hidden? Of course they know; we all know; but no one touches it."

Alberto had started work again, and the old woman bent down and murmured in his ear. "The lawyer runs up gambling debts, and Signorina Albertina gets into debt with all the scents and toilet things she buys. She's always washing herself, and she dresses well. But what's the good of that, if she never goes out? I help her, when she washes herself. She's as white as white can be, because she never goes out."

As she spoke, the old woman dropped her voice lower and lower, in a kind of guilty terror, and her eyes shone, and she pursed her lips

when she paused, as though she wished to hold back many thoughts
and words which flowered freely, but secretly, in her brain.

When she had left the room, the bricklayer thought, for a moment,
of his godmother who scented herself and did not find a husband.
There passed through his mind, for a few seconds, the idea of those
daily wedding preparations; and it was accompanied by rapid physical imaginings. He felt a sudden kindling of his blood; his movements
became quicker and more exactly co-ordinated; but in the end his emotion brought him back again, gradually, to his usual calm, and his
thoughts became mild and vague again, flowing along side by side without any necessary connection.

3.

Alberto knew that other visitors would arrive. It appeared that, in
the Casa Caramanico, the laying of these new bricks on the ancient
floors was a matter of interest to the whole family.

The young bricklayer did not understand the real reasons for this
general convergence upon the wing of the house in which he was working. He merely thought, casually, that they all liked him because he
was one of the Milone family who were retainers of the Caramanico
family, and that they all took pleasure in having a joke with him, to
pass the time.

The old man did not appear, that morning; about eleven o'clock,
however, Michele, the lawyer, arrived, wishing to see how the work of
repairs to his future abode was progressing, before he went out into the
square to collect the letters and converse with his friends.

The lawyer was forty years old and had decided, fifteen years before,
to take a wife; or else to leave home for the city; or at any rate to set up
a separate establishment from his old father, retiring into the other end
of the house. He wanted to start his legal career, to make a lot of
money, to have his own servants, to force his father to hand over the
share of the family property that would fall to him.

All these plans of his he, Michele Caramanico, the lawyer, would
communicate, in the morning, to the bricklayer, and then, later, to his

friends; in the evening he would talk about them, in a vague way, to his father, who would listen to him and say, fixing him coldly in the eye: "All right, then, that's understood; tomorrow you start your legal work."

The lawyer came into the room where Alberto was working, with his usual air of merriment. "Good morning, Alberto son of Albertina," he said; and he laughed in a harsh, childish way, as delighted with his old, jesting salutation as if he had been making use of it for the first time. "You're not working very hard, man," he went on. "Carry out my father's orders, man, not mine." Laughing, he went closer and closer to the young man, and then, all of a sudden, gave him a double pinch on his bare arms. The bricklayer clenched his teeth with the pain and jumped up in a flash.

The lawyer sprang back, holding out his walking stick. "On guard, man!" he cried. And, taking up the position of a duelist, he flourished his weapon two or three times in the air. Then he laughed again and went off. The bricklayer shook his head and started working again. He appeared to hold the conviction that the lawyer's little game was included in the list of his ordinary daily jobs.

A few minutes later his godmother also appeared. Her arrival was announced by a sharp smell of lilies of the valley and by a phrase from a little love song that had been in vogue ten years before, sung now in a thin, bleating voice.

Donna Albertina was a woman of medium height, pale and fat and with a superabundant bosom and hips. Her face was tiny, her eyes large and dull. Her walk was graceful and affected, like that of a schoolgirl; she moved with little, hesitant, staccato steps; but her breast and hips had the heavy movement of adult flesh.

Albertina came in, and the bricklayer rose to his feet and hurried to kiss her hand devotedly. For a few seconds she allowed her little perfumed hand to lie in the big, spatulate hand of the bricklayer; then she withdrew it and tapped him on the cheek with a tenderness at once playful and motherly.

The bricklayer pretended to be frightened, and she burst into loud explosions and trills of laughter; then she began to speak, between hiccups of laughter which made her bosom jump up and down. "You're frightened of me because I'm your godmother, and so I have the right to beat you. And beat you I shall. . . ."

And she began, in fun, to shower a rain of little slaps upon the young man's rough cheek.

Laughingly she went on: "If I like, I can take you up in my arms as I used to do when you were small."

And then she—she who was a weak woman, shorter by at least a foot —made as if to take him around the waist.

The bricklayer smelled the perfume of lilies of the valley which enveloped him like a puff of alcoholic smoke.

"No, don't do that," he said. "I'll lift you up, instead; look!"

And with sudden determination he extricated himself, imprisoned her in his sinewy arms, and began jokingly to swing her back and forth. Then he carried her over to the window and pretended he was about to drop his burden to the ground far below. Albertina gave little cries of fear and tickled his neck and thrust her fingers like a comb into his stiff hair.

4.

She was irresistibly attracted to the room where the bricklayer was working; her visits became more than usually prolonged and were not without moments of trepidation. But of Maria Vincenza, Donna Albertina had no fear. The old woman, in fact, used to say to her, when she saw her on her way to that part of the house: "Go on, go on, you need a little amusement."

And Donna Albertina certainly did need a little amusement. The little town where the Caramanicos lived had no other families of the same rank, nor were there any girls there who might have become friends of hers; nor, on the other hand, seeing how miserly he was, did her father willingly throw the house open for dinner parties or other entertainments.

Albertina, ten years before, had been the best match in the neighborhood. In the homes of clients or servants of the Caramanico family, and in those of innumerable matchmaking women, everyone spoke admiringly of her milk-white skin, of the heavenly sweetness of her voice, of the grace of her movements when she danced.

But, with the passage of the years, all the suitors who had been brought, after long negotiations and maneuvers, to the house, vanished away, one after another, when they came to realize that the old man had no intention, for the moment, of enriching a son-in-law.

It must also be added that, with the years, the little airs and graces of Donna Albertina had remained intact, even as her figure matured rapidly and swelled out with succulent juices like a September fig. The last candidates for her hand—who themselves had become gradually more and more middle-aged—found slightly ridiculous her little gestures and trills, her tripping, playful walk combined with the superabundance of her hips and bosom.

The young bricklayer, on the other hand, was enchanted by these things. That little chirping voice, that childishly pouting, tender prattle, that mixture of innocence and lasciviousness—all these put his heart in a flutter. And for some days now, even if he had wished to rid his mind of the pleasant pictures provided by his imagination, he would have been unable to do so. Donna Albertina came very often to see him and talked and laughed with her godson in a way both motherly and provocative. Sometimes she gave vent to an angry little burst of tears, which threw poor Alberto into an agony; he would look at his big hands with their spatulate fingers as though considering how immensely rough they were and how ill adapted to bringing consolation to his godmother.

5.

One day, in the early afternoon while everyone in the house was asleep, Albertina led the young man to a kind of little study adjoining the room in which she herself habitually took her summer siesta. In this little study were a number of old, broken-down pieces of furniture and some ancient iron-bound trunks that appeared disused and empty.

Donna Albertina pointed out one of these trunks, smaller than the rest, to the bricklayer, and said to him: "D'you know what's inside that one? All the important papers. The documents relating to all the family trusts. And here—you know what's in here?" she went on, pointing to a rough-looking safe fastened with screw bolts and fixed into one of the walls. "All Don Ferdinando's money, and our jewelry."

After a pause, she added: "D'you think you could open it?"

The bricklayer went close up to the wall, tried the crossbar that closed the safe, and then gave a sly smile. "With a chisel, I certainly could. It's easy." ·

She was looking at him with an anxious, ambiguous smile. Then, all of a sudden, she sank down onto a couch that stood in a corner and, arching her back, she sighed deeply. The movement caused her thin gown, which barely veiled her enormous bosom, to fall open. The bricklayer, his attention attracted by her sigh, turned and realized that she was naked. When she held out her hand languidly to him in sign of invitation, he approached stiffly, his throat parched. He clasped in his own the soft hand that invited him, and entered, intoxicated, into the atmosphere of perfumed flesh that rose from the sun-drenched couch.

6.

They ran away one morning just before dawn. The night before, Alberto, with due care, had emptied the Caramanico family safe.

They went by the lanes that sloped downward toward the valley, in the darkness of a night that had no moon but was cool and sparkling with stars.

A motorcar, driven by an acquaintance of Alberto's, was to await them at the Fontana dei Signori, on the main road leading to T——. Donna Albertina, stumbling and swaying on heels that were far too high, followed the heavy, assured footsteps of the bricklayer.

When they were inside the car she clung fast to her godson's shoulders and began to weep. Alberto suffered his usual embarrassment because of his big hands, which were incapable of making a caressing gesture. He did not squeeze her because he was afraid of hurting her, and he could find no suitable words by which to unravel the tangle of his feelings. All he could manage to say was: "Well, well, what's the matter, eh? Why? What's the use of it? No use at all. . . ."

The man at the wheel turned around from time to time and smiled in a knowing way, and waved his hand at his friend, as much as to say that she would soon get over it, that all women, as we know, burst into tears for no reason at all.

The farther they went, the more uneasy did Donna Albertina become; at one moment she even went so far as to say that she wanted to go back; and Alberto, with perfect docility, was willing to satisfy her and give orders to the driver to turn around. But then she changed her mind and was silent for some minutes; and it appeared that she must have gone to sleep on his shoulder, for the bricklayer was aware that her breathing was slower and heavier.

7.

Albertina awoke at dawn and welcomed the first trembling rays of daylight with a smile; her big, bovine eyes lit up; she freed herself of the tangle of clothes that she had clasped to her breast against the cool night air and wished to have the window opened.

She looked out and, as the sun rose higher, admired the reawakening plants and the splendor of the poppies at the sides of the road; and took pleasure in the sound of bells that could be heard from time to time in the soft air.

When they came to a bend in the road where there was a spring at one side enclosed in trailing plants and crowned by a tuft of infant oaks, with two wooden troughs covered in green moss, and she saw, all around, the wild flowers and smelled the smell of hay, she wanted to get out. She scrambled with some difficulty up the bank and, having reached the top of the slope, resumed her elegant, dancing gait, stooping to pick flowers and turning her laughing face toward the two men as a proof of her sudden access of gaiety.

The two young men, also, had got out of the car; the driver was a boy of about twenty, small in stature, with a lean, foxy face and untrustworthy eyes.

When Donna Albertina disappeared for a few moments behind the thick bushes near the spring, the driver went up to Alberto and made a sign to him, placing his forefinger to his brow, to indicate that the woman seemed to him quite crazy. Then he stood on tiptoe and, pursing his lips with a malignant expression, whispered something in his ear.

"Leave her here alone?" said Alberto, "and us go off with the money? Somebody'd come past and in two hours they'd arrest us. I'm going with her, d'you see? When we get to France we're getting married. I've got all the papers; my father saw to that. My father saw to everything."

The other man looked at him with a smile that was half sly and half ferocious. "You've stolen all the Caramanico money. I know that; you've got it all in that suitcase," he said, pointing to the car.

Then he was silent; and evidently some black thought was passing through his mind, for he had tightened his lips and was frowning. He turned, leaped into the car with one bound and tried, with precipitate, overhasty movements, to start the engine. Alberto saw what he was about, jumped on top of him, flung his strong, sinewy arms fiercely about him, and dragged him out.

"You're a traitor, you son of a bitch; and if you try that again, I'll strangle you," and he twisted his arms cruelly.

The other man was gasping with pain as he spoke. "What's the idea? I just wanted to test the engine. . . ."

"No, you didn't, you wanted to go off and leave us here; that's what you wanted, and I know it, you son of a bitch." Alberto relaxed his grasp, then took the little suitcase with the money and the jewels in it from inside the car, and said threateningly: "When she comes back we'll start again; and no more jokes."

The other man grumbled that he could no longer keep to his agreement, because something had gone wrong with the car, so they must get on with their own dirty work; as for him, he intended to turn back and would drop them at the first railway station. . . .

8.

He did, in fact, drop them at Marento station. It was a small station which had only two trains a day; one of them had left half an hour before they arrived, and the other did not leave till the evening. They decided to wait. They found a room in the only inn in the place and spent a few hours dozing and conversing in a melancholy fashion.

Albertina, during those hours, wept occasionally, laughed, grew sad again, and for long periods was silent. At table she declared the rough dishes prepared for them to be uneatable and sent the landlord's daughter out to buy biscuits. The ones brought to her were moldy, and she scarcely touched them. Everyone in the little village quickly got to know about the lady's strange behavior, and the gossips began discussing the pair, trying to interpret the inexplicable difference in their social standing. During the afternoon she wished to take the air for a short time, and they went out arm in arm, he stiff and very upright, she swaying as she moved and full of airs and graces. They soon had a trail of youngsters at their heels and heard the women whispering at their doors as they pointed their fingers at them and laughed, holding one hand in front of their mouths.

They went back to the inn, and he asked for the bill and paid it; and they went off to the station at least an hour before the train was due. They threw themselves down on a bench and sat silent for some minutes watching the railway lines and a small locomotive which was switching.

All of a sudden they heard a footstep behind them and turned. It was the Superintendent of Police. Alberto jumped to his feet. The Superintendent saluted the lady and said in a ceremonious tone of voice: "Are you Signorina Albertina Caramanico? And you"—he said to the man with a change of tone—"are you the bricklayer Alberto Milone?"

They both answered yes; and at the Superintendent's invitation they followed him obediently.

Although the Superintendent was anxious to do everything without any scandal, the name of Signorina Caramanico of L—— was by now on everyone's lips; the family was widely known, for its antiquity and its wealth, in the whole district.

The Superintendent took the young pair into his office. Standing there, his back to the window, was Michele the lawyer, Donna Albertina's brother, nervously twirling his bamboo walking stick. Beside him, seated, an elderly gentleman with an air of authority was taking long, thoughtful pulls at a cigar.

Albertina, when she saw her brother, ran over to him and clasped him tightly in her arms and started sobbing wildly, like a frightened child. "You see, Superintendent," said her brother, "this is the weeping of a woman who has been deceived and tricked. She had to go and visit a sick aunt at Vasto Aimone and she asked a person who was supposed to be trustworthy to go with her. This young man is her godson, Superintendent. It is he who has betrayed us; he emptied the family safe and took everything."

So spoke Michele the lawyer, while the sobs of his sister, as she pressed her tender bosom against his chest, gradually diminished. Albertina, helped solicitously to a chair, sat down and for a long time kept her eyes fixed on the floor, rubbing them continuously with her handkerchief and giving away, now and then, to painful sighs.

The Superintendent had sat down at his desk and grasped his pen. Suddenly he turned to the gentleman who was smoking the cigar and asked him: "And what do you think of it, sir?"

"The matter seems to me perfectly clear," he replied. "The driver who took them to Marento declared he had refused to go any farther when he understood that he had become involved in a disreputable affair. Milone had even gone so far as to strike him; he had two large bruises on his arms."

At this point Michele the lawyer resumed.

"You, young man, have always been treated as one of the family. For over half a century we Caramanicos have been looking after the spiritual welfare of you and yours, and you repay us by robbing us. Burglary further aggravated by the largeness of the sum involved— about twenty million lire, between liquid assets, jewelry, and bonds."

Alberto had remained on his feet, standing motionless; but his frightened eyes moved backward and forward with feverish vivacity, scrutinizing the hostile faces around him to try and understand what was happening. But his gaze rested most frequently upon the face of Donna Albertina, who continued to sigh, with her eyes upturned, now, to the ceiling. All of a sudden Alberto exclaimed violently, pointing his finger at her: "She knows all about it; she knows the whole story; we were going to get married."

"Get married?" said the lawyer crushingly. "And who broke open the safe with hammer and chisel? Did she?"

"No," said Alberto, "I did. But we were going to get married."

"Take it down word for word, Superintendent. The main fact is admitted by the accused," said the elderly gentleman. The Superintendent went on writing.

Alberto persisted, spluttering with rage. "We were going to get married. She said to me, 'You're able to open the safe, so open it, and we'll run away and get married in France.'"

"You're trying to protect yourself, young man," said the brother. "What time was it when you opened the safe?"

"Midnight."

"And was my sister present?"

"No."

"You see, then; it's very easy to say, 'She told me to, we were going to get married.' It takes two to plan to get married."

"But she did intend it; she intended the whole thing."

Here Donna Albertina sighed more deeply than ever, turned pale, and was seized with a kind of fainting fit. Putting up her hands to her brow, she said: "O my God, what confusion! What a strange business, O my God!"

Michele then said to the Superintendent that his sister felt ill, that it was impossible for her to remain present any longer at so unpleasant a conversation; if he would permit it, he would conduct her outside for a moment.

At a sign of agreement from the Superintendent, Donna Albertina, assisted by her brother, rose languidly and moved across the room; for an instant she fixed her tearful eyes upon her lover and her bosom heaved as she sighed.

As she came close to him, the bricklayer said, in a voice of pain: "You're going away, you're deserting me too; nothing but traitors everywhere. But *I*," he added, in a sudden access of rage, clenching his fists, "I'm good-natured enough, but I'm not to be trifled with. I . . ." And he bit his hands fiercely to prevent himself saying any more.

The Superintendent was uneasy and, fearing that the young man might commit some imprudence, placed himself in front of him.

"Superintendent, we were going to get married, it's God's truth," went on Alberto in a changed voice. "I took the money because we were going to get married; here are my papers—" and he took a bundle of sheets from the inside pocket of his jacket. "I left a hundred thousand lire for my father so that he could get the papers for her too. He was to send them to me as soon as we arrived in France."

"Who did the hundred thousand lire belong to?" asked the elderly gentleman quietly. "To you?"

"No," said Alberto, "I took them from there. My father told me to take them. He said to me: 'Why, you're going away and we shall be left on our own. I'm old; and how shall we get on if you're not there? . . . The reason the mechanic told you I wanted to run away alone was because I refused to give him a share of the money. He's a murderer, that man. Then I'll tell you what he wanted to do. . . .'"

Alberto spoke in a broken voice. The Superintendent and the elderly man listened to him coldly, winking at each other.

"My opinion is that the warrant should be upheld and he should be placed under arrest," observed the Superintendent.

"It's perfectly clear," answered the other man.

The Superintendent rang a bell; two policemen appeared, who, at a sign from their superior, seized the young man by the shoulders and hurled him through the door.

The young man tried, by wriggling, to escape their violence. But they were upon him again; they handcuffed him and pushed him out, striking him as he went, toward the stairs leading to the cells.

Alberto bellowed with suffering and rage, and the sound of his great, oxlike misery could be heard even in the room where Donna Albertina was sitting with her brother.

She turned her head gracefully in the direction of his crying and twice, three times, waved a slow farewell with her plump little hand.

GIUSEPPE MAROTTA

In a Lane of Naples

TRANSLATED BY ROBERT E. HILDER

Oh, ancient Naples, den of junk dealers, what could not happen when Christmas dawns over Vico Cannucce, the narrow street that struggled valiantly to remain true to Vincenzo Migliaro's * painting as it greets you from a neat wall in the Museum of San Martino . . . ?

Fluttering whiffs of cold that converge to generate vapor over the miserable back of Fanfariello, the tiny Sardinian donkey; an excited conference of muddy hens, exhausted from having combed the garbage with the patience of heirs who now seem to ask: Where, the dickens, is the will . . . ? A rusty-furred cat, vegetable-filled baskets, an armful of discarded bicycle tires, remnants of a cap, a shirt, a wooden top, once, perhaps, the treasures of a *scugnizzo* † who died at sunset last night or at dawn this morning; a wandering grinder whose shop consists of a wheel, a pedal-driven grindstone, a rag, and a perforated can from which compassionate drips of water mitigate the fever of knives and scissors subjected to the rude sharpening operation—and every sparkle that springs from the stone ought to be caught between two fingers and placed delicately in a manger.

What's the difference whether the glovemaker woman who sings today: "You know how tall the poppies are . . ." would have hummed a hundred years ago: "I'd like to be a goldfish—and swim out to the sea. I'd like to be caught by a sailor—and sold on the market—and bought

* Italian realistic painter born in Naples in 1828.
† *Scugnizzi*—little ragamuffins that roam Naples' streets.

275

by an innkeeper—and fried in a pan. I'd like to be eaten by my lover—
and remain forever in his heart. . . ."

Vico Cannucce never changes. If a bomb had destroyed it and
wiped it out during the last war, I would still tell you about it, sure
that it would rise again. Because, as all things in Naples, it is not made
of fickle stone but of unchangeable people.

There, in his cave, is the impervious cobbler Don Erminio Tagliamuollo. A trickle of old shoes dribbles over the floor, encircles his feet,
as if in blaming scorn or admiring reverence—it's for you to decide.

Essential, in this case, is his hump. You'll have to realize that Tagliamuollo is a hunchback and that right at this moment his mind is
filled to overflowing with thoughts more twisted and angular even than
his body.

These are the facts: Don Erminio has sprung from generations and
generations of hunchbacks. One of his illustrious forebears under the
rule of the Bourbons entertained good old King Fernando I for decades. When the French arrived in Naples, the witty and superstitious
monarch, champion of longevity, repented his having ejected the jester
from his palace after the latter had been caught by a master of ceremonies in the act of urinating into the resplendent royal top hat. From
Palermo, His Majesty informed the hunchback through secret chan-
nels that the offense had been forgiven. After which the King's expec-
tations came true, and in return for the royal forgiveness, he got the
throne of Naples back, still warm from Murat's buttocks, if I'm not
misinformed. The King declared, therefore, that an offspring of this
living talisman was required for his progeny. A little old maid, not less
hunched than her mate (just to avoid misunderstandings), was found
and used for the purpose, and this couple originated the uninterrupted
series of Tagliamuollos with the bulge on their backs.

There was no use for Don Erminio to have a well-formed, normal
mother, no use for him marrying a florid peasant girl from Apulia: the
iniquitous deformity continued to stretch out its hand and catch
every one of the descendants of the court jester. Aniello, the cobbler's
oldest son, was a hunchback, and so were Peppino and Erricuccio, who
came next in line. A fatality, an evil spell. These god-fearing souls did
not progressively arch their backs: They were born with undulated
spines right then and there, as if they had spent the usual nine months

hanging precariously from a vertebra hooked on a nail. Does that make it clear? Aniello is ten today, Peppino eight, and Erricuccio six. The fourth hunchback is expected any minute now. Filomena Tagliamuollo passed the deadline yesterday, Thursday. And as to Don Erminio's thoughts, who, in his position, could keep them quiet or at bay?

Another little hunchbacked male, all right—patience! But, as the cobbler is just now explaining to Don Vincenzo Torrusio, the dog-catcher, this is not the problem, this is nothing.

"First of all," he says, "there is the enigma of the sex. I, until now, have made the best of my calamity. Sure, my sons are hunchbacks, but they're males. Man is man. You don't measure a man by the inch. Handsome or ugly, complete or faulty, man functions, operates, produces. Look at me: I'm a working man, an effective entity which cures shoes and handbags just as you kill any old animal that crosses your path without a muzzle."

Whereupon Torrusio, in a darker mood: "Now, what has that to do with it?"

Don Erminio, somber: "A female, I beg your pardon, would be just as unsuited for my trade of a cobbler as she would be unfit to take your place as a lame executioner."

The dogcatcher: "Are you out of your mind? All I have is a seasonal rheumatic condition, and when I intervene I act by order of city hall."

"You didn't get my point. I just wanted to tell you, with all due consideration, that a penniless old maid has neither heaven to look up to nor earth to tread on. If the little innocent baby, which is on its way, is a girl instead of a boy, my dear Don Vincenzo, let me be frank with you: This time I shoot myself."

Torrusio, skeptical but friendly: "At Christmas? Jesus, you're crazy."

Don Erminio, with increasingly sinister determination: "I'm not. You put your finger on the sore spot yourself when you said: At Christmas. Since yesterday, Thursday, every day and hour count for Filomena and for the thing that is going to happen to her. And now follow me closely: This is the twenty-second of December, is it not? So, come today, come tomorrow, come the twenty-fourth, and probably Christmas Eve too. You follow me? Do I really have to continue? If the creature is born on the dot of midnight of the twenty-fourth, just as our Lord, I don't have to do anything to kill myself, I drop dead right then and there, quite simply and naturally as soon as they give me the news."

Don Vincenzo: "But why? Why? Is there a law against being born on Christmas Eve at midnight?"

Don Erminio: "Oh, you can do it. But at your own risk and under your own responsibility. Because chances are you're born a monster, maybe with the teeth and claws of a wild animal . . . a horrible, nauseating being, a major calamity."

Torrusio: "Jesus, you're right, that ought to be considered."

Tagliamuollo: "That's it. Now just imagine, if I become the father of a girl, of a hunchback (there can be no question about that), and of a werewolf to boot, Don Vincenzo, don't come near me: let me cut my throat right away with this honored and beautiful knife of mine."

Nonsense. Torrusio catches skillfully the cobbler's arm in mid-air; a keen eye and quick action are a must for a dogcatcher's trade. However, there are big events in the making. Erricuccio, Peppino, and Aniello break noisily into the picture; behind them flutter the skirts of breathless women. Tagliamuollo receives whispered and rapid information. This is it, Donna Filomena is in labor and how; she is eating the pillows; steady now, keep the boys busy, we and the midwife will take care of the rest. Yes, blessed women, thanks. The cobbler's nerves distend. With tender eye he caresses his offspring, this disheveled landscape of hunchbacks that unfolds and is lost to view behind his workbench. Time passes. Don Vincenzo relaxes, the whip and catch rope between his knees: anyway, in the imminence of Christmas, stray dogs are highly elusive, they must have an angel attached to their tails giving them miraculous warning when an ill-intentioned stranger emerges from the shadows of a house wall. The heart in the cobbler's asymmetric breast relents in its heavy drumming. Donna Filomena has always been a champion of efficiency and alacrity when it comes to the business of giving birth; so we shall not approach the forbidden midnight-deadline of the twenty-fourth, there will be no werewolves among the Tagliamuollos.

"Pray," Don Erminio orders his sons in a general way. Peppino, Aniello, and Erricuccio, stretched out over a field of leather scraps, mutter one Ave Maria after the other. "Oh, Virgin of Carmelo, oh, Mother Schiavona, give that it be no girl," whispers the father for his part, with complete assuredness that as to the other main feature, the hump, there can be no question. Outside, firecrackers burst at intervals while bengal lights flash across the sky; a shouting fishmonger asserts that his giant eels are possessed by seven devils and embody seven thousand delights, to which a prickly-pear vendor replies that whatever he may say, he who has not tried the intimate fragrance of his pungent fruit will never know what bride's lips taste like.

Hurry, time, hurry. One hour flies by, another follows. Suddenly Don Erminio and Don Vincenzo leap from their seats. Vico Cannucce is plunged into a sudden, short-lived silence, only to become alive again, vibrating and roaring, under the impact of something new. Disheveled women in flocks and swarms come tumbling down the stairs of the near-by houses and converge on the cobbler's grotto. Javarrone, the midwife, is at their head, brandishing a white bundle. She flings herself onto Don Erminio, shoving under his nostrils a moving odor of talcum and veins, and whispers something at his ears. Tagliamuollo tosses over workbench and stool and roars:

"It's a boy!"

He vacillates, regains control, lights up like a torch, and adds, as in delirium:

"He's straight, Madonna Mia, he's straight as a spindle!"

He would want to hurl himself onto the ground, bite into the floor that restrains him, prevents him from reaching the clouds; but just then his eyes fall on the three little hunchbacks emerging as if from the other end of the world and staring at him, their mouths wide open.

"Oh," he sobs in sudden fright (adult that he is, may the newborn Christmas sky forgive him) that his happiness has caused them deadly woe. Instead, Peppino, Erricuccio, and Aniello are already in the process of adjusting themselves to the new situation, here they are, dancing around the baby and shouting:

"Jesus, he's straight! Straight! Straight!"

Vico Cannucce laughs and cries. You, Migliaro, come down for a moment, mount your canvas and paint it again.

CESARE PAVESE

The Leather Jacket

TRANSLATED BY FRANCES FRENAYE

My father lets me spend my days
down at the boathouse. It gives me something to do, and at the same
time I can pick up a trade without even being aware of doing it. There's
a fat woman in charge now who's always shouting, and if I touch one
of the boats, she never fails to see me, even if she's down in the cellar,
and to yell out that it doesn't belong to me. Behind the boathouse
shack there are wooden tables and benches, but she won't let an outsider help her, and if I relay an order from one of her customers, she
tells her son to fill the glasses. I haven't set foot inside the shack for I
don't know how long, and it's even longer since I went upstairs to look
out at the boats and the water from Ceresa's window. No one comes
down here any more, and if my father thinks I'm picking up the trade,
he's got another guess coming.

This woman Pina doesn't know a thing. She treats her customers
about the same way she treats me. Not everyone that wears a leather
jacket can manage a boathouse. People must feel an urge to come, and
they must see on the boatman's face that he cares for boats and boating
and wants them to have a good time on the river. Ceresa was the right
sort. He always seemed to be playing a game, and he spent more time
in the boats than his customers. When Ceresa was around, there was
always something to laugh about. We went in shorts into the water,
boiled vats of tar for calking, bailed out the boats, and when the harvest season came around, we sat under the arbor for a snack, with a
bucket of grapes in the center of the table. The girls that came down

280

for boats used to hang around under the shed to laugh and joke, and one of them was always asking Ceresa to row her up the river. He would say that he couldn't leave his business and she'd have to come at sunrise. Once the little idiot actually did it, and then Ceresa told her that if she got up that early every day she'd never suffer from headaches.

The leather jacket that the woman throws over her shoulders whenever it rains is the one Ceresa used to wear. I remember how once, when a storm overtook us in a boat, he took it off and gave it to me. He was naked from the waist up underneath, and he said that if I were to live on the river, I'd have muscles like his when I grew up. He had a mustache, and his hair was blond from being exposed for so long to the sun.

Last year, some people stopped coming, on account of Nora. Nora started out by serving drinks, and she went home every evening. But beginning sometime last year, no matter how late I went away, she always stayed later, and when I came back the next morning she was there, hanging out of the window. She wasn't much to look at, at least I never heard Ceresa say so, but the boys and old men who bowled, back of the shack, were always calling her pretty. She would stand leaning against the door, holding her elbow in the palm of her hand, wearing a red dress, and looking at everybody without speaking. Once when I was sitting on the steps, waiting for Ceresa, she said: "Go on home, you little fool!" But at other times, when she saw me in a boat, dangling my feet in the water, she would simply laugh, and when Ceresa wasn't there and someone asked for an oar or a cushion, she would tell me to go get them from under the shed.

I didn't like it when Nora started to stay all the time at the boathouse. Before that, I used to speak of her the way the others did, as "a pretty girl," and that was all there was to it, but after she became so thick with Ceresa I began to think there must be something extraordinary about her, and it worried me not to know what it could be. They ate supper out under the shed, and I hung around for a while so that in case a boat came in I could lend a hand and they wouldn't have to get up from the table. They talked away, throwing a word at me every now and then, but a good deal of the time they simply winked at one another, and when Nora went to the kitchen for a plate, Ceresa sat silent, looking at the door. The way they talked together was different from the way they talked with me, and Ceresa, who always had a joke for everybody, didn't seem to be the same. He spoke slowly, drumming with his fingers on the table and looking up into the air, or else he waved the zipper of his jacket as if it were a fan, while Nora winked both eyes and stared at it, laughing.

Anyone could see that they were just keeping company, without any intention to marry. Nora never wore the kind of ordinary dress most women wear around the house; she had the red dress and a white one, which was even more beautiful, and once she had washed the dishes and swept the floor, she stood at the door, or went to look at the water, like the girls that came to hire a boat. When Ceresa called her, she came very slowly, as if she had nothing in the world to do. Actually, the day was long and full of all sorts of odd jobs. She served the oarsmen food and drink, washed shirts, and yet always found time to smoke a cigarette.

After Nora had ruled the roost for some time, Ceresa told me that one day we two would take a boat, the way we used to, and go up the Po one evening, beyond the dike. Nora never went out in the boat with us, because she said the water stank, and when we set off with nets and a basket to fish underneath the bridge, she laughed at us out of the window. When Ceresa went fishing, he wore only his leather jacket and a pair of very tight black bathing trunks. We jumped into the water and leaned the basket up against some stones; then while I held the boat, Ceresa scared up the fish with his hands. Beyond the dike there was a wonderful backwater, where you could always hope to get a basketful of fish, and he was always saying that one day we'd go up there early in the morning and not come back until night. One morning after another, I came to the landing, hoping that this was the right one, but there was always work to do, or Ceresa had to finish talking to Nora, or patch up a boat that had come in limping the previous night, and so our expedition was put off.

When I finally went beyond the dike, it was alone. One day Ceresa had business to conduct in Turin, and I was left with Nora, who was cleaning vegetables in a bucket under the shed. She looked at me without talking, and I got so bored that I told her I was taking the boat. A minute later I had gone. I stayed until noon on the water and came back thinking that probably Ceresa wouldn't turn up before dark and

I might as well go on home. But Ceresa was there, putting on his jacket in front of the window, laughing and calling me to come up-stairs. I had started toward the shack, when I saw Nora looking at me crossly from the kitchen, and I didn't have the courage to go in. "Ceresa's calling," I said, and went to put an oar under the shed. Nora stared and stared at me, until finally she went up herself.

Morning is the best part of the day, because you can hope for more then than you do at night. And at night I had to go home, because after supper Ceresa and Nora dressed up and went off, arm in arm, to the pictures, in Turin. The boathouse was deserted, and as for the arbor, that was closed right after sundown. Before Nora came, there was always someone around in the evening, and Ceresa used to give us a good time. He never felt the cold and stayed in his bathing trunks even after dark. It made me angry to hear Nora, who never got into the sun and must have been as white as a fish's belly, talking to him in such intimate terms and holding onto his arm. I'd have paid good money to know how to talk the way they did.

"You'll see," Ceresa said to me one morning, "when I get married, things will be just as they were before."

I was holding the bucket of tar and suddenly I wanted to cry. I didn't cry, though; I looked out at the river and held back my tears so he wouldn't laugh at me. I made sure Nora couldn't hear me from the kitchen, although of course I knew he really meant to marry her, and whatever I might say wouldn't carry any weight.

"I wouldn't do it," I said in a low voice. "After you marry Nora, she won't wear the red dress any more, and you're sure to quarrel."

"What were you talking about with Zucca yesterday, when he was here bowling?"

Ceresa always knew what was going on. Zucca, the fellow with the goiter, was actually talking with somebody else when he said that Nora was a donkey, and Ceresa had no business marrying her. I was only passing out the glasses.

"You're just a boy," said Ceresa, "so let that grown-up talk alone. And if Nora says anything to you, let me know."

But Nora never said anything to me. Sometimes she told me to go away. When Ceresa and I were working over a boat, she'd stare at us, with a bossy look on her face, from the door, and I couldn't be sure whether she was staring at Ceresa or at me. I waited for the subject of marriage to come up again so that I could tell him Nora was up to no good.

A few days after the question about Zucca, I was waiting in the boat for Ceresa to come down, but he never came. He had gone up for some cigarettes, and from the boat I could see the open window. It was a beautiful day and some customers might have come along any minute and taken Ceresa away, so I was in a hurry to get started. The air was so hot and still that the water didn't even lap against the boats. Then I caught a glimpse of Ceresa's back in the window; he was talking in the direction of the room and didn't turn around to call me. I looked up at the sun, squinted until I could see red and green spots, and was generally bored. It must have been some time before I saw Ceresa lighting a cigarette under the shed and asking me what was on the cards. I pointed to the oar, and he made a motion as if it were a bother but finally he jumped into the boat. He sat there without speaking and let me row all the way to the bridge. Then he jumped into the water and we began fishing. Every now and then he said something about the fish, dangling his cigarette from the corner of his mouth and straightening up at intervals to look at the water. I spoke of the motorboat, and we argued about whether or not it had a gasoline engine, but he didn't tease me as much as usual and talked to the smaller fish as he threw them into the bottom of the boat with a jeering: "Go on and die, damn you!"

That evening Zucca came by in his big boat and shouted hello.

"You're the cagey one," I said, emptying some water on the fish, and Ceresa looked first at him and then at me. Then he put his hand on top of my head and rubbed it.

But he hadn't had a fight with Nora. Women like to raise a rumpus or at least to cry, but we were always very quiet. Probably Nora spoke to him sometimes the way she spoke to me and said: "Go away, stupid," and Ceresa couldn't answer except by twisting her wrist and breaking it. Once, when two customers were there and he told her to mend a split cushion, she took the cushion and threw it into the water. Then she locked herself in her room upstairs and wouldn't answer the door. I went out with drinks to the tables in the rear, where no one had noticed. As for Ceresa, he didn't speak to me all day, but stayed out under the shed, filing and soldering an oarlock. He blew the bellows himself and picked up bits of charred coal and threw them sizzling into the river.

The next day the wooden gate was shut, and when I called, there was no answer. I didn't want anyone to come along and find out from me that there was trouble, so I went back home. The boathouse stayed dead for two days, and then when I was down by the shore in the morning, I saw a movement among the boats. Ceresa had come back, and so had Nora, who was standing in the window, changing her blouse. Ceresa was starting off with two girls, the kind that get undressed under the shed and squeal and carry on in a silly way. He was laughing at them and keeping the boat steady.

That evening there was a party in honor of Nora's return. Five or six came, between boatmen and customers; Zucca, Damiano, and the usual gang. They seemed very gay and joked and talked until midnight. They said Nora ought to go in swimming and they intended to get her a bathing suit the next day, one she could wear to serve the bowlers as well. Then the moon came out and made it as clear as day. Damiano brought in the wine, and they all started to play cards. I was keeling over with sleepiness, but I didn't want to go away, until finally Nora said: "Won't they be waiting for you at home?" and I realized the time had come.

From then on Nora was more and more gay, but where Ceresa was concerned her tongue grew sharper and sharper. All he did was laugh and shrug his shoulders. I was ashamed for him when she came out with a lot of stupid remarks in the presence of other people. She bought the bathing suit, a red one just like her dress, which she put on at noon in order to get some tan while she went to and from the shed and would have kept wearing indefinitely unless Ceresa had taken her by the arm and glared at her. She had a skin like pure cream, but she never went swimming in the river. When Damiano came, or Zucca's son, or some soldiers, she stopped to talk with them and get them to admire her. I don't know what it is they see in women. "Someday you'll catch on," Ceresa said to me once, "You'll have an eye out for them yourself." But it hasn't happened so far.

Then Ceresa had a fight with Damiano. It came about one day when I wasn't there, and I heard about it the day after. They came to blows and shouted so loud that the bus drivers on the other side of the river heard them. I stole a look at Nora, to see if she was angry, but as far as I could see she was scared more than anything else. There followed days when we stayed out under the shed without talking, and Nora wasn't to be seen. It was worse, really, when she came down into the kitchen and waited on the customers, because then I kept thinking she would make some sort of outburst. One day I looked for my boat—the one that I had built on the workbench under the shed when Ceresa would let me fiddle around there—and couldn't find it. Ceresa was sitting down, leaning up against a post, and when I asked him where it was, he said he didn't know. I ran into the kitchen to ask Nora, and she said, very quietly, that she'd used it for kindling wood in the stove.

Later on that day, Ceresa asked me why I didn't learn some trade.

"I want to be a boatman," I told him.

"You're crazy," he said. "Can't you see what a bad business it is? Tell your father he ought to start you out in a factory. Or else put you in the army."

I felt sorry, not for myself, because I didn't amount to anything, but for him, because he no longer cared about the river. I wanted to tell him to go ahead and marry Nora, so that he'd be better able to boss her around, but I wasn't too sure he'd give me any answer, so I pulled on my trousers and went home.

Nora woke up to the fact that she'd done me a dirty trick, because the next day she called me into the kitchen and got me talking. She asked me if I really wanted to be a boatman and if I wasn't afraid of drowning. I said I liked the business because it was Ceresa's. Then she asked me if I could take her out in a boat.

"Let's ask Ceresa if he'll let us go as far as the dike. And if tomorrow's a sunny day, we'll do it then."

The next day she put on her bathing suit and borrowed Ceresa's jacket. We took a picnic lunch, and she sat back on the cushions, while Ceresa laughed as I rowed her away. Once we had passed the bridge, I began to take long, slow strokes, and Nora asked me if we had much farther to go. I explained to her how to slip the oars into the water, and she had a try at it. She came to sit beside me and we nearly fell into the river. All women are alike. After that, she went back to the stern and asked me if I could swim in deep water. She knew that right under the dike was no place for swimming and said to stop at the mouth of the Sangone, where there was no current.

I tied up the boat and while she was looking made a perfect dive. Then I swam around in the Sangone and told her the water was colder than that of the Po. When I got back near the boat, where I could stand on my feet, I saw Damiano and a soldier on the shore. Apparently the soldier was a friend of Damiano's, but I had never seen him before. They came up to the boat and began to talk to Nora. I said hello to Damiano, but that was all. Then I climbed into the boat and sat where I had been sitting before.

I wasn't exactly pleased to see Damiano, because I knew he had a more powerful stroke than I did, and if Nora were to ask him to row us to the dike, I'd seem like a piker. But he and the soldier sat down on the shore and started joking. Nora fell in with their conversation and then she got out of the boat and said she wanted to go for a walk. The soldier put his hand on the zipper of the jacket and said with a laugh: "Better let in some air!"

He had a Neapolitan accent.

I was left by myself, thinking that if Ceresa were to know what was going on, there'd be trouble. Finally I went into the water so that anyone passing by wouldn't know the boat belonged to Ceresa. Nora came back when it was nearly dark and said we'd better not tell anyone we'd seen Damiano. I knew that much already.

The next day she wanted me to take her out again, this time to the Mulini, and I stayed away from the boathouse all afternoon. Between Ceresa's insistence and the way Nora had of looking at me as only an angry woman can look, I'd never have been able to wriggle out of it. I went back toward evening and found Nora wearing a skirt with the leather jacket over it instead of a blouse. Probably she had on her bathing suit underneath. She shot me a disagreeable look, but I was talking to Ceresa.

There were beautiful mornings in September, when a mist hung over the Po and we waited for the sun to break through. We had plenty of work to do at the forge and patching up the boats with tar, and Nora wasn't around in the early morning, because she had gone to market. Ceresa wasn't as talkative as he used to be, but I was happy to be there because I could see that he was indifferent to everything and willing to let me do what I wanted. Every now and then he found something to say, and I was there to keep him company.

The grapes ripened, and one afternoon we picked the ones in the arbor and set a bucketful of them on a table. Nora was there too, and we ate them and laughed all together. Nora said we'd have to watch out, or thieves would come in the night. Then, in order to show us where the thieves might hide the grapes, she opened the zipper of the jacket. I could see that she had nothing on underneath and caught a glimpse of something white and streaked, which certainly wasn't her bathing suit. But she closed it in a hurry. While we were having our snack, there were some soldiers sitting at another table, and one of them looked to me like the friend of Damiano's who had joked with Nora on the river. But all soldiers look alike, and it's impossible to tell one from another. When Nora brought them their beers, she didn't stop to chat.

An hour later, however, I saw them talking and laughing with Nora, while Ceresa was inside. I saw Nora lean over the table and the soldier stretch out his hand the way he had before, only this time he actually did pull the zipper down, and Nora burst into laughter. I couldn't take my eyes off them until I heard Ceresa at the door. He called me in, but I didn't talk to him.

A few minutes later I found myself alone on the bowling ground, with Nora and Ceresa inside. I waited to hear if they were going to quarrel, but everything was dead still. I was worried about the possibility of a boat's coming in or someone's wanting a drink, in which case I should have had to call Ceresa. Outdoors everything was quiet, darkness was coming on, and I felt cold. Over and beyond the trees I could detect low-flying birds, but there was not a single automobile from the city. Everything was as still as death. I felt ashamed and perhaps even afraid. I was still thinking of that white expanse of Nora. A shout rose up out of the everywhere, and I heard my name. A window opened and Ceresa called down: "Pino, go on home!" And almost immediately the window was closed.

I came back the next day, with my heart in my throat. First I walked along the bank and looked down at the boathouse, which lay quietly among the trees. Nobody was there. After lunch I began to say to myself: "Ceresa knows I didn't have anything to do with it." Then I saw a whole lot of boats in front of the boathouse, and two men in city clothes near an automobile at the beginning of the path. I realized that I couldn't get through and went around the field, the longer way. Men were moving about under the shed, but Ceresa wasn't there. Finally I came across Zucca's son, and he told me that Ceresa had strangled Nora and thrown her into the Po.

I wanted to see him, so as to tell him about that day at the mouth of the Sangone, but they cleared the premises, and when he came out, the automobiles drove away. That evening my father told me that the less I talked about it the better.

VASCO PRATOLINI

A Mistress of Twenty

TRANSLATED BY BEN JOHNSON

1.

Giovanni knew that Erina lived across the Arno, in the San Frediano quarter; but nothing more. "First of all, I'm finicky about my freedom": she had repeated this ever since the evening following their first encounter; and, charming him with her manner, saucy and demure at the same time: "Once I'm across the bridge," she had told him, "I'm unlike any girl you could ever imagine. So don't come sneaking around, because that would just end it all, before it's even started." She had taken his left hand, stroking it between her palms. He was wearing a wedding band on his ring finger.

She said: "You've finally talked me into it, this screwy idea of becoming your mistress. You see, I'm not afraid to say it, and I know the position it puts me in."

They were seated together in a carriage, riding back from the Picciolo Restaurant where, out one of the avenues, in a little reserved room, they had passed the entire afternoon.

He said: "I don't pretend that you love me—not yet at least."

Once they had crossed the bridge she asked to be let out, despite the rain; she reached for his hand again, through the window, and he kissed hers.

Now they were meeting in Porta a Prato, in a café-pastry shop that recalled to Giovanni memories of his adolescence and the years of his youth lived in those streets there on the outskirts of Florence; a café where he had then but rarely been able to stop. Twenty years had passed—more—and now, just beyond the gate, the road had been asphalted, and the roundhouse, near the Cascine Gardens, seemed to have been dislodged by the new constructions between. Nor was the café the same, either, its furnishings nor clientele; gone at that hour in the afternoon were the coachmen, the railway hands, and the sportsmen of the *Libertas*, replaced by couples, one, two, but not always, sitting at gay, print-covered tables.

It was wintertime; it was the winter of twenty-five, and Giovanni had had a new overcoat made, with collar and lapels of velvet plush; he lay the pack of Turkish cigarettes on the table and downed a cognac, then another. She always arrived late—young, a flower!, with her coat belted tight at the waist and falling a little below the knees, her long blonde hair combed smooth, with the bright-eyed, expectant air of a girl on the threshold of her first affair. Their trysts had been taking place for two weeks; it was mid-December, a bitterly cold evening, with the sky gray and as if frozen to the river bounding the horizon; he had waited for more than an hour and felt he had to say to her, but quite affectionately: "We're going out now. I want to get you a watch."

His rebuke apparently escaped her; she ordered her usual tangerine punch and, taking a cigarette, lighting it while he held a match for her, said: "I'd love to own a watch. In fact, I'll see that you keep your word, but I tell you again: I insist upon my freedom, and you aren't to get jealous. When you don't trust me any more, just drop me."

He interrupted: "You become increasingly necessary to me every day; you realize that, don't you?" Suddenly he was alarmed and—as usual—rhetorical.

Erina gazed deep into his eyes.

"It'll end with me really falling for you," she said.

She was a girl of San Frediano, with only her beauty in common with other girls of the quarter, fashioned as she was by life, yet young enough still to take her own words seriously, to issue them with a fitting glance. She said, and it was a victory for whatever remained in her that was still honest and pure: "But don't put any faith in anything I tell you. Putting on sincerity is just part of my strategy." Then she added: "You laugh, with that blissful look on your face, I know, because you're thinking that in a little while we'll be in our little room in the Picciolo."

"Don't be vulgar," he said, sounding ridiculous even to himself, and as if to dispel the offending remark with a gesture, summoned the waiter.

But a short while later they were indeed in their little private room in the Picciolo; supper was set before them, and, seated opposite each other, Erina said: "Do you still plan to give me a watch? Don't. It wouldn't be a surprise any more."

Her voice was sulky, babylike; she rose and went to the door, locking it from the inside. Standing there, with her hands behind her back, she said: "If you don't kiss me first, I won't eat."

This was her coquetry; Giovanni understood, entering into it with all the bluster and welled-up joy within him: now she was his mistress throwing open frontiers of promise, whose freshness and vitality he took pride in being able to hold in leash. Whenever she left the room for a moment, he would slip a hundred- or two-hundred-lira note into her purse, a thousand on the eve of her feast day, as she had happened once to bemoan the scanty condition of her trousseau, now with winter at the door—and after the watch there had come a cotton imitation fur piece for which she had expressed a desire,

By January, having given up the Picciolo, they went instead to a boarding house up on the hill, where, in a room registered in his name, frequently they spent entire nights together. One evening, in the first part of February, she told about herself all that, until then, he had shown a disinclination to hear. Her parents were still living and she had a younger brother and sister. And her father was a ragpicker.

"You know," she said, "one of those men who pushes a cart through the streets yelling *rags bottles junk give me your rags bottles* . . ." She imitated the cry, and he had to close her mouth with his hand; she bit it, drawing blood, titillated and thrilled by the cognac and their presence there. She spoke about herself, piecing truth and untruth into the self-portrait she considered appropriate: "You don't think for a minute my family knows I have a lover, do you? As far as they know, I'm at the tobacco plant, and nights like this I'm working overtime. Are you touched, Giannino?" She laughed her saucy, suspicious laugh and added: "No, don't worry, I won't shout any more. My handsome capon! When I've finished plucking you, will you hate me?"

He drew her against his breast.

"That day will never come," he said. "With each transaction, I become a richer man. What's more, don't get the idea I'm so awfully generous."

Provoking him, she said: "Wouldn't you say, it really depends on how good I am at plucking?" But again, in her excitement, she was only being ironic.

Giovanni said: "That's quite enough now. I don't care to continue this discussion. Take off your things, while I put some wood in the stove."

It was the night of February twelfth, 1925: a night long and filled with love, ending as dawn whitewashed the sill and the bell of San Domenico's rang with muffled tones through the quiet. A fire still smouldered in the stove, and the room was warm. Completely nude, Erina slid out of bed, her hands cupped beneath her breasts. Giovanni looked at the planes of her back, smiling, supine: at last exhausted, sleepy. She crossed to the window: "It snowed!" she cried. She let out the shutters; closing them again, in her right hand she was holding a snowball scooped from the window sill. Before Giovanni realized what she was up to and could jump, she had rubbed his genitals with snow. A sadistic, childish prank. He chased her around the room, knocking aside the obstacles she threw before him: a chair, another chair, the table, then the nightstand; and in the confusion following that night of love, unconsciously he relived, in a different and freer way, less inhibited, in a way vastly more befitting his character, twenty years later, his honeymoon. The same twenty years that separated his age from Erina's.

Erina surrendered, tumbling onto the bed, and he hugged her, he slapped her lovingly, he kissed her. He was tired and happy. A half-hour later, drowsing with his cheek on her breast, he said: "I want to make a lady of you. . . . I want to give you carriages and horses. . . ."

He awoke with the sun already high and Erina sitting beside him. With a sweater pulled on over her chemisette, a tray across her knees, she was dipping pieces of buttered bread into her coffee. Her hair was brushed back behind her ears, and her face and lips lay beneath a soft veil of powder and rouge. He gazed at her, the length of her torso, luxuriating in her beauty, brooding over the warmth of her body beneath the covers; and tenderly stroking her thighs, conscious of himself and his destiny.

"What beautiful eyes you have," he said.

She smiled down at him, still eating, sipping her coffee, and replied: "Like the sky, wouldn't you say?"

She was ironic and sharp, he mused, but like a child, and sweet—always so. His mouth felt pasty, and his breast burned as if the excess of smoking and cognac had slashed—as it actually had—a rivulet of flame down inside him.

"Didn't it snow?" he said.

"Of course," she replied, "just look! That's why I put up the curtains and wiped the window, to let in more sun."

Through the panes a snow field stretched off beneath the sun. Along the slopes of the Camerata, in the distance, shovelers were clearing the tram tracks; and the city far away, the campanili and the cupola of the Duomo rose like enormous stalagmites from the even, snow-blanketed plain of roof tops. Giovanni said—exactly what he was thinking—he was now sitting up in bed himself: "It's like a fairy-tale landscape, something out of a dream."

"Wake up!" she said. "It's eleven o'clock, time we were gone."

"Gone where?" he asked. "What do we have to do?"

He had stretched out beneath the covers again, talking as if to himself; actually, as if speaking his thoughts aloud: "You and your everlasting freedom! Tell me, why shouldn't I be jealous? We're always together as if for the first time. Why don't you want me to set you up in an apartment? You've never given me a good reason—"

"I told you last night," she interrupted. Placing the breakfast tray on the nightstand, she slid down beside him again. "I'm still living with my family, and I don't plan to become a kept woman."

"You don't have to put it like that!" he exclaimed. "You're more important to me than—"

"Than who? Tell me. Your family?"

This move—there was no doubt—had been planned ahead as part of her gambit, but planned or not, at that moment it was entirely un-called-for. He took offense and left off fondling her. Though it was not a sense of guilt that had provoked him: simply that such considerations, at that moment, were singularly out of place.

He said to her: "You don't need to make such comparisons. They are one thing—"

"And I'm another. Fine. Well, we'll just continue as we have till now. Have I ever asked you for anything?"

Giovanni thought back to the thousand lire he had slipped into her purse just two days before: and now, for the first time, it occurred to him that dear Erina was indeed dear; although by simply nuzzling against him, as she did, kissing him on the mouth, snaking a leg between his, she was able to dispel his irritation; that, and every thought in his head. Her body was warm and young, and she was freshly washed and scented with perfume he had given to her himself.

They had lunch served to them two hours afterward, eating with the table moved close to the stove and the curtains drawn over Florence in the distance. It was a winter's afternoon, dazzling with lights, the sky blue and radiant after a night of snowfall. She was tender and inexhaustible—the way he liked her. And that evening, still abed, together in each other's arms, they smoked and he told her of his most recent transaction, the third public sale he had participated in, from which he would realize even more than from the first two—one hundred thousand lire at one stroke; and he promised to take her on a trip.

"We'll spend a week together, a whole week, just you and I, in Venice maybe; I've never been to Venice." He paused, savoring the sound of his voice, then went on: "Or maybe Paris. What d'you say? I haven't been to Paris in over ten years."

He saw Paris before him, the Eiffel Tower, the first image that sprang to mind, and the Pam-Pam, where he had gone with Nella— and thus did Nella come to mind too. But it was not, this time, an importunate thought; quite the contrary. Nella returned to his side, along the Champs Élysées, on the hill of Montmartre, in a long dress reaching to her feet, with a large hat and parasol—it came late, that summer of nineteen-fourteen—like a porcelain doll on his arm: nothing now but a memory, for so different, so real was Nella today that he had had to awaken the memory.

"What d'you say?" he asked again. "There's a church, if you could only see it, up on a hill in Paris—called, I remember now, the Sacred Heart, the Sacré Coeur," he said, "simply a San Miniato's with lots of gold!"

Erina said: "It'd be wonderful, but think what it would cost, money you could use for other deals. You know, if I just had half of what you'll make from your last deal, I'd be set for life."

Certainly, this time her move had been well staged. She did not even need kisses and caresses to sustain it.

"What makes you think so?" he returned. "Fifty thousand lire would hardly set you up for life. I could do it—if you'd let me."

She lifted her piece to the far side of the board: "There's a stock of remnants in the warehouse under where we live. First they were holding them for the Fabbricone in Prato, but the Fabbricone went bankrupt—you must've heard about it, you being in business. And the stuff is just sitting there, waiting for the first comer. Tomorrow, there's no telling, Passigli may show up, or somebody else from the plants in Prato or Rifredi, and cart it all off for next to nothing. The owners of it are hard up. They've got high-grade remnants and I, I mean," she halted, "through my father, I—but I also happen to know myself—they know me—I could have the lot for less than anybody, and I could sell it blind. I could make a sure killing, just like you with your scrap iron."

He hugged her, slinging his arm around her neck: "What's my little dove doing, worrying her head about business, buying and selling?"

Erina wriggled free, bouncing up on her knees; she lay her hands on his chest, suddenly gay, as if brightened by an idea: "Why don't you take on this deal? Then give me a percentage. There are so many things I have to buy."

"Of course, why not?" he said. "But first I'll have to find out exactly what it involves."

"Let's go then!" she cried. "Come on, get up! We'll go now! Get a move on!"

She ripped back the covers and sprang to the floor, pirouetting on tiptoe in her chemisette, small and plump and blonde and happy. He yielded before her enthusiasm, surrendered to this lark, to his own state of mind, to a day and a night of uninterrupted ecstasy so suddenly, so naturally consummated, and now to Erina who, as she put her clothes on, danced around him, caressed and urged him to hurry, and sang: "I'm entering business! My darling is financing me! My financier darling!"

It was already evening, with a moon, and the road eerily moonlit, snow-lit, as the taxi came down the Circonvallazione; and then, presently, the mid-town streets, shorn of snow, crossing the bridge, thick with traffic, the taxi nosing its way through at walking pace. And then they had crossed the bridge, and he felt proud, sure of himself: the cab ride, in the still of the moon and the avenues banked with snow, the lights and din of the city, after their long, love-filled seclusion, had combined to make of him master of the world, had left a euphoria that overspread to the reaches of his unconscious; he reacted as if transported aloft by his own gestures and the soothing, tender presence of Erina to whom he, now having encouraged her in her childish plans, would cling forever, from whom he would exact fidelity and his proper rights as a lover. Erina startled him from his reverie, shouting to the cab driver to stop. The taxi pulled up on the corner of via Guicciardini, and she jumped out.

"Come along," she said to Giovanni.

She proceeded straight into the Café Old Fiorenza while he paid the fare. When he entered, he found her already seated, off at a secluded corner table. The place was small, furnished in imitation fourteenth century, with painted walls above the high wainscoting; it had never occurred to him to enter this café, and he was surprised by its elegance and by the fact that Erina had known it well enough to go to it so unerringly. He found her biting her lips, her eyes glistening with tears. The waitress came, and Erina ordered a cognac. "Double," she added, and her voice was choked. Giovanni's surprise mounted.

"What is it?" he pleaded. "I don't understand you at all."

"You don't un-der-stand me," she syllabized. "I was happy, and then, all of a sudden, I realized just how rotten I really am. I wanted to swing a deal myself, I wanted to take you down under where I live so that everybody would find out that I have a lover and that I get him business."

He smiled, his surrender complete; now, for the first time perhaps, fully convinced of being a seducer, and of Erina's honesty, her fidelity, her candor: vastly more than she had ever hoped for. He placed his hand over hers.

"All right," he said. "Give me the address, and tomorrow I'll go there alone and buy the remnants—"

"Tomorrow, no. It'll be too late tomorrow."

"Then I'll go now, by myself."

"No, they won't trust you. Besides, it's stuff they've already promised to somebody else. Only somebody living in the neighborhood, like my father—they'd make an exception only for someone like that."

"That means, then, that we'll have to wait for another opportunity," he said, smiling affectionately, a little fatherly—exactly the way he felt.

"But *this* is the opportunity!" she continued, obstinate, pouting. And suddenly gay again, childlike as shortly before: "Why not give the money to me? I'll go there and come back; then we can spend a little time together, later on, and I'll tell you how it went. You have the money, I saw it. You do have the money!"

He wagged his head benignly, still loving.

"My sweet, little baby," he said. "Yes, I do have the money; certainly I have it, but what I'm carrying on me now I have to pay out shortly, a little later this very evening."

"Ah! then you were giving me the runaround! How were you going to buy the remnants?"

"Silly, you never pay cash down for anything. At most you leave an advance," he told her, decidedly paternal now, with the very tone of voice one uses, deserted by imagination, having to explain to a child a story too big for its years. He went on: "At very most I'd have given them a promissory note."

"Make out a promissory note to me, then!" she said. "That way, tonight I can go and close the deal myself."

"But why do you insist so, Erina? You don't seem yourself."

"Because it's a wonderful opportunity," she said. "And then, just because."

He sought her eyes fixed in space before her: her wide blue eyes, the light in them, now as she returned his gaze, a stubborn, frightening blaze. In a deep voice, no longer aggrieved, instead conscious of each word, determined, she said: "I've made up my mind that I want to do this. Now take your choice: either give me the fifty thousand right now or make me out a promissory note; otherwise, between you and me it's all over."

"But, Erina," he answered. "Look, don't you realize—"

"I realize this: you made me a promise and now you don't want to keep it." She started to get up and he drew her back; the waitress brought their cognacs. She pushed her jigger away and repeated: "I've made up my mind, Giovanni; it's up to you: the money or the promissory note—one or the other."

"But this is perfectly silly," he declared.

"To you maybe, but lots of others wouldn't think so. There are plenty of men who'd find me worth fifty thousand. And, after all, I'm only asking for a loan."

He had a moment of lucidity, but only a moment of it, for then he said: "Darling, we've known each other for just over two months, and in a little while you'll have cost me fifty thousand lire."

Erina got up. And this time Giovanni had to go after her; he stopped to pay for the two untouched cognacs. He walked toward the door sensing that he had lost her, that he had lost her perhaps forever, and the prospect filled him with dismay: he was prepared to yield, when he reached the sidewalk he was prepared to give himself entirely into Erina's hands; he looked around to see which way she had gone. As it happened, she was only a few paces away, in the middle of the street, walking off toward Piazza Pitti. He hurried to catch up with her and took her by the arm.

"It's all right," he said. "It's a loan, then; and you can pay me back when you're able—never, if you wish. But this evening, at this moment, I can't give you the money. I'd miss out on too big a deal. And I'd be jeopardizing future ones, understand?"

They were on the corner of Via dello Sprone, under the ancient arch; she sank into his arms, laying her forehead against his breast, whispering through her tears: "There's a tobacco shop across the street."

A little later—in the shop he had bought a promissory note and, asking for pen and inkwell, had made it out to Erina for fifty thousand lire—they walked along Via Maggio; and it was only then that he noticed the biting air, the wind from the Lungarno clawing at them, cutting off their breath.

He said to her: "I left the date in blank, but be sure to wait a week before negotiating it. My money's all tied up and I'd have trouble try-ing to make good on it."

And to overcome his uneasiness, which lingered on, his having won back Erina notwithstanding—the promissory note was the first he had ever signed—he asked her: "Are you happy now?"

She nodded yes, wrinkling up her nose; and she quickened her pace, though it may have been only the thrust of the wind. They had come to the entrance to Borgo San Frediano: they were very near her house. She stopped, leaning her back against the wall of Via Maffia, the dark, lonely street, the site of her first adolescent affairs: but he was a man who had passed forty, a businessman and seducer experiencing his first successes—and his first promissory note.

She said to him: "Are you going home tonight? If you'd like, we can meet later on, in two or three hours."

"Wonderful," he said. "You're very sweet, Erina." Then he said: "Oh, no, I really can't. Tomorrow, yes; but not this evening. My son's expecting me. I promised I'd be back this morning."

Afterward, he watched her disappear up Borgo San Frediano, into the working-class bustle of the street, a buxom, well-proportioned figu-rine on spiked heels, in her brown coat, moving through the swarms of people, between tramcars and the carts and bicycles, following the sidewalk, then vanishing into the horizon where the fog swallowed up the lights. From the corner of Via Maffia, where he had remained standing, he hailed a taxi and asked to be driven across town to the suburban quarter of Rifredi: to a café quite unlike the Old Fiorenza where he had been with Erina a little earlier. The café in Rifredi was virtually deserted now during the supper hour. But there, with his elbows propped on a table, his hands closed one over the other in front of his mouth, Bugatti awaited him.

2.

"Thought you weren't ever coming," he said. He was unusually cheerful, and, decidedly out of character, gave Giovanni a resounding slap on the shoulder. "What d'you know, I was saying to myself, Gio-vanni must've started believing the papers. But then I said, that's no reason for him to miss an appointment. There's always a way out, no?"

Giovanni might have detected Bugatti's allusions, which would have been, unassisted by the papers, quite enough to alarm him, had he not remained with Erina, following her in imagination on into the back alleys of the quarter, bobbling along on her high heels, blonde and happy, with her purse on her arm, her hands plunged in the pockets of her brown overcoat, and his promissory note tight in her fist.

He answered: "I haven't seen the papers. What's up? Have the Exceptional Laws gone into force?"

"Of course not," Bugatti said, and his tone suddenly changed; guarded, contained, he was once again the man Giovanni had known for years past. "There's a general clamping-down to strengthen the position of the lira—that's the story—but because of that, I said to myself, it's possible that you had misread it as some sort of calamity. Actually, this clamping-down is a boon to people like you with ready cash."

"Naturally," Giovanni said.

"The Berta accountant, have you seen him yet?" Bugatti asked.

"Not him, either. I've been tied up all day long."

"No matter. I phoned him this morning myself. You'll be able to pick the material up from the roundhouse within the week; meanwhile, in the next couple of days, I'll arrange the usual bill of sale, thus completing your third and biggest transaction to date."

"Perfect!" Giovanni said. "All the more, as I've just taken on something totally different. You'll never guess—remnants, of all things! But high-grade stuff, at a price made special for me, and I don't have to be bothered with placing it, either."

Bugatti smiled his customary smile, a sparkle behind his glasses, and said: "Unfortunately, I can be of no help to you in this matter."

"You've helped me too much as it is. That's been my only complaint."

Giovanni slid the pack of fifty thousand-lire notes, which he had prepared in his overcoat pocket in the taxi, across the table top: "What do you say to a drink?" he said.

This time he took a strong Leghorn punch, and the lava flow inside his breast burned deeper.

A little later Bugatti walked with him to the tram. A Number 23, which would have let him off very near home; but he had to drop by the warehouse first, to pick up his brief case and valise and Fernando's erector set. He got off in Piazza Unità (always it was here, in this maze of streets not far from the station and the market, that his life was decided, and always in such a way that, much later, he had to turn over the situation in his mind) and bought a copy of the late edition of the *Nuovo Giornale* at the newsstand in Via Faenza. With hardly a chance to unfold the paper, the summary leaped from the page and clubbed him:

RAILWAY RECONSTRUCTION: THE DUCE'S HISTORIC DECISIONS

The Council of Ministers approves the appropriation of 300 millions for the electrification and construction of new rolling stock. Private speculation in this sensitive area of the national economy also blocked: salvageable material guaranteed entirely to the iron industry.

"The bastard! Double-crossed!" he cursed to himself.

A newcomer to business, yet a man of experience—however commonplace his experience may have been: that of a bureaucrat, of an unsuccessful union man—now that he had been struck directly between the eyes, he promptly acknowledged the fact with the fatalistic prescience of the foredoomed. And of the dispossessed. He recognized that the value of his scrap iron was automatically reduced and that that field of speculation was now exhausted; he would have to go into something new, entirely different—something, however, for which he was utterly unprepared. His first thought, suggested by his particular circumstances, and which gave him strength to stand up to the blow he had just received, was that, fortunately—fortunately!—he already had, without wishing it, undertaken something new. Something he could turn to good account: after all, the cases of ragpickers, of "remnant traders," to put it more delicately, who had piled up immense fortunes were so numerous and such as to have become proverbial. "A ragpicker worth his weight in gold," he said to himself along Via Faenza, across Piazza Madonna, on into Piazza degli Ortaggi, the square deserted, a lobby of wind. "Wheat thrives in dung." —And had his self-educative faculties been brought into play, he would have seen Erina high upon the wheatcocks of his imagination, atop the mountain of golden rags just as he envisaged her, as his Egerian Nymph, Aphrodite of Cnidus, his Sibyl of Good Fortune.

Arrived at the warehouse, he collected his valise and brief case and Fernando's erector set. Then he crossed Piazza del Duomo. In a tobacco-shop window, he noticed, along with cigarette lighters and tins of imported tobacco, some good-luck charms and bottles of perfume; he entered and purchased cigarettes; then—already on the way out—a thought occurred to him: he stepped back in and asked for a bottle of cologne—Coty—for Nella. He was, of course, and such did he feel as he prepared his role, a businessman returning to his family from Rome where, with the Ministry of Communications, he had just succeeded in negotiating a deal, a splendid deal, that would result in new bricks for the edifice of his wealth.

Upon reaching home, however, instead of the anticipated joyous welcome, the dining room illuminated, his wife and son rushing into his arms, he found the rooms silent, Nella worn with care, and Fernando delirious with a very high temperature. But the doctor, who was still there, was able to offer Giovanni a few words of comfort: Fernando had a violent case of scarlet fever which, if for no other reason than the suddenness of the attack, would run its course without complications; they might look forward to the youngster's speedy recovery. The child, although delirious, recognized his father at once; he took his hand and squeezed it, wanting Giovanni to remain with him at the bedside.

They both remained, Nella and Giovanni, sitting on either side of the bed, watching over their son. They spoke together softly. A faint shaded light burned on the night table. Giovanni's return had restored to Nella all of her courage; she mustered a wan smile for him. Fernando drifted off to sleep. It was midnight. Nella turned to Giovanni: "Are you pleased at least with your trip? How did it go? As well as you had hoped?"

"Yes," he said. "All quite well, very well."

Giovanni was strangely quiet, serene, astonished at his calm himself. In vain, he strove to impose a sense of anguish on himself which he did not feel; and recalling the hours he had spent together with Erina while his son lay at home "hovering between life and death," he tried to pretend remorse: the solicitude he offered himself found no response within his conscience. Actually, all that both his education and life had instilled in him, all that was conventional and declamatory, and to which his daily actions, his words and intentions themselves were subject, corresponded to nothing in his nature, whenever he was asked to confront elemental forms of affection or the ties of blood. Yet he was curiously moved by pangs of genuine distress and anxiety for the danger his son was in; and in a man without Faith, or even superstition, now at the mercy of fate, his anxiety and distress, only because these sentiments were honestly and sincerely felt, induced in him a calm: the stupor and quiescence of the deprived soul. Well, anyway, he was sure that Nella had already done everything possible in a practical way to help their son, to ease his suffering; and now, for Giovanni, nothing remained but to keep watch over him, to give him his sympathy, to see him through the disease, second by second, to wish him once again to be healthy and happy. And that, he was doing, by letting his hand lie in the hand of his son, by refraining from smoking, by resisting the recurring assaults of weariness and sleep. And to recall the origin of his fatigue, his sleepiness, was not to offend his position as a father, nor his son's love for him; nor, for that matter, Nella's affection, either: even for his wife his fondness was preserved intact, a rationalized fidelity; and, within his heart, she was not demeaned if he saw her as she was—just as she was: in the half-light of the room on the opposite side of the bed; not unlike himself, although less composed, haggard in the relaxed tension, and weary after the anguish of a day and a night spent alone watching over their child, as betrayed in her face and now by the way she sank into the armchair. To see her as she was, was only to remember her thirty-eight years, the little miseries and the barrenness accumulated over the long years during which she had had to look after a family on his office clerk's salary, at the same time vigorously defending before the eyes of the world her *petit bourgeois* origins which, as she said, she had "inherited." And the first strands of gray in her long chestnut-brown hair gathered into a large chignon at the back of her neck; the decline, ultimately, of her figure, natural though it was (yet far from irremediable): grown bulky at the hips, her breasts sagged, and wrinkles sprayed across her throat—to compare her with Erina did not mean to offend her; rather, all the more to respect in her everything that she represented in his life: companion, wife, and mother of his son. Giovanni was led then to the observation that he had never seen his own wife completely nude; suddenly, this reflection prompted by the memory of Erina who only a few hours before had lain nude in his arms, he was filled with a burning, lascivious desire to see Nella stark naked. He craved for her, making up to her in a way that was entirely new and unusual for him. He said: "I've brought you a bottle of cologne."

Her reply was even more unexpected, and disappointing: quite the contrary to what his state of mind besought: "I'll open it," she said, "when Fernando is well." Then she said: "Why not go and eat a little something, Gianni. So the maid can go to bed. It's too much to expect of her, to stay up any longer. She was with me all last night."

He demurred, mastering his first impulse, his inclination to obey: "Have her make a little coffee for me. That's enough."

Fernando was sound asleep now. Giovanni went to his room and slipped into pajamas and a dressing gown. Nella came to unpack and rearrange his clothes. The lights were on, and he could see her face, deadened by exhaustion, pale; her lips were dry, her pretty, black eyes bloodshot.

"Go to bed," she said, "if only for an hour. You've been traveling." And distractedly, as if to give her voice itself a cause for utterance: "What kind of weather did you have in Rome?" she asked.

"Oh, fine," he said, "fine weather," adding, in an effort to be more precise: "Only, yesterday evening there was a little sleet."

"Here it snowed all night long. And I can't remember when it's been so cold."

She prepared his bed, and he said: "I'll get into bed only for a moment, just long enough to go over an article here I'm interested in. Then I'll join you, and I want you to lie down, understand?"

She folded back the corner of the spread and, after Giovanni had got into bed, leaned over to tuck in the covers.

She said: "When Fernando's well enough, he'll need a change of climate. The city is no place to convalesce." She straightened out Giovanni's suit on the hanger, brushing the jacket and hanging it in the wardrobe. "Don't you agree?"

"There'll be time to think about it," he said.

"I've thought about it already. Since it'll be near the end of March, I've been considering Vallombrosa. What do you think?"

"Of course. A good idea," he answered, returning to the Nuovo Giornale, page one. Nella was about to leave; instinctively, she replaced the chair by the dressing table which Giovanni had moved.

She said: "It's lucky we have money now. Gracious! think, if it had happened five or six months ago!"

Alone, it was to more immediate matters that his thoughts turned: to his purchase, reduced in value by at least one half—at least that; and to the fact that he had sunk his entire fortune into this transaction. In his pocket he counted a scant two thousand lire which, within a very few days, would be eaten up by household and medical expenses. He thought of Bugatti's betrayal—Bugatti, who had certainly known beforehand how the tide was running, hence his impatience to close the bidding before the tenth! And of the fifty thousand he had delivered after the announcement had come out in the press! And of the promissory note, with the date in blank, given to Erina. A maze of circumstances confounding his reason, leaving him frenzied, benumbed.

An hour later, when Nella entered to tell him that Fernando seemed to be more comfortable and was asking for him, she found him asleep, serene, snoring lightly, and she did not have the heart to awaken him. She removed the paper tented on his breast, turned off the light, and returned to Fernando. She told him: "Daddy's sleeping now. But you'll see him in the morning. He told me that as soon as you're well, we're going to go to Vallombrosa, you and I, so you can rest. And Daddy will come to visit us on Sundays. And maybe he'll buy a car and come out every evening."

"A Mercedes, Mamma?"

"Perhaps."

"But a Mercedes is very big, you know, like a—like a—"

"Hush, Fernando, you mustn't excite yourself. If a Mercedes is really so big, then no. We certainly aren't millionaires yet."

"But Daddy's very good, isn't he, Mamma. Daddy's perfect."

"He's Daddy, Fernando," she said.

3.

There are days now, in March, of limpid skies and sunshine, and the air is warm; from the hilltop, away in the distance, one may discern the Anconella dredge plying the placid green of the river. And suddenly, without the horizon's darkening—simply a curtain of sheerest tulle across the sun—rain shatters down, and hail; and then, instantly, it is over: the sky is blue again, immaculate, and the sun shines. Yet, from this cloudburst, so abstract, so utterly unexpected, too brief to be convincing, the countryside emerges devastated, the city pavements sheeted with water, suburban lanes turned to wintry mire.

For Giovanni, this month of March was in every sense a memorable one: this the forty-third March of his life. When events (largely of his own making: as a result of his incompetence, his fatalism, and the rashness created in him by his first successes) marched one by one in succession to their logical conclusion, he was caught unprepared, confronted by a wall of hostility and intrigue he could not—we shall not say pull down—but not even dent. Though a man who, on former occasions, in war for instance, had proved himself both courageous and proud, and no less so, more recently, in dealing with insinuations however ironical, he now found himself to be cringing and petty whenever the moment specially demanded dignity. Thus, inept before responsibility, undertaking only whatever he felt would not further diminish his crumbling prestige, he fell back upon the most puerile sort of blackmail. The only thing that he fought desperately to defend, like a boxer his face, was the honor and harmony of his family, that they might stand aloof of his defeat until the very last. Or rather, until he had gained the upper hand; for once flattened and punch-drunk, naturally he risked losing his family as well, and in the most violent way.

For the scrap iron he had bid and paid two hundred thousand lire for—two hundred and fifty thousand, including Bugatti's commission —the manager of the Berta Works offered thirty thousand. With an expression of indignation, a portrait of the offended businessman, Giovanni strode from the office in high dudgeon. This, however unfruitful, had constituted his first energetic, dignified act; to be followed, moments later, by his second and last.

With the little change he had left, he took a taxi; it was morning and the Credito Toscano was still open. He had maintained a checking account there for the past six months; though now, having withdrawn money to cover his last purchase, his account had become purely symbolic, reduced to little more than a few hundred lire. He was ushered into the office of one of the directors, where he produced a bill of sale listing the property in his possession still lying in the roundhouse; on the strength of this, he asked for an immediate loan of fifty thousand lire.

He was very politely refused: "This policy cannot be broken," he was told by one of the vice-presidents, a certain Dr. Corsini, who wore a Fasces and "1921" in his buttonhole: a young, dark-haired man with mustaches and whiskers, the effeminacy and elegance of an actor. He added: "Particularly at this time: above all in this period of readjustment and defense of the lira. In fact, it is precisely because of the revision and general reorganization of credits and loans that a very slight exploitation, in depth, of resources is allowed. Defense of the lira is contingent upon the greatest possible increase of national industry and commerce, and also therefore—above all—upon the part played by trust companies, upon the greatest possible extension of faith to medium and small industry, to the medium and small businessman. . . . I notice, Signor Corsini," he put in parenthetically, "that we have the same name. Do you also have your doctorate?"

"No," Giovanni said, "a certificate in accountancy. And, unfortunately, as you can see, I'm not a party member."

"My word, what nonsense!" the other returned. "A good Fascist is nothing but an upright citizen. And you certainly are that: a client of ours, a public accountant. . . . But now, in conclusion, as regards your request, I'm obliged to say—let us discuss it again, say, in two months."

"In two months I won't need it," said Giovanni: unwittingly prophetic. "In two months I'll be in quite a different field. What I have just shown you represents the minimal part of the securities I now hold. But I am pleased, anyway, to find out exactly how far the Credito Toscano backs up its depositors. It means, from now on I shall take my deposits to a bank that gives something more than your measly five per cent."

He had walked to the door; still smiling, polite, his namesake Dr. Corsini came forward: "I should hardly say," he said, "that such language reflects any credit upon you. I well understand your annoyance; but may I point out that if you really had other securities, the ones you mentioned, you were ill-advised not to present them. Our talk would then have proceeded from a different basis. And lastly, if you actually are the big-time speculator you claim to be, evidence of which we fail to find, I should say that by your very request you injured your cause: you asked, wouldn't you say, for too little?" He opened the door, making way for Giovanni to pass: "My respects," he said.

The day after, his capitulation began. He had to return to the Berta Works, to see the manager, who kept him cooling his heels for two hours before receiving him: "Have you reconsidered?" he asked; and presently, mercilessly: "Your speculation in this field is finished, make no mistake about that!"

Giovanni needed money, mostly to cover household expenses, plus a thousand to keep Nella from even suspecting the disastrous state of his affairs.

"And I don't think there's any real likelihood of placing the material with another industry. But keep trying, if you have leads."

Giovanni ventured: "I can always dispose of it with a small firm, some private party."

"Think so? In any case, that's what you told me yesterday. The only reason I'm discussing it with you now is because my impression is that you're hard up for cash. That's the only reason. Then, of course, we've done business together before, and I didn't wish to appear discourteous. The best I can offer you is thirty-five thousand, but you'll have to decide whether you'll take it, immediately, here and now."

"Make it fifty," Giovanni said.

The manager took out his checks and drew up one for forty thousand. He passed it across to Giovanni and said: "Good luck, Corsini. And give our friend Bugatti my regards, when you see him. I haven't seen him myself in a dog's age."

At that time, whenever Giovanni had telephoned his office, Bugatti was "out at the moment." And Giovanni did not dare to call at his office both for fear that he encounter old friends and associates, and because, as if ostracized, Bugatti's staircase was now out of bounds to him. Fernando had taken a turn for the worse, his scarlet fever having become complicated by a slight pulmonary inflammation: consultants were required, a nurse night and day, oxygen, taxis, and doctors' fees; and during the month, five or six thousand lire were consumed by household and medical expenses. The remnant business was still hanging fire. He had met Erina twice, secretly, at their café in Porta a Prato, during the first week. And as soon as Fernando was no longer in danger of coming down with pneumonia, having cashed the check from the Berta Works, he spent another afternoon with Erina.

They met at the usual café. She arrived in a new *tailleur*, cut very short, above the knees, displaying her figure to great and provocative advantage; a dove-colored cloche matching her suit framed her face and the blonde curls lying against her cheeks: a kitten more than ever—the very way he liked her. He rose and kissed her hand; immediately, even before returning his greeting, she asked: "How's your child?" And then, quickly: "Now don't ask me if I've sold the stuff yet; or rather, we'd better talk about it right now, so we won't spoil the whole afternoon. Nothing's settled yet. I went to Prato yesterday with my father, but they didn't offer us enough. It's best to hold out—you agree, don't you?"

She sat with her legs crossed, futilely trying to pull down her skirt; each time she shifted position her thighs, halfway up her dress, were visible, and Giovanni, as if a stranger to her body and she were now offering it to him for the first time, grew gradually more excited. She sipped her cognac and remarked offhand: "The people we got the rags from have to negotiate the promissory note. That's what you say, isn't it—'negotiate'? Anyway, they've got to have money. They asked me if I would pay up the note or else if they could release it, in which case—I'm only telling you what they said—they want to know what date to write in and what address—the warehouse?"

This was what Giovanni had expected; he felt his blood curdle, venturing: "Couldn't they at least wait until your father has sold the rags? And you—couldn't you, just this one time, accept a small profit? It's the sort of thing, you know, you have to be prepared for in business. You can't expect every hand to be a slam. At the moment, darling, I'm on my uppers—that's the expression. But our trip—don't worry—is only postponed for a few weeks."

She sat listening to him with perked-up ears, less like his kitten than a tigress. And God alone knows how much of the commercial talk came through to her, for she promptly gave it her own, more vulgar interpretation; she left Giovanni speechless when she said: "What? Say that again! You want your fifty thousand back? You didn't give it to me?"

Giovanni felt faint. He fingered his Turmac. The jigger of cognac stood before him. But his voice, this he recognized: the voice of a man smiling in the teeth of pain. Yet hardly a voice: rather, a distant echo, a thousand miles distant, as if his tonsils, suddenly ballooning in his throat, were about to choke him. He summoned up strength, and a manner, in one swallow downing half the cognac left in his glass: "Sort of disappointed, aren't you?" he mocked. "Just as I had planned, to have a little fun with you!"

Erina, eying him mistrustfully, sat tight-lipped with her thighs now more than half visible; they were not alone in the café, and the waiter was young and was looking at her too. With a glance to match his words, Giovanni said: "Pull down your skirt!" And, as she did not see fit to respond, continuing to stare at him, suspicious, her eyebrows cast in a frown, the expression, he felt, really that of a tigress cub: "Shall we go?" he asked her.

At that, Erina exploded; as shrill and flushed with anger as he, in his simulated emotions, had been husky-voiced and petty, she screamed: "Come off that pull-down-your-skirt crap! Shall *who* go? I don't take talk like that, brother! And I halfway feel you're still trying to pull something. But get this: there's not much left to pull! That chicken feed—you can just forget it!" Then, suddenly sensing that her outburst had been too violent, that she had shown her hand too hastily, she shifted ground: "You've really disappointed me. You had been so generous, giving me such a present, and I had made all kinds of plans. I wanted to put up a laboratory."

She didn't say what sort of laboratory, and Giovanni didn't ask. He puffed at his cigarette, unable to draw his eyes away from her legs.

She went on: "Really, are you really having trouble? I'm sorry. Excuse me if I lost my temper. Sure, Giannino, I'll sell the stuff right away . . . and whatever they give me, they give me. And I'll return the fifty thousand immediately," she smiled, very sweetly, "but as a loan, of course, with interest. How much interest will you give me?"

"Will a hundred per cent do?" Giovanni said.

For the first time—at last!—he had detected a note of imposture in his mistress's voice. She was slipping from his grasp. He dreaded the thought; but at least she was still there. Her presence excited him. And he turned to the single task of regaining her confidence in him.

Taking out his wallet to pay the waiter, he pretended to fumble, and let the pack of thousand-lira notes bounce out onto the table, the twenty-five or thirty that remained of the payment received from the Berta Works, which, once he had chosen a bank—not the Credito Toscano—were destined for deposit.

It was a naïve strategem, a ruse much too obvious to deceive a Sanfrediana now and for some time well along the road we might euphemistically call "to perdition." Actually, of the two, Giovanni was the one being "taken," and he ought to have recognized it, a moment later, when she said: "You'll have to excuse me, but I've got to hurry home."

She did not even care to fabricate a pretext. His surprise, his insisting, pleading, and, when they had left, about to raise his voice, as he took her by the arm, his telling her, "Be nicer, I have some say-so over what you do"—all this notwithstanding, she wrenched free and halfshouted at him: "Some *what*? You have a say-so? You have a say-so over what *I* do? You can stop kidding yourself now!"

They had come to the entrance of Ponte Sospeso. She opened her purse and handed a coin to the tollkeeper; then, turning to Giovanni, added in a sharp, peremptory tone: "I think you'd better stay on your side of the bridge. We'd best let a little river water run between us for a time—until your screwed-up ideas straighten out a bit."

Unheeding, he followed after her; contrite, he had begun to plead with her again, imploring forgiveness. He followed her on to the tramcar from Legnaja and followed her off only two stops later, under Porta San Frediano. Evening had fallen; she stepped back close to the wall of the gate, into the half-shadows, standing away from the traffic and pedestrians.

"If I were you, I'd steer clear of San Frediano," she warned. Her voice was one of menace and naked insinuation.

"And what do you mean by that?" he answered. "You have protectors?"

Threat for threat, he replied with whatever vulgarities he needed to counter Erina's. The three-months-old enchantment, begun in the private dining chambers of the Picciolo, proceeding to Room Number 8 of the Belvedere, now lay shattered. His mistress had revealed to him her true self, and there remained, as far as he could see, but a single way of winning her back: by bullying her. He was still fond of her, as she was, as she showed herself actually to be; her ferocity and vulgarity took on an unexpected charm, arousing in him an animal attraction, there being this sensual warp in all healthy, virile men. This match, at least, he hadn't lost; he was holding cards, he felt, that could turn the game in his favor. But he was deluding himself; again, once again, deluding himself, and—as always—mainly *about* himself: about his courage and his fund of self-reliance, clearly all spent ten years before in the mountains of the Trentino.

He said to her: "Well, beautiful, now I suppose you'll have me hauled in for corrupting a minor." He had taken her by the arm and again she had wrenched free. "Let me meet your Alphonses. What are they—ragpickers like yourself?"

She was no longer Mary Pickford or the young Maria Campi: simply a little whore from San Frediano, her degradation laid bare, old for her twenty-three years, old for the life she had lived.

She said: "Look, I warned you. You just have to take a few steps. I live in Via Camaldoli, and you know it."

The "few" steps lengthened into twenty, thirty . . . there was a corner to turn, a little stretch of ancient wall, halfway along which he asked her to stop, his animus, his voice, both completely re-formed. He turned to her: "Why must you be so mean with the one who loves you?" And as she had started on again, he said quickly, the words tumbling from his tongue: "You know I can't do without you. Erina, I'll buy you a ring, I'll give you five thousand lire, I'll let you negotiate the note."

"Ahhh," she said, and she slackened her pace. "Now we can talk. —Not because of what you offer me, understand; but I see your tone has changed."

A half-hour later, as it was already evening and he would have to be home before midnight, forgoing the intimacy of Room Number 8 in the Belvedere, they found themselves toasting their reconciliation in champagne, in one of the little reserved rooms of the Picciolo: a reconciliation sealed by a quick embrace, by Giovanni's having given her the promised five thousand lire, and by a rendezvous agreed upon for two days later.

The afternoon of the following day—Nella had insisted, and there had been no way Giovanni could see to refuse—another medical consultation took place at Fernando's bedside; the attending physician, supported by two specialists, announced a marked improvement in the child's condition, definite progress toward convalescence. The visit cost a thousand lire, and Nella seemed a new person. Fernando's fever had subsided to normal, and he was allowed to play with his erector set, mounting the pieces on the pillows.

Participant in the family rejoicing, Giovanni left the house shortly after the doctors, he, like Nella, with a sense of release from an incubus, which, in his case, had blunted his faculties and left him, during the past two weeks, incapable of judging his own actions. Walking the streets, he meditated. He started for the warehouse: the ideal place to concentrate on the turn taken by his business: a business which, in truth, had ceased to be—but for that reason the ideal place! And on his position which, for the first time, he seemed to see clearly, in all its drama and insolubility—exactly as it was. And in its full frightening measure, he appraised his conduct: his innocence in giving Bugatti the fifty thousand lire, his panic which had abated after dumping his stock of railway parts on the Berta Works, the pettiness he had relapsed into in conversation with his banker namesake.

His reflections had begun directly he was out of doors, unraveling in his mind as his legs bore him along Via de' Pepi, Via Pietrapiana, Via dell'Oriuolo. By the time he came into Piazza del Duomo, he had absolved himself of blame: "I lost my head worrying about Fernando," he decided. He plotted muddleheaded revenge against Bugatti, the Berta Works, and the whole Corsini clan; daydreams all, not one of which crystallized into a plan of action. He went into Bottegone's and ordered a vermouth at the bar. He had need of something to distract his mind. A physical need—of companionship, of love; he regretted not having agreed to see Erina that evening. He headed for the warehouse of his friend Adamo Maestri, the paint dealer, and found it closed. The thoughts which had driven him out of doors, toward his own warehouse, now, once again, turned him in that direction. Down to his last few dozen thousand lire, he had definitely to decide upon a new career for himself.

It was a late March evening, and he was wearing his gray topcoat, still new despite its two years; during the winter of twenty-four, he remembered, cutting corners on his office clerk's salary, it had served him in the coldest weather. At his newsstand in Via Faenza he bought a paper; under streamer headlines he found *The Full Text of the Duce's Directives to the Ministry of Communications Regarding Railway Renovation.* He turned the page and immediately, in the first column, saw an account of the investigation into the Matteotti crime. There—in Via Chiara, a small street, at that hour deserted—with a single, abrupt fidget of annoyance, he folded the paper in two, tore it in half, into quarters, and scattered it along the sidewalk; then, walking back, he kicked it down a gutter drain with his foot. He came into Via Panicale, circling around the market, for months now a familiar neighborhood; and not until that moment, there in the deserted, silent square, walking beneath the eaves of the vegetable stalls, emptied of carts and the people and traffic and shouts that glut it from dawn till noon, not until then did Giovanni hear the trumpets of Destiny sound forth.

There was his street. Providence itself had led him there, had willed that he rent a warehouse that was near the market: he would become a wholesaler! Of fish or fruit, of greens or earthenware or rolls—whatever he chose! Or a wholesale paint dealer, a competitor of Adamo Maestri's: would they be any less friendly because of this? Of course not! But why necessarily a competitor? They could go in together!

He dug the bunch of keys from his pocket, opened the lock and raised the shutter door: on the entry floor lay two envelopes: one from the Credito Toscano and the other from Erina; optimistic—with none of the apprehension recent experience ought to have implanted in him —he fancied that he could guess the contents of both letters: the bank, of course, was apologizing for having refused him the loan which, now, after more closely examining the matter, it felt quite differently about; and Erina—sweet, lovable, generous Erina—had been moved to scribble a few kind words to him in final apology for her harsh words of the evening before, and perhaps—yes, perhaps!—to tell him that her father had sold the remnants and that tomorrow he could count on having the fifty thousand lire.

He switched on the light inside the glass cage and sat down, delighted, touched; and with unconscious, but consequently mistaken, trepidation, took the paper knife and slit open the letter from Erina.

Actually, he had heard the resolute blare of the trumpets of Jericho!

Dearest Gianni [his mistress wrote],

Im writing to tell you something which youll be pleased and displeased to hear but because it means something to my future youll agree Ive done right since you love me even tho we must separate. Id made up my mind yesterday but then I didnt have the courage to tell you. Well this is what Ive done—Ive joined a niteclub troupe and today at noon I leave therefore when you receive this letter Ill all ready be gone. Im not telling you where because I must think only about my art at least in the beginning. You know that Ive all ways dreamed of this and now finally I have the chance. Later on Ill write you cards and tell you where you can reach me so you can give me news which Ill be glad to hear because you are all ways in my heart.

Lots of Belvedere and Picciolo kisses from your

Kitten

By the way do you know that the rag business didnt work out. I didnt even get back half and I shall have costumes made because I am the one that must do that so that when I dance and sing I think of you.

Giovanni had no sooner read past the signature, the charming little pseudonym Erina preferred to her actual name, than his gaze came to rest on the letter from the Credito Toscano: only then did he notice in the upper left-hand corner of the envelope, printed in fine type and underlined, the words: EXCHANGE OFFICE. To open it was hardly necessary, like staring at the sun in midsummer to satisfy oneself of its existence. The promissory note which he had released with the date in blank was due to mature the following day, on demand of a Brunetto Pisselli. That, at least for Giovanni, was really a pseudonym.

VITALIANO BRANCATI

The Cavaliere

TRANSLATED BY FRANCES FRENAYE

On Maundy Thursday of 1943, a feeble cry came out of the ruins of the Palazzo San Placido in Catania:

"I'm Cavaliere Luigi Arcidiacono!"

The excavators stood with their picks suspended in mid-air, and finally someone went to call the army captain who was in charge.

"Captain, somebody seems to be alive!"

The captain ordered complete silence and bent over the rubble with one hand curved around his ear. A moment later, the cry rose again:

"Help! Help! I'm Cavaliere Luigi Arcidiacono!"

"Perhaps we can get him out, if we hurry," said the captain.

"Here's hoping!" said one of the workers.

"It would be a damned shame to lose a *cavaliere*!" said another, starting to laugh, just as the guns to the north rang out again and the sky was filled with white smoke. Soldiers and workers alike took shelter, echoing the cry of: "Here, here!" while bombs rained down upon the half-destroyed city and its wounded and dead, its empty streets and houses, where many a heartbeat had been stilled and buried forever. . . .

A cloud of smoke rose up into the sky. Many of those who had been bewailing their dead were plunged into silence, and their fate struck the survivors with the same terror to which they themselves had been prey. Some of the wounded, who had called for help, received fresh wounds in answer to their prayer. And others, who had been buried and then partially dug up, were buried again. After which, the workers and soldiers finally emerged from hiding, followed by the captain, a

317

priest, several nuns, and an old man in his second childhood, who had escaped from his evacuated relatives and come back on foot to the city, stopping passers-by to ask: "Are there women in those planes? A fine lot they must be!"

The ruins of the Palazzo San Placido had been hit again, but in a very curious manner, so that the cavaliere was closer to the surface than before and his voice sounded more distinctly, while at the same time he was apparently unable to hear the answers addressed to him from the street, and his rescuers' work was impeded by the danger that some of the remaining walls might crumble and precipitate a landslide. They had to take some boards from a wooden fence and set them up as supports of the masonry. Meanwhile, darkness was falling, and they sat down to rest, leaning up against the boards.

"What do you suppose the cavaliere's up to now?" said one of them. And he added, raising his voice: "Cavaliere, how are you doing? Have you gone to bed?"

"You damn fools!" said the captain. "He may be dead!"

"With every bomb, another cavaliere bites the dust!" put in one of the soldiers.

"What sort of a cavaliere do you suppose he is, anyhow?" asked another, and then, with an expression of mock terror: "If he's a Knight of Malta, God help us!"

"Don't tell me that! My legs are trembling with respect! . . . What is a Knight of Malta, anyhow?"

"A cavaliere that has four-fifths noble blood!"

"Well, I wish him joy of it! But he'd be better off today if he were a lizard or a cockroach."

They talked on in this vein until midnight, when another alarm drove them to the shelter. Even there, after every crash, they spoke of the cavaliere.

"That one must have finished off the cavaliere!"

"Easy up there, boys; spare the cavaliere!"

"That was it, Cavaliere! So long!"

"What shall we do without our cavaliere?"

"Dinner is served, Cavaliere!"

Before dawn, the workers and soldiers ran back to the ruins. With renewed vigor they dug their picks and shovels into the rubble all the way up to the handles and pulled them angrily out again, displacing masses of sand and stone. But no voice came from below.

"I miss you, *Cavaliere!*" a corporal groaned.

But all of a sudden, just as the sun came up, the voice emerged, clearer than ever: "Help, help! I'm *Cavaliere* Luigi Arcidiacono! Call my wife and son!"

Workers and soldiers embraced, slapped each other on the back, and waved their picks and shovels in the air.

"Good for you, *Cavaliere!*"

"Hurrah for the *cavaliere!*"

"He's a tough bird, the *cavaliere!*"

Around eleven o'clock, the local Fascist party leader, skinny as a crow in his black uniform, with a gilt chicken on his cap, arrived upon the scene. He strutted about the ruins, while one of the workers bent over close to the ground, made a trumpet of his hands, and called out: "Touch wood, *Cavaliere!* The Big Dud is here!"

The captain lit a cigarette, with such obvious signs of disgust at having his work interrupted that finally the leader, after looking around for a moment and tapping his boot with his riding crop, got back into his car and drove rapidly away, leaving the odor of a shroud behind him.

"To hell with him!" said the soldiers and workers, crossing their fingers, and they went to work with their picks and shovels even harder than before.

"If the *cavaliere's* not out by noon, I'll spit in my eye!" said one.

"I'll cut off my balls!"

"I'll cut off my balls and hang them around my neck!"

But when noon came, in spite of all their efforts, the *cavaliere* was still buried, and so he was that evening.

"This is an impossible brand of *cavaliere!*" the workers grumbled.

"He's a *cavaliere* with the evil eye upon him."

"Perhaps our Saint Agatha simply doesn't like *cavalieri!*"

They slept for only a few hours that night and were back on the job by three o'clock in the morning. Meanwhile, the news that under the ruins of the Palazzo San Placido there was a man buried alive, who called out every half hour: "I am *Cavaliere* Luigi Arcidiacono!" had spread all over the city, covering great spaces with every bound because of the rarity of the inhabitants, who were dispersed in shelters, hospitals, and the innermost recesses of their own houses.

Around the middle of the next day, when the workers had hacked their way far enough to exchange actual conversation with the victim, his son, Rosario Arcidiacono, arrived like a whirlwind upon the scene.

"So you're his boy?" they said, crowding around him. "And you didn't know he was here? He was caught far from home, is that it? What's your father like, tell us. Is he short, tall, thin, fat, or what? We're asking you in order to prepare ourselves for the moment when we actually pull him out!"

The son did not answer. He scratched at the dirt with his hands and lowered his head among the rocks as if he too wanted to bury himself alive.

"Papa!" he cried.

"My booooy!" came an answer from below. "My booooy!"

Just then a bell started ringing.

"A bell!" exclaimed one of the workers. "I hadn't heard one in so long, I'd forgotten such things existed. Who can be ringing it?"

"It must be Pietro Simili," said a soldier. "He came back on leave last night and swore he'd start the bells ringing."

Sure enough, in the nearby church tower, a soldier was pulling the bell rope with all his might and main, and soon other bells began to answer.

"It's the Gloria! God help us, the Gloria!"

Some women who were standing in line before a bakery stopped fighting for first place and fell weeping upon one another's necks.

"It's Holy Saturday!" exclaimed one of the workers, throwing down his shovel and looking gloomily at the ground. The others followed his example and sat down, with their hands hanging between their legs and a disconsolate look on their faces. Just then another peal, as keen and silvery as the tinkle from a horse's collar, rang out directly above them. From underground came a frightened cry.

"What is it? The air-raid alarm?"

"No, it's the Gloria," said his son, in a low, almost ashamed, voice.

"The Gloria!" There was a pause, while from under the stones came a sound of thrashing and wriggling. "Where's your mother?" asked the cavaliere.

"She's at home!" said the son, and he whispered into a soldier's ear: "Wounded!"

"Listen, Rosario, tell your mother to sell her rings and necklaces and earrings, everything she's got, and pay those men a thousand lire a minute! Every second here is hell!"

"Cavaliere!" one of the workers interrupted. "We don't need money to keep us going! We'll stick at it until we drop, don't worry!"

"If only I could get out for Easter!"

"Do you think he will?" asked the son, pressing a handkerchief to his mouth.

"Who can say?" sighed the worker. "Jesus Christ got out of the tomb. . . . But tell us, how did your father come to be a *cavaliere*?"

Just then they heard a loud noise from the direction of the sea. The women in front of the bakery began to shout, and the workers took hold of Rosario Arcidiacono, who was crouching among the ruins and looking up at the sky as if he were waiting for something to fall, and dragged him away to the shelter. The noise was repeated, to north and south, followed by a faraway echo of gunfire. A stranger ran to the shelter door and told the soldier on guard: "There under the remains of the Palazzo San Placido, a voice is shouting: 'Go away, Rosario, go away and get under cover!'"

"It must be the *cavaliere*," the soldier said.

"The *cavaliere*? What the devil do you mean?" said the other, his eyes wide open in surprise.

Their conversation was brusquely interrupted. In a portion of the sky so remote that it seemed to be above the sky proper, were two, three, four, five, minute silvery creatures. They moved slowly and solemnly, almost with an effort, like birds of prey held back by some strange trepidation, perhaps by their own ferocity, which assumed such proportions as they drew near the target as to stun their own wings. Then, all of a sudden, they picked up speed and flew very straight and fast, with a sparkling stare in their expressions, as if they were fascinated by the prayerful fear upon the faces of their future victims and could not but look at them intensely. An avalanche of roaring, whistling, crashing sounds, accompanied by rays of black light, which contrasted with the absolute darkness of the bombed buildings, fell for ten minutes upon the city.

Rosario Arcidiacono put his hands over his ears and eyes, and a worker added his hands as well. The soldier who had been standing watch at the door made mute signs of a last blessing and opened his mouth to form the syllables: "The cavaliere! ..."

The worker moved his lips as if to ask him to repeat what he had just been saying, and with his thumb and middle finger the soldier made motions representing a man on horseback and then reiterated the blessing. When the raid was over, three men held Rosario back from running to the ruins, forcibly loaded him into an ambulance, and took him home.

"Why won't you let me go to my father?" he protested.

A half-hour later they came back from the cavaliere's house and joined the circle of their fellows, who were standing where the ruins of the Palazzo San Placido had been heaped up before, and where now there was only a large ditch.

"He wasn't so very noble, or so very rich, either," said one of the three. "I saw his pictures. He was a fellow no taller than this, who was always photographed with a black hat and a cane."

"What did he do for a living?" a soldier asked.

"He sold second-hand books."

"And did he really have the title of cavaliere?"

"Cavaliere, my eye! He didn't have any title."

"Silly ass!" exclaimed a man with a squint. "He didn't have anything and he wasn't anybody, and yet when he was pinned under the rubble like a trapped mouse, just look what his imagination prompted him to say! Cavaliere! Silly ass!"

For the next two nights the bombers did not return. The sky, from whose edges men had rolled stones down upon men, live rocks rolling down the banks of a pond full of frogs, was once more moonless and taciturn, but there was a rosy light of spring in the air, which went along with Easter. The workers and soldiers were sleeping outdoors, around the ditch, at the foot of the steps of the church, which, now that the Palazzo San Placido was gone, dominated the main street of the city. One soldier imagined he saw the cavaliere's black hat outlined against the cross of the bell tower and said as much to his companions.

"Silly ass!" murmured the man with a squint, half awake and half asleep. "He didn't have anything and he wasn't anybody, and yet his imagination prompted him to call himself *cavaliere!*"

"What do you suppose has become of him?" asked a soldier. "How come we haven't found even a little finger?"

"He's gone where all the rest of us poor beggars are slated to go!"

"Silly ass!" said the man with a squint. . . . "*Cavaliere!*"

The next night after that, a sound of hammer beats on the pavement awakened all the men. They sat up, but before they could ask: "What is it?" the sound was upon them, like a clap of thunder rolling from one point of the horizon to another. Over the rock-clogged street, with all the impetus of a cannon ball, ran a dazzling white horse, without either reins or saddle, and disappeared into the darkness of the night.

"He must have run away!"

"I don't believe it!"

"That's the horse of our *cavaliere*," a soldier said laughing.

"Silly ass!"

"He's gone to join his master! . . ."

"Silly ass! . . ."

For many nights to come, the little group continued to talk about the *cavaliere*, until finally they were broken up, scattered, and some of them killed by war. But men's words live behind them. A crowd of beggars, watchmen, and night owls of various kinds kept alive the legend of the *cavaliere*, and the empty space left by the loss of the Palazzo San Placido came to be known as the Piazza del Cavaliere, where his memory is cherished and reigns as solemnly as the church in the background.

In this legend, the *cavaliere* is not benighted and vainglorious, or a stocky man always dressed in black. He is young, tall, and strong, and his eyes are covered with a veil of alternating severity and sorrow. When the Palazzo San Placido was knocked down, he made an arch of his shoulders and for two whole days held up the ruins. Under this arch a little girl cried, slept, and called out: "I'm hungry! I'm scared!" to her mother, and lived to tell the tale. When the local Fascist leader toured the ruins, the *cavaliere* recognized his footsteps as surely as a tree knows the feel of a kite's claws that have perched on it before, and, stretching his arm out from a hole in the ground, he reached up, struck him across the shoulders and sent him tumbling at a worker's feet, while his cap with the gilt chicken rolled along the ground. When the stones were finally removed, the cavaliere jumped up, handed the frightened little girl over to a nun, sat down on a bench, and stayed there for an hour, looking very pale, and without eating or drinking. Indeed, he couldn't be budged, even when the city suffered the cruelest raid of the war. There he sat, staring up at the sky with a severe and sorrowful expression. "Cavaliere!" a soldier shouted from the shelter door. "Come on in here!" The cavaliere gave him a look so sad that it seemed like a large tract of heaven filled with rain and with thousands upon thousands of angels adding their tears to the downpour. Then he shifted his gaze to the point on the horizon where the airplanes always appeared. "The first blood drawn will be that of a child and shoot up in the air!" prophesied the cavaliere.

And after the first explosion, a spout of gleaming red drops shot quite incredibly upward. They were tiny drops and very far away, but everyone could see them just as clearly as if they were in his own handkerchief. The red cluster climbed up and up, turning from red to silver on the way, until it stopped to quiver like a group of stars in the twilight sky. "Get in the shelter!" the cavaliere shouted. "It's my turn now!"

The soldier dived in and, crouching on the floor, with his hands over his ears, he heard the next street machine-gunned and torn to pieces without pity. But once the raid was over, the cavaliere was gone. A streak like a violent outpour of spittle, left by machine-gun fire, defiled the façade of the church, all the way to the feet of the Saviour standing in a niche. But what of the cavaliere? Not a single sign, not a hair, or fingernail, or even a thread. Disappeared, completely disappeared! . . .

But that night, in the bell tower, a bell rang all alone. Even now, at certain twilights, when the black-suited sexton's arm is weary, an invisible hand grasps the rope, and after pulling it slowly from one side to the other, gives it a superhuman yank. Then, amid the mild tones of the Ave Maria, the bell hits a clear, high note, sweet and powerful at the same time, like a cry of celestial challenge. When they hear this sound or cry, people bow their heads and make the sign of the cross.

There are some that pale and tremble. They are not old men, women, or children, cowards, weaklings, or doves. These, on the contrary, feel encouraged and breathe a sigh of relief. Those that tremble, whether they be under arms or under shelter, are from the ranks of the violent and the pitiless; they tremble among a mass of black clouds and kites and vultures. And those, who in heaven or earth have said or borne on their wings the motto: "I have never trembled!"—these tremble more than any others.

GIUSEPPE BERTO

Aunt Bess, in Memoriam

TRANSLATED BY BEN JOHNSON

The legend of my father, prospector in the Klondike, fell off rapidly after I reached my twelfth year. It was a decline that was to bear significantly upon my life. Until then, meek-looking and puny as he was, my father had been in my eyes a stupendous combination of Buffalo Bill and Henry Ford. He was afterwards deflated to his modest self as summoner, a title still used in our town to designate the man at city hall who, on starvation pay, performs the duties both of doorman and house messenger. In the latter capacity my father enjoyed the prerogative of a rickety bicycle which, though property of the Commune, was actually his. But after my twelfth year even the occasional and abusive use of that wheel did not suffice to restore to him his glory as a sourdough in the Klondike.

This disenchantment, coming as it did during the formative stage of my mental development, brought on regrettable consequences. Such, I would say, was its effect upon my brothers as well. In any case, following a normal physical development, we turned into listless, irresponsible youths, cynics at heart, and fairly brimming with envious contempt for all those hardy, industrious folk, assured of their meals, in whose midst fate had deposited us. Alone in escaping this ruin was our sister Peggy; born somehow a number of years after us, she had been able to draw profit from hearing accounts of my father's prospecting adventures which we, by then completely broken of the spell cast by this unlikely tale, punctuated with smart remarks and snickers.

There was a point, indeed, when the analytic spirit, so highly developed in us, succeeded even in trying to destroy the belief that our father had ever been in the Klondike at all. But counter to the destructive drive of our intelligence, there were several irrefutable facts. Apart from our names—Tom, Mike (yours truly), Johnny, and Peggy; apart from the existence of a photograph of a man, clumsy-looking as a bear, and perfectly capable of being our father, posed in front of a snow-covered mountain; apart from the determination every Sunday morning with which the man who had fathered us, foregoing mass, set out to pan for gold along the banks of our gentle plains river; apart from all this—there was Aunt Bess: a remote and mysterious personage who once each year, at Christmas, sent us a package of presents from an inconceivable place called Wichita Falls, Texas, U.S.A.

Time was needed before we got to the real essence of Aunt Bess. Whose sister, our father's or our mother's, was she? And why was it that our grandparents—Tom, in fact, made two bicycle trips hoping to clarify the situation—why was it that our grandparents chose to ignore her existence? And why did our mother turn pale and glare at her spouse whenever she was mentioned? Quite briefly: Aunt Bess was not an aunt at all. She was merely someone with whom our father had taken up during his glorious American adventure.

Once this detail was clear to us it would seem that the scant consideration we accorded our father, the municipal summoner, would increase a jot or so. Something, at any rate, *had* happened in America. Aunt Bess, clearly, must have been one of those marvelous western vamps—the kind that dances and shows her thighs through a slit in her skirt, singing huskily as she slinks from table to table plucking men's billfolds, one of those that finally, when her lover-bandit arrives, blows out all the lights in the saloon with her six-shooter. Our father, in his getup as lover-bandit, must have been enamored of her, and it must have been on her that he had squandered his fabled sacks of Klondike gold.

But not even this was effective. The true story emerged a little at a time, usually on Sunday evenings when Father came home drunk and would proceed with unwitting candor to comment on his past exploits. He had not acquired any gold in the Klondike. He had gone, certainly, urged by brashness and a childhood companion of his. After the death there of his companion, he was left with nothing. And so, on the heels of colossal failure, he had started for home, drifting from town to town across the vastness that is America, literally dying of hunger. And it was this person whom Aunt Bess had chanced to meet. Moved by pity for him, she took him in, she fed and reclothed him, and, slowly falling in love with him, would even have agreed to marry him if he, homesick for the Motherland, had not first touched her for the wherewithal for his return trip and then left. What a damned disgusting story! Admittedly, we had no clear notion as to what America was like, or Wichita Falls, or Aunt Bess, but we certainly knew the Motherland: the handful of houses surrounding the dilapidated one we lived in ourselves, where our chickens enjoyed utter freedom to scatter their droppings at will, the post of town summoner with its ridiculous stipend and, poor thing! our mother who, though scarcely to blame, was as far from being the heroine of a Western as one might imagine. If our father had preferred all this to America, then he was nothing, to our mind, but a plain fool. And in his entire life, past and present, there has arisen nothing indeed to convince us to the contrary.

We even came to hate him.

At mealtime, contemplating in turn the cabbage and pigskin soup before us, the tablecloth that went for weeks before being changed, and lastly our father's loutish face and the downcast look on our mother's, we could not but think how vastly different our lot would have been if that fool had not come down with homesickness for his Motherland, and we, instead of our mother's, had been Aunt Bess's children. We had gone so far as even to decide upon American professions for us. Tom would have been a pimp, Johnny ringleader of a gang of crooks, and I, the lazy idealist, a lighthouse keeper to whom beautiful women would flee in hiding from the police. Our sister Peggy never played with such ideas, and, anyway, we ourselves rarely admitted her to our projects. Aged seven, she seemed to care not a fig about her brothers or parents, let alone Aunt Bess. Years came and went, Aunt Bess at Christmastime continuing to send us playthings which would have been ideally suited for infants in diapers. And our mother—jealous or simply practical, there was no telling—sold them to the vestrymen who, praised be, were rich and always had new children, grinding out as they did one a year. And despite its completely subsidiary use, the Christmas package remained proof of a sentimental bind that would not break.

Why, then, didn't our father just drop everything, wife and all, and take us to America to live with Aunt Bess, who was still in love with him? Or why, in recompense for her great unrequited love—why didn't Aunt Bess send for us three brothers to become her adoptive children? Obviously, she must not have been aware of our miserable circumstances, our father having failed to advise her. Whereupon we resolved to study English by ourselves, so as to be able to write her a letter of explanation. Working at it for an entire week before giving up, it marked our only significant effort during adolescence. And then, on the point of stepping into life itself, we found ourselves dismayed by the prospect, already defeated, and imbued with such moral principles as would have made even the natives of Guiana blush, and without— excepting our passion for motion pictures—there developing in us any worth-while inclinations. And looking back, we now marvel that the world went on, all the same.

It went right on.

One evening our father came home completely transformed: he was attired in stiff jack boots, riding breeches, and a gray flannelette jacket buttoned to the neck, a cap with Bulgar visor, and sported a curious emblem which it had recently been decided, he explained, was the ancient insignia of the commune. It made us laugh. Not him, though; for within, a change had taken place, the uniform being but a pale exterior expression of it. He spoke of the new concept of the state, of the new orders that were at last providing the nation with an ethical dignity, of the respect owed the authorities, however significant or insignificant they were, under which latter heading he was modest enough to place himself.

Although we regarded these doings with our usual cynicism, and our mother seemed genuinely disturbed, the change was not without certain concrete advantages. Cabbage and pigskin soup made fewer and fewer appearances at table, being replaced according to the season by home-cooked hams and salami, by geese and turkey and fattened capons, while the strain that attended digestion of these delicacies was effectively alleviated by the light wine, imbibed to extravagance, that was produced by the neighboring countryside. The poor niece of a second cousin of my mother's was invited to live with us to help speed up various household chores, and she promptly assumed the rank of ill-treated menial; but being an energetic baggage, she bore up well, and Tom soon found in her, as presently did Johnny and I, a source of personal delight.

We began honestly to lose interest in our American and domestic destinies alike: to tell the truth, one had to appreciate that the old fool, once having surpassed his fiftieth year, had begun to conduct himself with a measure of decency and cleverness in regard to the practicalities of life. The New Order, though—repeated censuses and a need to own an identity card with prescribed photograph—left scarcely any impress upon our peaceful peasant population in whom respect for constituted authority was no different from their desire to remain on amicable terms with whomever was in command. But progress was evident: our rural folk, previously known by the vulgar term "peasants," who had been considered mere citizens of some kind of spiritual realm and had therefore made donations exclusively to the parish priest, now started to notice the existence of an administrative community, so that their gifts came with increasing frequency to be directed also to the town hall, where, though it was the villagers' intention that they reach the secretary of the commune or the mayor himself, they were ably expropriated by our father and brought home. The flannelette uniform with the badge in front had some importance.

But all this was but a trifle compared with what was to come.

With the aid one Sunday of four or five of his associates, our father stopped worshippers as they were leaving mass and herded them over to the front of the town hall. There the Tricolor was unfurled from the center balcony. Out from behind the flag stepped our father, no longer embarrassed by his puny physique, dressed completely in black and wearing on his head a sort of kettle with a tassel dangling from it. Little by little, his assistants managed to prod the countryfolk from their lethargy, and after some time the piazza was rocking with shouts and applause. Presently our father made several solemn gestures to calm them. Then he spoke. We had never suspected him of such—I shan't say oratorical powers—but great vocal power. His voice, slightly gravelly but powerful, ranged out over the rickety fences enclosing the tumbledown houses, over the lodging house and the church, and into the open countryside where, as it was, there happened to be nobody to listen to him. Still, even the disparity between half-functionary that he was and the rank to which he aspired had some effect upon his audience. Though not neglecting to mention the New Order, the citizens' reborn conscience, and the obligations incumbent therefrom upon everyone, our father orated for the most part about himself. It is cause for wonder still, how, by means of a few simple arguments, he was able to transform himself from a plain fool into something of a national hero. He cited himself, in fact, as a man who, scorning the facile lures by which the plutocratic powers had sought to enslave him, had abandoned a mercenary position to return to his Motherland, even to suffer, yet to contribute his energy, his intelligence, his devotion to the greatness of the nation. At the conclusion, in part spontaneously and in part prompted by their neighbors' examples, the audience applauded at length (though it was questionable whether the address had had any real effect upon them). However, it did have effect elsewhere, and in considerably higher quarters. A few days afterward an order came down from above naming our father as political head of the town.

It was a big thing, one which—why deny it?—gave rise to a little uneasiness. The political authority, of course, was entirely separate from the administrative, and there was no objection to the fact that the town's political leader was a lowly summoner at town hall. All the same, it was embarrassing. One need only think that our father, though attired in gray flannelette, was the lowest flunky, not of the mayor or the secretary, but of the meanest functionary in the commune. Whoever wished, on the pretext of wanting a message carried to the farthermost limits of the municipal realm, had the right to order him off on an eight-mile bicycle trip. Yet it was enough for him simply to assemble four cats in the piazza, don his black costume, and appear on the balcony, and suddenly he was equal if not superior to the mayor himself. And it was common knowledge that, such visible honors aside, it was also enough for him simply to whisper the right word in the right place and without further ado the mayor and secretary and entire municipal clique would come tumbling from their jobs. Not that our father wore the air of such a man, not that he would consider graft. Just that the possibility existed.

One evening he came home a little excited. Vainly he offered his summoner's uniform with attached stipend to Tom, me, and Johnny, in turn. We turned it down flatly. He, however—the following day he had an office in the town hall, all for himself, appointed with a large table and a brand-new leatherette writing set, a gift from the mayor. What he did there, no one ever learned. In all probability, nothing, because nobody ever gave him anything to do. But under that arrangement the embarrassing aspects of hierarchical interdependence were successfully avoided; and ultimately reaching a point where he drew down a salary more than triple his former one, he also sheltered himself from all risk of having to pedal off on those eight-mile bicycle trips. In respect to our fears that along with his gray uniform the gratuities attached thereto would likewise pass, they were shown to be utterly without foundation. In fact, the peasants were quick to realize that side by side with and perhaps slightly higher than the religious and administrative authorities, there existed a new one—the political. This, our father kept them aware of by means of patriotic ceremonies and Sunday morning discourses which, by continually harping on the same strings, acquired increased formal perfection and successfully galvanized the masses, both.

All this did not stand in the way of his being a good father. Indeed, his greatest efforts were put to providing us with gainful employment, gainful but completely honorary in view of our unseemly attitude toward all work. I, the most ingenuous of us three brothers, once actually found myself seated in the provincial grain depot. A week later I tendered my resignation, because I got bored just sitting around and because, to put it in a nutshell, it was not in the least necessary for me to get out of bed before everyone else to bring home the bacon. We had plenty of money at that time. We had moved into a respectable house, one in keeping with our father's new position. We had even changed our names. Tom had become Tommaso, I Michele, and Johnny Giovanni. A simple enough thing, on the face of it. But for Peggy, since no one could make out its derivation, recourse to a drastic innovation was demanded, and with a decision that affected her not one whit nor jostled her a single foot from her road, she was patriotically renamed Italia. Peggy, or rather Italia, having attained her thirteenth year and by then considerable physical development, went on vegetating in undisturbed silence.

Our nationalization was due as well to a steady fading from the memory of Aunt Bess. Poor Aunt Bess, victim of political upheaval! We found ourselves thinking of her less and less. Her ever-the-same Christmas toys arrived punctually; but with never a word about them, they were passed out, as personal contributions from the chief, with other gifts from the political Santa Claus, by our mother, who, dressed in black, distributed them to the neediest and politically most worthy children during a gala patriotic ceremony. Meanwhile, in our hearts, we no longer had many reasons to lament our aborted destiny. It may have been the result of a more mature view of life(plus time), or in consequence of the propaganda treating the scant amount of happiness being enjoyed in America; in any case, we had concluded that if we had been Aunt Bess's children, we should have been faced with work in one form or another, and for us, that, at least for the time being, was unnecessary. It is quite true that politics poison the mind. Through no fault of hers, Aunt Bess came to be thought of with indifference and even resentment, or simply not thought of at all, and yet she persisted in that really sweet habit of hers, of sending us gifts at Christmas. Only the war was a bar to her generosity.

But our entry into war—oh, what an epic, what a great day that was! It came at harvest time, but our father succeeded all the same in getting every peasant, every last reaper, into the piazza. Except for a woman to tend the fires, no one remained at home. Toward evening, as light, sultry gusts of wind carried the lowing of unmilked cows in from the countryside, our father stepped out onto the flag-draped balcony, flanked by the mayor and the priest. What he did there will long abide in the memory of those who lived at that moment in our history. He sweated, he wept, he kissed the flag, and flung his arms into the air calling upon God as his witness, he blessed those on the frontier who were beginning the sacrifice, and he cursed the enemy with such vehemence that at the conclusion, fourteen strapping young peasants, called by heaven only knows what atavistic warrior spirit, came forward and submitted their names to him as volunteers. This was topped off by a terrific drinking spree, during which all the patriotic hymns, starting with those of the Risorgimento, were sung with tear-filled eyes.

That evening our father came home late. He may perhaps have drunk beyond his measure, success itself may have gone to his head, or he may really have been sincere, since he was taking everything so damned seriously. He looked at us with such contempt as to freeze the grins on our lips. "You," he bellowed in his drill sergeant's voice, "you —my own flesh and blood—why haven't you signed up?"

Tommaso, assuming the right of the first born, replied first. He said that it had never even entered his mind, that he was getting along pretty well as it was and could see, therefore, no reason to alter his estate. He remarked that a father's duty is to safeguard the lives of his offspring—not to send them off for slaughter. And, he added, if our father was such a wretch as to forget his paternal duties, he for one was not going to forget his own as a son, to remain at home at the side of his aged mother to assist her and provide succor in the event of such need.

Except for some slight variations on this theme, Giovanni and I expressed the same opinion as that of Tommaso. Overtaken by an almost epileptic seizure, our father implored and cursed us; he threatened to cut off our meals and to deprive us of all future assistance —but all to no avail. And in that atmosphere of impending tragedy, one by one the fourteen volunteers came to announce that they had reconsidered, that the idea did not appeal to their families, that their duty would be more effectively discharged at home, tilling the fields: in sum, that they would not honor their original pledge.

Our father retired to his room. All night long we could hear him pacing back and forth. It was for us as well a tragic night: we found it difficult to remain cynics with our father's football clumping in our conscience. Then, at daybreak, the front door slammed and silence descended upon the house. All that day and for some days thereafter our mother moped about, now and then staring at us as if she thought we could tell her where he had gone. Then, one Sunday afternoon, he returned. He was wearing a gray-green uniform that was too large for him, and above it his lined face and white hair combined to present a pitiable sight. They had taken him despite his advanced age. Though attached to the Regimental Warehouse in the next town, his assignment was completely temporary inasmuch as he had already put in for front-line duty. Our mother was moved to tears. Whether it was from patriotic pride was not clear, but she wept, anyway. We, however, confined ourselves to giving our father—the soldier—looks of stern disapproval. What had possessed him? Did he doubt perhaps that without him the war would be won, all the same? Didn't he realize that, carried away by his lunatic ambition, he was risking destroying his family's position of well-being? Of course, these were things that escaped him. But we—we who had never aspired to any vainglory whatever—could already discern before us the abyss into which we were to be thrown.

The drop was swift. One of the townsmen, whose main exertions had gone into our father's political rise, delivered an undistinguished address in his praise—a speech from which one gathered that our father had already laid down his life in battle. With a selection of the most flattering details, he retraced his life—so completely dedicated to the welfare of the Motherland; he said that his life had received in its very nobility every conceivable reward, including the highest and most coveted, that of wearing the uniform and of marching off in the worthiest of company to be immolated in the defense of the communes and sacrosanct ideals. Finished with the praise, the speaker hastened to add that unqualified as he was, he felt that in the absence of the town's political chief he must shoulder that burden himself. And from that moment onward the political presents were rerouted to contribute toward the prosperity of another family.

Quite frankly, at the town hall they comported themselves more decently. Pretenders to the seat and writing table in the room where our father, luxuriating in serene prestige, had spent his later years were not few. The wiliest and most favored was the priest's brother, a man who, having received a free education in a seminary, had forsaken religion and was now on the lookout for any job that turned up. But the mayor refused all comers with a statement which, when relayed to us, filled us equally with pride and hope. Said he: "The post belongs to a warrior and shall be given to no one: it remains his for the day he returns as victor." The pride that this awakened in us was both honest and real. Unfortunately, any hope that to such high-mindedness there would be attached payment of a monthly check was in vain. The commune passed on to our mother no more than the usual allotment which the government had decreed for the families of conscripts. With which pittance we were able not even to buy cigarettes.

It is clear how things work in this world: one misfortune drags behind it another. Presently we were left even without a serving girl. The poor niece of our mother's second cousin got herself quite inexplicably pregnant and was sent forthwith back to her home town. Thus, while all about us the peasants were enriching themselves in the black market, stuffing their mattresses with thousand-lire notes, the last exterior mark of our respectability fell. And once again we had cause to lament our father's lack of foresight: Why did he not see to it that we were born among peasants? In our misery, only the house was saved, thanks to a law that forbade the eviction of servicemen's families even if it so happened that they were in arrears in their rent payments. A providential law, and one that rescued us from death by starvation. Our house, in fact, had become too large for us, and upon receipt of a reasonable sum of money, we turned over use of two rooms to a wealthy businessman who had been left a little addled by the first experiments in saturation bombing.

Meanwhile, our father, a trooper at the Regimental Warehouse, continued to make his Sunday appearances in town. He got down out of the bus with his satchel under his arm and headed for home without a word to anyone. The peasants milling about in the piazza noted his satchel and then winked at one another with distrustful irony: there, they thought, goes a smooth operator, a man who has found a way to make money and cover his movements to boot. Once in the house, our father handed his satchel full of dirty laundry to his wife, and then, having kicked off his shoes and unwound his puttees, lowered his feet into a basin of near-boiling water. And in that domestic attitude, some of his military pride melted. "My children," he would say in a discursive tone, "things are not going badly at all." By "things," naturally, he meant the war. Though it would have been interesting to examine the source of his optimism. The worse things became, the more he perfected his reasoning to show that victory was near. Unless he had become, very unexpectedly, a wag, by victory he actually meant victory for our side.

But one Tuesday night he appeared at the house, several days before he was due: he had walked the fifteen kilometers from the city. As he undressed, he had a large fire prepared. Then, exercising great care, taking them one by one, he dropped the various articles of clothing that made up his uniform into the fire, saving out only his shoes. And, pausing to study himself in the mirror, "They're not going to take me prisoner," he said. "I'm too old: the enemy will never suspect that I'm a soldier."

As dawn approached, the walls of our house began to shake with the rumble of passing American tanks. Watching from the window, every so often our mother scurried back to report to our father, who was locked in the closet under the staircase, taking notes. These, in his view, were valuable snippets of information which, come the propitious moment, would contribute toward victory. That pastime of his lasted three days, because then the war ended, and our father, though still not budging from the closet, had to give up the comfortable thought of hoping for the enemy's defeat.

Till then our rural folk had favored neither one side nor the other, but finally presented with such opportunity, they took up positions, naturally, alongside the conquerors. They came streaming into the piazza to celebrate the victory. But they felt the absence of a leader, having become so accustomed to one. Compelled, of course, not even to consider our father, they settled on a poor devil who, in times past, when properly soused, used to sing the *Internationale* at the top of his lungs and who, in consequence, whenever a big wheel in the government or the party or the royal family rolled through town, was put in the lockup for a few days. In a word, he was a subversive, and they hurried off to get him. He was brought out onto the flag-draped balcony of the town hall. His appearance there was made in a black shirt, because in the turnover of regimes, all who had possessed incriminating clothing had speedily got rid of it by making donations to the poor. And he had found it almost incredible, the fact that finally he had a virtually new shirt to wear. In any case, he was the only person in town with the right to dress as he wished, and the crowd cheered him. Contrary to the belief of those who thought he would be incapable of getting out a single word, he instinctively struck the new democratic mode of expression and bawled out: "Friends!—a toast to victory!"

The binge that followed sufficed to drown the memory of the one, it too of historic proportions, that had solemnized our entry into war. When evening fell, the entire town was reeling. And in that epic atmosphere our father was risking martyrdom. No one had anything against him—I should make that clear—but, after all, a political overthrow is a political overthrow, and this time it was a serious affair. All the same, before setting out with the intention of hanging him, they dispatched an advance party to warn him so that he might escape. And, perhaps for the first time in his life, our father ran away. He hid himself in a barn in the country, and though everyone knew where he was, no one dreamed for a moment of going after him.

But now what were we going to do? Already we were terribly underfed; it was no easy thing for us to assemble sufficient calories each day to guarantee our being alive the next morning. Our tenant, the gentleman to whom we had given asylum throughout the difficult years of war, learning that the fighting was really over, returned to his own city in the wake of a heated argument in which he made the absurd demand for restitution of the two months' rent he had given us in advance. No sooner was cause for fear eliminated than he was showing himself to have not the merest trace of understanding. And we were left utterly alone.

At one moment our salvation looked as if it might come from our sister. Having completed her silent development, she had become a very good-looking girl. And though basically one would not suspect her of any intelligence at all, with the end of hostilities she provided some evidence of reasoned adjustment to circumstances. Having dropped her ridiculous name of Italia and resumed the old one of Peggy, she would leave the house empty-handed and return late in the evening with stocks of chocolate, American cigarettes, and cans of something labeled "Meat and Vegetables," which proved edible. Later on, she occasionally appeared with a representative of the American detachment that was stationed in town, various fellows whose names were either Joe or Jimmy or Bob, and announced: "This is my fiancé." Relieving him of the cans he was carrying, we would cook a fine meal, to which he was also invited, since, poor boy, so many thousands of miles from home, he could appreciate a meal in familia.

Shortly thereafter, unfortunately, the detachment was transferred to a near-by city, and Peggy, who at that time was seriously in love with a sergeant named Harry, went after it. And we plunged headlong into misery blacker than ever. Weakened by hunger, broken by adversity, we found ourselves passing long hours in silence, looking and sighing at one another from time to time, wondering how we should be capable of retrieving ourselves from our predicament. It was from one such siege of meditation that one day the name of a person all too long forgotten suddenly re-emerged: Aunt Bess. Aunt Bess could save us. She had won the war. She represented the mightiest and wealthiest nation in the world. And she had an obligation to us, since, if it had not been for the dim-wittedness of our father, she could easily have been our mother. Which meant that our salvation was her responsibility.

We decided to write her a letter asking for help.

The letter was written one afternoon while Peggy was at home paying us a visit and letting us meet her fiancé, whose name was Bill. We explained to Peggy what we wanted written, Peggy re-explained it to Bill, and Bill then put it in writing. He did it, frankly, with a certain difficulty and some uncertainty, but we were confident that in one way or another he would succeed in making Aunt Bess understand that our father, who had always secretly longed for her, was dying of hunger and that we, his children, were in no less dire straits, and that if Aunt Bess had so much as a grain of responsibility, once a week she would have to send us a big box full of cigarettes and food.

The letter was posted by air. It may be said that from that moment onward we lived for the most part simply on the hope of what was on its way. It was a fairly long wait and threw our bony structures into really fine relief. But at last, one day—a day we had spent trying to recall the precise circumstances that had attended our having something solid between our teeth—the first package arrived. It was not very large, to tell the truth, especially when placed alongside our hopes, but, anyway, it was a package. And we three of us began feebly to unwrap it. The first thing to appear was a letter, which was put aside, mainly because reading matter wasn't exactly what we needed, and then because, in any case, there was no one present who could read it. Under the letter, well packed in crumpled strips of cellophane, nestled a little red bag tied with a red, white, and blue ribbon, the colors of the American flag, and then we seemed to realize that not only Aunt Bess, but an entire continent had come to our rescue. Except for the little bag, there was nothing else—no chocolate, no cigarettes, no canned pork. Only the bag, which contained the powder of a substance of indefinable color. We licked our fingers and stuck them into the powder to taste it. Its taste was even more indefinable than its color. To me, personally, it tasted like dehydrated peas. Tommaso, however, rather thought it was soybean flour, and since no one of us, including him, had ever seen or eaten soya, his judgment was perfectly reliable. But Giovanni asserted that it might well be a synthetic food, that the powder could easily prove to have the nutritional value of a bull. And since he was the only one of us who kept up with scientific advance, this final hypothesis was rather comforting. And we turned to the subject of how to eat it. Following a brief discussion, we settled on stew. All considered, it was the most sensible way to use the powder, vegetable, animal, synthetic, or whatever it was. I set to work immediately, dissolving the powder in water. Meanwhile Tommaso went out to steal some wood, and Giovanni went to appropriate some representative samples of the vegetables growing in a neighboring garden, these items, of course, being indispensable in the preparation of stew.

The idea of a meal in the making sharpened our hunger. Huddled around the fire, we watched for the first signs of boiling, hoping almost that when boiled the substance would transform itself into something entirely different—the hind quarter of a bull, or—how was I to know? —a turkey, say. Instead, it boiled for a few minutes and nothing happened. And so, since the powder was obviously not going to change, we pronounced it cooked; and if the vegetables were still a little raw, it was just as well, since, as is known, heat destroys vitamins. The stew was then ladled out and we fell to. It did not have a bad flavor at all; rather—but this certainly was due to our hunger—we found it downright tasty. Anyway, it was something to eat, and once inside it gave one a sense of well-being. When the meal was over, we continued to sit about the table, letting ourselves bask in that sense of well-being.

Then Peggy came in. Curiously, without a fiancé and without any canned goods. She had had a misunderstanding with her Americans and was a little down in the dumps. Scarcely paying any attention to us, she went over to the sideboard. There she sulked for a while and, casually fingering the letter that had accompanied the package from America, she exclaimed: "Good gracious, Aunt Bess is dead!"

We stared at her, incredulous.

"She's really dead," Peggy repeated, taking up the letter. And she read, translating it:

My dear Italian friends,

I, the one who is writing you, am Alice Smith. Your letter has been delivered to me. I regret to inform you that dear Bess has passed on. It happened during the war. It may have been perhaps, the thought that we were at war with you that brought her life so prematurely to a close. You were the love of her life and she bequeathed herself to you. She left instructions that her body be cremated and the ashes be sent to you. With this parcel I am carrying out her will.

Sincerely yours,
Alice Smith

His careful preparation for the unpleasant moments in life notwithstanding, Tommaso turned pale and staggered for the door.

"Where are you going, Tom?" Peggy called.

"To the graveyard," he answered, without stopping.

Giovanni and I were right behind him.

DOMENICO REA

Piededifico

TRANSLATED BY FRANCES FRENAYE

The convent of the Sisters of ——,
in a town not far from ours, was an abode of true Christian joy, lying
between a hill with a famous name and the blue sea, which reflected a
heavenly light upon it. The convent itself, four stories high, and the
outbuildings around it had no bars across their windows or any other
defenses against the world outside. The nuns wore a light-blue habit
and a flapping starched cap. Their faces were round and red like those
of the nuns described in the *Decameron*, but these contemporary
sisters were good women who had given up all their worldly goods, and
in many cases a princely title as well, in order to dedicate themselves
to contemplation and the care of old people and children, two groups
which were more often than not ragged and infested with lice and had
mastered a large vocabulary of oaths before they learned to say father
and mother.

Besides a free elementary school, with a boarding department for
older pupils, the nuns tended and instructed, with a view to preparing
them for a holy death, a number of aged men called "Old Christians,"
most of them quite innocent sinners: retired porters and messengers,
beggars who never let a good chance go by, and former teachers without a pension, like those who had taught at the bankrupt Lotto School.
These gathered every evening in the chapel for Benediction. They sat
on the benches occupied by the schoolchildren earlier in the day and
were less inclined to open their ears to the preaching of the Sister
Evangelist than to open their eyes to the big basket of sandwiches,

chocolate, and preserves, which was the prime motive for their coming from so far and then jousting with their crutches for the seat nearest to it. Finally, the Sister Evangelist, a nun with the face of a Saint Catherine of Siena, came along and said authoritatively. "Peace be with you, brother beggars in Christ!"

On this particular evening she scrutinized her charges one by one and suddenly asked an owl-eyed individual: "What's your name?"

"Zoppiniello, Sister."

"Do you know anything about the sausages?"

"I haven't seen any sausages for the last ten years, Sister," said the eighty-year-old fellow, mopping his eyes.

"And what about you?" she asked, turning upon a cripple. "Do you know anything about the *provolone* cheese of Santa Maria?"

"How can you suspect me, Sister?" he protested, rising up from his bench. "Don't I look like a gentleman? Like the last leaf on a noble tree? Oh, what shame I've had to go through since I've been poor!" And in his agitation he came down on his crippled leg.

"Well, then, which one of you is Piededifico? Is there any Old Christian by that name?"

The old men looked critically at one another, trying to ferret out the secret. Finally, one of them, who was the focus of all their eyes, started sobbing.

"Sister, they've got it in for me because I still have my teeth!" he shouted, waddling like a seal toward the altar with a cane to propel him along on his flat feet, as if he were seeking a revelation from God, which, however, was not forthcoming.

"Come, come, Old Christians, who could it have been? Which one of you has taken hams and sausages from our cellar?"

The Sister Evangelist knew well enough. She had already done penance, and this was her first evening back on the job. Only by proving that Piededifico had never been among her charges could she stand up to the Mother Superior, who blindly insisted that he was one of them.

"You have only to look into the eyes of those dear old babies of mine to see their innocence," said the Sister Evangelist. "And Piededifico has a piercing, blue, evil stare in his."

After all that she had taught them about respecting other people's property and treading in the Lord's way, surely no one of those present could have fattened himself on the stores of the convent. Especially as this convent was one that kept nothing for itself, not even the sea or the walnut trees, as Saint Alessandro Manzoni has it.

Who, then, was Piededifico?

First of all, a man able to isolate and distinguish the odor of sausage among a thousand (Neapolitan) smells. Doubtless a Neapolitan himself (although this does not imply that the thief was a Neapolitan) with a wife and children to support, and lionhearted for the simple reason that he had nothing to lose. His name, it was found out from the police, who failed to ascertain, however, whether or not he was an Old Christian, was—Piededifico.

He was lean, unsteady on his pins, and always in the company of his wife, who in her turn inevitably appeared with one infant in arms and, between her feet, two older children with bad complexions and an air of overgrown babies about them. She wore a single, unbelted, sacklike garment, and her offspring performed acrobatics on her body, hanging onto her hair, hands, and sagging breasts, as if she were some sort of trapeze.

The family lived off begging. But since in the world at large and this town in particular, beggary is off the gold standard, Piededifico, who had once exercised the profession in a bustling business section of the town, which was now as abandoned as if the plague had struck it, had moved himself and his family to the luxurious residential quarter where the convent was located. There he sat on the ground, flanked by his miserable family, around a circle traced in the dust, which was supposed to represent a receptacle for the generosity of passers-by. His eyelids were half closed and the curly lashes served as a sort of curtain, behind whose shelter he could reflect upon the vicissitudes of his life, which were too dire to be faced up to squarely.

And yet once upon a time Piededifico had been well enough off. A beggar by both heredity and upbringing, he belonged to the class of specialists known as "rats." These specialists study the comings and goings of rodents, their ways of breaking into groceries and delicatessens, and leaving the surface of stolen objects so intact as to defy perception. And when they cannot emulate the creatures which they are spying on, they simply catch them and sell their meat under a dif-

ferent name to beggars of a lower class than themselves, who are occasionally glad to have a sandwich of some indefinable kind with their
glass of wine. Ah, the good old days! ...

Now Piededifico, veteran of the wars, beat the sidewalks of a high-
class street, as if it were an ice bed, with his former job swept away
from under him by the pervading poverty of the town and no notion
of anything to which he could turn his hand.

"Have pity upon the children of a starving mother and father," said
his carefully trained sons to every well-heeled passer-by, and if the pity
wasn't forthcoming, they broke into invectives as diabolical as those
which lizards throw at anyone that dares cut off their tails. If, on the
contrary, the well-heeled individual did come across, Piededifico
sighed: "Ah, poor me, the starving but devoted father!"

Meanwhile, bending his head and lowering the curtain of his eye-
lashes, he wondered what he was going to do next. His wife sang and
his children danced around him while he rewarded the next comer
with a pious: "Here's a long life to you!" Or else, when he saw that the
offering was no more than a single lira: "Death to you and all the lice
in your hair!" After which he half closed his eyes again and returned
to his meditations.

It must have been while he was meditating thus that Piededifico
sniffed the presence of ham in the vicinity, and it seemed to him like
an oasis on his stomach's horizon. The first time he paid no heed,
thinking that it was a last-gasp olfactory hallucination. Then the genu-
ineness of the odor concentrated itself in his nose and swept through
his brain like a resurrecting wind until it became pointed, positive, and
compelling, as if it were a scruple calling upon him for confirmation.

Actually, the ham smell was rounded out with several others: calves'
and goats' milk cheeses, sausages put up with peppers and sharp *provolone*, whose shape he guessed from its scent and found more provocative than a pair of female buttocks, besides other alimentary
essences as attractive as a spring meadow. With a: "Quiet, there!" to
his family, he proceeded step by step, for the next three hours, under
the guidance of his nose, to follow every whiff, until, finally, with a
smile of a rat that has got into the larder, he came to the source of all
happiness.

Having let his wife in on the secret, he lost no time in drawing up a plan. He noticed that every week a commissary truck arrived from the Vatican, and one day, under the pretext of helping to unload, he made his way into the courtyard and thence into the cellar. Here, after the truck had gone and the cellar door had been locked, he rolled out of a barrel and looked at the lay of the land. One part of the cellar contained the supplies just brought in and the other the delicacies accumulated by the nuns and their chaplain: huge rounds of cheese, piled up like automobile wheels in a corner; hams suspended from the ceiling like hanged men, whose bodies had slipped down under the noose around their necks; rolls of lascivious red sausages, dripping oil; and boxes upon boxes of chocolate, preserves, white flour, and all the other good things which adorn a life of ease and prayer.

In order to keep his head and protect himself against so great a variety of attractions, Piededifico decided to try them all, and his stomach, which had been hollow when he came in, became as large as that of a pregnant woman. But even in this condition he started to plan future operations and to pick out a barrel where he could hide in an emergency, deprived of everything but wine. When night came, he talked through a grating between the ceiling of the cellar and the street, where his wife lay flat on her stomach to listen.

"My dear, it's in the bag, and a piece of very good business, I can tell you. There's a little bit of everything in God's creation." He spoke in a low voice, and his wife answered plaintively: "No doubt you're quite right, my love, but give me a taste of something, so I can have an idea. . . ."

"You shall taste everything, of course you shall, but lower your voice and be calm."

"You've eaten," she said with muted resentment. "You're not trembling with hunger as we are, and to tell the truth I feel as if I didn't know you."

"We want something to eat, too," said the children, and when they got no answer, they repeated their demand in a loud shout.

Piededifico was furious. Smoke poured out of his voice and flames from his eyes, and the children cried: "The ogre! The ogre!" and ran away in a flood of tears. Their mother went after them, picked them up by the seats of their pants, and knocked them against the ground, thereby causing them to cry and swear all the louder. She gathered them up and held them face to face, saying: "Shut up there, or I'll bash your heads in proper!"

But they only continued to cry and swear through their noses. In her agitation, she went back to the grating and managed to slip her thumb and forefinger through it in such a way as to pinch one cheek of the waiting Piededifico.

"Either give us something to eat or I'll report you to the police!" she told him. "Just look at the condition of these children!"

Unable to wrench his cheek from her grasp, Piededifico said imploringly: "Let me go! Dear little woman and kids, you'll have to forgive me if I can't feed you right away. Come back tomorrow with the pushcart, but for heaven's sake be quiet about it, and you'll be satisfied with the generosity of Piededifico."

With which he seized three sausages and passed them, slice by slice, to his wife, along with several dozen American crackers. After, thus assuaged, she had gone away, Piededifico went back to work, humming to himself, taking a bite here and there as he pleased and reflecting upon the glories of honest labor. "It's all my father's fault that I ever became a beggar," he said to himself. "Because he practiced the trade in a golden age, he had to go and say: 'Come with me, my boy, and learn to beg! Why can't a son ever follow the advice of his father? Don't you see I have your good at heart?' And to think that all this time I might have been in the arduous but satisfying business of a grocer! There's a real business for you! Wherever you go, you touch cheeses and pigs' feet and butter! It's just my bad luck! . . ." And he munched and munched, feeling renewed faith in life and giving thanks to the Madonna of Pompeii.

Beginning the next evening, his sons came with the pushcart and loaded it with the good things which their father passed up to them, carefully sliced so that they would pass through the grating. In the course of a day he was able to slice about two hundred pounds, and no one was the wiser. The system was foolproof, except for the noise of the cart wheels, which the boys wrapped in rubber tubing. Piededifico saw nothing criminal about his new occupation, since a man must make a living off whatever he can find, and if he finds nothing, then he must take whatever comes along. And he took a long-range view of the job, as is proved by the fact that he made himself a bed in the barrel and hung up a mirror with which to admire the fat he was putting on every day.

Indeed, things might have gone on indefinitely, if one summer evening an old nun hadn't been driven by the heat to seek a breath of fresh air on the convent roof, which overlooked the surrounding houses and streets, including the stony alley leading to the main door. This alley habitually rang with the shouts and footsteps of the children pouring out of the convent school, and on this July night it echoed the clang of the iron wheels of the pushcart, which the boys had had to strip of their rubber tubing because when the cart was heavily loaded the wheels refused to roll and carry it along. Now, when the nun saw this monstrous apparition, she took it, in the manner of her kind, for a manifestation of the devil and shouted at the top of her lungs: "Chaplain! Watchman! Sisters!"

In a split second the Mother Superior, the chaplain, the watchman, and all the nuns poured out onto the roof, armed with bottles, broomsticks, pillows, and other domestic weapons. The good nuns were capless, so that the stars looked down on their bare, shaven heads. Before the cart could get out of the alley, a host of angry neighbors raised such a racket that Piededifico's sons left it there, overturned, with its shafts sticking up into the air and its contents spread out all over the ground, and fled, half jumping, half flying, like chickens before a storm.

Piededifico trembled in his barrel, and it was this trembling that betrayed his whereabouts, shortly before dawn, to the small army of policemen and nuns who were scouring the cellar. His trousers wouldn't close around his waist, and a big flap of shirt was sticking out of them. He had a two-weeks' beard on his face and looked altogether like an Old Christian of the younger generation. For this reason, the Mother Superior, who had feverishly tormented herself with the question of "how a man could have broken into the cellar," threatened the Sister Evangelist with such drastic penance as stones on her prayer stool in the chapel and on the pillow of her narrow bed, because she had neglected the most elementary precautions.

"You ought to escort those wretched old codgers that come to Benediction one by one to the door! I always told you so!"

And then she turned her attack upon the equally gentle nun who kept accounts: "I saw her with my own eyes treating the men who came in on the truck with as much consideration as if they were princes. Just look at the woe these two softhearted Sisters have brought upon us! Something has got to be done!"

She compelled them to stand weeping on either side of her, like culprits beyond all hope of appeal. And when the lamp fell upon Piededifico in his barrel, the Sister Evangelist cried out in terror: "Jesus, give us light! Let Your truth shine upon our darkness!"

Under the first shower of questions, Piededifico said that he was an Old Christian, while the Sister Evangelist, who was kneeling among the lanterns and barrels, prayed desperately: "No, Jesus, no!" He was born a Christian, he maintained, and such, even at the risk of being called old, he felt himself to be. But a few minutes later he changed his story and said that he was one of the truckmen who had brought the Vatican supplies, thus throwing the Sister Accountant into transports of panic.

"I called for help for two days in succession, Sister Lady," he said to the Mother Superior, distinguishing her from the rest by the disapproving curl of her pinched lips. "I have no connections at all with the pushcart people. After I've lived all my life, come heat, come cold, in honorable poverty, would you make me out a thief?"

"How do you know there's a pushcart mixed up in it?" asked the chief of police.

"How could I help hearing the racket above me? But I got locked up in here by mistake, I tell you. I came down on the Vatican truck to help with the unloading. And you owe me money for the loss of so many working days!"

"Jesus!" exclaimed the Sister Accountant. "If all truckmen are so young and strong, shed Your light upon our human errors!"

"Don't bring Jesus into it," said the Mother Superior peremptorily. And, turning to the convent monitors, she added: "Place these two in custody. They will be questioned at a special meeting of the Disciplinary Council later in the day."

The two Sisters, the Evangelist and the Accountant, broke into a mystical chant as they were led away and disappeared in the light of dawn which filled the patch of sky beyond the open cellar door.

Meanwhile, Piededifico said to the chief of police: "Just tell me this:

doesn't robbery mean taking other people's belongings away? I haven't anything to do with that pushcart gang; if you face me with them, I can prove that. And all I have on me is lice. I didn't rob, I tell you, I simply ate. What else could I do? I thought about it for two days, and then I started eating."

But the chief of police wanted to cut a handsome figure in front of the Mother Superior, who with her bald head and scornfully curled lips looked like no less than a Roman emperor. So he tightened the handcuffs around Piededifico's wrists and said vaingloriously: "We knew all along that something was going on. And we were just waiting for the opportune moment. . . ."

While Piededifico, not unmindful of his wife and children, philosophically concluded: "I saved my life and gained weight in the bargain. Now I must lose it all and waste away in prison. Why, I ask you, why? Jesus, shed light and give me an answer!"

CARLO BERNARI

It's All a Question of Degree

TRANSLATED BY FRANCES FRENAYE

"We always make our own weather,"
Corresio thought to himself, but this particular evening came on him
all of a sudden, with the impact of an unexpected cold wave. Corresio
was waiting for "someone" at the door of the Café Garisci, "to make
some money." His hand was swollen and he had difficulty in holding
it out to the benefactor who was stepping out of the warmth inside,
leaving behind him a trail of familiar and welcome odors, to which a
man was tempted to attribute color, as if in the process of dressing a
doll, with so many oh's for buttons. Oh! the changeless red of the
strawberries; oh! the yellow of the orange; oh! the brown of coffee and
chocolate. . . . How many colors! Isn't the whole world made up of
color, when you come down to it? That is easy enough to see, but how
many of us see what is inside the color, the shading and degree? Corresio cut short these thoughts in order to hold out his heavy hand to
the man coming out of the café, a hand of stone, which was able to
steal, beg, and perhaps even open a door, but not to create a hundred
different whites from a whitewashed wall.

"You're a person of taste," he began, sacrificing his "whites" to
words of the most conventional kind, "and you have an eye for painting. May I show you some pictures I've been working on for the last
few days?"

"Good Lord, no! And then I haven't a penny in my pocket."

"As if everyone didn't know who you were! You can take the pictures with you, and I'll come to your office tomorrow."

351

"For heaven's sake! I'm sick of pictures."

"But pictures are always good business. A permanent investment. . . ."

The painter put more hopes in querulousness than in tears. But the obdurate Chiurato, owner of so many pictures, had, with no intention of offending Corresio, stored most of them in his cellar. Corresio was perfectly aware of this, and it didn't in the least bother him.

"For just a few lire I'll give you everything," he insisted. "You're a man of taste and you have an eye for painting."

He did not really think so at all.

"Yes," said the millionaire, who couldn't help being pleased by the compliment," but you've chosen a very bad day. I'm in no mood to talk about anything serious, don't you understand? To hell with it all! Let's talk about ice cream, or movies, or the latest hats, or girls. . . . There are so many things to talk about. . . . Can't you think of anything but painting?"

The thing to talk about was a nude, perhaps of the model who had posed for it. But they had reached the rich man's car, and his chauffeur was holding open the door. Chiurato got in and motioned the painter to follow. He'll change his mind when he sees them, Corresio said to himself, patting the newspaper in which they were wrapped.

"I've spent thousands and thousands on pictures," the rich man said as the car started, "and to be quite frank with you, I'm sorry. Yes, I regret it with all my heart. What drove me to it, I ask you? What good do pictures do me? Do I really enjoy looking at them? Perhaps, at first glance, a picture takes my eye, and since I have the means to do a good deed . . . well, you know the rest. But where is it written that I have to go on that way for the rest of my life? Just tell me where! If I'd spent half the money for something practical, the government would have given me a medal. Well, then, just a whim, a matter of self-indulgence, you say? But even a whim has to have a counterbalance of one kind or another. Put your mind on that. A man like myself, who had the good luck, (and the brains) to build up an entire country, no less, wasting his money on pictures! I could never forgive myself that!"

"But as I was saying, it's an investment!" protested Corresio, who hardly dared hope any longer.

"An investment, you say! That sort of investment leads straight to bankruptcy!" He dropped this sentence from the corner of his mouth and lit a cigarette.

The sky was one purple cloud, with a fringe of sea foam all around it. The car wound slowly up a curving street and stopped in front of a gate high up over the bay. Corresio, with his paintings under his arm, practically ran after the master of the house, who had started up a ramp that looked like a white arm suspended in the air. Then they went up a marble stairway, through a hall, and came to a halt near a window which looked out over a sea of black leaves.

"Just look!" the rich man said solemnly.

"Do you want to see them?" asked Corresio, pointing to his roll of canvases.

"No, there's something I want to show you. You artists have a lot to learn from the so-called average man. I have a collection that will make your eyes pop. . . ."

"Pictures, you mean?"

"Pictures, indeed! Do you think that every collection is a picture collection?"

"Is it books, then?"

"Something much more rare!" the millionaire said with a smile. "You'll be gaping," he added, with his mouth hanging open.

"Do you mean it?" asked the painter.

"See if you can guess!"

"I give up," said the painter, listening to a clock strike the hour. At almost the same moment, part of the purple cloud split, revealing an area of dark, heavy sky. Corresio suddenly imagined that his wife had died in the process of waiting for him.

"Can one die of expectation?" he asked.

"What sort of a question is that? You artists are an odd lot. One dies of death. When death comes along, it's all over. But nobody dies of cold or hunger or expectation?"

The rich man stared at him, then muttered something quite incomprehensible and started through the empty house, which was lit only by the incandescence of the storm. He walked ahead, without putting on a single light, holding up his forefinger as straight as a needle.

"This way," he said. "Straight ahead. Take it easy. The doors are open."

The succession of rooms impinged upon the painter's sense of smell, with their various kinds of furniture: dusty antiques, then heavy walnut, ultramodern lacquers, and Victorian veneers. From the mixture and overlapping of various woods, which released the odor of their resins into the stuffy air, he could guess at the bad taste of a man who had indiscriminately piled up everything he had bought at an auction or bankruptcy sale. Near a window which looked out over a bare metal network, Chiurato forced the painter to stop. With a motion of his hand he pointed out the "beauty" of winter's effect upon his garden, then mumbling again, he went on up a winding stair. Through the embroidery of the wrought-iron steps, Corresio saw just above him his host's socks, trousers, and even his long underdrawers, whose sloppy ends revealed the man's essential vulgarity. It seemed impossible that a man who had got dressed with so little care should have so many big-business projects in mind, one more profitable than the other. Perhaps it was his preoccupation with all these things that prevented him from lacing his shoes or buttoning his waistcoat or tying his underdrawers neatly around his ankles. On these reflections, the painter came into a large room, which, in spite of the fact that it had been several times made over and redecorated, still had the air of a recently covered porch and a smell of peat and rust about it. Just then two spotlights went on simultaneously.

"Come on in!" said the rich man, as the painter paused at the threshold. In order to reach him, Corresio had to squeeze through a narrow space and climb a circular stairway. Standing on a platform beside his host, he saw that the room was occupied by a cardboard relief map of Italy, complete with mountains, valleys, houses, steamers, and trains. The whole peninsula was there and everything that pertained to it. The two bright lights lit up the model, which smelled of glue and fresh varnish, like a children's book or a newly built sample fair.

"You were talking as if there were nothing so rare as pictures," said the rich man, raising his hand as if to pull aside an invisible curtain. "But here, I tell you, is the rarest thing in all the world. Every one of our railway lines is there. I built it in 1908, but I've changed it to keep up with the latest improvements. For instance, I've just electrified the line between Rome and Naples and now I'm building the Porretta tunnel."

"Wonderful!" said the painter.

"Wonderful, is that all? Aren't you going to say it's fascinating? Instructive? Important? That even at the Ministry of Communications they have nothing to beat it? . . . Do you see that red point up there? It's where a landslide is blocking traffic. . . ."

"What, you even have landslides?"

"What do you mean, 'even'? Aren't there landslides on the railway lines? Of course, I can't have my slides move on the same day as the real-life ones. I have to wait until a day later. There is a clipping service which sends me news of everything that happens on the railways. Of course, sometimes months go by without anything interesting: any landslides, or collisions, or broken bridges. As a matter of fact, there hasn't been a single accident this whole last week."

"That takes the fun out of it," the painter remarked.

"Exactly. I come up here for an hour every evening, and if everything goes smoothly, what fun is there in it for me? I know all the train movements by heart."

"Couldn't you stage an imaginary accident every now and then?"

"Are you crazy? What about the schedules? The schedules are all made up and if a train leaves, say from Naples, then it's got to arrive at Rome in time to make connections with the train leaving for Milan. If there's a real disaster, I can let everything slow down, but I can't do it just for a whim. That would be positively criminal!"

He came down from the observatory, motioning to the painter to follow. In a few steps he was at Milan, where, with a match, he lit the fire in the locomotive of a departing train, then he ran quickly to Naples, to switch on the electric current of two others. At Trieste he readied a steam engine to go to Rome, then he hitched up two locals leaving from Brindisi. He ran up and down the map, with the soles of his shoes creaking, until finally he stopped and said: "Steam trains out of Milan and Brindisi are all set. The electric trains from Rome and Naples will cross at Formia, where they have a two-second stop. . . ."

He looked at his watch, blew into a whistle, ran to Turin and repeated the operation. When these three trains had started, he was off to Ancona to prepare a steam train for Rome. Soon miniature trains overran the whole peninsula, making their way among its vast network of tracks. Green and red lights flashed on before and after them; station bells rang, trains plunged screeching into dark tunnels and came out of them clouded with steam, which was gradually dispersed over the green grass on the map. The plains of Lombardy, the mountains of Emilia, and the Tuscan fields shook as if from an underground tremor. And the rich man, watch in hand, seemed like a baby, a big, bald baby, confounded by the intricacy of his toy.

"Look here," he said, from somewhere near Bologna, where a train was entering a tunnel. "Just see how fast it goes . . . marvel! Look how it's speeding there, to make up lost time."

"Why? Is it late?" asked the painter, sticking one finger into the lake of Bracciano.

"Of course. Didn't you realize that?"

"And is it going to reach its destination at the scheduled time?"

"What do you mean by 'reach its destination'? And what do schedules have to do with it?" And after a moment of perplexity, he looked at his watch and asked: "Where's that Brindisi Local? Why is it skipping stops again?"

"Again?"

"Yes, yesterday evening it was up to the same tricks. After Bari it went at breakneck speed, without stopping, even for water. Little beast!"

He was interrupted by a clap of thunder which rent the air outside. The preceding flash of lightning had lit up the night and at the same time put out the spotlights. The tops of the cypress trees in the garden stood out beyond the windows like the tufts of great paintbrushes, dipping into the smoky, black sky.

In the silence that followed, the miniature steam trains, casting red shadows behind them, continued to chug over the darkened map. Without being able to see each other, the two men looked helplessly on at the disaster. The train from Rome speeded through the Aversa station just as the Brindisi local was pulling in, and in the inevitable collision, cars were overturned, while a burning locomotive set fire to the map.

"Fire! Fire!" shouted the painter in a childish voice, of which he was suddenly ashamed. He did actually feel like a child, a poor child, guilty of envying a rich one.

"Fire!" echoed the rich child. "And why aren't you getting out of the way?" He took an extinguisher down from the wall, pushed the painter aside, and directed a jet of water on the flames. Corresio felt the fire in his own breast. He let it burn for a moment and then, as if to placate it, stretched out a disrespectful hand, disconnected the locomotive, and, hiding behind the peaks of the Apennines, tiptoed out of the room. Behind him lay Italy, dark and deserted. He went down the circular stair and ran through the apartment all the way to the door.

Outside, the freezing cold had turned into big drops of rain. By flights of stone steps and short cuts, Corresio came down from the fashionable part of the city to the alleys of the center, where Christmas bagpipers were still playing in front of wall shrines that glittered with votive candles. Little metal images of souls in purgatory simulated the tortures of the damned as they danced in the flames, but every one of them was redolent of warmth, comfort, and kindness, while Corresio was aware of nothing but cold, a cold so intense that it made his own hand seem extraneous to him, like somebody else's hand in his. And this extraneous hand was holding a stolen object, which he showed to old Don Ernesto, who sat in a rocking chair in the back room of his junk shop at Donnalbina. The junk dealer looked at the toy and said he didn't know what he could do with it. Never in all his life, he said, had he dealt in such "nonsense." He wouldn't take it in his hand but glanced skittishly at it, as if he were afraid that the slightest display of interest would imply that he was making a bid.

The painter walked through more alleys, with sheets hung out over them to dry in spite of the recent rain, until he came to Santa Maria la Nova. Chair caners ate their supper on the church steps, between one job and another, while coppersmiths beat out metal sheets with a sound like that of a hundred bells. He walked up and down the steep streets between Santa Maria dell'Aiuto and the Ecce Homo, until at the locality known as Le Campane di Donnalbina, under a bombed building, he discovered the shop of Camillo Scognamillo, filled with brass bedsteads, worn statuettes under glass bells, lamps, and candelabra that could not possibly be lighted. Camillo wore a rose plush shirt and a jersey scarf around his neck, with a cap too small for his head perched on a mop of bushy hair. Until he moved, he looked like another piece of furniture. Finally he got up and took the toy into his hand, looked at it inside and out, carried it over to the kerosene lamp, raised the wick, dipped some sort of pick into a basin of liquid, and then stuck it into the top of the locomotive.

"Where did it come from?" he asked.

"It's a present someone gave me."

"That's right. It couldn't be anything else. And now it's a question of finding someone stupid enough to buy it. How much did it cost when it was new?"

"You don't expect me to ask the price of a present, do you?"

It wasn't really stolen, although the act of selling it could only be the consequence of stealing. He would have to make sure that he wasn't parting with it forever. For in that case it would be stolen. "Stolen," did you hear? Then would Corresio, the kindly painter, the man of the subtle shadings, be an ordinary thief?

"How about three hundred?" asked Camillo.

"I don't want to sell it, after all," said the painter, reaching out a hand to take it back.

"Four hundred, then. I can tell you need the money."

He did need it, all right; perhaps his nervousness was visible on his face or in his unkempt beard and shabby clothes. Why hadn't the rich man guessed at his need so quickly? Automobiles, servants, trains, yes, even trains, and still he hadn't understood something so simple! . . .

"Leave me your address," said Camillo, putting four hundred-lire notes into his hand.

It was nearly nine o'clock, and the butcher was pulling in his marble-topped tables, taking down his hooks, and putting the meat away in the icebox, when Corresio came along, uncertain whether to ask for a quarter of a pound of ground meat, a big piece with a bone, or some head sausage.

"Give me a capon," he said in answer to the butcher's questioning look.

He took the bird by its legs, stuffed the packet of entrails into his pocket, and rushed out. Everyone stared at him as he sat in the tram with the plucked bird on his lap. What must he look like? He remembered a picture entitled "Young Man with a Chicken," in which a pair of white hands were laid on the white (or was it yellow?) meat. Always a question of shading and degree. He found his house dark and his wife in bed, for the sake of keeping herself warm.

"Giò, why are you so late?" her voice said out of the darkness.

The painter came in and walked over to the bed without answering.

"Did he give you the money? Did you have to wait long? Poor Giò!" And she leaned her head against his shoulder. "Why, you're perspiring all over! Have you been running?"

"Why isn't there any light?" asked the painter.

"Oh, something's broken. We had hail, you know."

"Hail?"

He hadn't noticed; in fact, he was perspiring.

"You'll catch a cold," he said at last. "Get back under the covers."

Then he took off his coat and lighted a candle. The flame revealed his wife huddled up in the bed and rubbing her feet to warm them. Her white breasts and hands and gown caught his painter's eye; he thought of the "Weary Night" and the "Young Man with a Chicken." "It's all a question of degree," he thought, and then he stared at his own purple hands, which had no feeling left in them, the poor hands that he had to carry through life just as he had carried them to the academy of painting, hands that didn't know how to draw or paint or do anything useful.

There was a knock at the door, and Camillo, the junkman, came in, with a short black jacket over his rose plush shirt. He had the toy in one hand and his cap in the other, and he stepped forward until the sight of the woman in bed brought him to a halt.

"I've thought it over," he said, "and I find that I can't make the deal. We come from the same part of the world, so let's have everything out in the open. I've thought it over and come to get back my money."

In the draft from the half-open door the flame of the candle flickered, alternately shrinking and enlarging the shadows of the men on the wall. One of them was too large and the other too small. And the small one was too small to be caught and the large one too large to be hurt by any of the blows directed at him. The woman peered through the sheet at the battle which the two shadows were waging in order to form a picture of something human. Finally, Camillo's shadow appeared to be somewhat placated and said: "Give me back my money!"

"Why should I?" asked the shadow of the painter, flapping like a sail.

"I've already told you why. I don't want to get into anything shady. Those times are gone forever. I've thought it over, I told you. Can't a man think twice about something?" And he pointed to the roof of the locomotive. "There's a gold piece here that's worth at least a thousand lire."

"Well, what of that, if I'm satisfied with what you gave me?" Corresio asked him.

"It might be all right that way. But the fact is that if they haul me in for something like this, they'll make me pay through the nose for it. I've got to take care to stay within the law. Surely you understand. . . ."

He looked around the room, noticing the easel and the pictures on the walls.

"My dear sir . . ."

"But I've already spent two hundred lire," said the painter, taking the rest out of his pocket.

And with the hand that had warmed up sufficiently to be his own again he pointed to the chicken, which was lying beside his wife on the bed. Camillo lifted up the bird, balanced it in the palm of one hand, waved the hand that was holding the cap, and walked toward the door. There he stopped to look around again.

"Is today something special? Perhaps the lady's birthday?" he asked, pointing a finger at the bulging sheets.

The painter looked around too, trying to discover what had made the junk dealer think this was a special day. Rags, pictures, dirt . . . Perhaps it was the chicken. The chicken is a holiday bird, when it's stiff and cold and can't crow or cluck any longer, when it has nothing more to contribute to man's happiness and is reduced to a series of gradations of white.

"Yes," said the painter, "it's my wife's birthday."

He couldn't take his eyes off the rigid whiteness of the bird, which hung from Camillo's hand over the warmer white of the sheets. Isn't it all a question of degree? If he were to take the white out of the sheets and substitute it with green or reddish-brown, everything would die in his hands.

"If that's so, then please excuse me and let me give her a present too."

Corresio smiled. Was there festivity rather than famine in his eyes? Or had the junk dealer chosen to read it there? Chiurato, too, might have better understood his hunger, if he had cleansed it of the element of poverty and held it up to him like this: "Mr. Millionaire, I'm the happiest man in the world, and I'm bored because I have absolutely nothing to do. . . . Just think, I have to go buy a chicken and take it back to the house for my wife's birthday."

"So will you allow me to make a present to your wife?" interposed the voice of Camillo.

Corresio shrugged his shoulders, and the junk dealer stretched out his hand to lay the chicken on a table near the door. Then he touched his cap and disappeared. The bulging sheets moved, and the lanky body of Signora Corresio, once an artist's model, but now gray of hair and voice, emerged from under them.

"What's happening, Giò?" she asked, looking at the locomotive, which Camillo had left on the table beside the bed. "Does it run?"

"So fast that he gave it a good medal!" Corresio told her.

"Then make it go!"

"I'd have to have tracks and signals. . . ." He picked up the toy and heard a plaintive gurgle. "Well, perhaps it's a Diesel."

"Then all you have to do is light it, isn't that so?"

"Yes, but then . . ."

"Use the candle."

There was a lever as tiny as a baby's fingernail, and a valve no more than large enough for a baby's piss to go through. Perhaps that was the thing to open and the place to apply the candle.

The woman stopped up her ears in the fear of an explosion, but the flame did not flare up, and instead went through the locomotive until it came out in smoke from a stubby stack on top. The creature murmured like a pot on the fire, then the murmur became a lament and a purr. Corresio put the toy down on the floor and raised the lever.

The locomotive began to dart in and out among the legs of the chairs and tables, which the woman gradually pushed over against the wall. It jerked over the fissures between the tiles and made their hearts beat faster when it ran into a piece of furniture or its wheels whirled idly around while it was jammed up against a protruding corner. They couldn't help laughing to see how, in spite of its tiny size, it was stubbornly resolved to accomplish its function. It was like Paperino, in the story, when he couldn't have his own way and began to garble his words. Be good, little train, go fast, because today's a special day.

The candle went out, and the train's headlight was reflected on the red tile, two indications of color. Corresio, lying prone across the bed and watching the toy's wild gyrations, felt his wife's body against his hip, while the locomotive, unaccustomed to such trackless travels, bumped up against something in the darkness. The flame under its belly was motionless and orange against the red of the gleaming tile. Corresio remembered the "Young Man with a Chicken" and the "Weary Night."

"Do you see those two reds together, my dear?" he said. "It's all a question of shading and degree."

G. B. ANGIOLETTI

A Poor Ghost

TRANSLATED BY ANGUS DAVIDSON

As soon as evening descends over the town, the ghost begins to get ready. In his room, shadow gradually envelops him, diminishing his outline, dissolving his solidity. When he puts a sheet over his shoulders and steps in front of the mirror, he himself is frightened by the grayness of his hands and by the black eye sockets in his whitened face. He is a ghost.

This ghost is a poor devil from the slums, a long, lean creature with a big, bony nose and yellowish eyes like a cat. He started pretending to be a ghost from sheer hunger, and now he has the job of terrorizing a girl who is vacillating at the advances of a young man living in the same quarter. Tonight he has to pull her hair, to break something, to appear suddenly to her like a corpse, and then immediately disappear again into the darkness. He has not entirely understood why this plan should be effective, but for many years now he has given up trying to understand. He has been a paid hooligan, a mountebank, a charlatan, and a hundred other things, ready to serve anyone who would pay him. He has never managed to be independent, and if, at first, he blamed the world in general, and then his own crazy, cantankerous character, now, at the age of forty, he no longer blames anyone. Someone pays him, and he pretends to be a ghost. After all, it is a trade that requires courage.

Having entered the girl's room, the phantom starts to work at once. He arranges a black thread, with a small hook tied to one end, so that it dangles right over the pillow; he ties another thread to the back of a chair, and yet another to the handle of a jug. He is helped by the amused expression on the face of the newly risen moon. Then the ghost hides behind a curtain and waits. He feels sleepy and would like to lie down and sleep on the low bed with its cover of pink with little white flowers. It looks soft, and it smells of jasmine. He thinks of the girl's pleasure at waking there each morning, having her breakfast brought to her, stretching her arms, eating good fresh rolls and then turning, in her own youthful warmth, to enjoy a little more sleep.

The door opens and golden light pours into the room. The girl is truly lovely. She is rather small but well-formed, her hair is black and wavy, her eyes brilliant, with very long lashes, her skin smooth and dark. Her light dress gives a feeling of extreme cleanliness, of something precious, not to be touched. She smiles at herself in the looking glass, gives herself a kind of little curtsy, tries to look at her little nose, with its dilated nostrils, in profile. She is pleased and contented. She sits down on the bed and starts undressing, singing meanwhile.

The ghost takes note of her bare arms and shoulders, of her broad, rounded knees. And a sudden access of modesty makes him blush beneath the flour smeared over his cheeks, so that he lowers his eyes, trying not to see this paradisiacal loveliness. He is discouraged at his own wretchedness, at the foolish task he is about to undertake against a creature who is so trustful of the world. He even tries not to listen to the rustling sound of falling garments, and an infinite bitterness whispers to him to make good his escape.

But he decides he is being ridiculous, and, with an impudent grimace, makes up his mind to look. Too late. The girl is already in bed, her loosened hair covering even her shoulders; and she is still smiling, so that there are dimples in her full cheeks, and under her chin her throat curves away lovingly toward her breast. She is so charming that he feels a longing to caress her; to hear her laugh, to feel her little velvety hands on his face. The ghost is seized with a feeling of yearning, protective friendliness for this beautiful creature; he would like to stay there all night long, looking at her and enjoying an immense peace like a mountain in springtime.

Now the girl has put out the light, and soon afterward the sound of the warm breathing of sleep can be heard. Then the ghost is seized with exasperation again. The darkness is his enemy, bringing his own ill luck before him again, reminding him of hunger and sleeplessness; love's shy apparition has vanished, and nothing is left but the fixed idea of the money promised him. He loses no more time.

He pulls a thread, and the hook hanging above the pillow gives a tug at the sleeping girl's hair. She awakes with a heavy sigh, turns her head, closes her eyes again sleepily; but a stronger pull makes her cry out with pain. The ghost is in a hurry now; he would like to do everything all at once, in order to make his escape from this nightmare. A chair suddenly falls over and starts running across the floor, knocking against other chairs; the jug flies through the air, diaphanous in the clear moonlight; fearsome blows resound against the wardrobe. In the midst of this hell let loose the girl clutches the bed convulsively, groaning as though she were being suffocated; but, from very terror, she is unable to scream. This is the moment for him to appear in front of her waving his arms, but the ghost is kept glued to the spot by an immense feeling of shame. He feels miserable, inhuman, he longs to vanish like a spirit, but is conscious of his own solidity, his heaviness, his animal quality. There are a few moments of complete silence, and then the victim leaps like a flash from the bed, snatches slippers and dressing gown and is already out on the landing making the whole neighborhood tremble with her piercing shrieks.

The ghost, too, having collected his threads and hooks, rushes away like lightning toward his own room. A woman who had come to her window sees him and falls back fainting. A moment later he is stretched out on his pallet, feigning sleep. His heart hammers inside his bony chest, hurting him as if he had been struck with a stone.

In the meantime, the news of the incredible thing that has happened travels like wildfire from house to house; lights appear in windows, and the entire neighborhood is astir. Drinkers come out from inns, sellers of watermelons run with their big knives toward the haunted house. As for the ghost, he appears, in his ragged, beggarly clothes, outside his room, rubbing his eyes and asking, in bewilderment, what has happened. No one pays any attention to him; he is the poor devil who never knows anything.

The possibility that spirits may really exist sends everyone out of

their wits. Women get into each other's beds and lie there, clasped together, trembling; they jabber ceaselessly and seek omens for public
lottery numbers until they fall asleep exhausted. Even the men, who do
not believe in ghosts, stop short for a moment in terror at the sight of
clothes dangling on hangers in dark rooms. But the spiritualists of the
town are triumphant; they make tables dance up and down all night in
order to call up the welcome supernatural guest.

The aforesaid guest, after watching the turmoil for an hour, is now
asleep and dreaming upon his pallet. He dreams of a shining waste,
where he is walking without fatigue. Panthers with brown and golden
coats come to meet him and touch him lightly, gently. An unseen
woman is singing. Then a panther lies down at his feet, and he too lies
down, rests his head against its warm, gently heaving flank, and falls
asleep. He sleeps and dreams he is asleep. He is happy.

Next evening the ghost has to start work again. The man who is paying him is not satisfied. And, since the house is now watched inside, a
change of tactics is required. Climbing over his own window sill, the
ghost walks along the parapet and stops in front of the girl's open
window.

A shimmer of moonlight begins to radiate over a roof top; then the
full moon rises and reveals the lovely sleeping girl. Her sleep is heavy
yet sweet, as the lovable seriousness of her face shows. The ghost con-
templates her in bewilderment, possessed again by that same feeling of
hopeless friendliness. Might she not possibly rise and come to the window, smile at him and take him pityingly by the hand? Perhaps even
kiss him, in a calm and kindly way? Then it would not matter to him
even if he fell into the street. After all, he would never receive any
other gesture of love. But of course such a thing is impossible; his idea
is fantastic; he is nothing but a clumsy scarecrow. Then, in exasperation, he starts knocking with his knuckles on the windowpanes.

The girl—just as if she had been waiting only for this sound—awakes
immediately. She sees the phantom, deathly pale, ghastly, infinitely
dismal dressed up in its sheet. A real ghost indeed. Without even utter-
ing a cry, she flies from the accursed room; and then her voice echoes
again, shrill and piercing, through the lodging house.

Hundreds of people collect in the street, as though they had popped up out of the ground, and point in horror at the ghost, which, standing erect on the parapet, has started slowly, almost solemnly, waving its arms. They all rush away, shouting, and the ghost feels himself lord of the whole neighborhood. For the first time in his life he counts for something; there is a whole crowd of people who are frightened of him. He has a feeling of exaltation at this unexpected triumph, and goes on waving his sheet like a flag of death. When a few people reappear timidly around the corners of the street, he sends them flying again with a burst of sinister, inhuman laughter.

But, from inside the room, two strong arms seize him by the shoulders, lift him up, twist him around into the room. He is surprised at feeling the pain of being thus held fast, surprised to find himself alive, with the full weight of his bones and of his fear. He plunges back into his old unhappiness.

When he can, he looks into the face of the man who has made him prisoner. It is the same man who paid him to pretend to be a ghost, and who now imposes silence upon him with a hand over his mouth, preventing him even from breathing. The ghost closes his eyes and allows himself, in utter humiliation, to be handcuffed by two policemen.

Before going downstairs, he has just time to see the instigator of his crime embracing the girl on the landing. And she is kissing him, with a long, full kiss whose honey taste can be imagined. Small and shapely, her long lashes lowered, she lingers obediently in the arms of the traitor.

In the street, the crowd receives the poor devil with shouting and whistling. Stones fly. Irritated at having to protect him, the policemen make him run in front of them. They will put him in prison, but he will not speak. For those two love each other. The man is young and strong, the girl beautiful, gay, affectionate. They will get married. She will sing all day long and will wear a light gown that falls open at her soft breast; she will pass long hours at the window, and the whole neighborhood will be in love with her. But him she would never love, long and bony and big-nosed as he is, with those yellow catlike eyes, and always out of luck. Best not to speak.

And so he goes stumbling forward, absent-minded, half in a dream. Someone has to pay so that others may be happy. He is one of those who pay. Never mind. But one kind of envy is born in that tired heart of his. Envy for the real ghosts, those who travel solitary about the world, who are light in substance, made of smoke, and who feel nothing, neither weight nor fatigue, nor yet this obscure thirst for love.

MARIO SOLDATI

Nora

TRANSLATED BY CLAIRE MURRAY

I am a lawyer with an office in Turin.

On last July seventeenth, or perhaps it was the eighteenth (I don't remember too clearly), I was in Vicenza on an inheritance case. I had arrived in the morning and wanted to leave the same evening to spend the night in Milan so as to be back in Turin before noon of the following day. Because my client was willing to settle for a modest sum, I rushed through the interviews with his opponents wherever possible. But they were rich country people, stingy, fussy, and stubborn. The settlement I offered, ridiculously low from my client's standpoint, did not seem fair in their eyes. They were old uncles and aunts and whole families of distant cousins, who were quarrelsome by nature and constantly at odds with each other. And each one was receiving advice from a different contentious partisan.

Using as excuses the paralysis of an eighty-year-old uncle, or the delicate health of some aunt or other, they would not get together on a single meeting place. So between proposals, counterproposals, and arguments, I spent the whole day going back and forth, in a fierce sun and burning heat, from house to house, from office to office. It was not until after eight at night that I finally obtained signatures from all concerned.

The last train for Milan had already left. It meant I had to spend the night in Vicenza. I hurried over to the Roma Hotel and was lucky enough to get a room. I left my brief case there and went out to find a restaurant. It was almost nine o'clock, yet because of the blackout and the wartime curfew, there was still light in the sky, a soft green above the dark houses. The city was already deserted and still, except for German patrols marching down the main thorough-fare, the sound of their hobnailed boots echoing in the doorways. I looked for, but couldn't find, the restaurant where I had eaten well a couple of years before and where I had hoped to be able to eat again. Through the portico I saw a light showing under the black curtain of a store that was still open. I entered in the hope of getting some information.

It was a de luxe tobacco store, perhaps the best in town. A dark woman, somewhat heavy and, at first glance, rather beautiful, was sitting behind the counter under a soft light, against a background of orderly, brightly colored shelves. Through a small door to the side, you could see that the back of the store was arranged as a combination kitchen and dining room. It was all neat and tidy, however, and a thin, bent old woman was preparing supper over a gas plate. The aroma that emanated from the store, the stillness and cleanliness of the place, the restful beauty of the tobacco saleswoman, and the in-stinctive though unjustified thought that these two women were alone caused me—in the few seconds between crossing the threshold and reaching the counter—to wish earnestly to stay and eat there. Of course, it was a ridiculous wish. Or rather, it was not so much a wish as a passing whim.

"Some Toscani cigars, please," I said to the clerk. Lazily she pushed the cigar box so that it slid across the counter. As she did so, it seemed to me that I had seen her somewhere, that I knew her.

I bent over the cigars and pretended to be concerned over my pur-chase, at the same time making an effort to remember where I had met this handsome brunette.

At first, I thought I might have met her in this same tobacco store when I had passed through Vicenza two years before. But, some-how, this simple explanation didn't satisfy me and I continued my reflections while I tested the cigars, examining them closely.

"No more than five, sir; it's not allowed," warned the tobacco clerk in a strange voice that was harsh and discourteous, yet bored and affected at the same time; it bore no trace of Veneto accent and was in sharp contrast to the known hospitality of the place and the customary politeness of tobacconists in general.

"I know, I know," I answered hastily, raising my eyes and staring at the woman. "Here, I'll take two." While I was paying, I added: "Excuse me, but can you tell me what street will take me to the restaurant called *L'Aquila d'Oro?*"

"I'm not familiar with these parts," she replied, more rudely, this time, throwing me a side glance that was quick yet searching: a glance that bore some absurd hidden meaning as if she had seen me before and had no desire to renew the acquaintance. Just at that moment a German soldier entered, and at once she smiled at him, asking in a loud tone: *"Bitte, was wünschen Sie?"* *—anxious to please and devoting herself to him as if I no longer existed.

What kept me from leaving then? Anger at having been treated badly and the stupid desire for some kind of revenge? At that time, that was my justification for the decision to remain. But perhaps I had been drawn to the woman because of her impudent air, and that mysterious glance of hers had disturbed me, made me curious, confirmed my first impression; I must have met her somewhere and had some sort of an encounter with her.

As one pretext for remaining, I looked about for the cigar-cutting machine. I saw it farther down the counter, beyond the body and arm of the German soldier, who was selecting post cards. I made a motion to the clerk to pass it to me. She pretended not to see me. Then I circled the German to reach that end of the counter, and the cutter, and, taking the trouble to be ever so accurate, I measured and remeasured the distance of the blade from both ends of the first cigar—and finally cut a second cigar only after the German's departure.

"Then you aren't from Vicenza?" I began casually. "I've been here before and don't recall having seen you."

"No, I've been here only two months. Why?" She smiled slowly in a manner that was ironic and ambiguous at the same time.

"Because—because—if you had been here, I'd have recognized you; in fact, I think we have met before...."

"And I don't think we have, sir," she said in a tone of finality that dismissed me. But again, as she said "sir," she had smiled in that ironic

* "What do you wish?"

way of hers, narrowing those eyes that had a glint in them, as if she were thinking: "We certainly *have* met before, and I know how and where, but you don't remember, and I don't want to tell you."

"I think we have met before," I insisted, expecting to receive a sharp retort. "In Milan, but not here in Vicenza. I don't know, I don't remember. Perhaps in Milan?"

"Oh, no," smiled the woman pityingly, staring at me as if I were out of my head.

"In Rome? Perhaps in Rome. That's it. Rome!"

"My dear man, it's no use."

"I'm sorry." I now wanted to close the subject as far as the acquaintanceship was concerned, yet still continue our conversation. "It's obvious that I am mistaken."

"It is," she replied dryly; but, guessing that I wished to continue talking, she turned at once and called, "Mamma!" with the idea of discouraging me, and moved toward the entrance to the rear-room. She stopped there, her back turned, determined to give me no further opening.

She had broad shoulders, and a body that was strong and well-built, now that I could see her figure to the knees from a better advantage. The old woman came up to her with a casserole in her hand and they exchanged words in a low voice.

"Then you can't tell me where I can get a bite to eat?" I said loudly to get back her attention.

"Eat?" she said, turning roughly. "Don't you know that if you don't hurry you'll find every place closed? Furthermore, in a few minutes we'll be closing, too. Closing—my good man—closing! Do you understand?"

At these words, which were more than clear enough, I determined to make every effort to stay, partly from stubbornness, partly from the desire to decide where I had known this woman; or perhaps it was because of a strange power that attracted me to her, or maybe simply because I would not have eaten as well in the usual restaurant as in the rear of this store.

"Yes, I understand," I answered. "But I am so tired that I really don't feel like going out to look for a restaurant. I would pay anything to eat here."

"You're crazy," she retorted, serious and annoyed. "Come on, now, get out at once," and with a confident sense of authority she took me by the arm and led me to the outer door, where she raised the curtain and said, pushing me out, "Come on, get going."

"Wait a minute, Signora, perhaps I didn't make myself clear. I didn't say I didn't want to pay."

"Come on, get going. This isn't a restaurant."

On an impulse, I grabbed her wrist (it was very narrow and she had a small, thin hand, in strange contrast to the fullness of her body), and, forcing her to lower the outside screen, I spoke in a muffled undertone, so that not even her mother could hear from the back.

"I'll give you a thousand lire if I can eat here with you."

Again, now that I think back on my motives for making such a proposition, I can remember none. I am a dignified professional man, conservative, the father of a family, by nature economical, and never in my life have I gone in for wild behavior.

Sudden passion? Oh, no, I recall distinctly that in that moment I was not thinking, at least not exclusively, of the possibility of an amorous interlude. My chief thought was that I had to know who this woman was and where I had met her. I had to, that was all. In that instant I experienced the irrepressible drive that a "must" carries with it, unfortunately all too rarely, and which is translated into action before it has been fully recorded in one's consciousness.

Anyway, one thing is certain: the effect of that absurd proposal was magical: the woman's face froze while greed and spite fought for supremacy. For the first time she appeared pleasant and her mouth, which was given its ironic expression by the prominence of her lower lip, seemed to smile kindly. She studied me another instant, looking at me closely, searching me from the depths of her little black eyes. Finally, still silent, without freeing her wrist, she twisted it till she could show me her open palm. She lowered her glance to her palm, making her meaning clear, looked up at me again, smiling more openly, and said in a tone of expectancy: "Well?"

I got the point, of course. I took out my wallet and put a thousand-lira bill into that small hand with its pointed red nails which folded on it as if on a prey.

"Help me to close," were her first words after she had tucked the bill between the great full breasts revealed by the low-necked summer dress, and she handed me a long hooked pole. We went out into the dark and deserted portico.

"Come on," she said, brushing against me. Still blind because the light inside had been bright, I had to take her arm—fat and warm though it was—in order to find my way. She had used the familiar form of the verb, and while it did not surprise me, it was disturbing. That wasn't what I wanted—at least not what I was after first of all. Still, she couldn't have taken my proposal any other way.

It suddenly occurred to me that she might be a professional and had worked in a bordello. Perhaps that was where I had seen her! But I realized at once that it was impossible. It was more than twenty years since I had been in one; and twenty years ago she couldn't have been more than ten years old.

We reached a display window, only a few yards away, on the corner of an alley. German footsteps could still be heard here and there in the night, reverberating against the tiles under the portico, and there was also their chorus singing—at times religious, at times drunken—which seeped outward in subdued tones from the interior of dwellings.

The tobacconist pointed out a ring high up on the edge of the blind and with this gesture practically ordered me to pull it down.

"My name is Amneris," she said, as we returned through the dark to the store. "But you can call me Nora."

Nora? I had heard this name before. Someone had mentioned it at some time or other, someone close to me. But it was a distant memory, fleeting, uncertain, the memory of a name that had appeared in a dream.

Let me make it clear that no ethereal image was conjured up even in my memory when I heard the name "Nora." On the contrary, I felt at once as if the depth had been sounded, that "Nora" was right. It was the name of the mysterious, vulgar woman now walking arm in arm with me, and it was the name of the woman I remembered having known sometime in the past. In other words, the woman I had known was this one and not one who resembled her; it was she and no other.

I lowered the store blind after letting Nora in and left a narrow space so that I, by bending nearly in two, could also slide through.

Nora rudely burst out laughing and looked at me with curiosity, as if she saw some defect in me she had not noticed before.

Surprised, I asked her what was the matter.

"Finish closing," she said, pointing to the blind. Then she explained, laughing all over again: "Do you know what I was thinking, when I saw you on your hands and knees? That it would have been fun right then, to pull the blind down all the way and crush you like a rat! Ha! I'd love to have done it! Ha! Ha!"

I can't say I enjoyed the joke. And I swear to Heaven that if it hadn't been for the crazy urge, increasing by the minute, to remember where I had known her, I would have left without eating, letting her keep the thousand lire.

I put the light out in the store and went to the back. The table was set. The mother added a place for me. Now that I saw her close up, she was a repulsive old woman, with a sharp nose and chin, hair that was gray and sparse almost to baldness, a shifty glance, a shuffling step.

Nora made me reach for a large jar of mushrooms in oil that was on top of a cupboard, and we began eating them while waiting for the soup to be ready. Pointing to the mushrooms, she said in an undertone, "Of course, you'll pay me extra for these," as if she had to keep up appearances in front of her mother; "with the price of oil these days, such a jar is like gold!"

At such insatiable, uninhibited, and professional venality, so characteristic of whores, it occurred to me again that she must have worked in a bordello; in fact, I felt convinced of it. But that did not help in the least to answer my question; on the contrary, it only complicated the matter. The entire time we ate, we conversed prosaically, I remaining impartial throughout, on the war, on the high cost of living, on the Germans, and on the probable outcome, but I did not take my eyes off her for a moment. I watched her every motion and gesture, convinced that any moment, in a flash, I would remember.

She ate sensually, almost rapaciously. And she was both sensual and rapacious in appearance. She sat across from me, and I could study her minutely now. Her hair, as black and shiny as the wings of a crow, crowned her high forehead and formed thick curls that clustered behind her temples and ears and fell about her shoulders. Her eyes were not very large, nor were they particularly small. They changed in appearance from one moment to the other, depending on whether she narrowed them ironically or dilated them to a stare that commanded obedience. Her mouth was small, her lower lip protruded in an offensive sneer. But most striking of all, because it was in such contrast to the fullness of her cheeks, the roundness of her chin, and, indeed, to all her features and members except her hands, was her nose—a fine line, somewhat aquiline, and so thin and pointed that it seemed but a skin-covered beak. One wasn't aware of this bad feature at first glance; indicative as it was on a closer and lengthier examination, of the woman's character, it might have seemed repulsive, and yet again, it might also have served as a disarming weapon against one who was attracted to her immediately. Alcina, Armida, Circe must have been like her. In their fatal beauty there must have been a flaw which, betraying as it did their wickedness, was the salvation of admirers who were lukewarm and undecided, yet doomed those others who fell madly in love at first sight.

Where had I seen that face? I studied it carefully, feverishly, the way you rack your memory for a musical theme that you know well but cannot place. You have it. You think you remember. But no, it's another aria leading you astray, hopelessly off the track. You have to start all over again and painfully reconstruct the atmosphere and cadence that seem to suggest the theme.

Toward the end of the meal, I began to question her subtly, insidiously. But she avoided my questions by pretending to miss the point. After the fruit, she got up to clear the table. She took the fruit bowl from the table and moved away to the credenza. In that instant, as she raised her fat arms, bare to above the elbows, and placed the fruit bowl on the credenza, I remembered and again saw those arms performing that same task. Emilio's maid! The maid of my poor friend Emilio Ferrero. I had become aware of her two years ago, during my last visit to Rome.

I believed I knew the explanation for the woman's determination to keep quiet. She had recognized me and didn't want me to remember her in a position inferior to that of tobacco clerk. For this reason I decided to keep my recognition to myself and, now that my curiosity had been satisfied, to leave as soon as I could.

But, when she turned back from the credenza, one glance was all she needed to realize that I had recognized her. Perhaps my eyes betrayed my inner satisfaction; perhaps instinct told her. The fact remains that she came over to where I was seated, close enough to touch me with her body, and, staring at me from above, eye to eye, she said quietly: "You remember now, huh!"

"No, what?" I answered, pretending.

"Oh, nothing," she said with a smile. But I gave in at once!

"Yes, in Rome, at Professor Ferrero's home."

"I knew you remembered," and, still smiling, she added: "Now what? Are you satisfied now?"

Satisfied? Now that I knew, it no longer mattered at all. I regretted the thousand lire. I found that house and the woman repulsive and wanted only to get away.

The sudden death of my poor friend, Emilio Ferrero, had occurred in Rome about a year before as a result of heart failure and was not entirely unexpected by his relatives and acquaintances, grieved though they were. However, I had been his only companion during his extraordinary adolescence and a confidant of his early, lofty ambitions. I had then followed his successes in a governmental career and had seen in his increased leisure nothing more or less than a gradual renunciation of his ideals. In the last years I had guessed at some secret and tragic corruption. For me, therefore, Emilio's death had been a disturbing mystery. His wife, a few days afterward, had gone mad and was still a patient in a sanitarium. His relatives, and hers, had been notified at the last minute and had arrived in Rome only in time for the funeral. Furthermore, it was strange that no diaries, memoranda, or notes were to be found among his letters, although I knew he had some, since he had shown me his notebooks one day, without opening them. Also, why had the usually so correct and punctilious Professor Veracini not answered my questions when I inquired about Emilio, but replied only that he would be glad to see me, and not to fail to call on him when I came to Rome? I was always reluctant to visit Rome and was persuaded to do so only when I had a case in the Supreme Court. And suddenly, here in the rear of a tobacco store, all these little details came to my mind. Perhaps Veracini wanted to talk to me about Emilio. I wanted to talk to this maid about Emilio. She had been in the service of the Ferreros for more than a year and certainly should know more than I did concerning the death of my poor friend. All the same, it seemed a sacrilege to discuss Emilio with her. I felt that I should not have remained.

Her strange beauty repelled me, yet at the same time, I was fascinated—and disturbed. I feared, for a moment, that I had exaggerated the vague doubts concerning Emilio's death, which I had been feeling for several months, so that I might have a pretext for talking to the tobacco woman and remaining there. Veracini would say this fear was a subtle trick of the devil's. Thinking of Emilio's death, no, I hadn't exaggerated. In my simple way, for a moment I pretended I had exaggerated to prove to myself that I had not exaggerated, and that I should stay and investigate the mystery.

The desire to get to the bottom of Emilio's death had in itself no inner motive. I would have completed my research, if not here, then somewhere else and among other people.

As always happens when we tell ourselves that our conscience was bewildered while instead it was torn by a struggle between two opposite sentiments, duty and pleasure, the matter was decided for better or worse by an external circumstance which settled things more or less and gave the will a chance to exert itself in a particular direction. And so, somewhat upset and inwardly confused, I rose and, murmuring some word of farewell, headed for the door. Nora was looking at me and smiling indifferently; perhaps she already knew what to expect of me. All the same, I had picked up my hat and was putting it on.

And suddenly I remembered. It was also in Rome when, late at night—I had left Emilio after a long visit (it was the last time I saw him)—yes, also in Rome, that she had given me my hat in the hallway. I remembered I was startled to find her still up, since it was after three A.M. and Emilio's wife had retired before midnight. When I had expressed my surprise, Emilio said: "Oh—it's our faithful Amneris— Oh! don't you know Amneris? Let me introduce you. Mr. Costanzo, a lawyer ... Miss Amneris ... ," and he mentioned a surname I don't recall.

But I remembered Amneris perfectly and the absurdity of the introduction (introduction to the maid!) so late at night in the silence and darkness of the vestibule. Amneris, or Nora, was holding open the door to the stairway, which had vast windows that looked upon the Parioli gardens, and because of the blackout, the vestibule light was screened. I had said good-by to Emilio again, kissing him first on one cheek, then the other, as we always had done the few times we saw each other over the years. And I had gone down the wide stairs bathed in blue light, thinking over painfully what he had told me of himself that night, of his wife, of the ill-chosen life he had led, and I wondered why he had felt it necessary to introduce me to the maid in that way, almost as if she were nobility.

Then why was it, after having been so struck by that introduction and having thought of it several times, that I had not recognized her the minute I stepped into the tobacco shop? It may have been that Rome and Vicenza are so far apart, or a difference in the woman's environment, or perhaps her beauty had had some effect on me in the evening in the subdued light in the store.

Anyway, now she was here before me, Signora Amneris, and she was smiling as she handed me my hat—and she must have recalled that moment in the past because she exaggerated the gesture and bobbed ironically in a maid's half-curtsy.

I took my hat, ready to go, at the same time asking her, somewhat distractedly and without realizing that I was starting a conversation, if she had been with Emilio until the time of his death.

She said she had, and had stayed on even afterward, the very last to remain. His wife had been taken off to a sanitarium, and at the request of Emilio's relatives she had taken care of the house until the furniture could be removed. She told me this as she walked me through the half-dark store to a small glass door—which connected with the passageway to the street. I stopped and, leaning against the counter in a darkness broken only by a strip of light from the rear of the store, I asked her how Emilio had died, and to tell me all about it.

"Cheerful conversation, my dear fellow! Don't you know how he died? Of course, you knew! He had heart trouble. What do you care, now?"

What could I have answered?

Describe my long-standing friendship, my affection for Emilio?

If I lacked the will power to go away, at least I would have enough sense not to discuss Emilio with this woman. If I reproved her for her cynicism, I would only be lowering myself. I kept still, therefore, and in some sudden reversal of conscience I felt I would be committing less of a sin if I did not bring the memory of my friend into a whim of the hour.

I moved near her. In the darkness, her black eyes shone as she smiled. I seized her waist, pulled her close to me, felt myself enveloped in her perfume, her warmth, her soft flesh.

When I reopened my eyes I had a strange vision. I was leaning against the counter, and Nora, in my embrace, had her back to the door. The glass of the door, shining against the darkness of the passageway, reflected the dim light of the rear of the store. In that dark mirror, I had seen momentarily outlined the smooth, spectacled face of a German officer.

In one instant he seemed to be standing behind me, in the store.

"What happened? What's the matter with you?" asked Nora.

"There—a German behind the door!" I answered, feeling that some German, looking for cigarettes, perhaps, had passed the door and had stared through the glass spying on the tobacco store's interior.

"How silly you are, darling!" She ran swiftly to the door, opened it, and rushed out.

I heard her steps clatter on the tiles of the passageway, pause, start up again more slowly, farther away, and then stop again. After a minute or two, she returned calmly and began carefully to close a wooden door outside the one of glass.

When I protested feebly that I had to leave to go home: "I should say not. You're to stay here to sleep."

I didn't answer. Then she moved closer, encircled me with her arms, and murmured, as she gazed at me: "What will you give me if I let you sleep with me?"

For some time, I lay motionless in the darkness. Through the open window I could see the wall of a courtyard, the top of a young tree, bathed in a soft gray light, the reflection perhaps of the moon that had meanwhile risen. The heat was oppressive. The unfamiliar room, the heavy, cheap perfume of the woman who lay next to me, and remorse for what I had done, tormented me. And I kept thinking of Emilio. It seemed as if I was only now beginning to understand the strange conversation we had had that last night. I seemed only now to be able to measure the despair into which he had fallen. I was like a man who has heard of a distant land from his friends or his books and who sets out for that land only to find, on reaching it, a surprising panorama far different from what he had imagined, seas more vast, loftier mountains, more populous cities: similarly, I now saw before my eyes the desolate landscape Emilio had described to me, and, thinking back over my recent moments of pleasure and the consequent shame, I was overcome by my own feeling.

Was I a friend to Emilio that night in Rome? Yes, perhaps. In fact, I remember having listened to his words with the closest of attention, reproving and comforting him, and persuading him not to despair. Does friendship exist where there is not complete understanding? At that time, I had not understood what Emilio was telling me. And now I felt myself almost his accomplice, while he was now relieved of his problems and suffering, and had no further need of my aid.

Next to me, I heard Nora's breathing. I don't know why, but it did not sound like the breathing of a human being. I felt as if I were sharing a bed with an animal. Could I express to her any of the thoughts passing through my mind?

She would have laughed at them all. Her life, a continuous exposure to meanness, egoism, and greed, had left her impervious to anything that did not concern her own interests. She had no understanding of the rest of the world, not even of the simplest and most commonplace of things, unless they represented to her either a threat or gain. "Me! Me!" she had said a few minutes before, as she gazed into my eyes. "Me!" She experienced pleasure only when paid and only when she could think continuously of herself.

I raised myself up on one elbow and saw as I leaned over her that she was not asleep.

"What's the matter with you? What do you want?" she asked calmly, raising a gentle hand for me to kiss.

"Nora," I said quietly, and with no more hesitation, "I'm leaving. I'm going to the hotel," and I started to get out of bed.

"Keep still," she said roughly. "I have no desire to get up and open the door for you."

"I can let myself out."

"You can't. The outside door is locked from the inside. Keep still and go to sleep. Quiet!"

I stretched out on the bed again and tried to fall asleep. But it was impossible. With every passing moment, the situation became more and more insupportable. I tossed and turned, feeling as if I were about to suffocate.

"Keep still. Will you let me sleep?" she snapped after a time.

"I'm thinking of my friend. That's why I can't sleep."

"*The dead sleep and the living keep the peace.* Don't you know the proverb?"

"But he was my dearest friend."

"And what am I?" She burst into loud laughter. "Am I not your dearest friend? Am I not dearer to you than he is—if he were alive? And dearer than your wife, and your children, and everything you have in the world, and dearer than God and the Madonna? Say it, that I am dearer to you than anyone else. Come on, say it! Why can't you understand that one moment of my sleep is worth more than all your thoughts and worries. What do you think I am, anyway?"

"I'm still thinking of my friend and how he must have suffered before he died."

Nora laughed heartily. "Suffer? Suffer, my eye! Quite the contrary! He felt fine, and especially in that particular moment. So long, good night," and she turned heavily, showing me her back.

With determination I got out of bed and began to dress. Nora's vague, strange words merely shocked me at the time, and I feared that if I did not get away at once, I might again lose the desire to leave. I dressed quickly and quietly. For a time Nora neither moved nor spoke. Finally, when she suddenly realized that I meant business, she stood up on the bed like a Fury and, nude as she was, flew at me, pressing her nails into my arms, crying chokedly: "You think you're going to leave like this? You're crazy. Give me two thousand lire."

Then I had the presence of mind to burst out laughing.

Highly indignant, she shouted: "You're laughing? You have the nerve to laugh at me?" She raised a hand as if to slap me, but I didn't give her time and slapped her first. Then a brief struggle took place. I grabbed her wrists to keep her from scratching me. She tried to get away by throwing herself face down on the bed, twisting about in angry convulsions.

Eventually she stopped puffing and, nearly bleating with rage, repeated stubbornly: "Give me two thousand lire."

"Five hundred," I retorted.

"A thousand five hundred."

"Five hundred."

"A thousand."

"Five hundred."

There was a long pause. I still held her wrist, waiting for her reply. She decided: "All right, five hundred. But let me go."

I released her and, taking my wallet, I went over to the window for better light.

"Five hundred, plus the mushrooms, makes six hundred and fifty," she called from the bed hopefully.

I pretended not to have heard.

"Here," I said, handing her a five-hundred-lire bill.

"Come on, come on, I have to go."

Beaten, she got up, put on a bathrobe, and stepped into her slippers. She led me down the stairway into the store, opened the inner door, and walked me to the main door, which she opened with a huge key.

I was about to go out without further words, but she blocked the doorway and, speaking for the first time in a sweet, gentle tone, she said: "Come, let's part as friends. Won't you give me a little kiss?"

I went out through the portico and I think I must have covered the first hundred yards to the street corner almost at a trot, without glancing backward.

When I came out on the cross street, bathed in moonlight, I slowed down and walked at a normal pace to the Roma Hotel.

The summer night was quiet and airless, the walls of the houses reflecting the heat of the day. Nora's terrible, yet absurd, words re-echoed in my ears: "Suffer? Suffer, my eye! Quite the contrary! He felt fine, and especially in that particular moment." What did those words mean? When I heard them I had felt only that I had to get away at once.

I've already said that many of the circumstances of Emilio's death had been disturbing me for several months. What had happened? Heart disease? Yes, that was the diagnosis of the doctors who certified his death. But his regular physician said he had never noticed any signs of cardiac trouble. It's true, of course, that Emilio had not seen his regular doctor for more than a year, but still . . . I was consumed by a thousand doubts and suppositions, and now there was added Nora's incomprehensible statement. Perhaps Emilio did not die of heart disease. Did he kill himself, then? At one time, I had thought that. And now, had not Nora's allusion, in its macabre sarcasm, seemed to point to suicide?

With these sad thoughts, I entered the hotel. As soon as I reached my room, I lay down. But I couldn't fall asleep. I looked out of the window across the tree-lined courtyard, into the tranquil moonlight, and in an effort to find a solution to the mystery that was torturing me, my thoughts drifted back to Emilio's life, back to the earliest recollections of our adolescence.

One by one, I slowly reviewed the noble goals which his home training and religious and academic education had helped him to set for himself on the conclusion of his university work; and one by one, thinking back over the progressive decadence in which I found him on each of my trips to Rome, I tore them down again, one by one. Then I remembered clearly his ultimate despair.

My reaction was like that of a jealous man who has for a long time nourished suspicions which he has nevertheless been able to put behind him. Suddenly he is brought to realization by a single tiny fact or gesture or word and, in a flash, is able to assemble all the infinitesimal doubts that he thought he had forgotten—to visualize in one instant the truth that had been concealed from him so obstinately over the years. In such a way, I now saw and knew everything about Emilio, his life and his death, in that sudden enlightening statement of Nora's. It was the key to the door on which I had been knocking in vain for so long.

In this story I have been careful to substitute a fictitious name for that of my poor friend. But if I were to tell his whole story now, his family could not fail to recognize him. And for that reason, I shall withhold it for the time being.

DINO BUZZATI

Strange New Friends

TRANSLATED BY FRANCES FRENAYE

Stefano Martella, president of an insurance company, had spent almost half a century living, sinning, and making his pile on this earth before he died. He awakened from death to find himself in a marvelous city, full of impressive buildings, straight, broad streets, parks, well-stocked shops, sleek automobiles, theaters, and well-fed, fashionably dressed people, all splendid to look upon under the sunny sky. He was walking quietly along a boulevard with an agreeable new companion to show him the sights. "I knew it," he said to himself. "I worked hard all my life long, looked after my family, left my children a respectable fortune, and in short did my duty. So here I am in Heaven."

His companion said that his name was Francesco and that he had been there for ten years.

"Are you happy?" Martella asked with an ironical smile, as if the question were utterly superfluous.

"I can't very well say no," the other answered, staring at him. And they both laughed over their little joke.

Was Francesco an official host or was it out of sheer courtesy that he played the part of escort? He led Martella from one street to another and to sights each one more remarkable than the one before. Everything was spotlessly clean and in perfect order, with no unpleasant sound or smell to spoil the harmony. They walked quite a distance, and still the somewhat stout Martella did not feel tired.

At one corner a handsome car, driven by a liveried chauffeur, was waiting.

"This is for you," Francesco said, beckoning to Martella to get in, and they proceeded to drive about. On the streets the newcomer saw men of various ages and social conditions, all well dressed and healthy. They had kindly expressions on their faces, and only occasionally did he notice something like a mildly bored stare. "That's natural enough," he said to himself. "They can't go around wearing a beatific smile all day."

Finally they stopped in front of one of the handsomest houses they had seen.

"This is yours," said Francesco, bidding him go in. Martella's earthly estate was a miserable hovel by comparison. The place was up to fairy-tale specifications, complete with a parlor, study, library, billiard room, and other conveniences too numerous to mention. Outside there were a formal garden, tennis courts, a riding ring, a swimming pool, and a pond stocked with fish. And everywhere servants awaiting his orders.

They took an elevator to the top floor, where there was a music room, one side of which was an immense glass window. Martella marveled again at the view. As far as he could see the city had no end; there was an infinite extent of rooftops, domes, skyscrapers, pinnacles, and fluttering flags. Only church towers were missing.

"Aren't there any churches?" he asked his companion.

"There's hardly any need for those here," said Francesco, apparently surprised at the ingenuousness of such a question.

"And what about God?" Martella asked. Deep down inside he didn't much care, but it seemed to him no more than polite to ask after the master of the kingdom. "It seems to me that I remember learning in the catechism when I was little that in Paradise we were to enjoy an eternal vision of God. Can't we see Him from up here where we are now?"

Francesco gave a slightly mocking laugh.

"My dear fellow, excuse me for saying so, but it seems to me that you expect a little too much." (What made him laugh in such a disagreeable manner?) "Every man has a Paradise of his own, of course. What do you care about seeing God, since you've never believed in Him?"

Martella did not insist. After all, it was quite true that he didn't care.

To visit the whole house would have been too much of an undertaking for one time, but they inspected its main features, and Martella saw that it promised to offer him a very comfortable existence. Then Francesco proposed taking him to his club and introducing him to his friends. On the way out Martella couldn't resist satisfying his curiosity by asking slyly: "What about women? Are there any pretty women around?" (Of course he had seen some perfect beauties along the way, but what he wanted to know was whether in a place like this a man of his age, and so on, could, without losing his dignity, hope to . . .)

"What a question!" exclaimed his companion, still with the same mocking air. "Why here in Paradise, there's plenty of everything!"

At the club, which was housed in a building that might have been a king's palace, seven or eight obviously distinguished gentlemen greeted Martella as heartily as if he were an old friend. He had the feeling that he had met two of them before, that they were business acquaintances or perhaps rivals upon whom he had once put something over, but he couldn't be quite sure. In any case, none of them gave any signs of recognition.

"So you've just arrived, have you?" said the oldest of the group, a white-haired individual who looked at him almost overeagerly. "And very happy to be here, I suppose."

"Oh, very happy, indeed," said Martella, sipping a cocktail that someone had offered him. "I couldn't be anything else."

"What do you mean by that?" asked a thin fellow in his thirties, with a face somewhat like that of Voltaire and a bitter twist to his lips. "You speak as if our kind of happiness were practically obligatory."

"Don't make your usual fuss," said the old man, who seemed to be annoyed. "As a matter of fact, it is inescapable. All the things that used to bother us before (and he made a gesture which Martella soon realized was the conventional way of referring to life on earth) have been done away with."

"Absolutely all of them? Even bores?" Martella asked, trying to be witty.

"I should hope so," said the old gentleman.

"And what about illness? No more common colds?"

"Illness? What do you think it means to be in Paradise?" retorted the old man, placing a somehow scornful stress on the last word.

"Never fear," echoed the thin man, looking hard at the new arrival. "Don't expect to have any illness; it simply dosen't exist."

"What makes you think I'm expecting any? I've had about enough, I should say," Martella said, pleased with his own spontaneous wit.

"You never can tell," said the thin man, and it was impossible to tell whether or not he was serious. "It's no joke not to look forward to staying in bed a few days with fever or having a good toothache. . . . We're not allowed to so much as sprain an ankle!"

"What makes you talk that way?" said the old gentleman. "The lack of such afflictions is no calamity." And he added, to Martella: "Don't pay any attention. He's a great tease."

"Yes, so I've noticed," said Martella with a deliberately casual air, although he actually felt embarrassed. "It's plain that there's no suffering here."

"No suffering, that's it exactly, and hence no hospitals or sanitariums or asylums of any kind," said the old gentleman.

"Just so!" said the thin man. "Tell him everything."

"Well, as I have just said, we have no suffering," said the old gentleman. "And nobody is afraid. You're not likely to feel your heart pounding."

"Not even in case I have a bad dream or a nightmare?"

"Why should you have a nightmare? I don't have dreams at all any more. I'm sure I don't remember dreaming since I came."

"And desires? Don't you wish for anything?"

"What should we wish for? We have everything. What is lacking?"

"And the so-called pangs of love? What about them?"

"Nothing of the kind, naturally. No desire, or love, or hate, or regret, or war. . . . Everything's perfectly quiet."

At this point the thin young man got up, with a hard look on his face.

"Don't think of such things," he said to Martella emphatically. "Just put them out of your mind. We're all happy, do you understand? You'll never be tired or thirsty; you'll never be heartsick over a woman or toss on a bed of pain, waiting for morning to come. We have no longing, or remorse, or fear, not even the fear of going to Hell. We're happy, don't you understand?" (Here he hesitated a second, as if he had just thought of something unpleasant.) "There's one thing in particular— at first one doesn't think of it, but it's very important. There's no death, of course. We can't possibly die; isn't that wonderful? We're de-fi-ni-te-ly exempt from dying. . . . Time passes, but yesterday and today and tomorrow are all the same, and nothing can happen to us." (Here his voice took on a solemn tone.) "Death! Do you remember how we used to hate it? What a shadow it cast over our lives? Do you re-member the look of cemeteries? The cypress trees? The votive lights on the tombs? The ghosts that walked by night, with clanking chains around them? And the discussions we held about the mystery of the hereafter? Well, all that's forgotten. Here it's very different; we're perfectly free and have no sensation that the grim reaper is knocking at the door. That's real happiness for you!"

The old gentleman was listening apprehensively to this peroration. Now he broke in to say: "Leave that kind of talk alone, I tell you. How can you lose your self-control?"

"My self-control? What does that matter? Why shouldn't he know?" said the thin man mockingly. Then he turned to Martella. "You've come here to rot, too, don't you understand? And thousands like you arrive every day. They find a house and car, theaters, women, amuse-ments, and they never suffer from illness, or sorrow, or unrequited love, or fear, or anxiety, or remorse, or desire. . . ."

This was too much. Quietly but firmly, three of those present, includ-ing the old gentleman, pushed the young man out the door, as if he were guilty of violating the strict code that governed their common ex-istence. The speed of their punitive action showed that scenes of the same kind must have taken place before. Even after the young man had been pushed down the stairs, he shouted back to Martella: "Just look at the fine buildings and gardens and jewels, and amuse yourself if you can! Don't you see that we've lost everything? Don't you know yet that . . ."

But here his words were choked off, as if someone had gagged him, and the sentence ended in a mumbling which Martella could not fol-low. But by now this hardly mattered. A haunting voice seemed to whisper in his ear the words that the other had not been able to get out: "Don't you know yet that we're in Hell?"

Hell? With all these buildings and flowers and handsome people? How absurd! But as Martella looked around, his heart turned over. He saw six or seven implacable, smooth-skinned, mysterious faces, with set smiles upon them. A servant came up to offer him another drink. He took a sip with disgust, feeling completely alone and abandoned by humankind. Then slowly he regained his self-possession, met the gaze of his new friends, and joined their desperate conspiracy. With woeful faces, all of them together tried to smile.

ITALO CALVINO

One Afternoon, Adam . . .

TRANSLATED BY BEN JOHNSON

The new gardener was a boy with long hair and a cloth band on his head to keep the hair in place. Now he was coming up the walk, with the watering can full and his free arm outstretched to balance himself. He sprinkled the nasturtiums carefully, as if serving creamed coffee: in the soil, at the base of the plants, a dark stain fanned out; as soon as the stain was large and soft, he tilted the can back up and moved on to another plant. Gardening surely was a fine occupation, because everything could be done so leisusely. Maria-nunziata stood watching him from the kitchen window. He was already a grown boy, though still in short trousers. And with his hair so long, he looked like a girl. She paused in her dishwashing and tapped on the windowpane.

"Boy," she said.

The new gardener looked up and saw Maria-nunziata and smiled. Maria-nunziata began to giggle in reply, and also because she had never seen a boy with such long hair and with a headband like the one he was wearing. Then the boy signed to her with his hand, "Come here," and Maria-nunziata giggled again, at the funny way he gestured, and commenced to gesture herself to explain that she had to wash dishes. But the young gardener beckoned to her a second time and pointed to the pots of dahlias with his other hand. Why was he pointing at the dahlias? Maria-nunziata opened the window part way and leaned out.

"What is it?" she asked, and she began to laugh.

"Say, want to see something nice?"

"What?"

"Something nice. Come down and see. Quick."

"Tell me what it is."

"I'll make you a present of it. Something nice."

"I have dishes to wash. Then my mistress will come, and with me nowhere around."

"Do you want it or don't you? Come on, hurry."

"Don't go away," Maria-nunziata said, and she closed the window. When she came out of the back door the boy-gardener was still there, watering the nasturtiums.

"Hi," Maria-nunziata said.

Maria-nunziata looked taller than she was because of her beautiful cork-platform shoes, which, though it was a pity, she wore at work, as she wished. But she had the face of a child, small and framed by curly black hair, and legs, too, that were slender and childlike, although her body, puffing out her apron, was already full and nubile. And she laughed constantly: she laughed at everything, said by her or by others.

"Hi," said the boy-gardener. His skin was brown, on his face and neck and chest: maybe because he was like this all the time, bare to the waist.

"What's your name?" asked Maria-nunziata.

"Libereso," said the boy-gardener.

Maria-nunziata laughed and repeated: "Libereso . . . Libereso. . . . What a name, *Libereso!*"

"It's a name in Esperanto," he said. "In Esperanto it means Liberty."

"Esperanto," said Maria-nunziata. "Are you an Esperanto?"

"Esperanto is a language," Libereso explained. "My father speaks Esperanto."

"I'm Calabrian," said Maria-nunziata.

"What's your name?"

"Maria-nunziata."

And she laughed.

"Why do you laugh all the time?"

"Why do they call you Esperanto?"

"Not Esperanto: Libereso."

"Well, why?"

"Why do they call you Maria-nunziata?"

"It's the name of the Madonna. My name is like the Madonna's and my brother's is like San Giuseppe's."

"Sangiuseppe?"

Maria-nunziata shrilled with laughter. "Sangiuseppe, oh! Giuseppe: not Sangiuseppe! *Libereso!*"

"My brother," said Libereso, "is called Germinal, and I have a sister named Omnia."

"That thing now," said Maria-nunziata, "let me see what you have."

"Come with me," said Libereso. He put the watering can on the ground and took her by the hand.

Maria-nunziata stopped: "First, tell me what it is."

"You'll see," he said, "and you'll have to promise to take good care of it."

"You'll give it to me?"

"Yes, I'll let you keep it."

He had led her to a corner near the garden wall. The potted dahlias there were as tall as they.

"Over here."

"But what?"

"Just wait."

Maria-nunziata peered around from behind his shoulders. Libereso bent down to move a pot; he moved another one standing near the wall and pointed to the ground.

"There," he said.

"There what?" said Maria-nunziata. She didn't see a thing: only a shadowed nook with damp, mold-rotting leaves.

"Look, it's moving," the boy said.

Then she saw a leaf-covered stone moving; no, a moist something with eyes and feet: a toad.

"*Mamma mia!*"

Maria-nunziata had fled, flouncing between the dahlias with her beautiful cork-platform shoes. Crouching beside the toad, Libereso laughed, his teeth white in the brown of his face.

"You're scared! It's only a toad! What're you afraid of?"

"It's a toad!" Maria-nunziata wailed.

"A toad. Come here," Libereso said.

She pointed at it with her finger. "Kill it."

The boy raised his hands, almost as if to protect it. "I don't want to. It's good."

"Good? It's a good toad?"

"They're all good. They eat worms."

"Ah," said Maria-nunziata, but still hanging back. She bit the neck of her apron and tried to see, averting her eyes.

"Look how nice he is," Libereso said, putting his hand down.

Maria-nunziata approached: she had stopped laughing and was watching with her mouth agape. "No! don't touch it!"

Libereso, with one finger, caressed the back of the toad, greenish gray and mottled with running warts.

"Are you crazy? You'll get burned, you know, if you touch it, and your hand will swell up."

The boy held out his large brown hands, his palms laminated with yellow calluses.

"Not me," he said. "He's so nice."

He had picked up the toad by the scruff of the neck as if it were a kitten and placed it in the flat of his hand. Maria-nunziata, still biting the neck of her apron, came closer and crouched down.

"It gives me goose flesh. *Mamma mia!*" she said.

They were both crouched behind the dahlias, Maria-nunziata's pink knees lightly touching against the brown-burned, peeling knees of Libereso. Libereso caressed the toad with the palm and back of his hand, catching it from time to time, when it tried to slip down.

"Maria-nunziata, you pet it, too," he said.

The girl burrowed her hands in her lap.

"No," she said.

"No?" he said. "Don't you want to?"

Maria-nunziata lowered her eyes and, glancing at the toad, lowered them again quickly.

"No," she said.

"But it's yours. I'm giving it to you."

Her eyes were beginning to mist; how heartbreaking it was not to accept a present—no one ever gave her presents—but a toad, that toad turned her stomach.

"I'll let you take it inside, if you wish. It'll keep you company."

"No," she said.

Libereso put the toad down, and it promptly hopped away and squatted in the leaves.

" 'By, Libereso."

"No, wait."

"I have to finish the dishes. And my mistress doesn't want me in the garden, anyway."

"Wait, I want to give you something. Something really nice. Come with me."

She followed him along the graveled walks. He was a strange boy, this Libereso, with his long hair, and picking up toads like that with his hands.

"How old are you, Libereso?"

"Fifteen. And you?"

"Fourteen."

"Already, or going to be?"

"On the Feast of the Annunciation."

"Has that come yet?"

"What, don't you know when Annunciation Day is?"

She had begun to laugh again.

"No."

"Annunciation Day, that's when they have the procession. Don't you go to the procession?"

"No."

"In my town there are really fine processions. My town's not like here. We have big fields full of bergamot trees, nothing but bergamot. And everybody works picking bergamots, from morning till night. And there were fourteen of us brothers and sisters, and we all picked berga-mots, and five died when they were babies, and my mother got tetanus, and we all spent a week on the train coming to Uncle Carmelo's, and eight of us slept in a garage. Say, why do you have such long hair?"

They had stopped beside a bed of trumpet lilies.

"Why not? You have long hair, too."

"But I'm a girl. If you have long hair, you're like a girl."

"I'm not like a girl. It's not by the hair that you tell boys from girls."

"It's not by the hair?"

"No, not by the hair."

"Why isn't it by the hair?"

"Want me to give you something nice?"

"Will you?"

Libereso went and began to rove among the lilies. They were all in full flower, their white chalices open to the sky. Libereso peered into each trumpet, with two fingers digging out something and stuffing it into his fist. Maria-nunziata had not entered the bed and watched him, laughing silently. What was Libereso doing? He had now examined every lily in the bed; he came out with his hands held forth, one over the other.

"Open your hands," he said.

Maria-nunziata cupped her hands but was afraid to put them under his. "What do you have?"

"Something nice. You'll see."

"First, let me see."

Libereso opened his hands a little and let her peep in. His hands were crawling with rose beetles: rose beetles of every color. The prettiest were green, and then there were reddish ones, and some that were black, and one even that was a deep blue. They buzzed and slid across one another's sheaths, kicking their tiny black feet in the air. Maria-nunziata ran her hands beneath her apron.

"Here," Libereso said. "Don't you like them?"

"Yes," Maria-nunziata said, but kept her hands hidden.

"They tickle when you hold them in your hand. Want to see?"

Timidly, Maria-nunziata held out her hands, and Libereso let the colored insects tumble down.

"Don't be afraid. They won't bite you."

"Mamma mia!"

It hadn't occurred to her that they might bite. She opened her hands; and, released, spreading their wings, they vanished, the gorgeous colors at once becoming a black coleopterous swarm in the air, alighting in the trumpets.

"What a pity; I want to give you a present and you don't want me to."

"I must go wash dishes. If my mistress finds me outside, oh, the fuss she'll make."

"Don't you want a present?"

"What will you give me?"

"Come."

He continued to lead her through the flower beds.

"I have to return soon to the kitchen, Libereso. Then I have to clean a chicken."

"Ugh!"

"Why ugh?"

"We don't eat the meat of dead animals."

"You have Lent every day, then?"

"What?"

"What do you eat?"

"All sorts of things, artichokes, lettuce, tomatoes. But my father doesn't want us to eat meat from dead animals. Or coffee and sugar, either."

"And the sugar on your ration card?"

"We sell it in the black market."

They had come to a cascade of thick-stemmed plants, entirely stellated with red blossoms.

"Oh, aren't they beautiful," Maria-nunziata said. "Do you ever pick any?"

"Pick any?"

"To take to the Madonna. Flowers are for the Madonna."

"Mesembrianthemum."

"What?"

"This plant is called Mesembrianthemum in Latin. All plants have Latin names."

"Mass is in Latin, too."

"I wouldn't know."

Libereso was glancing aside, up among the branches winding along the wall.

"Look!" he said.

"Look at what?"

A lizard, green with little black markings, sunning itself.

"I'll catch it."

"No!"

But he crept up on the lizard, his hands open, cautious, slowly . . . and pounced, snatching it. Now he was grinning, pleased with himself, with that brown and white smile of his. "Look, he's trying to get away!"

At one moment the lizard thrust its puzzled little head from Libereso's clasped hands, then its tail would appear. Maria-nunziata laughed, too, but took several jumps backward, pressing her skirt between her knees, each time she saw the lizard.

"I see, then, that you don't want me to give you a present," Libereso said, a little crushed, and reluctantly put the lizard down on a little wall. The lizard darted off. Maria-nunziata kept her eyes downcast.

"Come with me," Libereso said, taking her by the hand again.

"What I'd like is a little tube of lipstick so I could paint my lips on Sundays for the dance. Also, a black veil to put over my head, later, to wear to the Benediction."

"On Sundays," Libereso said, "I go to the woods with my brother and we fill up two bags with pine cones. Then, in the evening, my father reads out loud from books by Élisée Reclus. My father has hair all the way down to his shoulders and a beard down to his chest. And he wears short pants, summer and winter. And I draw pictures for the Federazione Artistica Italiana show window. The men with top hats are the moneybags, the ones with kepis the generals, and the ones with round hats the priests. Then I paint them with water colors."

There was a fishpond with round water-lily leaves floating on the surface.

"Shhhh," Libereso said.

Under the water they saw a frog coming up, its green legs stroking sharply and pausing. Floating on top, it climbed onto a lily pad and squatted in the center.

"There," said Libereso, lowering a hand to seize it; but Maria-nunziata said: "Uh!" And the frog leaped back into the water. Now Libereso was searching again, with his nose just above the water.

"Down there."

He plunged his hand in, withdrawing his clenched fist.

"Two at a time," he said. "Look. One on top of the other."

"How come?" asked Maria-nunziata.

"Male and female stuck together," Libereso said. "Look at what they do."

He wanted to put the frogs in Maria-nunziata's hand. Maria-nunziata did not know if she was afraid because they were frogs or because they were male and female stuck together.

"Leave them be," she said. "You don't have to bother them."

"Male and female," Libereso repeated. "Then they'll make tadpoles."

A cloud passed across the sun. Suddenly Maria-nunziata's heart sank.

"Oh, it's late! My mistress must surely be looking for me."

But she didn't leave. They continued to wander together through the garden, and the sun had gone in. Now came an adder. It lay behind a bamboo hedge, a little adder: a glass snake. Libereso let it coil around his arm and he caressed its head.

"I used to train adders once. I had ten of them, and one was real long and yellow, one of those water snakes. Then it shed its skin and got away. Look at this one, the way it opens its mouth, and the forked tongue. Pet it. It won't bite you."

But Maria-nunziata was afraid of adders, too.

Then they went to the rock pool. First, he let her see the water jets; he opened all the valves, and she was very pleased. Then he showed her the goldfish: a lonely old fish whose scales had already begun to turn white. There now: the goldfish was something Maria-nunziata liked. Libereso began to troll his hand through the water trying to catch it; it was difficult, but afterward Maria-nunziata could put it in a bowl and even keep it with her in the kitchen. He caught it but, so that it wouldn't suffocate, left his hand in the water.

"Put your hand in. Caress it," Libereso said. "You can feel it breathe. It has fins like paper and the scales prick you, but only a little."

But Maria-nunziata did not wish to caress the fish, either.

In a petunia bed the soil was soft, and, scratching with his fingers, Libereso dug up an earthworm, very long and very soft.

Maria-nunziata ran away emitting little screams.

"Put your hand here," Libereso said, pointing to the trunk of an old pear tree. Maria-nunziata did not understand, but she put her hand down; then she shrieked and ran, plunging it into the pool. She had raised it covered with ants. The trunk of the pear tree was crawling with tiny Argentine ants.

"Look," Libereso said, placing his own hand against the trunk. The ants climbed up across his hand, but he didn't move.

"What are you doing?" Maria-nunziata asked. "Why get ants all over you?"

His hand was already black; now the ants were climbing up around his wrist.

"Move your hand," Maria-nunziata whined. "You're getting ants all over you."

The ants climbed up his bare arm; already they had reached his elbow.

His arm, now, was covered with a pall of tiny black moving specks; already they had arrived at his armpit, but he didn't budge.

"Libereso, take your hand away Put it in the water!"

Libereso laughed. Some of the ants were migrating from his neck up onto his face.

"Libereso! Anything you want! I'll take all the presents you give me!"

She threw her arms about his neck and began to wipe the ants away.

Libereso removed his hand from the tree, smiling white and brown and nonchalantly brushing his arm off. But her gesture, obviously, had touched him.

"Well, then, I'm going to give you a wonderful present," he said. "I've made up my mind. The most wonderful present I can give you."

"What?"

"A porcupine."

"Mamma mia! . . . My mistress! My mistress is calling!"

Maria-nunziata had finished washing the dishes when she heard a pebble clink against the windowpane. Libereso was below holding a large basket.

"Maria-nunziata, let me come up. I have a surprise for you."

"You can't. What have you got there?"

But just at that moment her mistress rang, and Maria-nunziata disappeared.

When she returned to the kitchen, Libereso was gone. He was not inside and he was not under the window. Maria-nunziata went to the sink. Then she saw the surprise.

In each plate which she had put to dry hopped a frog, an adder lay curled in a saucepan, there was a tureen full of lizards, and mucid snails were leaving iridescent streaks across the crystal ware. In the dishpan full of water swam the lonely old goldfish.

Maria-nunziata shrank back a step, but noticed a toad under her feet, a large toad. It must, actually, have been a female, for it was followed by an entire brood, five little toads in a row, all vaulting in little hops across the black and white tiles.

ELIO VITTORINI

Uncle Agrippa Takes a Train

TRANSLATED BY FRANCES KEENE

My uncle, his face wrapped in his Bedouin scarf, cannot look out into the night. He can only look up, at the luggage rack full of suitcases and packages dimly illumined by a bluish light, or down, at knees, legs, hands, elbows. Or he can look at the faces of those sitting across from him, some of them fallen in shadow on their breasts, others caught between darkness and the wan light, exchanging smoke and breath in the gentle undercurrent of men's melodious night talk on trains.

My uncle, as well as being short, is a very thin man. He always was, even when we were children, and his name, Uncle Agrippa, was synonymous for us with "Uncle Stick" or "Uncle Bean Pole." Wherever he sat down, there was always room for another person. Consequently, as now in his travels, he is always squeezed in between two others, one of whom takes up three-quarters of his seat.

He leaves Syracuse or Milan, Genoa or Rome, in a seat next to the window he has picked out hours earlier. But half an hour after the train starts, some big fat character jams himself in between my uncle and the window. Then, pushing him toward the next traveler, crushing him against the man or woman who happens to be sitting on the other side, little by little he deprives my uncle of all his space on the seat.

"Excuse me," my uncle says.

He draws back a hand that has been crushed under a fat buttock and smiles at the usurper to show that he is not annoyed. Thus he tries to make himself comfortable between his two neighbors and keep the peace. He talks to them; he talks to everyone in the compartment, sometimes perched on the edge of his seat when his neighbors lean back, sometimes disappearing behind them when they sit forward. But he can never look out at the night, for to do that he would have to press his face against the window and wipe a little steam from the glass now and then.

Besides, someone is always standing between the seats blocking a good part of the window. The aisle in the middle of the car, too, is always full of people sitting on their own baggage or on the floor. And my uncle, who manages to sleep only through the first hours of darkness, endures periods of paralysis during these long nights in which, while no one talks, he must sit with his little body and his little head quite erect. His face covered to the eyes by his striped scarf, he observes the others opposite and beside him with eyes that, no longer sparrowlike, have become a Bedouin's eyes, sharp, narrow like those of an old Arab nomad, the nomadic American Indians, the Mongols of the steppes, or the muleteers of my home town.

The silence hasn't lasted long—it must have been only fifteen minutes—and the train has stopped. A man who has been sleeping across from my uncle wakes up.

The train begins to move again. The man's arms are crossed on his chest. My uncle is still looking at him as he did while he was asleep. But when the man looks at my uncle in turn, Uncle pulls his scarf down below his mouth: "Marinese," he says to him.

The man raises himself a little, while my uncle stretches out his right hand.

"Marinese?" asks the man.

And my uncle: "That's my name."

"Ah," the man exclaims.

He brings his large bovine face forward, and his eyes and cheeks are shadowed by the hat brim he pulled down when he went to sleep. He yawns. Did he say "Ah," or did he just yawn? He uncrosses his arms and, as he lowers his stubby hands to his knees, my uncle catches one of them in his.

"Ah," says the man, "pleased to meet you."

He hastens to scratch an ear.

"We hadn't introduced ourselves," my uncle says to him.

And the man: "That's true."

"It was already night when you got on," my uncle says.

"And I had to stand up quite awhile," the man answers.

"An hour," my uncle tells him. "The gentleman whose place you took got off at . . ." He asks, "What's the name of that place?"

"I don't know," the man answers. But he adds, "I was lucky that man got off."

"Somebody always gets off at one station or another," my uncle tells him. "Even at two in the morning. Even at three."

At this point he pulls his scarf back up above his mouth and meditates for a little. At two in the morning! At three in the morning! They get off at a little station whose name the conductor doesn't even call out, and then good-by! The train goes on while they stay behind. Strange travelers! What will they do in a little country station at two in the morning? But there are even people who get on at that hour! My uncle looks at the man facing him, studying the shadow his bovine face casts on his chest.

"Isn't it strange?" my uncle says to him, for he always takes the train where it's made up and gets off only at the end of the line.

"Ah," the man replies.

This is what my uncle wants, to be able to talk while he can't sleep, just to have someone awake with him who will at least say "Ah" now and then when he says something.

"Oh, is that so?" the man says, as my uncle tells him of the days and nights his trips last and tells him too how each of his destinations is always, sooner or later, the place from which he must again depart.

"Do you know why?" he asks.

Since the man with the bovine face doesn't pick up the question, he himself does. "Why?" It is extremely important that the question be asked because the answer is the long story my uncle has been telling about himself ever since he made his first trip. He loves to tell this story, he wants to tell it. And if each new person he meets on the trains does not ask him the question, my uncle asks it of himself.

"I'll tell you why," Uncle says.

"I suppose it must be on business," Cow Face says.

My old uncle hesitates a few seconds as if it really were, in some sense, on business. Then, tilting his head to one side, he says, "Not exactly."

"Ah, no?" the man says.

And my uncle: "No, sir. I have nephews and grandnephews and my working years are past. I live on a pension."

"Lots of people go into some kind of business after they've been pensioned," observes Cow Face.

"I, instead, had to get away from work altogether," my uncle says. "I had the kind of job that tires a man. I was a railway road worker. I had forty years of shoveling on my back, and was I happy to be given a chance to rest!"

"But if you travel, you can't be resting. You must hope to get something out of it."

At this, my uncle stops holding his scarf. It's down under his chin now, and his little old face is snuggled into it from his sharp jaws around to his ears. He meditates without covering his mouth. He smiles.

"Maybe I'll get something out of it in the end. But it's business of another kind," he says. "I had only nephews and nieces, all children of my sister's, and everyone called me Uncle. But what's an uncle? No man in the world can be satisfied to be just an uncle. You see a beautiful girl and you're nothing to her, you're only her uncle. You can be sure she doesn't care a fig for you. On the contrary, she likes to make fun of you: whereas she fears and respects her father and pays him all kinds of attention. So I thought sadly about my old age, when I would be just an uncle."

"Lots of uncles are respected," the other man says. He speaks this way, always a little vaguely, as if he were hoping to drop out of the conversation as soon as my uncle left him in peace. "While," he adds, "many fathers are not!"

"Yes," says my uncle.

He's well able to agree with anyone who has judgments to make about life. Any philosophy can be his, too. But he goes on at once: "Finally, after ten years, my wife died. She'd been barren but I thought perhaps I still had time to remedy the situation. I was forty, but I remarried, and three years later my daughter was born and began to grow."

Cow Face yawns. His broad jaws gape open, and he tries to cover the sound of the yawn with words. "It's better to have childhen when you're younger."

"That's right," says my uncle.

Hadn't he thought just this all his life? But he was happy at forty-five to have a child who was going to grow into a beautiful girl and he no longer thought sadly of his approaching old age. I can swear to this: I used to see him in our home town where I lived until I was drafted. And I knew him as a sprightly man, always joking and whistling, always good company. And when his second wife died, it seemed as if his life's dream had been to live alone at sixty-five with his young daughter.

"Men are egotists," observes Cow Face.

My uncle doesn't go on right away. Egotist? It's not a word with much meaning for him. He looks attentively at the man who said it. He might be inclined to agree with him.

"Sure, we are," he says. "I was like a bridegroom with my daughter, and, as I'd always imagined, it was a happy old age. I had my supper prepared by my daughter. I had my white collars ironed by my daughter."

Cow Face begins to get interested.

"You see?" he exclaims. "Men are so egotistical that you probably wouldn't have liked it if she'd gotten married."

He lowers his voice toward the end of his sentence. He still hasn't made up his mind to stay awake for the whole trip. But my uncle's answer rouses him.

"Never," my uncle answers. "I would never have permitted it."

"You see?" the man exclaims. He's roused by this answer and irritated at being roused. He clenches his hands on his knees. "By God!" He beats his fists on his broad knees. "At least you're honest!"

"Always have been," my uncle answers him.

Now he's speaking pensively; his striped scarf has slipped up again and covers his mouth, but he goes on talking without pulling it down, in a voice smothered by the wool and still gentle as, in his absorption, he himself is gentle.

"Why should she have left me?" he says. "She was so young. She was twenty-two in 1943. She could have waited until I was dead before making a new home."

He talks without looking at the man; now it's another passenger, the big foreman, who is looking at him.

"Certainly, I don't deny," he observes, "that every man would enjoy having a young daughter at his side until the end. . . ."

"Who can deny it?" my uncle says to him.

"But today young people have their own ideas, too," the foreman continues, "and the first thing many men look for in a wife is a girl who has an independent attitude toward her parents."

"I don't know," says my uncle, "but in any case my daughter was quite independent in her dealings with me. . . ."

Here Cow Face interrupts him. "You mean to say she's dead?" he asks point-blank.

"Oh, no," my uncle answers.

"You spoke of her as if she were no more."

"Yes," says my uncle, "for now she isn't with me any more."

Cow Face doesn't let it go with a simple exclamation.

"Yeah," he mutters. "It was bound to happen." And he looks at my poor uncle, studies him, is at last curious about this little person.

"Disappeared," says my uncle. He doesn't look at his questioner now, but he himself knows that he is being looked at, that he is an object of curiosity; he is embarrassed, he lowers his eyes yet he wants it this way. He could easily have avoided telling anyone his business.

Or does he talk about it to see what he can find out? He certainly can't ask after his daughter if he doesn't tell the story first.

"Are you looking for her now?" Cow Face asks, genuinely interested. "And you're a railroad pensioner?"

He looks my uncle up and down, studies him in detail. There is a look of satisfied amazement in his no-longer-sleepy eyes.

"I think you're the uncle I've heard about," he says. "Haven't you been traveling back and forth since forty-three looking for your daughter? Haven't you been to Milan fifteen times since April twenty-fifth?"

Now the young man who is standing against the middle window, bracing himself by holding onto the wooden railing above my uncle's head, lifts his face which had been buried in his arms. His eyes, dark with weariness, can be seen searching about desperately in the feeble light. He sees the big man in front of my uncle and mutters; he sees my uncle and mutters. Then he buries his face in his arms again, dragging on the railing, while his body, limp with fatigue, twists against the rack into a new and therefore somehow comfortable position.

"What's the matter with him?" the man asks. He is at ease now, awake and delighted to be awake, a lively traveler.

"Him?" answers my uncle. "He's been sleeping on his feet since before you got on. If he hadn't been asleep, he could have taken the place where you're now sitting."

Cow Face laughs heartily, though his laughter sounds choked.

So that's how it is. A bond of confidence is sealed between him and my uncle. And with his short hands, he squeezes my uncle's knees through his baggy trousers. "So?" he says.

But my uncle needs no encouragement to go on talking. He's ready to repeat what he's been repeating ever since the first trips he made in November and December of forty-three between Syracuse and Messina, Syracuse and Palermo, Syracuse and Salerno, Syracuse and Bari, Syracuse and Naples.

"Do you think she was kidnaped?"

"I've never considered such a thing. Why should anyone have kidnaped her?"

"I imagine she was a beautiful girl."

"She certainly was. Rather on the order of my sisters, who don't look at all like me. They're tall and full-blown. They took after our father; I'm like our mother, who was a bit like an old broomstick, and a little like the bristles, too!"

"Tall and full-blown! That's saying quite a bit. At twenty-two she could easily have caught the eye of some passing soldiers. You had the Moroccans in these parts. You had the Poles, too."

"Not in our part of the country. We only had the Americans. And in any event, my daughter wasn't the type to give people ideas like that."

"Oh, well, for soldiers it's enough to watch a girl walking from behind! If she's well upholstered, they get ideas, all right. Didn't she have something . . . underneath?"

"She had more than that to attract their attention—her eyes, for instance. And whoever looked into them—good-by! Even if he'd had the kind of ideas you're talking about, he would have forgotten them."

"That doesn't mean . . ."

"Yes, it does. You know something? Any man would have wanted her as I had her: as a daughter, or else as a wife or a mother, whatever you like, but not in order to make a stupid wreck of her in some gang. For that matter, my daughter had fingernails and knew how to use them. No one in the world would have been able to touch her if she hadn't wanted him to."

"So you think," asks Cow Face, "that she wanted to?" He sounds a little afraid but he asks the question just the same.

"What?" my uncle exclaims.

The young man holding onto the baggage rack moves slightly again. And another sleeper stirs; a woman moves.

But the face of the standing youth is different from the one he had revealed before; it is no longer dark with a tortured need for sleep, only troubled, as if he hadn't been able to close his eyes since he last stirred. Nor is his body soft any longer, like that of a man tied to a knot of weariness. It is soft in a more self-aware way. And looking down, he murmurs with greater coherence. It's a sting coming from the obscurity of his mouth, while he leans against the rack, thrusting his head back and grasping the other railing, too.

"To disappear," answers Cow Face.

"Oh, of course," my uncle says. "She wasn't the kind to disappear unless she wanted to."

"So you put all the blame on your daughter?"

"I blame her for having wanted to leave me alone."

"And you don't blame her for all the rest?"

"What all-the-rest?"

"Why, everything a girl's likely to do when she runs away from home."

"What could she have done? Go first to one place, then to another. . . ."

"Surely, you don't think she travels alone. . . . She must certainly go with someone."

"It doesn't matter whether she goes about alone or with other people. I think she left with a truckload of them."

"Soldiers?"

"Soldiers."

"Then she must be with a soldier. She must go around from place to place with him. Maybe even one place with one of them and another place with another. That's how these things go."

"Sure thing, she'll go now first with one, then with another. If she doesn't like the place she happens to be, she's the kind of girl to find somebody right away who'll take her somewhere else."

"Then you know the kind of life she must be leading. . . ."

"I know, I know. Not a suitable life for a girl of twenty-two."

"Twenty-five by now. She might easily get sick."

"She was healthy and strong. But I don't deny that she might have taken sick."

"Of course. It goes without saying!" Cow Face shakes his head in commiseration. His face is quite dark by now, shaded by the overhang of hat and nose, broad lips, and chin. "You're looking for her all up and down the whole countryside! And you want to find her! What would you do with her if you did find her? What if you found her in a hospital? What would you do with her then? Would you take her home, even if she were rotten with some disease?"

My uncle, though small and thin, is not a nervous man. He never gestures when he speaks; whatever he says, he remains quite still.

"Of course," he says. "Why shouldn't I take her home if she were sick?"

Cow Face looks at him attentively. "You're the first man I've met who'd be willing to take back a daughter with a shameful disease."

My uncle asks: "What shameful disease?"

"Those . . . ," answers Cow Face. "What would you like to call them? There are those diseases, after all, which tell the shame of every girl who goes to bed with men."

"But my daughter," says my uncle slowly, "doesn't go to bed with men."

"Ah, no?" says Cow Face. "Extraordinary!" And he looks at my uncle intently. "She runs away from home after men; she goes around the world with men, yet she doesn't go to bed with men!"

"Why should she?"

"But did she run away or didn't she?"

"She wanted to do that!"

"Isn't she running around with one after another?"

"She might like that, too. She'd be seeing the world."

"Then she must go to bed with men."

"You shouldn't talk like that," my uncle says mildly. "Do you know her? No, you don't. She wasn't the kind who'd want to do that. And she's never done what she doesn't want to do."

"But," says Cow Face, "excuse me if I insist. One can learn to want something, too."

"No," says my uncle. "My daughter was against that. She didn't know anything about it, and she didn't want to."

"You must admit," says Cow Face, "that the men she found herself going around the world with knew about it and wanted to continue to know more about it."

"I admit that."

"But this means they must have wanted to with her, too."

"What could they have done with someone like her? They couldn't help seeing that she was an innocent baby, and then they would certainly have changed their ideas about her. And they would have lost their taste for it, too." My uncle, at this point, has the look of one who considers himself profoundly wise. "Things of that sort are pleasant to do only with people who like to do them." And he draws his striped scarf that makes him look like a Bedouin up to his eyes which have suddenly gone hard.

But the big foreman can't agree with him. He pays no more attention to him.

The foreman looks up at the young man. He hears him murmur again and sees that now he has thrust his hands into his pockets inside his bundled-up person. And he sees that the others have awakened in that dismayed silence of those who wake on trains. He sees the woman wake up too, the one who had turned in her sleep. As he observes them in turn, he says: "Extraordinary! This little man has a daughter twenty-five years old who spends a little time here, a little there, in the company of men, yet he pretends to believe she doesn't go to bed with them. . . ."

"Who?" shrieks the woman. But then she thinks it over, "Oh, yes, of course," she says. "Uncle Agrippa!"

Biographical Notes

CORRADO ALVARO

Born in 1895, in Calabria, Alvaro migrated to the north of Italy and was graduated in literature and philosophy from the University of Milan. He took part in World War I and was badly wounded on the Austrian front. After his recovery, he began a brilliant journalistic career as a foreign correspondent for leading newspapers.

Alvaro has traveled widely in Europe, the Near East, and Russia and made long sojourns in Paris and Berlin. His literary activity at home was restricted, however, because of his hostile attitude toward the Fascist regime. When the Germans occupied Rome in 1943, Alvaro had to flee and go into hiding.

One of the most important novelists of the Fascist and post-Fascist eras, he has described his life experiences in the autobiographical *Quasi Una Vita* (1951), which has been translated into various European languages. Among his novels and short story collections, most of which have also been translated into many languages, the most important are *Vent'Anni*, *Gente in Aspromonte*, and *Età Breve*.

"The Wedding Journey" ("*Viaggio di Nozze a Napoli*") is taken from the collection *L'Amata alla Finestra*, Bompiani, Milan, 1936.

GIOVANNI BATTISTA ANGIOLETTI

This Italian European, born in Milan in 1896, has lived for many years in France, Czechoslovakia, and Switzerland as the director of Institutes of Italian Culture. He is well known in Paris, London, Oslo, and Brussels as he is in Rome. He has lectured on literary topics in almost every European country, has associated with practically all the leading writers of our time, and was influential in introducing to his fellow countrymen the latest trends of world literature through his essays in various periodicals, of some of which he was editor in chief.

Angioletti has written some twenty-six volumes of prose and poetry. At present, he is living in Rome, where he directs the literary programs of the Italian Radio.

"A Poor Ghost" ("*Lo Spettro Spaurito*") is taken from *Narciso*, published by Mondadori, Milan, 1950.

GABRIELE D'ANNUNZIO

Poet, novelist, storyteller, and man of action, d'Annunzio (1863–1938) early became a prominent figure in Europe. Born on the shores of the Adriatic into an aristocratic family, he started writing at fifteen and by the beginning of the twentieth century was considered the main exponent of the Romantic revival in Italy. His innumerable love affairs, particularly one with the celebrated actress Eleonora Duse (which he unreservedly described in his novel *The Flame of Life*, 1900), the scandals which accompanied his extravagant mode of life, his attempts to pose as a man of the Renaissance, his lavish entertainments, his oddities and his duels, made him a highly sensational personality.

By 1910, pursued by creditors, he went to live in France, where he wrote plays and film scenarios in French. When Italy entered World War I, d'Annunzio returned home, joined the armed forces as a pilot, and extolled his own military exploits in sonorous chants. In 1920 he led an expedition for the occupation of the town of Fiume, which the Treaty of Versailles had failed to give to Italy, and created an international incident. Forced to abandon Fiume, he went into retirement on the Lake of Garda and spent the last years of his life in a haughty solitude. Despite all the attempts of Mussolini to make him a friend of the regime and to exploit his nationalistic and aggressive tendencies, he remained rather cool to Fascism.

His novels (*Giovanni Episcopo*, 1892; *Le Vergini delle Rocce*, 1895; *Forse che Sì, Forse che No*, 1910), his plays (*La Città Morta*, 1898; *La Gioconda*, 1898; *Francesca da Rimini*, 1902; *La Nave*, 1908), and, in particular, his poems (from *Poema Paradisiaco*, 1891, to the three volumes of the magnificent *Laudi*, 1903–1912) had a strange and almost unwholesome attraction for his contemporaries. Among the forty-nine volumes of his collected works there are several books of short stories, such as *Le*

Novelle della Pescara, Terra Vergine, San Pantaleone, written in the late eighties.

"The Wake" ("*Veglia Funebre*") is taken from the volume *Le Novelle della Pescara,* Mondadori, Milan, 1945; this story was not included in the English version of *Tales of My Native Town,* published by Doubleday, Doran, New York, 1920.

RICCARDO BACCHELLI

Bacchelli was born in 1891 into a wealthy and socially prominent family in Bologna. His whole life—apart from his travels—has been devoted to study, mostly of literature and history, and to writing. By 1927 he had established himself as a successful novelist with his *Diavolo a Pontelungo* (*The Devil at the Long Bridge*), in which he dealt with Mikhail Bakunin's attempts to introduce Socialism in Italy in the sixties.

Even more popular was his epic *Il Mulino del Po* (*The Mill on the Po*)—a family chronicle of three generations of millers, from the Napoleonic wars to our own times (1938–1940). His other works are *Il Rabdomante* (1936), *Il Male d'Africa* (1937), *La Cometa* (1951), a fantastic satire.

"An Etruscan Harvest" ("*La Tarantula*") is taken from the first volume of *Tutte le novelle,* a two-volume collection of some ninety stories published by Rizzoli, Milan, 1953.

CARLO BERNARI

Born in 1909 in Naples into a middle-class family, Bernari studied philosophy at the start of an interesting and complex intellectual development. He began writing at an early age, and at twenty-five published *Tre Operai,* a novel, considered a milestone in the history of Italian neorealism. Next to his novels (*Speranzella,* 1949, and *Vesuvio e Pane,* 1953), he has written many short stories.

"It's Only a Question of Degree" ("*E una Questione di Tono*") is taken from the volume *Siamo Tutti Bambini,* published by Valecchi, Florence, 1950.

GIUSEPPE BERTO

Berto took part in the last war, was made prisoner in Tunisia, and sent to a prisoner-of-war camp in Hereford, Texas, where he remained until 1946.

There he wrote his first novel, *Il Cielo Rosso*, brought out in Italian in 1947 and translated into English (*The Sky Is Red*).

After *Le Opere di Dio* (1948), he became interested in motion pictures and adapted stories and novels for the screen; he has also written scenarios for several successful Italian films.

He was born in Mogliano in 1914. He is now living in Rome and his time is equally divided between writing *novelle* and turning out scenarios.

"Aunt Bess, In Memoriam" will be included in the next collection of his short stories.

MASSIMO BONTEMPELLI

Born in Como in 1884, Bontempelli has been a teacher, a journalist, a poet, a rebel, an Academician, a Senator, a left-wing sympathizer. His literary career has been as checkered as his life. Among his varied and prolific literary productions, the most widely known are: *La Vita Intensa* (1926), *Eva Ultima* (1923), *Vita e Morte di Adria* (1931), *Gente nel Tempo* (1936), *Miracoli* (1938), *Giro del Sole* (1941).

The stories in this anthology, "Linaria" and "The Sleeping Beauty" ("*La Bella del Bosco Addormentata*") are taken from his collection *L'Amante Fedele*, Mondadori, Milan, 1953.

GIUSEPPE ANTONIO BORGESE

A Sicilian born in the province of Palermo, G. A. Borgese (1882–1952) became an important figure of Italian cultural life in the first quarter of this century. Critic, scholar, professor of European literature at the universities of Naples and Rome between 1917 and 1930, he published in 1921 his novel *Rube*, an exposure of the impotence of the Italian pseudointellectuals. He has also written numerous short stories.

An ardent anti-Fascist, Borgese was compelled to leave Italy for the United States in 1931. He taught at the University of Chicago, published *Golia*, an analysis of Mussolini's regime, in 1934, and was active in various cultural and political organizations. He dreamed of a World Constitution, and after the liberation of Italy went home and fought against extremists both of the left and of the right. Among the twenty volumes of his various works, there are several collections of tales.

"The Siracusan" is taken from the collection under the same title, and "The Boy" ("*Il Ragazzo*") from *Tempesta nel Nulla*, both published by Mondadori, Milan, in 1950.

VITALIANO BRANCATI

Born in Pachino, Sicily, in 1907, Brancati began his literary career in 1932 but did not achieve popularity until the publication in 1947 of his *Bel Antonio*, which Emilio Cecchi compared to an *opéra bouffe* successfully conducted by a maestro.

"The Cavaliere" is taken from the collection of short stories, *Il Vecchio con Gli Stivali*, published by Bompiani, Milan, 1949.

DINO BUZZATI

Born in Belluno, on the Lake of Como, in 1906, Dino Buzzati has been active as a journalist and fiction writer since the early 1930's. He is the author of *Barnabò delle Montagne* (1933), *Il Segreto del Bosco Vecchio* (1935), *Il Deserto dei Tartari* (1940; translated as *The Tartar Steppe*, Farrar, Straus & Young, New York, 1952), and *I Sette Messaggeri* (1942).

"Strange New Friends" ("*Strani Nuovi Amici*") is taken from the collection *Paura alla Scala*, Mondadori, Milan, 1949.

ITALO CALVINO

Pavese and Vittorini encouraged this young writer, born in 1923 in San Remo, on the Riviera Ligure, close to the French border. In 1947 he made his literary debut with a war novelette, *Il Sentiero dei Nidi di Ragno*. In 1949 his collection of short stories, *Ultimo Viene Il Corvo*, won him the high approval of the critics. His other novelettes, such as *Il Visconte Dimizzato* (1952) and *Formiche Argentine* (1953), confirmed the promise of his earlier work. He is at present living in Turin and is an editor for the Einaudi publishing house.

"This Afternoon, Adam . . ." ("*Il Nuovo Giardiniere*") is taken from the volume *Ultimo Viene Il Corvo*, Einaudi, Turin, 1949.

EMILIO CECCHI

Born in Florence in 1884, Cecchi began his literary career as a journalist. He contributed to various Florentine periodicals and, after World War I, was a leader of La Ronda group. He has served as foreign correspondent for a number of newspapers and has written brilliant travelogues on England, Holland, Mexico, Africa, and the United States—the latter under the title of *America Amara*.

Translator of Chesterton and Stevenson, and the author of a history of English literature, he has published numerous comments on current American fiction and once taught a course at the University of California. His essays, art criticisms, and short stories soon gave him the well-deserved reputation of one of the best contemporary Italian stylists. His whimsical and poetic works have been collected in such volumes as *Pesci Rossi* (1920), *La Giornata delle Belle Donne* (1924), and *Corse al Trotto* (1936). Cecchi continues to contribute critical essays to leading Italian periodicals, and his evaluations are extensively quoted.

"Aquarium" and "The Visitors" are taken from the new edition of *L'Osteria del Cattivo Tempo* (written in 1927), Mondadori, Milan, 1950.

GIOVANNI COMISSO

Giovanni Comisso was born in Treviso in 1895. He studied law, fought in World War I, and took part in d'Annunzio's expedition to Fiume. As a journalist, he has traveled extensively throughout Europe, Africa, and Asia and has written vivid travel books. The success of his *Al Vento dell'Adriatico* (1928) and *Gente di Mare* (1929), for which he won the Bagutta Prize, made him devote himself entirely to literature. A bachelor, he lives in the solitude of his farm not far from Venice, dividing his time between his desk and his vegetable garden.

Among some twenty volumes of his works, the most important are: *Il Delitto di Fausto Diamante, Storia di un Patrimonio* (1933), *Avventure Terrene* (1935), *I Due Compagni* (1936), *Le Mie Stagioni* (1951), an autobiography.

"Mario and Fortune" ("*La Ricchezza di Mario*") is taken from the collection *Un Inganno d'Amore*, Mondadori, Milan, 1953.

GRAZIA DELEDDA

A native of Sardinia, Grazia Deledda (1871–1936) is probably the most popular Italian woman writer after the Neapolitan, Matilda Serao. After winning the Nobel Prize in 1926, her works were translated into many languages. During her lifetime she published some fifty volumes of prose, among which *Elias Portolu* (1902), a novel of tragic passion, is considered her masterpiece. *Canne al Vento*, a chronicle of peasant life, is also held in high esteem. The numerous collections of her short stories in which she depicted the simple folk of her native island have enjoyed great success.

"The Sardinian Fox" ("*La Volpe*") is taken from *Chiaroscuro*, first published in 1917 and reprinted in Volume I of *Romanzi e Novelle di Grazia Deledda*, Mondadori, Milan, 1941.

GIOVANNI GUARESCHI

Giovanni Guareschi began his journalistic career in the thirties, contributing to comic magazines and newspapers. During the last war he was interned in Germany. After his release, he wrote his book about the priest Don Camillo and the Communist mayor Peppone, which has been translated into many languages and was successfully made into a screen play. He was born in Milan in 1908.

"The Petition" is taken from *Don Camillo and His Flock*, published in 1952 by Farrar, Straus & Young, New York, and is included here by permission of the publishers.

FRANCESCO JOVINE

Jovine studied law and was active as a journalist. His literary reputation began after World War II with the publication of his sketches, *L'Impero in Provincia* (1946) and *Tutti I Miei Peccati* (1948). *Le Terre di Sacramento* (1950) is considered his best novel. He was born in 1902 in Campobasso, in the Naples region. In 1950 he died of a heart ailment.

"The Flight to France" ("*Fuga in Francia*") is from a posthumous collection published in 1953 by Einaudi, Turin.

CARLO LEVI

Carlo Levi was born in 1902 into a well-to-do family in Turin. In 1924 he took his medical degree, but he seemed more interested in the arts than in medicine. He became a painter and was strongly drawn to literature. Intellectually an anti-Fascist, he became actively opposed to the regime when he joined the clandestine Justice and Freedom organization. He was arrested twice while working for this group and finally exiled to a forsaken village in the southern province of Lucania where he wrote his first book, *Christ Stopped at Eboli*. In 1945 this first novel became a best seller in Italy as well as abroad, and it made its author internationally famous. His second novel, published in 1951 by Farrar, Straus & Young as *The Watch*, was also widely read. During the liberation, Levi belonged to the resistance movement and directed various liberal publications. Today he lives in Rome, atop a Renaissance palace, in a large studio filled with his canvases and his papers.

"The Massacre in Vallucciole" was originally written in 1945 for an underground newspaper during the German occupation. Before the story could go to press, the Germans raided the paper's editorial offices. The editor, who would have been shot had he been found with it, was forced to burn the piece. Later Levi rewrote the story much as it was first set down and kindly offered it for translation in this anthology.

GIANNA MANZINI

This writer has published several collections of short stories which were highly praised by the critics—notably, *Venti Racconti*, *Tempo Innamorato*, *Rive Remote*. She was born in 1902 in Pistoia. In 1924 she was graduated from the University of Florence and has been a teacher as well as a writer. At present, Manzini is living in Rome.

"An Indiscreet Madrigal" ("*Il Madrigale Indiscreto*") is taken from the collection *Ho Visto il Tuo Cuore*, published by Mondadori, Milan, 1949.

GIUSEPPE MAROTTA

Giuseppe Marotta was born in Naples in 1909. An English translation of his *Oro di Napoli* was published in 1949 by Dutton, New York.

"In a Lane of Naples" ("*Natale al Vico Canucce*"), which the author offered for this anthology, will be included in a collection of his short stories soon to be brought out by Bompiani, Milan.

INDRO MONTANELLI

Instead of following the example of his noble ancestors who were statesmen and scholars, Indro Montanelli has led an adventurous life as a war correspondent and peripatetic newspaperman. Born in Tuscany in 1909, he has traveled from Africa to Finland, and from Russia to America. He has written about his experiences in several books—*XX Battaglione Eritreo* (1936), *Ambesa* (1938), *I Cento Giorni della Finlandia* (1940), to mention only a few.

An exceedingly popular journalist as far back as the Fascist regime, Montanelli has written numerous short stories and is the author of a very witty book about Mussolini (*Il Buonomo Mussolini*, 1947). After the fall of Mussolini, however, he concentrated on writing his *Incontri*, which consist of his interviews and sketches of world celebrities. These were published in newspapers and later in book form (the third volume of the series was brought out in 1953). Some of those portrayed have protested over the Montanelli pieces, but most of the subjects have liked them—or pretended to do so.

"His Excellency" was first published in the magazine *Il Borghese* (March, 1950), under the title "*Il Generale della Rovere*."

ALBERTO MORAVIA

Alberto Pincherle, who writes under the pseudonym of Alberto Moravia, was born in Rome in 1907. He became well known at the age of twenty-two when his novel *Gli Indifferenti* (*The Time of Indifference*), a study of superfluous characters, was acclaimed by critics and readers alike as a pessimistic, but highly significant, work of the period. Since this first success, Moravia has been one of the most widely read and translated Italian authors.

Among his books, the most successful were: *Le Ambizioni Sbagliate* (1931), *Romanzi Brevi* (1937), *La Romana* (1945), and *Il Conformista* (1950). His numerous short stories, usually published in periodicals, have formed several collections.

"The Unfortunate Lover" ("*L'Amante Infelice*"), written in 1942, is taken from *I Racconti* (Bompiani, Milan, 1952), which contains twenty-three tales, and will be included in a volume of Moravia's short stories to be published by Farrar, Straus & Young in New York and Martin Secker & Warburg in London.

ALDO PALAZZESCHI

Aldo Palazzeschi was known before World War I as a poet and extravagant futurist. The name of his cat figured as that of his publisher on the jacket of his first book of poems. At first more interested in painting than in literature, he was forty-seven when he won his reputation as a prose writer with the publication of his childhood recollections, *Stampe dell'Ottocento*. The novels *Sorelle Materassi* (1934) and *Fratelli Cuccoli* (1948) have gained him an important place in contemporary Italian literature. The author was born in Florence in 1885.

"Love Letters" ("*Lumacchino*") is taken from *Palio dei Buffi*, Valecchi, Florence, 1938.

ALFREDO PANZINI

Alfredo Panzini (1863–1939) was born into a middle-class family in Senigallia, Le Marche, on the Adriatic. He studied in Bologna under the famous poet Carducci and, after graduation, began a long and uneventful career as a schoolteacher. He wrote assiduously, led a peaceful life of devotion to his wife and children, read a great deal, and traveled moderately. He retired in 1927 to Bellaria, a quiet village on the Adriatic, where he spent the rest of his days like an ancient sage practicing the virtues of tolerance, frugality, and contemplation.

As a young man, Panzini had had to pay from his own not-too-well-filled pocket for the publication of his first book of fiction. It was not until he was forty-two that G. A. Borgese brought him to the attention of readers and critics. His sentimental and ironic sketches, stories and travel impressions (*La Lanterna di Diogene*, 1909; *Santippe*, 1914; *Novelle d'Ambo I Sessi*, 1918; *Viaggio di Un Povero Letterato*, 1919; *Il Mondo E Rotondo*, 1926), and various novels and tales were widely circulated after World War I and during the first years of the Fascist regime.

"The Mistress and the Master Speak" is taken from *Padrone Sono Me* (1922) and was reprinted by Mondadori, Milan, 1939–1940, in *Romanzi d'Ambo I Sessi*.

GIOVANNI PAPINI

The son of a poor, atheistic cabinetmaker and a deeply religious country woman, Giovanni Papini was born in Florence in 1881. There he was educated and earned his living as a teacher, journalist, library clerk, and employee of the Museum of Anthropology. His main occupation, however, was always that of a passionate reader, a prolific writer, and an active member of all Florentine *avant-garde* circles. A symbolist in his first book of short stories, *Il Tragico Quotidiano* (1906), he next became a romantic and a decadent with the novel *Un Uomo Finito* (1912). For a time, he edited the literary magazine *La Voce*, and in 1913 he joined the futurists and wrote violent polemic tracts.

Papini married a simple peasant girl and in 1921, at the age of forty, returned to the candid faith of his mother. His world-renowned *Life of Christ* (1923) attested his reconversion to Catholicism. His numerous essays and books of philosophy, religion, and literary criticisms, as well as his collections of short stories, continued to appear in an uninterrupted stream during the Fascist regime.

"The Cloud Maker" ("*Il Fabbricante di Nuvole*"), "The Mask Factory" ("*La Manifattura delle Maschere*"), and "Madmen's Congress" ("*Il Convegno dei Pazzi*") are taken from the author's witty book of tales, *Le Pazzie del Poeta*, published by Valecchi, Florence, 1950.

CESARE PAVESE

A man of many literary accomplishments, Cesare Pavese was born in 1908, the son of a respected Piedmontese lawyer. He studied at the University of Turin and at the age of twenty, a candidate for the Doctor's degree, wrote a dissertation on Walt Whitman. Pavese has himself written poems which show the influence of Whitman and Edgar Lee Masters. His excellent translation in 1932 of *Moby Dick* was followed by translations of Sherwood Anderson, Dos Passos, Gertrude Stein, Faulkner, Defoe, Joyce, and Masters. His version of the *Spoon River Anthology* enjoyed great success in postwar

Italy. Pavese's numerous translations, as well as his fine essays on American writers (later collected and published in book form), were largely responsible in the 1930's for Italy's increased interest in American literature.

The writer was arrested in 1935 for anti-Fascist activity and was exiled to Calabria. His work in fiction did not receive recognition until 1941, when his novelette, *Paesi Tuoi*, stirred and surprised the critics. Some of his later successes were: *Il Compagno* (1946), *Dialoghi con Leuco* (1947), *Prima che Il Gallo Canti* (1949), *La Bella Estate* (1949), and *La Luna e I Falo* (1950; published as *The Moon and the Bonfires* by Farrar, Straus & Young, New York, 1953). Before committing suicide in 1950, Pavese had worked as an editor in the Einaudi publishing house.

"The Leather Jacket" ("*Giacchetta di Cuoio*") is taken from the *Feria d'Agosto* collection, Einaudi, Turin, 1946.

LUIGI PIRANDELLO

Pirandello (1867–1936) was fifty-four when the extraordinary success in 1921 of *Six Characters in Search of an Author* made him a playwright of world renown. His paradoxical dramas subsequently thrilled and puzzled the audiences of Europe and the two Americas. He won the Nobel Prize in 1934 and died two years later as the greatest Italian dramatist of the century.

Long before his name appeared on the billboards of Paris, London, New York, and Buenos Aires, he was well known in his own country as an accomplished master of the short story. His twenty-four volumes of tales (*Novelle per un Anno*), brought out annually, beginning with 1900, as well as his novels, the first of which was *Il Fu Mattia Pascal* (1905), established him as a leading Italian storyteller, ranking with Verga and d'Annunzio.

Son of a prosperous Sicilian mineowner of Girgenti, Pirandello refused to become a businessman and devoted himself to studies of philosophy and classical literature in Rome and in Bonn, Germany. After taking his degree, he came upon very hard times. His father's industry collapsed, his wife became insane, and he had to struggle against many difficulties. But he never ceased to write, even while teaching at Teachers College in Rome. Recognition came slowly, and it was not until 1917 that critics and readers alike were unanimous in their praise of his short stories. While hardly known outside of Italy, Pirandello's stories are extremely popular in his own country, where they are published in numerous reprints.

"The Bat" ("*Il Pipistrello*") is taken from the collection *Il Scialle Nero*, the latest reprint of which was brought out by Mondadori, Milan, in 1950.

VASCO PRATOLINI

Like Gorki, with whose name he is often associated, Pratolini had a very difficult childhood. He was born in Florence in 1913 into a family of poor artisans and has had to earn a living since the age of nine. At various times during his youth he has been an elevator operator, a printer's devil, a salesman, and a soda-fountain clerk.

His literary career began in 1938 when he became associated with a local magazine called *Campo di Marte*. In this also he was beset with hardships, but success finally came to him when he started publishing books based on his life experiences (*Via de' Magazzini*, 1942; *Il Quartiere*, 1945; *Cronache di Poveri Amanti*, 1946; *Mestiere di Vagabondo*, 1947; *Un Eroe di Nostro Tempo*, 1950). Most of Pratolini's works have been translated into English and other languages.

"A Mistress of Twenty" ("*Amanta di Vent'anni*") was first published in *Botteghe Oscure*, Vol. VIII, Rome, 1950. It is part of a longer narrative which describes Florence under the Fascist regime and which is scheduled for American publication by Prentice-Hall, New York.

DOMENICO REA

Before emerging as a writer and chronicler of Naples, where he was born in 1921, Rea had tried his hand at a number of things. He has been a textile worker, a clerk, an emigrant to South America, a civil servant, and an administrative officer of the Neapolitan Museums. His collections of short stories, *Spaccanapoli* (1947) and *Gesu Fate Luce* (1950), for which he was awarded the Viareggio literary prize of two million lire, were well received by the public and have assured Rea a place of honor among the postwar writers.

"Piededifico" is taken from *Gesu Fate Luce*, Mondadori, Milan, 1950.

IGNAZIO SILONE

Ignazio Silone was born in 1900 in Pescina dei Marsi, in the Abruzzi. His real name is Secondo Tranquilli. His father was a small landowner, his mother a weaver. At the age of fourteen he was orphaned when his home was destroyed by an earthquake in which his mother and all his sisters and brothers, but one, perished. His father and other brother and sister had already died in various tragic circumstances.

Silone was educated in the Jesuit and other Catholic schools. Because of his very poor health, he thought there would be no point in his going on to the university, and, instead, threw himself into politics. In 1921 he visited Russia, returned a Communist, and became editor of *Il Lavoratore*, a Communist daily in Trieste. In 1922 the premises of the paper were burned by the Fascists. Silone escaped, but his one surviving brother was arrested and beaten to death in jail. Silone went underground and continued his anti-Fascist activities in Italy and abroad.

In 1929 he broke away from the Communist party, and in 1931 he was smuggled across the border to Switzerland where he remained in exile. There he wrote *Fontamara* (1933), which was translated into seventeen languages, *Bread and Wine* (1936), *The School for Dictators* (1938), a play, and various essays on Fascism. In 1935 his short stories were translated into English under the title *Mr. Aristotle*. From 1940 onward, he resumed political activity by organizing the underground groups of the Socialist party in Italy. In 1944 he returned to Rome and was elected a member of the Italian Constituent Assembly (1946–1948). He has now gone back to writing and intervenes only occasionally in politics as an opponent of Communism and Fascism. His most recent novel, *A Handful of Berries*, was published by Harper & Brothers in 1953.

"Return to Fontamara" first appeared in *Tomorrow*, Vol. VIII, No. 2, 1949, New York. We offer a revised translation of the piece by Darina Silone, the author's Irish wife.

MARIO SOLDATI

Mario Soldati is equally well known as a writer of fiction, an art critic, and a film producer. He was born in Turin in 1906. His books include *Salmace*

(1929), *America Primo Amore* (1935), *La Verità sul Caso Motta* (1941), *L'Amico Gesuita* (1943), *Fuga in Italia* (1947), and *A Cena Col Commendatore* (1950), which was published by Knopf, New York, 1953.

"Nora" ("Dinner with Commendatore") appeared in the periodical *Prosa* (No. 2, March 1946, Mondadori, Milan) and is included here by the author's permission.

ITALO SVEVO

Ettore Schmitz (1861–1928) was born and educated in Trieste and was active as a businessman, manufacturer, banker, and industrialist. Under his pen name, Italo Svevo, his two novels *Una Vita* and *Senilità* were published in 1883 and 1898 respectively. But these volumes remained unknown to the public and were ignored by the critics. James Joyce, who taught him English while he was in Trieste, discovered Italo Svevo and called his works to the attention of the French writers Valéry Larbaud and Benjamin Crémieux. Actually, it was through France that Svevo first became known to a small group of admirers in Italy. The novel *Senilità* was published in England by Putnam and in America by New Directions under the title suggested by James Joyce, *As a Man Grows Older*.

By the time he had published *La Coscienza di Zeno*, 1923 (translated into English in 1930 as *Confessions of Zeno*), his reputation was established. Since his death, his influence has continued to grow. The publication of his posthumous works only confirms the opinion that Italo Svevo must be placed among the leading Italian writers of the century.

The piece offered here, "This Indolence of Mine" ("Il Mio Ozio"), is from the collection *Corto Viaggio Sentimentale* (Mondadori, Milan, 1949), a book of short stories Svevo was working on just before he died. The story was first published in *The Hudson Review*, Vol. IV, No. 4, 1952, under the title "This Indolence of Mine" ("*Il Mio Ozio*").

BONAVENTURA TECCHI

Although mainly recognized as a novelist and short-story writer, Bonaventura Tecchi is also a professor of German literature who has written literary histories and critical analyses. He was born in 1894 at Bagnoreggio (Viterbo). After World War I, in which he was wounded and made prisoner, he devoted himself entirely to teaching and writing. Tecchi has traveled widely, lectured abroad, and has taught at the universities of Padua and Rome.

Among some fifteen volumes of his fictional works, the most popular were: *Tre Storie d'Amore* (1932), *I Villatàuri* (1935), *Giovani Amici* (1940), *L'Isola Apassionata* (1945), and *Creature Sole* (1950).

"A Day in Venice" ("La Partenza") is taken from his collection of short stories written from 1937 to 1940, *Presenza di Male*, Bompiani, Milan, 1948.

GIOVANNI VERGA

The parents of Giovanni Verga (1840–1922) were wealthy Sicilians from Catania, who wanted their son to become a lawyer. In order to prove his artistic abilities, Verga composed a long novel at the age of twenty-one and left his home town in search of fame and excitement. He contributed to newspapers in Rome, Florence, and Milan and had many adventures and love affairs. He wrote numerous stories and novels about fascinating and treacherous ladies, such as *Eva* and *Tigre Reale*. When he tired of being a man about town and was bored with parties and amorous intrigues, he returned to Sicily. There, in the sunny quiet of his old bachelor home, he wrote his best stories. Instead of sentimental and pseudoromantic narratives about high society, he described the customs and passions of the peasants, fishermen, and impoverished nobles of The Big Island.

The great fame he dreamed of in his youth did not, however, come to him during his lifetime. In 1920 he was made a senator, and died two years later. Only then did the critics and public realize that they had lost a great writer in Verga. National recognition was followed by international repute. D. H. Lawrence, who translated Verga's stories, did a great deal to introduce the Italian realist to the English-speaking world. Verga's collections of stories (*Vita dei Campi*, 1880; *Novelle Rusticane*, 1882; *Cavalleria Rusticana*, 1884) and his two novels (*I Malavoglia*, 1881; *Mastro Don Gesualdo*, 1889) made him the leader of the verist school of literature. The general public became acquainted with his name through Mascagni's opera, inspired by Verga's *Cavalleria Rusticana*.

"La Lupa," translated by D. H. Lawrence, is included in this anthology by permission of The Dial Press, New York, from their edition of *Cavalleria Rusticana*, published in 1928.

ELIO VITTORINI

A writer of varied and complex interests, Elio Vittorini has been active in political and artistic circles and has belonged to left-wing, anti-Fascist organizations. Although never a party member, he has been in sympathy with Communism. In 1950, he publicly declared his spiritual and intellectual break with the Communist ideology.

Born in 1908 in Siracusa, Sicily, Vittorini studied in Milan, where he published his first book of short stories, *Piccola Borghesia* (1931). He has also produced two influential anthologies: *Scrittori Nuovi* (with Falqui, 1930) marked the passage from fragmentism to sustained narrative; *Americana* (Bompiani, 1943), a collection of American short stories, greatly impressed the younger generation.

His most important works are: *Sardegna Come Infanzia* (written in 1932, published in 1952), *Conversazione in Sicilia* (1941), *Uomini e No* (a novel of the resistance, 1945), *Il Scipione Strizza l'Occhio a Frejus* (1947), and *Garofano Rosso* (1948).

"Uncle Agrippa Takes a Train" ("*Lo Zio Agrippa Passa in Treno*") is taken from *Donne di Messina*, Bompiani, Milan, 1949. The English translation of this book is scheduled for publication by New Directions, Norfolk, Connecticut.

ABOUT THE EDITOR

ALTHOUGH HE was born in Novgorod Seversk, in Russia, Marc Slonim lived part of his childhood in Italy and studied for four years at the University of Florence before matriculating at the University of Petersburg. Since 1917 he has lived in Italy, Prague, Paris and the United States, where he is now teaching comparative literature at Sarah Lawrence College. He is the author of two major studies of Russian literature, The Epic of Russian Literature and Modern Russian Literature. Besides translating Turgenev into Italian, he has written and published a great deal in that language, and most of the authors whose work is included in this volume have been his personal friends.